CW01666576

MAESTRA

MAESTRA

L.S. HILTON

Best wishes

ZAFFRE

First published in Great Britain in 2016 by

Zaffre Publishing
80–81 Wimpole St, London, W1G 9RE
www.zaffrebooks.co.uk

Copyright © L.S. Hilton 2016

The moral right of the author to be identified as the author of this work has been asserted in accordance with the Copyright, Designs and Patents Act, 1988.

All rights reserved. No part of this publication may be reproduced or transmitted in any form or by any means, electronic or mechanical, including photocopy, recording, or any information storage and retrieval system, without permission in writing from the publisher.

This book is a work of fiction. Names, characters, businesses, organizations, places and events are either the product of the authors' imagination or are used fictitiously. Any resemblance to actual persons, living or dead, events or locales is entirely coincidental.

A CIP catalogue record for this book is available from the British Library.

Hardback: 978 1 78576 003 7
Trade Paperback: 978 1 78576 083 9
Ebook: 978 1 78576 002 0

1 3 5 7 9 10 8 6 4 2

Printed and bound by Clays Ltd, St Ives Plc
Typeset by IDSUK (DataConnection) Ltd

FSC
www.fsc.org
MIX
Paper from responsible sources
FSC® C018072

Zaffre Publishing is an imprint of Bonnier Publishing Fiction, a Bonnier Publishing company
www.bonnierpublishingfiction.co.uk
www.bonnierpublishing.co.uk

To the Norse God of Everything,
with thanks.

Prologue

Heavy hems and vicious heels swooped and clacked over the parquet. We crossed the hallway to a set of double doors, the low hum within indicating that the men were already inside. The room was lit with candles, small tables positioned between sofas and low dining chairs. The waiting men were dressed in thick black satin pyjamas with frogged jackets, the sheen in the weft of the fabric offsetting their starched shirts. An occasional heavy cufflink or slim watch flashed gold in the candlelight, an embroidered monogram rippled beneath a flamboyant silk handkerchief. It would have felt silly, theatrical, had the details not been so perfect, but I felt hypnotised, my pulse slow and deep. Yvette was being led away by a man with a peacock feather pinned in his cuff – I looked up and saw another man approaching me, a gardenia like my own in his lapel.

'So it works like that?'

'While we eat, yes. Afterwards you can choose. *Bonsoir*.'

'*Bonsoir*.'

He was tall and slim, though his body was younger than his face, rather hard and lined, with greying hair swept back over a high forehead and large, slightly hooded eyes, like a Byzantine saint. He led me to a sofa, waited while I sat and handed me a plain crystal glass of white wine, clean and flinty. The formality was arch, but I liked the choreography. Julien clearly appreciated the pleasure of anticipation. The mostly nude waitresses reappeared with small plates of tiny lobster pastries, then shavings of duck breast in a honey and ginger paste, tuiles of raspberries and strawberries. Gestures at food, nothing to sate us.

'Red fruit makes a woman's cunt taste so beautiful,' my dinner companion remarked.

'I know.'

There was some quiet conversation, but mostly people watched and drank, their eyes moving from one another to the swift movements of the waitresses, who had dancers' bodies, I saw, slim but strongly muscled, their calves full over their tight boots. Moonlighting from the *corps de ballet*? I saw Yvette dimly across the room, being fed almond-stuffed figs with a sharp-tined silver fork, her body laid out like a serpent's, one dark thigh a hint between the red silk. Solemnly, the waitresses circled the room with candle snuffers, dimming the lights in a cloud of beeswax, and as they did so I felt the man's hand on my thigh, circling and stroking, entirely unhurried, and an answering tautness between my legs. The girls set out shallow lacquered trays containing condoms, small crystal bottles of monoi oil, lube decanted into bonbon dishes. Some of the couples were kissing, happy with their matched partners, others rose politely and crossed the room to find the prey they had selected earlier. Yvette's robe was tumbled about her parted legs, a man's head dipped to her. I caught her eye, and she smiled, luxuriously, before letting her head fall back among the cushions with the ecstatic motion of a junkie nodding out.

PART ONE

OUTSIDE

1

If you asked me how it began, I could truthfully say that the first time, it was an accident. It was about six in the evening, the time when the city churns again on its axis, and though the streets above were full of the sharp wind of another piss-miserable May, the station was stuffy and humid, squalid with discarded tabloids and fast-food wrappings, irritable tourists in garish leisurewear crammed amidst the resigned, sallow-faced commuters. I was waiting on the platform for the Piccadilly line Tube at Green Park after another fabulous start to another fabulous week of being bullied and patronised at my super-fabulous job. As the train on the opposite side pulled away, a low collective groan rippled through the crowd. The board showed that the next Tube was stuck at Holborn. Someone on the tracks, probably. Typical, you could see people thinking. Why did they always have to top themselves at rush hour? The passengers across the line were moving off, amongst them a girl in crippling heels and an electric-blue bandage dress. Last season's Alaïa via Zara, I thought. Probably on her way to Leicester Square with the other rube losers. She had extraordinary hair, a great cascading plum-coloured mane of extensions with some sort of gold thread bound through them that caught and held the neon light.

'Judeee! Judy! Is that you?'

She started waving at me enthusiastically. I pretended not to hear.

'Judy! Over here!'

People were beginning to look. The girl had hobbled precariously close to the yellow safety stripe.

'It's me! Leanne!'

'Your friend's waving to you,' said the woman next to me, helpfully.

'I'll see you upstairs in a min!' I didn't hear voices like hers very often anymore. I'd never expected to hear hers again. She obviously wasn't going to disappear, and the train showed no sign of appearing, so I settled my heavy leather briefcase across my shoulder and pushed my way back through the crowd. She was waiting on the gangway between the platforms.

'Hiya! I thought it was you!'

'Hi, Leanne,' I tried gingerly.

She tripped the last few steps towards me and threw her arms around me like I was her long-lost sister.

'Look at you! Dead professional. I didn't know you lived in London!' I didn't point out that this was probably because I hadn't spoken to her in a decade. Facebook friends weren't really my style, and nor did I need to be reminded, ever, of where I had come from.

Then I felt like a bitch. 'You look great, Leanne. I love your hair.'

'I don't go by Leanne anymore, actually. It's Mercedes now.'

'Mercedes? That's . . . nice. I use Judith mostly. Sounds more grown up.'

'Yeah, well, look at us, eh? All grown up.'

I don't think I knew, then, what that felt like. I wondered if she did either.

'Listen, I've got an hour before work.' *Werk*. 'Do you fancy a quick drink? Catch up?'

I could have said I was busy, that I was in a rush, taken her number like I was actually going to call it. But where did I have to get to? And there was something in that voice, strangely welcome in its familiarity, that made me feel lonely and reassured at the same time. I had just two twenty-pound notes in the world, and there were three days before payday. Still, something might turn up.

'Sure,' I said. 'Let me buy you a drink. Let's go to the Ritz.'

Two champagne cocktails in the Rivoli bar, £38. I had twelve on my Oyster card and two in hand. I just wouldn't have much to eat until the end of the week. It was stupid, maybe, to show off like that, but sometimes you need to show the world a bit of defiance. Leanne – Mercedes – fished enthusiastically with a fuchsia shellac nail extension for the bobbing maraschino and took a cheerful slurp.

'That's dead nice, thanks. Though I prefer Roederer now, myself.'

Well that served me right for being flash.

'I work round here,' I volunteered. 'Art. In an auction house. I do Old Masters.' I didn't, actually, but then I wasn't sweating that Leanne would know a Reubens from a Rembrandt.

'Posh,' she replied. She looked bored now, fiddling with the swizzle-stick in her drink. I wondered if she was sorry she had called out to me, but instead of feeling annoyed I had a pathetic feeling that I wanted to please her.

'Sounds it,' I said confidentially, feeling the brandy and the sugar soothing their way into my blood, 'but the pay's crap. I'm skint, usually.'

'Mercedes' told me she had been in London for a year. She worked in a champagne bar in St James's. 'Reckons it's classy, but it's full of the same dirty old gits. Nothing dodgy,' she added hastily. 'It's only a bar. The tips are amazing though.'

She claimed she was making two grand a week. 'Puts weight on you, though,' she said ruefully, prodding her tiny belly. 'All that drinking. Still, we don't have to pay for it. Pour it into the plants if we have to, Olly says.'

'Olly?'

'He's the owner. Eh, you should come down sometime, Judy. Moonlight a bit, if you're brassic. Olly's always looking for girls. D'you want another one?'

An older couple in black tie, probably on their way to the opera, took the table opposite us. The woman ran her eyes critically over Mercedes' fake-tanned legs, her shimmering cleavage. Mercedes swivelled in her chair, and slowly and deliberately uncrossed and recrossed her legs, giving me and the poor old bugger next to her a flash of black lace G-string, all the time staring straight into the woman's eyes. There was no need to ask if anyone had a problem.

'As I was saying,' she said, when the woman turned beet-faced to the cocktail menu, 'it's a laugh.' *Laff.* 'The girls are from all over. You could look smashing, if you got a bit dolled up. Come on.'

I looked down at my black tweed Sandro suit. Nipped-in jacket, flippy pleated skirt. It was meant to look knowingly coquettish, professional with a little Left Bank spin – at least that's what I told myself when I clumsily mended the hems for the umpteenth time – but next to Mercedes I looked like a depressed crow.

'Now?'

'Yeah, why not? I've got loads of stuff in me bag.'

'I don't know, Leanne.'

'Mercedes.'

'Sorry.'

'Come on, you can wear my lace top. It'll look ace with your tits. Unless you've got a date?'

'No,' I said, tipping my head right back to catch the last drops of bubbles and angostura. 'No, I haven't got a date.'

2

I read somewhere that cause and effect are safeguards against contingency, against the terrifyingly inaccurate mutability of chance. Why did I go with Leanne that day? It hadn't been worse than any other. But choices are made before explanations, whether or not we care to know it. In the art world, there are only two auction houses you really need to know about. They're the ones who make the hundred-million-pound sales, who handle the collections of desperate dukes and socially anxious oligarchs, who funnel a thousand years' worth of beauty and artisanship through their museum-quiet rooms and turn it into hard, sexy cash. When I'd landed the job in British Pictures three years ago, I had finally felt like I'd made it. For a day or two, anyway. I soon twigged that that the porters, the blokes who did the actual lifting, were the only people who cared anything about pictures. The rest of them might have been flogging matchsticks or butter. Despite the fact that I'd been employed on merit, despite my hard work, diligence and generally rather impressive knowledge of art, I was forced to admit that as far as the standards of the House went, I was distinctly not made of awesome. After a couple of weeks in the department, I had realised that no one there really cared if you could tell a Breughel from a Bonnard, that there were other, more vital codes to crack.

There were quite a few things I still liked about my job at the House after three years. I liked walking past the uniformed doorman into the orchid-scented lobby. I liked the satisfyingly reverent looks the clients reserved for "experts" as I climbed the imposing oak staircase, because naturally, everything about the House looked like three centuries' worth of imposing. I liked eavesdropping on the conversations of the identikit Eurosecretaries, their French and Italian vowels flicking as crisply as their hair. I liked that, unlike them, I wasn't angling to snare a passing hedgie in the tendrils of my blow-dry. I was proud of what I had achieved, winning an assistant's position after a year of interning in British Pictures. Not that I intended to remain in the department for long. I wouldn't be spending the rest of my life looking at pictures of dogs and horses.

That day, the day I bumped into Leanne, had started with an email from Laura Belvoir, the deputy head of department. It was headed 'Action Immediately!' yet there was no text in the body. I walked across the office to ask her what she actually wanted. The bosses had recently been on a management course and Laura had really got behind the idea of desk-to-desk digital communication, though unfortunately she hadn't yet worked round to typing.

'I need you to do the attributions for the Longhis.'

We were preparing a series of conversation pieces by the Venetian artist for the upcoming Italian sale.

'You want me to check the titles in the warehouse?'

'No, Judith. That's Rupert's job. Go to the Heinz and see if you can identify the subjects.' Rupert was the head of department, who seldom appeared before eleven.

The Heinz Archive has a huge catalogue of named images – I was to look up which particular English lordlings on their eighteenth-century gap year gaieties might have sat for Longhi, as identification of particular individuals could make them more interesting to buyers.

'OK. Have you got a set of photographs, please?'

Laura sighed. 'In the library. They're marked as Longhi-slash-Spring.'

Since the House occupied a whole block, it was a four-minute walk from the department to the library, and it was one I did many times every day. Despite rumours of it being the twenty-first century outside, the House was still run largely like a Victorian bank. Many of the employees spent their days plodding round the corridors delivering scrips of paper to one another. The archive and the library were hardly even properly computerised; often one stumbled across little Dickensian ghosts wedged despairingly into obscure cubby holes between mounds of receipts and triplicate photostatted accounts. I retrieved the envelope of pictures and went back to my desk for my bag. My phone rang.

'Allo? It's Serena onna desk. I've got Rupert's trousers here.'

So I schlepped to reception, picked up the vast bag from Rupert's tailor, couriered over the 500-odd metres from Savile Row, and took it back to the department. Laura looked up.

'Haven't you gone yet, Judith? What on earth have you been doing? Well, since you're here, please could you get me a cappuccino? Don't go to the canteen, go to that nice little place in Crown Passage. Get a receipt.'

Coffee fetched, I set off on foot towards the archive. I had five photographs in my bag, scenes at the Fenice theatre, the Zattere and a coffee house on the Rialto, and after working through the boxes for a couple of hours, I'd made a list of twelve positive identifications of sitters who had been in Italy contemporaneously with the portraits. I cross referenced the Heinz index with the pictures so that the attribution could be checked for the catalogue and took them back to Laura.

'What are these?'

'The Longhis you asked me to do.'

'These are the Longhis from the sale six years ago. Really, Judith. The photos were on my email to you this morning.' That would have been the email with no content.

'But, Laura, you said they were in the library.'

'I meant the electronic library.'

I didn't say anything. I logged on to the department's online catalogue, found the correct pictures (filed as Lunghi), downloaded them to my phone and went back to the Heinz with a flea in my ear from Laura for wasting time. I'd finished the second lot of attributions by the time she was back from lunch at the Caprice, and got on with cold-calling invitees who hadn't RSVP'd to the private view for the sale. Then I wrote up the bios and emailed them to Laura and Rupert, showed Laura how to open the attachment, took the Tube to the Applied Arts depository near Chelsea Harbour to check on a silk sample which Rupert thought might match with a hanging in the Longhis, discovered to no one's surprise that it didn't, walked most of the way back because the Circle line was stuck at Edgware Road and detoured to Lillywhite's on Piccadilly to pick up a sleeping bag for Laura's son's school camping trip, reappearing exhausted and grimy at 5.30 to another reprimand for missing the departmental viewing of the paintings I'd spent the morning working on.

'Honestly, Judith,' Laura remarked, 'you'll never make any progress if you're haring about town when you could be looking at the works.'

Twitches on invisible threads aside, maybe it wasn't all that surprising that when I came across Leanne at the Tube station a little later, I really did feel like a drink.

3

My interview at the Gstaad Club that night consisted of Olly, the giant, morose Finn who was proprietor, maître d' and bouncer, looking me over in the lacy nude blouse I'd hastily shuffled on in the loos at the Ritz.

'Can you drink?' he asked me.

'She's from Liverpool,' giggled 'Mercedes', and that was that.

So for the next eight weeks, I worked Thursday and Friday nights in the club. Not hours that most people my age would welcome, but after-work drinks with the team weren't really a big feature of my career. The name, like everything else about the place, was a dated stab at fake class; the only thing that was real about the club was the truly eye-watering mark-up on the champagne. In fact, it didn't look much different from Annabel's, the has-been nightclub a few streets away in Berkeley Square. Same Sloane-Ranger yellow walls, same bad-good pictures, same collection of tragic paunchy older men, same lounging gaggle of girls who were not quite hookers but who always needed a little help with the rent. The job was simple. About ten girls gathered half an hour before the club opened at nine for a pick-me-up dispensed by Carlo the bartender in his immaculately pressed but slightly whiffy white jacket. The rest of the staff consisted of an ancient babushka who took the coats, and Olly. At nine sharp he unbolted the street door and made the same solemn joke.

'OK girls, knickers off.'

After opening, we sat about chatting, flicking through celebrity mags or texting for an hour until the customers started to drift in, almost always alone. The idea was that they would pick the girl they liked and take her to sit in one of the pink-velvet swagged alcoves, which was known rather bluntly as 'getting booked'. When you were booked, your objective was to get the punter to order as many ridiculously overpriced bottles of champagne as possible. We got no wages, just ten per cent on every bottle and whatever the customer chose to leave. My first night, I reeled away from the table halfway through the third bottle and had to ask the babushka to hold my hair while I made myself throw up.

'Stupid girl,' she said with gloomy satisfaction. 'Is not for you to be drinking it.'

So I learned. Carlo served the champagne with huge, goldfish-bowl sized glasses, which we would empty into the ice bucket or the flowers as soon as the customer left the table. Another strategy was to persuade him to invite a 'friend' to share a glass. The girls wore pumps, never open-toed sandals, as another ruse was to teasingly persuade him to sip some out of your shoe. You can pour a surprising amount of champagne into a size 39 Louboutin. If all else failed, we just tipped the stuff on the floor.

At first, it seemed miraculous to me that the place stayed open at all. It seemed positively Edwardian, all the heavy-handed flirting and the exorbitant fee for our company. Why would any man bother when he could order up whatever he wanted on his I-Hooker app? It was all so painfully old-fashioned. But I gradually realised that this was exactly what kept the guys coming back. They weren't after sex, though plenty of them could get a bit frisky after a few goldfish bowls. They weren't players, these guys, even in their dreams. They were ordinary middle-aged married blokes who for a few hours wanted to pretend to themselves that they were on a real date, with a real girl, a pretty girl, nicely dressed with decent manners, who actually wanted to *talk* to them. Mercedes, with her talons and her extensions, was the official naughty girl, for customers who wanted something a bit more racy, but Olly preferred the rest of us to dress in plain, well-cut dresses, not too much make-up, clean hair, discreet jewellery. They didn't want risk, or mess, or their wives finding out, or probably even the embarrassment and trouble of having to get it up. Unbelievably pathetic as it was, they just wanted to feel wanted.

Olly knew his market, and he catered to it perfectly. There was a tiny dance floor in the club, with Carlo doubling as DJ, to give the idea that at any moment our chap might spin us off into the disco night, though we were never to encourage this. There was a menu, with perfectly acceptable steak and scallops and ice cream sundaes – middle-aged men like to watch girls eat fattening puddings. Obviously, the knickerbocker glories stayed down just as long as it took us to make a discreet trip to the loo. Girls who took drugs or who were too obviously slutty didn't last a night – a Polite Notice by the gents proclaimed that it was Strictly Forbidden to offer to Escort any of the Young Ladies Outside the Club. They were meant to aspire to us.

I found myself looking forward to Thursday and Friday nights. With the exception of Leanne (I couldn't really think of her as Mercedes yet), the girls were neither friendly nor unfriendly; pleasant but incurious. They didn't appear interested in my life, perhaps because none of the details they revealed about their own were real. The first night, as we swung a little unsteadily down Albemarle Street, Leanne suggested I choose a name to use in the club. My middle name was Lauren; neutral, untelling.

I said I was studying history of art part-time. All the girls seemed to be studying something, business administration mostly, and perhaps some of them were. None of them were English; clearly the idea that they were working in the bar to try to better themselves struck some sort of Eliza Doolittle chord with the punters. Leanne was flattening out her raucous Scouse – cushion came out as 'cashion'; I modified my own accent, the one I used at work, which had become the voice I dreamed in, to make it a little less obviously Received Pronunciation, but to Olly's evident satisfaction, I still sounded relatively 'posh'.

At my day job, on Prince Street, there were those million tiny codes. Anyone's placement on the social scale could be calibrated to the *n*th degree at a single glance, and learning the rules was a lot more difficult than identifying paintings, because the whole point of those rules was that if you were on the inside, you never had to be told. Those hours of carefully teaching myself how to speak and how to walk might have passed the test with most people – Leanne, for instance, seemed bemused and grudgingly impressed by my transformation – but somewhere inside the house was a hidden casket of Alice in Wonderland keys that I would never possess, keys that unlocked ever tinier gardens whose walls were all the more impregnable because they were invisible. At the Gstaad, though, I was the token 'toff' and the girls, if they thought about it at all, believed there was no distinction between the WAGs and the superannuated debutantes who occupied adjoining pages in *OK!* magazine. Of course, in a deeper sense they would have been right.

The chat at the club was mostly about clothes, the acquisition of designer-branded shoes and handbags, and men. Some of the girls claimed to have steady boyfriends, many of them married, in which case it was the done thing to complain about their boyfriends endlessly; others were dating, in which case it was the done thing to complain about their dates endlessly. To Natalia and Anastasia and Martina and Karolina it seemed a self-evident truth that men were a necessary evil, to be endured for the sake of shoes, handbags and Saturday night trips to Japanese restaurants in Knightsbridge. There was a lot of analysis of texts, their frequency and affection, but any emotional response was reserved for the possibility that the men were seeing other women or failing to provide sufficient gifts. Plots and counter plots – with elaborate iPhone ruses – ensued, there was talk of men with boats, men with planes even, but I never got the sense that any of this involved pleasure. Love was not a language any of us dealt in; fresh skins and tight thighs were our currency, only of value to those too old to take it for granted. Older men, it was generally agreed, were less bother on the whole, though they came in for a good deal of raucous shrieking about their physical deficiencies. Baldness and halitosis and the Viagra-grind was reality, though you would never have known that from the coquettish messaging that formed communication between the girls and their men. This was the way of their world, and they kept their contempt and their occasional tears for the rest of us.

For the first time, in the Gstaad, I had what felt like girlfriends, and I was a bit ashamed of how happy it made me. I hadn't had friends at school. I had had quite a few black eyes, an aggressively haughty attitude, a truanting issue and a healthy appreciation of the joy of sex, but friends I didn't have time for. Beyond explaining that we had met up north, Leanne and I had an unspoken agreement that we had been teenage chums (if not actively taking part in holding someone's face in the lavatory cistern could count as being chummy) and never referred to it. Apart from Frankie, the department secretary at the House, the only constant female presence in my life had been my flatmates, two earnest Korean girls studying medicine at Imperial. We had a cleaning rota pinned up in the bathroom which we all stuck to politely enough and beyond that there was barely any need for conversation. With the exception of the women I met at the particular kind of parties I liked to go to, I'd only ever expected to encounter hostility and scorn from my own sex. I'd never learned how to gossip, or advise, or listen to the endless rehashings of thwarted desire. But here, I found I could join in. On the Tube, I swapped reading the *Burlington Magazine* and *The Economist* for *Heat* and *Closer*, so that when the talk of men palled I too could fall back on the endless soap opera of film stars. I invented a broken heart (implications of an abortion) to explain my lack of dates. I was Not Ready, and I enjoyed being advised that it was time to Get Closure and Move On. My odd nocturnal excursion I kept strictly to myself. It suited me, I realised, this strange little concentrated universe, where the world outside felt far away, where nothing was quite real. It made me feel safe.

Leanne hadn't lied about the money. Exaggerated, maybe, but it was still pretty extraordinary. Counting my percentage on the bottles as cab fare home, I was making about 600 a week clear in tips, crumpled twenties and fifties, sometimes more. A fortnight took care of my pathetic overdraft, and a few weeks later I took the Sunday train to an outlet centre near Oxford and made a few investments. A black Moschino skirt suit to replace the poor old Sandro, an achingly plain white Balenciaga cocktail dress, Lanvin flats, a DVF print day dress. I finally had my NHS teeth lasered in Harley Street, I made an appointment at Richard Ward and had my hair recut so that it looked subtly the same but five times as expensive. None of this was for the club. For that I got a few simple dresses from the high street and tarted them up with patent Loubie pumps. I cleared a shelf in my wardrobe and carefully placed most of my acquisitions there, wrapped in dry-cleaner's tissue. I liked to look at them, count them through like a stage miser. When I was little I had devoured Enid Blyton's boarding school books, St Clare's and Whyteleafe and Malory Towers. The new clothes were my gymslip and my lacrosse stick, the uniform of who I was going to be.

He started coming in after I had been at the club a month. Thursday was usually the Gstaad's busiest night, before men up on business went back to the country, but it was pouring outside and there were only two customers in the bar. Magazines and phones were not allowed as soon as the punters appeared, so the girls were listless, popping out to crouch under the awning for cigarettes, awkwardly trying to protect their hair from frizzing in the wet. The bell went and Olly came in. 'Sit up straight, ladies! It's your lucky night!' A few minutes later, one of the grossest men I had ever seen swung a vast belly into the room. He didn't even attempt a bar stool, but thumped down immediately on the nearest banquette, waving Carlo irritably away until he had removed his tie and mopped his face with a handkerchief. He had that slatternly look which only really extraordinary tailoring can solve, and his tailor had clearly been overwhelmed. His open jacket revealed a taut cream shirt stretched over the gut which rested on his splayed knees, folds of neck swagged over his collar, even his shoes looked overstuffed. He asked for a glass of iced water.

'Haven't seen Fatty for a while,' someone hissed.

The form was for the girls to talk animatedly, with a lot of hair tossing and glances beneath our lashes, looking as though we just happened to be there, unescorted in our smart dresses, until the client made his selection. The fat man was a quick chooser. He nodded to me, the flabby mottled curtains of his cheeks swishing back in a smile. As I crossed the floor I noted the regimental stripe on the discarded tie, the signet ring embedded in the swell of his little finger. Eeew.

'I'm Lauren,' I smiled breathily. 'Would you like me to join you?'

'James,' he supplied.

I sat down neatly, legs crossed at the ankle, and looked at him, all twinkling expectance. No talking until they ordered.

'I suppose you want me to buy you a drink?' He said it grudgingly, as though he knew how the club worked but still felt it an imposition.

'Thank you. That would be lovely.'

He didn't look at the list. 'What's the most expensive?'

'I think –' I hesitated.

'Just get on with it.'

'Well, James, that would be the Cristal 2005. Would you like that?'

'Get it. I don't drink.'

I gave the nod to Carlo before he changed his mind. The 2005 was a violent three grand. Three hundred up to me already. Hey, Big Spender.

Carlo carried the bottle over as though it was his first-born son, but James waved him away, uncorked it and dutifully filled the goldfish bowls.

'Do you like champagne, Lauren?' he asked.

I allowed myself a wry little smile. 'Well, it can get a bit monotonous.'

'Why don't you give that to your friends and order something you want?'

I liked him for that. He was physically repellent, true, but there was something brave about the fact that he didn't require me to pretend. I ordered a Hennessey and sipped it slowly, and he told me a little bit about his profession, which was money, of course, and then he heaved himself to his feet and waddled out, leaving £500 in new fifties on the table. The next night, he came back and did exactly the same. Leanne texted me on Wednesday morning to say that he had come to ask for Lauren on Tuesday, and on Thursday he reappeared, a few minutes after opening time. Several of the girls had 'regulars', but none so generous, and it gave me a new status amongst them. Slightly to my surprise, there was no jealousy. But, after all, business was business.

4

Once I'd started working at the club, the daily humiliations of my life in the department were thrown into glaring relief. At the Gstaad, there was at least the illusion that I held the cards. I tried to tell myself that it *amused* me that my straight life, my 'real' life, separated by just a few London streets from Olly and the girls, was bereft of any value or power. At the club, I felt prized every time I crossed my legs, whereas at my actual job, the one that was supposed to be my career, I was still pretty much a dogsbody. Actually, the Gstaad and the world's most elitist art store had more in common than it was comfortable to admit.

Working at the House could be disappointing, but I still remembered the first time that I had really *seen* a painting, and that memory still glowed within me. Bronzino's allegory, *Venus, Cupid, Folly and Time*, at the National Gallery, in Trafalgar Square. I still find the picture soothing, not only for the mannered, mysterious elegance of its composition – playful and innocently erotic, or darkly reminiscent of mortality and death – but because no scholar has so far advanced an accepted theory of what it means. Its beauty lies somewhere within the frustration it provokes.

It was a school trip to London, hot hours in a coach with the smell of sausage rolls and cheese crisps, the popular girls yakking and squabbling in the back seats, our teachers looking strangely vulnerable in unaccustomed casual clothes. We had gawped through the gates of Buckingham Palace, then plodded down The Mall to the gallery in our navy uniform sweatshirts – just pin on the name badge and you're ready for the call centre. Boys skidded on the parquet floors, girls made loud, coarse remarks at every nude we passed. I tried to wander away alone, wanting to get lost in the seemingly endless rooms of images, when I came across the Bronzino at random.

It was as though I'd tripped and fallen down a hole, a gasping sense of quickly recovered shock, the brain lagging behind the body. There was the goddess, there her boy child, there the mysterious old man standing over them. I did not know then who they were, but I recognised, blindingly, that I had not known lack until I watched those delicate colours glow and twine. And then I knew desire too, the first sense that I knew what I wanted and what I didn't have. I hated the feeling. I hated that everything I had known suddenly looked ugly to me, and that the source of that feeling, its mysterious pull and lure, was shining at me from this picture.

'Rashers is perving on that naked woman!'

Leanne and a couple of her cronies had caught up with me.

'Fucking lezza!'

'Lezzaaaaaah!'

Their harsh, screeching voices were disturbing the other visitors, heads were turning, my face burned with shame. Leanne's hair had been an orangish blonde back then, viciously permed and gelled into a peruke on her crown. Like her friends, she wore thick tan foundation and smudged black eyeliner.

'They really shouldn't let them in if they can't behave,' I heard one voice saying. 'I know it's free, but –'

'I know,' interrupted another. 'Little animals.'

They looked at us as though we smelled bad. I wondered if we did, to them. I hated the disdain in those smooth, educated voices. I hated being lumped in with the others. But Leanne had heard them too.

'You can fuck off an' all,' she said aggressively. 'Or are you fucking lezzas too?'

The two women who had spoken looked, simply, appalled. They did not remonstrate, just walked calmly away into the deeper galleries. My eyes followed them hungrily. I turned to the girls.

'They might complain. We might get chucked out.'

'So what? It's last here anyway. What's your problem, Rashers?'

I'd already got pretty good at fighting. My mother, when she bothered to notice me at all, was gentle with my blacked eyes and bruises, but mostly I tried to hide the evidence. Even then, she regarded me as a changeling. I could have started in on Leanne right there, yet – maybe it was the picture, maybe the knowledge of the women behind me – I didn't want to. I wasn't going to demean myself like that, not anymore. So I didn't make anything of it. I tried to wrap myself in contempt like a fur coat, to show them that they were so far beneath me that they weren't worth my attention. By the time school was over, I'd made a pretty good job of convincing myself of that. I had saved for two years for my first trip to northern Italy as a teenager, working in a petrol station, sweeping up bleached worms of hair in a beauty salon, slicing my fingers on foil cartons in the Chinese takeaway, dripping blood into the Friday night drunks' sweet-and-sour pork. I'd provided myself with a gap year in Paris and later a month's foundation course in Rome.

I had thought things might be different when I got into university. I had never really seen people who looked like that, let alone a place that looked like that. They belonged together, those beings and those buildings; all those generations of effortless entitlement melded honeyed stone and honeyed skin to an architectural perfection in every time-polished detail. I had lovers at college, yes, but if you look the way I look and, frankly, like the things I like, maybe girlfriends won't ever be your thing. I told myself I didn't need them, and besides, between the library and my part-time jobs there hadn't been much time for anything except reading.

I didn't stick to the books on my course list: along with Gombrich and Bourdieu I read hundreds of novels, scouring them for details of the customs of the strange country of class, of how to speak, the vocabulary that marks out those who belong to the invisible club from those who don't. I worked endlessly at my languages: French and Italian were the tongues of art. I read *Le Monde* and *Foreign Affairs*, *Country Life* and *Vogue* and *Opéra Magazine* and *Tatler* and polo magazines and *Architectural Digest* and the *Financial Times*. I taught myself about wine, about rare book bindings and old silver: I went to all the free recitals I could, first for duty and then for pleasure; I learned the correct use of the dessert fork and how to imitate the accent on which the sun has never set. I knew better by then than to try to pretend I was something I was not, but I thought if I became a good enough chameleon, no one would ever think to ask.

It wasn't snobbery that kept me at it. Partly, it was relief at being in an environment where confessing to an interest in anything apart from fucking reality shows wasn't an invitation to a cracked jaw. Mostly, when I had skived off school, it was to get the bus into town to visit the Picton Reading Room at the Central Library, or the Walker Art Gallery, because those quiet spaces breathed something more to me than the beauties they contained. They were – civilised. And being civilised meant knowing about the right things. However much people pretend that doesn't matter, it's true. Disclaiming that is as foolish as thinking that beauty doesn't matter. And to get amongst the right things, you have to be amongst the people who possess them. Since one also likes to be thorough, knowing the difference between a hereditary and an honorary marquess always comes in handy.

When I first arrived at the auction house, it seemed to have worked pretty well; the edges were smoothed off. I got on well with Frankie, the department secretary, even if she had a voice that sounded like a memsahib ordering her bearers over the plains and friends to whom she actually referred as 'Pongo' and 'Squeak'. Frankie fitted in a way I never could, quite, but at the same time she seemed to be floundering a bit in the brash new tide of money that was slowly seeping into the House. The art world had woken from its genteel slumbers in a billionaire's playground, where girls like Frankie were slowly becoming extinct. She had once confided to me rather mournfully that she would prefer to live in the country but that her mother thought she had more chance of 'meeting someone' with a job in town. Though Frankie was an avid reader of *Grazia*, she never seemed to follow any of the makeover tips – she wore an unironic velvet hairband and her arse looked like a giant tweedy mushroom. Once I had to steer her gently away from a truly disastrous turquoise taffeta ballgown on a sneaky dash to Peter Jones. I didn't think her mother needed to worry about ordering the engraved invitations anytime soon, but I admired Frankie's unapologetic style, her magnificent disdain for diets and her perennial optimism that she would some day meet 'the One'. I really hoped she would – I could see her in a Georgian rectory, dishing out fish pie in front of the Aga to an adoring and wholesome family.

Sometimes we had lunch together, and whilst I couldn't get enough of her Pony Club childhood, she seemed to like hearing about the (strictly edited) escapades of my own upbringing, too. Frankie was definitely one of the things I liked about my job: the other was Dave, who worked as a porter in the warehouse. Dave was pretty much the only other person at the House whom I felt actually liked me. He had left a leg just inside the Iraqi border in the first Gulf war and got into art documentaries while he was convalescing. He had a fantastic natural eye and a quick mind; his passion was the eighteenth century. He'd told me once that after what he'd seen in the Gulf it was sometimes the only thing that kept him going, the chance to be close to great pictures. You could see the love in the tender way he handled them. I respected the sincerity of his interest, as well as his knowledge, and I'd certainly learned more about pictures from Dave than any of my superiors in the department.

We flirted, of course, the nearest I ever got to water-cooler banter, but I also liked Dave because he was safe. Beneath his occasional saucy joke, he took a rather old-fashioned, paternal interest in me. He'd even sent me a congratulations card when I got promoted. But I knew he was happily married – his wife was always referred to as 'my missus' – and to put it bluntly it was relaxing to be around a guy who didn't want to fuck me. Aside from rococo art, Dave's other pleasure in life was garish 'true crime' paperbacks. Marital cannibalism was a popular trend, with many a disgruntled wife serving her husband as a pâté accompanied by a nicely chilled Chardonnay, and Dave, whose encounters with weaponry had been efficient and gun-shaped, delighted in the Shakespearean ingenuity of their fatal instruments. It was astonishing what you could do with a pair of curling tongs and a penknife if you put your mind to it. We had many a happy double-fag break in the dusty area of the warehouse, analysing the latest trends in gruesome murders, and I wondered sometimes how his interests connected, whether the prettified gods and goddesses who cavorted delicately through the canvases Dave loved were a solace for the violence he had witnessed, or an acknowledgement in their often erotic beauty that the classical world was as brutal and cruel as anything he had witnessed in the desert. If I was impressed by Dave's self-taught expertise, he was sometimes embarrassingly respectful of my own specialist status.

One morning after my latest evening with James, a Friday in early July, I had a few minutes before the department opened, so I ducked into the warehouse to find Dave. It had been a long night at the Gstaad and my retinas felt raw with smoke and sleeplessness. Dave clocked it when he saw I had my sunglasses on at 9 a.m.

'Rough night, darlin'?'

He produced a mug of sweet tea, two Nurofen and a Galaxy. Nothing like crap chocolate for a bad head. Dave kindly maintained the fancy that like many of the other girls who worked there I lived a dazzling social life amongst the reeling toffs of Chelsea. I didn't enlighten him. Once I felt human enough to remove the shades, I got a pad and my tape from my case to start measuring a small series of Neapolitan landscapes for the upcoming 'Grand Tour' sale.

'Shocking,' Dave remarked, 'putting that on at 200 reserve as a Romney. It's barely a "school of".'

'Shocking,' I muttered in agreement, pen between my teeth. One of the first things I'd learned at the House was that the reserve is the minimum price a seller requires a piece to fetch. I jerked my head towards his back pocket. 'New book, Dave?'

'Yeah, I'll lend it to you if you like. Smashing.'

'Remind me when Romney was in Italy?'

'1773 to 1775. Rome and Venice, mostly. So, this bloke's wife did him in the Cuisinart. In Ohio.'

'As if, Dave.'

'As if that's a Romney.'

My phone pinged with a text from Rupert, the head of department. I had to get out on a valuation the minute I'd taken the notes up.

At his desk Rupert was treating himself to what was probably his third breakfast of the morning, a sausage sandwich that had already oozed mustard onto one of his heavy double cuffs. I'd be off to the dry cleaner again later, I thought ruefully. What was it about me and fat men? He gave me an address in St John's Wood and the client details, and told me to get a move on, but as I reached the door of his office, he called out to me.

'Er, Judith?' One of the many things I hated about Rupert was his affectation that my first name was 'Er'.

'Yes, Rupert?'

'About these Whistlers –'

'I read up on them yesterday, like you told me.'

'Er, yes, but please remember that Colonel Morris is a very significant client. He will expect absolute professionalism.'

'Of course, Rupert.'

Maybe I didn't hate Rupert so much, I thought. He was trusting me with a serious valuation. I'd been sent on a few jobs before, minor things, even out of London a couple of times, but this was the first opportunity I'd had to speak to a 'significant' client. I took it as a good sign, that my boss's confidence in me was growing. If I could judge the price right, accurate but appealing to the seller, I could score the deal for the house by acquiring the pieces for sale. Whistler was a major artist, one who attracted serious collectors, and could mean serious money for the House.

To celebrate I charged a cab to the department's account, even though we juniors weren't permitted cabs. That budget was reserved for vital transportation such as fetching Rupert from the Wolseley round the corner on Piccadilly. I let it off a few streets from the address so that I could walk quietly under the summer-heavy trees by the canal. My head was clear now, and there was a scent of wet lilac from security-walled gardens. It made me smile to think that these streets, with their gangs of solemn Filipina nannies and Polish workmen installing vast basement pools, had once been little more than a vast and notorious high-class brothel, where women waited behind heavy plush curtains, arranged like Etty nudes, for their lovers to call on the way home from the City. London had always been and would always be a city of whores.

A beady laser eye scanned over me as I rang the bell at the ground-floor flat. The client opened the door into the creamy double-fronted stucco himself. Somehow I had expected a housekeeper.

'Colonel Morris? I'm Judith Rashleigh,' I introduced myself, holding out my hand, 'from British Pictures? We had an appointment about the Whistler studies?'

He snorted a greeting and I followed his Cavalry-twilled rump into the lobby. I'd hardly been expecting a dashing officer, but I had to prevent myself from recoiling as the yellow-nailed claw of his hand briefly grasped mine. Vicious little eyes twitched above a greying Hitlerish moustache, which clung to his upper lip like a slug on a ski jump. He didn't offer me a cup of tea, leading me straight into a stuffy drawing room, where fussy pastel drapes made an odd, provincial contrast with the extraordinary paintings on the walls. The Colonel drew the curtains as I gazed at a Sargent, a Kneller and a tiny, exquisite Rembrandt cartoon.

'What wonderful pictures.' At least ten million's worth. This really was going to be a proper valuation.

He nodded smugly, treating me to another walrus snort. 'I have the Whistler drawings in my bedroom,' he wheezed, skittering towards a second door. This room was yet more dim and close, with an unpleasant acrid smell of dried sweat cut with astringent, old-fashioned cologne. A large bed, made up with sheets and hairy moss-green blankets, took up most of the space. I had to sidle round it to reach the bureau, where five small pictures were lined up. I took out my torch and examined each one thoroughly, checking for the consistency of the signature and very gently unfastening the frames to check the watermark on the paper.

'Lovely,' I said. 'The preps for the *Thames Sonata* series, just as you suggested.' I was quite pleased with the sound of my own confident, efficient attribution.

'I didn't need you to tell me that.'

'Of course. But you are thinking of offering them for sale? They wouldn't be quite suitable for the Italian show, but they'd be perfect for the spring catalogue. Naturally you have the provenances?' Provenance was key in this business – the trajectory of a picture from the artist's easel through its various owners and salerooms, the paper trail that proved it was genuine.

'Naturally. Perhaps you might like to have a glance at these while I hunt them out?' He handed me a heavy album. 'They're late Victorian. Most unusual.'

Perhaps it was the two grasping hands which were scrabbling at my buttocks, but I had a depressingly clear idea of what the Colonel's etchings were going to look like. Nothing I couldn't handle. I simply twitched the hands off and opened the album. Not bad, for nineteenth-century porn. I turned a few pages as though I was actually interested. Professionalism, that was all I needed. But then I felt one of those hands creeping around my breast, and suddenly his weight was on me, pushing me abruptly down on the bed.

'Colonel! Let me up immediately!' I gave him my best outraged-head-girl voice, but this wasn't feeling like panto anymore. His body pressed heavily on my lungs as he rolled sideways to try to get those repulsive cuspate fingers under my skirt. The green blanket was stifling me; I couldn't lift my head. My attempts to buck him away were obviously doing something for him, as he planted a foully wet kiss on my exposed neck and hauled his body further over mine.

I was breathing in shallow gasps – I couldn't get any air, and that was making me panic. I really don't like that. I tried to work my palms beneath me to throw him off in a press-up, but he pinioned my right wrist to the bed. I managed to turn my face to the right and sucked foetid air from beneath his armpit. Sweat drenched the front of his Viyella shirt and the bunched wrinkles of his face pulsed next to mine. This close, his teeth were hideously tiny, browning foetal stumps.

'What do you think?' he gasped, narrowing his boiled eyes seductively. 'I've got lots more like that. Videos too. I bet a little bitch like you would love that, eh?'

His stomach was gibbering against my back. I gave him time to fumble at his fly. God knows what he thought he'd find there. Then I bit his hand, as hard as I could, feeling the flesh give under my jaw. In the moment it took him to squeal and rear up, I'd grabbed my bag, found my phone and aimed it firmly at his crotch like a pistol.

'You little –'

'Bitch? Yes, you said that already. Problem with dogs is, they bite. Now. Get the fuck away from me.'

He was nursing his hand. I hadn't drawn blood, but I spat at him just in case.

'I'm going to call Rupert immediately!'

'I don't think so. You see, videos are a bit behind the times, Colonel Morris. We've gone digital. Like my phone. Which can film this and automatically email it to all my friends. Though there's no magnifying glass if you're planning to pull out whatever you're hiding in your trousers. Have you heard of YouTube?'

I waited, keeping my eyes on his face, feeling my vertebrae tense inside my shirt. There was still no way I could get past him in that cramped space unless he was prepared to let me. I inhaled and exhaled very slowly. This was a very important client.

'Thank you so much for your time, then, Colonel. I won't take up any more of it. I'll have someone from the warehouse come to pack the drawings this afternoon, shall I?'

I had another brief moment of panic at the front door, but it was unlatched, closing quietly behind me with a heavy click. I kept my back straight as far as Abbey Road. I breathed in for four, held for four, out for four. Then I cleaned my face with a wipe from my bag, tidied my hair and called the department.

'Rupert? It's Judith. We can send someone for the Whistlers this afternoon.'

'Er, Judith. Did everything, er, go alright?'

'Why shouldn't it have done?'

'No, er, trouble with the Colonel?'

He knew. Sweaty fucking Rupes *knew.* I kept my tone smooth.

'No trouble at all. It was quite – manageable.'

'Good girl.'

'Thank you, Rupert. I'll be back at the office soon.'

Of course he knew. That's why he'd sent the pretty one instead of doing such a significant valuation himself. Why are you such a mug, Judith? Why did you believe that he might have sent the departmental nobody on a major call unless the client expected a little extra? He was clear in his own mind, wasn't he, about what I was good for?

Then, just for a few seconds, I leaned against a wall and hid my face in my arms, letting the adrenalin surge through me. I was shaking so hard I felt the muscles of my stomach ache. I felt coated in the stink of Colonel fucking Morris and I was so furious I felt winded, like something had punched out my heart. I made a fist of my face in the effort to keep the sobs back. I could cry, I thought. I could press my face to the grainy London brick and weep for all the things I didn't have, and the unfairness, and how bloody tired it made me. I could cry like the chippy little loser a part of me still was, because I just had to take this shit. But then if I cried I might not stop. Couldn't have that. This was nothing, nothing. I caught myself thinking that Rupert might actually be grateful to me, because I hadn't done the obvious thing, screamed harassment and insisted on the police, but I squashed that down along with my waver of self-pity. It was a waste of time for me to expect praise, just as it was a waste of time to be bitter about it. I might not have the right name, or have gone to school or on fucking shooting weekends with the right people, but I didn't resent the Ruperts of the world, and I wasn't insecure enough to despise them. Hate is better. Hate keeps you cold, keeps you moving fast, keeps you lonely. If you need to make yourself into someone else, loneliness is a good place to start.

When I had gone for the interview at Prince Street, Rupert had boredly shown me a few postcards to identify; elementary stuff – a Velazquez, a Cranach. I wondered then if he'd bothered to read my CV and, later, when I mentioned something about my Master's, realised from his expression of perturbed surprise that he hadn't. The last postcard, which he pushed slyly across the table, showed a slim half-nude girl wound in gauzy draperies.

'Artemisia Gentileschi, *Allegoria dell'Inclinazione*,' I had answered without hesitation. For one tiny moment, Rupert actually allowed himself to look impressed. I'd had that postcard on my wall ever since my trip to Florence at sixteen. Artemisia was the daughter of a painter, the most brilliant of his apprentices, one of whom raped her while they worked on a commission in Rome. She took him to court and, after being tortured with thumbscrews to prove she was telling the truth, she won her case. Her hands were her future, and she risked them being twisted beyond recovery, so blazingly did she demand justice. Many of her paintings were famously violent, so much so that critics had a hard time believing that a woman had painted them, but I had chosen this one because Artemisia had used her own face as her model.

She was twenty-one when she made the picture, unwillingly married off to a third-rate court painter who sponged off her talent, but she showed herself, I thought, as she wanted to be, unashamed, her rather plain face serene, holding a compass, the symbol of her own determination. I will choose, the picture said to me, *I* will choose. Like all teenagers when they fall in love, I had been convinced that nobody understood Artemisia like I did. The object might have been unconventional, but the feeling was just the same. We were so alike, she and I. For sure, if she hadn't died in the seventeenth century, we could have been Best Friends Forever.

It was Artemisia who got me the job. That interview was the only time that Rupert ever saw me, that is, saw a person rather than a negligible presence. But even then, what he saw was a perfect, clever dogsbody who would do his grunt work and never complain. Now, leaning dry-eyed against a suburban wall, I felt a little skein of love twisting back towards my sixteen-year-old self, standing there in the Casa Buonarroti with her earnest book bag and her terrible clothes, wishing I could appear like a ghost from the future and tell her that everything was going to be alright. Because it would. I wasn't going to go to the police. Rupert would fire me as soon as they'd taken my statement. No. I could take this, I could make it alright.

5

Getting home that evening my nerves were fizzing, and I told myself that after Colonel Morris I deserved a bit of a party. I texted Lawrence to see if there was anything going on at his place that night. Lawrence was an acquaintance from my early days in London: rich, dubious and placidly addicted to heroin. I'd got to know him around the scene, which like all special-interest hobbies is a pretty small world. Now he organised more private affairs at his home in Belgravia and suggested I swing by the Square about eleven.

Lawrence's parties supposedly cost £150, but I knew he'd let me in for nothing. I unlocked my bedroom door and let my head fall back against the silk kimono hanging there, breathing in the scent of clean linen and geranium oil from my little ceramic burner. I looked at my books, my neatly made bed, the Balinese-print shawl hung over the foul Venetian blind, and I couldn't stand the sight of any of it. All cheap, all so pathetically optimistic. Not even the folded promise of the beautiful clothes in the hunchbacked melamine wardrobe could soothe me. I rustled through my things, trying to work out how I felt. Nothing too aggressive. Underneath, I needed to be soft, feminine; on top I would be the cat who walked by herself. I chose coffee-coloured Brazilian-cut lace shorts and a matching bra. Over that I slipped on loose combats, a black tee and Converse. I'd change into heels when I got there – I could afford a cab these days, but I wanted to move, to clear my lungs of the lingering spores of the Colonel's blanket. I took a luxurious time making up my face to make it look as though I hadn't made up my face and walked over to Belgravia.

The still-white stuccoed streets seemed wrapped in secrets. It was always so calm here; whatever sins were concealed behind those plutocratic porticoes were safely swaddled by money. Lawrence was leaning in the doorway of 33 Chester Square, smoking, as I approached. Probably grabbing some peace from the commune of rackety Soho exiles which inhabited his attic, sponging and drinking and fancying themselves artists: in theory the fee for the parties kept them in smack and vinyl. I'd sometimes thought of asking for a room myself, to save the rent, but the atmosphere was too messy; it would distract me from the future I needed to make.

'Hello, lovely.' Lawrence was wearing blue velvet trousers with a grosgrain stripe and an ancient white shirt, the frayed cuffs gaping over his skinny wrists.

'Hey, Lawrence. Who's here? Who's pretty?'

'Well, darling, you, now.'

'Are you coming in?' From the length of Lawrence's vowels I thought he was probably going to nod out right there on the doorstep.

'No, darling, not yet. Off you go. *Amuse-toi.*'

The party was in the basement but I went for a wander first, imagining, as I always did, how I would live if such a house were mine, how I would change the rooms, colour and furnish them. There was no one to see me run my hand over the sensuous curve of the eighteenth-century banister, the solid certainty of its polished mahogany. I had learned from the smarter interiors magazines that it was wrong for houses to look too 'done', that the hideous Seventies green corduroy sofa squatting in Lawrence's drawing room was as much an ineffable mark of his class as his voice or the way he wore his fraying shirts, but I imagined how the room would look rewashed in Trianon *gris*, with just a few perfect pieces, spare and exquisite, and myself serene amongst them. Chester Square was a much better antidote to Colonel Morris than my snotty little pep talk earlier. Desire and lack, I told myself, and the space between them, was what I had to negotiate. I sometimes saw my life as a web of tightropes to be walked, stretched between what I could give, or make believe I gave, and what I would possess. I wriggled out of most of my clothes and slipped on a pair of black suede Saint Laurent pumps, then I stalked round the room, trailing my fingers over Lawrence's lovely, neglected antiques, touching them like talismans. You, I thought, you and you and *you*. I practically skipped down the basement stairs.

As I stepped through the black shantung curtain I saw a blonde girl I recognised from other parties going down on a fortysomething guy, professionally sweeping her hair away from her face so he had a good view of her mouth, taking the whole length of him in one smooth swallow. I'd seen her around; she was Russian, but she called herself Ashley – Lawrence usually mixed a couple of rentals with his guests to keep the party going. I walked past them and took a drink from Lawrence's barman-cum-bouncer, who stood formally against one of the glossy black walls with a tray of champagne flutes, as imperturbable as if he were serving canapés at a diplomat's cocktail party. I tried a sip, but I didn't need it.

'Is Helene here?' I asked. Another regular at Lawrence's.

'Over there.' He cocked his head.

Helene was lying on a black velvet chaise longue, her breasts spilling like syllabub out of an embroidered corset.

'Hey, Judith darling.'

She lifted her face to me and I bent down to kiss her, taking her tongue, slightly sour with champagne, into my mouth.

'Lawrence said you'd be coming over. We were waiting for you, weren't we?'

A boy looked up from where he had been kneeling between Helene's generously rounded thighs. I wouldn't have wanted her body myself, but I had a little kink for her belly, the soft pale spread of it. I ran my hand luxuriously over the full mound, exploring its give and sheen.

'This is Stanley.'

'Hello, Stanley.' He stood up and swooped down again to kiss me too quickly for me to have a sense of his face. His mouth was wide and not too sloppy; he had that young man's smell of wet hay underneath his cologne. I ran my hands speculatively over his naked back as he pulled me closer, feeling the muscles winged under his shoulder blades. Nice.

Helene was idly dangling a pair of handcuffs, bright steel, proper police issue. 'I said to Stanley you might like to double dip?'

'Sure, lovely. Where would you like me?'

'Underneath. Will that be nice, Stanley?'

He nodded. He didn't look as though speech was one of his gifts. I settled next to Helene on the chaise and we began to kiss again, me stroking the delicious dips and roundness of her body, she slowly working off my knickers and gently placing a finger on the lips of my cunt. I took her nipple in my mouth and sucked, swirling my tongue over the areolae until she made a little purring noise, then pushed two fingers inside her. Always that exquisite tightness, so soft, so very soft. I could feel the want inside me now, so I manoeuvred myself face down, wriggling underneath her until our bodies were aligned, my face in the velvet seat, her luscious belly settled in the small of my back. I reached up my right arm and she did the same. Stanley fumbled a bit as he cuffed our wrists together, but he managed it.

'There,' Helene murmured, 'isn't that pretty?' He took her first, straddling my legs and going into her from behind so I felt his balls and the heat and juice of her against my arse. I worked my left hand under my clit where the weight crushed it against me and began stroking. I was eager now, wanting his cock up me, lifting my hips in time with Helene as she took him. I heard her gasp as he pulled out, and then the head of his cock, smooth in the condom, was against my own lips and he slid easily into me, using his hands on Helene's arse for purchase. He got me close, then went back to Helene, fucking her harder until her body tensed and bucked above me, then entered me again. I was praying for him to last until I was over the edge, then he got me there and she rolled off to the side, her cunt wet against my thigh, and finished him in her mouth. I lay there, breathing, one leg falling to the floor, gaping, my own juice cooling on the fluttering lips of my pussy. This was the rush, for me. Not merely the purity of sheer carnal pleasure but the way that being splayed and screwed by a stranger made me feel so free, so untouchable.

6

That turned out to be the last party I went to in London. Now I was working at the Gstaad Club I needed to take care of myself, to give time to sleep and running as well as my actual career. I told myself that I had to dismiss the incident with Colonel Morris. The old bastard had failed at his pathetic attempt, and the only thing that really mattered to me was the endgame. I had pulled off the valuation and that was all that counted at the House. So I had to stay tight and fresh, even if that meant setting the alarm for five to bang out my laps of Hyde Park before leaving for the office. After James began waddling into the club with his showers of fifties I began to have regular facials and manicures and paid for a couple of expensive Pilates sessions at the gym. Thanks to my new reading material, I knew that this was not extravagance, it was Me Time, and Investing In Myself. James was now accepted as my regular and on Thursdays and Fridays Olly said I didn't need to get booked by anyone else, though sometimes I would sit with another man if I was asked, so James had to wait alone, watching me intently until the obligatory bottle was finished and I could sashay across the dance floor with a welcoming smile on my face.

I couldn't help fantasising about what I could do if I could keep old James interested. My job in British Pictures barely paid minimum wage. Although my education had been basically free, I had still taken out a graduate loan for £10,000 when I finished studying to cover rent and expenses. Soon I would have to start paying it back. I had reckoned I was good enough to get a less junior position before the payments fell due so the risk had seemed worth it, but the debt would be called in in the autumn, a scant couple of months away, and until I'd begun at the club I'd just been subsisting. With a thousand a week from James, plus what I could earn on the side from other customers, I could hope to start paying back the loan and breathe a bit, maybe even get a flat on my own. I opened a savings account and watched the numbers begin to stack up.

It was clear from the start what James wanted, but his arrogance was overlaid with an air of diffidence, as though he didn't quite know where to begin. Like most men, his favourite topic of conversation was himself, so it was easy to draw him out. He had a wife, Veronica, and a teenage daughter, who lived in Kensington, near Holland Park. He claimed to like reading philosophy in his spare time, though his idea of serious thought was more 'Jesus CEO' than Kantian aesthetics. Still, we got quite a lot of mileage out of that. I asked him to recommend a few titles and Googled the reviews so it seemed as though I had read them. Veronica managed the house and sat on various charity committees. I wondered about her, a little, about whether she knew, or cared, where her husband spent his evenings. I doubted she did. Did they fuck? I couldn't imagine James being capable of it – even if the oestrogen produced by all that flab hadn't eaten his cock he could barely get up the stairs of the club without risking a coronary. But as our evenings together unfolded, he was keen to convince me that he'd been quite the dog in his day. Oh, he'd had a gay old time, had James. The older married woman in St Moritz, the sisters on Cap Ferrat. He was old enough to claim to have been a debs' delight, and I came in for a lot of anecdotes about 'gels' who gave in in shooting brakes and London squares, madly hilarious house parties and Soho nightclubs. Apparently, what was left of London Society in the Seventies had been an erotic paradise for the morbidly obese.

'Biccie, Judith?' asked Frankie, the department secretary, pulling my mind back to the meeting as she pushed a plate of chocolate digestives over the conference table. Laura frowned. We were having what Rupert called a High Priority Consultation – me, Frankie, Rupert, Laura and Oliver the portraiture expert, who was slightly thinner and less pomegranate-coloured than our boss.

'No, thanks,' I whispered back.

Laura frowned at us and ruched up her pashmina further over the ravages of her Barbados tan. I changed my mind and took a biscuit. At least Frankie offered some gentle female solidarity, unlike Laura, who mostly treated me like an unsatisfactory housemaid.

'Here they are,' said a girl's voice. A tall blonde with artfully ratted hair was breathlessly setting down a pile of new catalogues.

'This is Angelica,' said Laura. 'Angelica is joining us on work experience for a month. She's just finished at the Burghley in Florence.'

If Dave had been there I would have rolled my eyes. The Burghley offered history of art courses for rich thickies too monumentally idle to get into even a pretend university. They got a year in Renaissance Disneyland on the assumption they might absorb a bit of culture by osmosis between spliffs, and a nice little certificate.

'Welcome to the department, Angelica,' said Rupert pleasantly.

'It's so good of you to have me here,' she replied.

'Angelica is my god-daughter,' added Laura, winching her Botox into a beam. That explained that then. I sat up a bit straighter.

'Now,' said Rupert, 'big event today, boys and girls. We've got a Stubbs in.' He passed round the catalogues. They looked like programmes for an eighteenth-century opera. *George Stubbs*, announced the cover, *The Duke and Duchess of Richmond Watching the Gallops*.

'Oooh,' squealed Frankie, like the good sport she was, 'A Stubbs!'

I could see why she was excited. George Stubbs was a hugely profitable artist, known for fetching prices over twenty million. I had a bit of a soft spot for him myself – he was from Liverpool, like me, and despite having actually bothered to study anatomy, meaning that his paintings of horses were some of the finest the eighteenth century had produced, he was still dismissed by the Royal Academy in his own day as a 'sporting painter' and denied full membership. I was curious to see which of his works we'd got.

'You'll want to read this thoroughly,' put in Oliver. 'I've been working on it for quite some time.'

I flicked swiftly through the pages, but when I came to the main illustration I suddenly felt cold. I had seen this picture before, and there was no way it belonged in a catalogue.

'Rupert, I'm sorry,' I said, 'but I don't understand. This is the picture I saw in January, the one at the place near Warminster?'

'Don't worry, your assessment was fine. I went back to have a look at it myself. Couldn't have expected the intern to pick up a Stubbs!'

I hadn't picked it up, because it wasn't a Stubbs. And I wasn't an intern anymore, as Rupert knew perfectly well. I'd worked hard to be able to make that kind of judgement. I tried again.

'You didn't say –'

Rupert cut me off with an awkward laugh.

'Wanted it to be a surprise. Now –'

I interrupted. 'But I was certain. I took photos.'

'The picture was cleaned, Judith, after I brought it in. The details you correctly identified were later overpaintings. Is there a problem?'

I knew better than to challenge him again. 'No, of course not.' I forced myself to look enthusiastic. 'How thrilling!'

A two-week view was planned for September, to precede the sale. Rupert thought the picture sufficiently important for a stand-alone auction. Oliver thought it should be integrated into an assembled sale. Laura talked about which collectors to alert. Frankie took notes. I was too shocked even to amuse myself with what thoughts might be tumbling through the vast and empty expanses of Angelica's brain. I managed to ask a few diligent questions at the end as to arrangements for the private view, so I could memo the events girls, and then casually asked if they were hilling in the warehouse that afternoon.

'I thought I could take Angelica down to have a look,' I suggested in a friendly voice.

Hilling, as I explained to Angelica as we made our way through the dusty confusion of passages that was the basement, was the house slang for unloading works, so called because they had to be wheeled up a slatted ramp into the warehouses. It was an opportunity for the juniors to see the pieces up close as they were unpacked in the viewing room before the experts came down. It was really extraordinary,

I explained, to see masterpieces displayed on an everyday wooden bench instead of the sanctity of a gallery. Angelica was engrossed in her phone.

'Yah,' she managed, raking a hand through the blonde mass, 'I saw loads in the Uffizi. Like, uh, Branzini?'

'I think maybe you mean Bronzino?'

'Yah. Him.'

As I'd hoped, Dave was there. He and a colleague were hilling ten Pompeo Batonis for the upcoming 'Grand Tour' sale.

'Looking good, Judith, looking good. You got a new fella?'

'You know you're my only boyfriend, Dave,' I flirted back. I'd ordered a whole bagful of true crime from Amazon and bashed the paperbacks around a bit. As I introduced Angelica I handed them over and said I'd found them as a job lot in the Marylebone Oxfam.

'What's on today?' I asked, for Angelica's benefit, as what passed for her concentration was still focused on her phone.

'Batoni in Rome.'

'Italy!' I squawked. 'Perfect, Angelica! Why don't you help with the measuring?' I made a smoking motion to Dave and he limped out into the butt-filled basement area with me for a fag.

Quickly, I filled Dave in on my trip to Warminster. Rupert said he'd had a call from a pal who had an antiques place in Salisbury, who had seen the picture at a dinner party and thought it might be the real thing. I'd only been sent originally because Rupert had been off shooting. The owner of the house, an ex-Guardsman who introduced himself without irony as Tiger, explained that his family had been there for about a century; he thought the picture had been bought by his great-grandfather. I didn't ask too many questions, as Rupert had enjoined me strictly not to even hint that we thought the picture might be genuine.

I had taken the picture from the dining-room wall and repositioned it in the window seat for the best light. At first, I could see what Rupert's friend had been so excited about. The composition was arranged rhythmically, with a group of ladies, gentlemen and grooms occupying the left background, watching three horses who seemed to be galloping across the down towards the spectator. The horses were beautifully rendered, two chestnuts and a grey, their limbs spread in racing symmetry; the colours were muted, as though on a misty morning, with only the red liveries of the grooms competing for the light with the sheen on the horses' coats. Looking closely, though, I had been less impressed by the group of spectators, who seemed lifeless and fussy, their space cluttered with the accoutrements of an elaborate eighteenth-century picnic. They threw the composition off balance, distracting from the graceful descent of the animals, the people dominating the canvas in a way which had seemed to me uncharacteristic of Stubbs. Uncertain, I had found what seemed like a too-positive signature, then turned the canvas around to check the backing. A small label was glued to the frame, with the name 'Ursford and Sweet', a long-defunct London gallery. The label carried a title, *The Duke and Duchess of Richmond Watching the Gallops*, and a date, 1760. Behind the figures in the picture was a signpost that read 'Newmarket'. Stubbs was the finest equestrian painter of his day, perhaps of all time, but so far as I knew he had never worked at Newmarket Racecourse. I had brought a *catalogue raisonné* with me, the latest compendium of all known Stubbs works, so I flipped through the plates until I found another representation of the same Duke and Duchess watching horses exercising at Goodwood, dated 1760. There was a similarity between the faces, though it was more period generic than personal – I supposed now that must have been what convinced Rupert. It was quite possible that Stubbs should have painted his patrons at Newmarket, though the catalogue made no mention of it, nor of the existence of the picture before me. A newly discovered Stubbs would have been a major event, and majorly profitable, so it was with regret that I had photographed the picture carefully and made a thorough summary in my notes, adding my own opinion, that it was a period mock-up, at the bottom. Then I had had an hour before my train, and Tiger had offered to show me the stables. I didn't think Dave needed to know about my own jolly little gallop around the paddock.

'So it's weird, Dave. I wrote it up in January as a "school of" and now in summer it turns up as a Stubbs. And the Newmarket signpost is gone – Rupert said it was an overpaint that was removed at cleaning – and the signature's in a different place.'

'Where did you say it came from?'

'The owner said his great-grandfather bought it. It was labelled from Ursford and Sweet in Bond Street; they've not been there since the war.'

'Well, you say it was eighteenth century, though?'

'Yes –'

'So Ursford's must have got it from somewhere.'

'Not here. Rupert would have put that in the catalogue if the provenance was ours.'

'The other place?'

Like Oxford and Cambridge, it was taboo for the two leading auction houses in London ever to mention one another's name.

'It could have been a private sale, of course, but there's a good chance it was them. It would take forever to get the permission to use their archives, though.'

'Well, I've got a mate in the Old Masters warehouse there. He can get you into their archive, no problem. You could do it today, on your lunch. Why are you so keen anyway?'

'I don't know. I just wouldn't like there to be a mistake.'

I couldn't tell Dave that my sudden transformation into Nancy Drew was because I thought I saw a way to finally get some recognition in the department, by saving their faces from a very public error. Stubbs was news; the British always preferred their masterpieces to have an animal in them. I felt excited; I was imagining my brilliant disclosure at the next departmental meeting, maybe even a congratulatory lunch in the boardroom, a real promotion. To show that I was worth something more than getting the likes of Colonel Morris hot under the collar. It would be a chance to succeed for the right reasons, talent and application, a chance to prove that I could do a proper job.

Officially I had an hour for lunch, but it was easy to go over as the other members of British Pictures seemed to consider it their ancestral right to take three, and I made it across Piccadilly to New Bond Street with forty minutes in hand.

'You're Mike? Dave's friend? I'm Judith Rashleigh. Thanks so much for letting me do this – we've got a bit of a rush on in the department.'

I smiled when I saw the paperback sticking out of the back pocket of Mike's jeans: *Shattered: The True Story of a Mother's Love, A Husband's Betrayal and a Cold-Blooded Texas Murder.*

'I can get you in, then I'm off on my lunch. Fine that you're in a hurry, but if anyone asks why you haven't got a permission slip from the department head, it's nothing to do with me, OK?'

'Sure. We really appreciate it. As I said, we're a bit manic. Thanks again.'

Our rival's archive was housed in a beautiful panelled gallery, with a view over Savile Row. They hadn't been computerised yet either, and looking over the long rows of heavy double bookcases dating back to the early 1700s, it was difficult to believe that the most impressive mechanical brain might not melt into a sulking puddle at the prospect of such chaos. There were several other people working, most of them around my age, interns and assistants longing for their lunch, surreptitiously messaging. None of them paid any attention to me.

If the painting's original dating of 1760 was accurate, there were about 150 years between the its creation and the closing of Ursford's in 1913. Ursford had opened in about 1850, but the label on the picture had been typed, which would place the gallery's acquisition no earlier than 1880, so it was logical to start there and work forward. Luckily, the two houses used the same system, so I started with the index cards, each of which recorded a single painting, often with a photograph, and details of the sale date and price. Updating the index was one of the dreary jobs I was used to. There were many Stubbs sales, but none of the descriptions corresponded to the painting I had seen. There were also several 'school of' classifications, pictures in the style of the named painter, and of the period, but not necessarily by the artist, five of which were dated between 1870 and 1910. One of these did correspond to the possible Stubbs, identification code ICHP905/19, meaning that it had been an Important Country House Pictures sale in 1905 with the painting as the nineteenth lot. I rushed back to the stacks and gripped the handles of the case labelled 1900–1905 with both hands, hauling them until a wide enough gap appeared. The cases were on castors and it was a hard job to force them far enough apart to get into the stack to read. I sidled in and moved quickly down the row until I came to 1905, in search of an 'Important Country House Pictures'. There it was. *Property of an Earl: The Duke and Duchess of Richmond Watching the Gallops*. Sold to W.E. Sweet, Esq., knocked down at 1,300 guineas. The Earl of Halifax, I guessed, one of the largest Stubbs collections in the country. So it was genuine. I couldn't help feeling perversely disappointed. My brilliant plan to rescue Rupert from a catastrophic misattribution was a non-starter. It was quite respectable – some earlier expert had misjudged the real thing for a 'school of', that was all. It had been my mistake. Still, at least I could contribute some useful information about the provenance. Rupert had to be pleased with that.

I walked back along the Burlington Arcade, looking into the windows of the cashmere shops and the enchanting gilded jewel box of the Ladurée *macaron* shop. I thought I might get myself a good classic jumper with some of my club money. Still, there was something nagging at me. Thirteen hundred guineas was a significant sum in 1905, yet in the excitement about the Stubbs in the department, no one had mentioned the reserve. I visualised the catalogue, the numbers printed discreetly on the back page: 800K. Absurdly low. It didn't make sense. If the picture was as genuine as it appeared to be, why would Rupert have agreed to set such a small minimum asking price?

Only Frankie was in when I got back to the department, munching a vast cheese toastie from the greasy spoon in Crown Passage. It was damp outside, as per usual, and I couldn't help noticing that her jacket, slung over her chair, smelt strongly of Labrador. It made me feel affectionate towards her.

'Frankie,' I asked, 'do you remember where you put the notes I brought back from Warminster a few months ago? The Stubbs research?'

'They should be with the material for the upcoming sale. Rupert's so excited!'

'Yes, yes, of course. I just wanted to have a quick squiz.'

She reached behind her and picked up a file, which she leafed through, shaking her head. 'No, they're not here. Just Rupert's own notes and the photos after the cleaning. Shall I have another look?'

'No, no worries. Sorry to disturb your lunch.'

Something about this was still scratching at me. I checked a number in the office diary and went to make a call in the dingy departmental loo. Mrs Tiger answered. I hadn't met her; she had been visiting her sister in Bath, which was perhaps just as well, given what Tiger could do with a riding crop. She sounded pleasantly floral.

'This is Judith Rashleigh. I came down to Warminster a few months ago. Your husband was kind enough to let me have a look at your equestrian painting.'

'Oh, yes. Well, we were pleased. What can I do for you?'

'You must be very pleased with the attribution?'

'Yes, well, we always knew in our hearts that it wasn't really a Stubbs. The chap gave us a jolly good price though.'

'The buyer?'

'The chap who came down.'

'Of course,' I said quickly, 'Rupert.'

Mrs Tiger hesitated. 'No – I don't think that was the name.'

'Oh.' I tried to sound casual to cover my confusion. 'My mistake. Well I was just wanting to make sure you had our details in case there's anything else you'd like us to look at. We like to follow up.'

'You've been very kind, suggesting another gallery.'

'That's – um – no trouble. I don't want to take up any more of your time, but you don't happen to remember the name of the man who came down, do you?'

Her voice became slightly wary.

'No. Why?'

I muttered something full of jargon, thanked her and hung up. I sat down on the loo to think. Mrs Tiger had ruefully acknowledged that their picture was not a genuine Stubbs. She had sold it, and had been pleased to get a decent price for a 'school of'. Yet the picture we were selling in the department was the same one.

I took another look at the catalogue we were preparing. The picture was to be listed, in the conventional style, as 'Property of a Gentleman'. I had naturally assumed the 'gentleman' was Mr Tiger, but apparently not. Rupert's story tallied with my research at the other archive: the picture had been misattributed, so whoever had discovered it was real had to be the mysterious 'chap' who had bought it from the Tigers and now planned to sell it through us. Bad luck for the Tigers, though I was hardly going to be stupid enough to tell them that. If the 'chap' had fiddled them, it wasn't our business – he had apparently paid fair whack on a hunch and was getting his reward. Still, it didn't sit right. I felt antsy, oddly apprehensive, a feeling that stayed with me until Rupert breezed in about three, after what had obviously been yet another good lunch, and muttered something about a meeting at Brooks's. They actually provide pillows there for the members to nap in the library in the afternoon.

'I'll see you tonight, then, Angelica,' he said on his way out.

Angelica didn't even bother looking up from her urgent texting. 'Yuh, sure, Rupes.'

I was wondering what 'tonight' was when Rupert paused at my desk, fumbling in his briefcase.

'Er, Judith. Thought you might like to come to this,' he said, handing me a stiff envelope. 'Angelica's coming along. Bit of socialising. Look smart!'

'I'll do my best, Rupert.'

'I'm sure you will. You always look, er, very nice. See you later then!'

I left the envelope where he'd dropped it for a bit, in case Angelica thought I didn't know what I'd been asked to, but when I opened it I had a hard time keeping the grin off my face. Rupert had given me an invite to the Tentis party at the Serpentine Gallery. Tentis & Tentis were a huge architecture firm who had just finished a conversion in the City which contained some of the most expensive flats in London. The sleb magazines at the Gstaad Club had been full of it. Rupert had managed to flog them a job lot of uncollected sale remnants dating back to the Eighties to adorn the billionaires' walls. It had taken me a week to cobble together the provenances. The party was to celebrate a forthcoming collaboration with the Frieze Masters art fair. Rupert had actually asked me. There would be photographers – the girls at the club might see it. Maybe even the slags I'd been at school with would see it.

The dress code at the base of the thick, classic cream board said 'Black Tie'. I didn't have a long dress, but this was no time for economy. I clock-watched until exactly 5 p.m., ran up to the bank on Piccadilly, then hailed a cab. By six, I was back at my flat, via Harvey Nicks, with a cotton dress bag containing a plain Ralph Lauren black silk column which fastened over one shoulder with an almost invisible gold chain. It had been stupidly expensive, but I wouldn't think about that. I could make it good at the club. I wasn't terribly interested in Rupert's opinion of my fashion sense, but this was the first real opportunity I'd had to network with serious people. I wanted to look perfect.

But I dithered over jewellery. The dim little diamond studs my mother had given me for my twenty-first had been pawned in Hatton Garden ages ago, so I took the view that no jewels would always be more stylish than bad jewels and went without. The dress didn't need a thing underneath it, just simple heels. I begged Pai's black Gucci clutch to finish it. Hardly any make-up, just mascara and a berry stain on my lips. I ordered a taxi so as not to arrive feeling ruffled. The expression on the cabbie's face as I got in told me everything I needed to know.

A crowd of paps waited at the end of the red carpet which stretched out from the glass pavilion in Hyde Park, glowing pink and mauve like a retro spacecraft. A couple of them clicked off a few obliging frames, just being polite, I supposed, but it made me feel good. The hum of the party throbbed towards me, unified, organic, like the murmurings of some massive beast. I handed my invite to an attendant, who waved me through, and closed my eyes for one delicious anticipatory second, preparing to take it all in.

How would Cinderella have felt if, when she finally did make it to the ball, she found herself at an estate agents' office party? The huge pots of Jo Malone candles couldn't disguise the smell of one massive, acrid champagne belch. Hundreds of pasty men in bad suits were crowded round the free bar with the excitement of Mormons let loose in Atlantic City. Wherever Tentis & Tentis had found their rentacrowd was obviously a Moët-free zone. I spied the tiny head of a superannuated supermodel poking out of the scrum like a stick of bewildered celery, but apart from her it could have been Friday night in All Bar One Hammersmith. I had a horrible pang of regret over the Harvey Nicks receipt on my bureau. The only other person who hadn't ignored the dress code was Rupert, whose gut had created his own mini-VIP section around him. He was talking to someone I vaguely knew, a gallerist named Cameron Fitzpatrick. I caught Rupert's eye, and he came barrelling towards me. Few men fail to be improved by black tie, and Rupert was one of the few, but for once I was glad to see him. 'Rupert,' I called sociably, waving the clutch at him. 'Hi!'

He looked momentarily confused.

'Oh, er, Judith. Righto. I was just going, actually. Got a dinner.'

'I don't want to keep you, but I did a bit of extra work on the provenance of the Stubbs?'

'What?'

'At the departmental meeting today? That Stubbs?'

'Judith, must dash, we'll talk tomorrow,' he threw over his shoulder as he bolted.

My only other hope of a spot of small talk, Fitzpatrick, had by now vanished in the crowd. I pushed my way to the bar through a gaggle of micro-dressed girls with shoes that

Coleen Rooney probably wanted back. I couldn't even enjoy the looks they were giving me. They'd obviously heard about bootylicious being powerful, but that was as far as they'd taken that particular thought. Channelling your inner goddess by shovelling your arse into a skirt that practically announced your last visit to the waxer was not perhaps the best route to female emancipation. I guessed their evening would end in a half-hearted lap dance at 3 a.m. in the Vingt Quatre for a crowd of mayonnaise-covered sub-Sloanes. Not like me, oh no. Not like Judith the successful art dealer-slash-hostess. I didn't really want a drink, but I took two glasses to give me something to do. I re-crossed the room slowly, pretending I was taking it to someone, but my heart wasn't in it.

Angelica hadn't bothered to show. She might know nothing about paintings, but her life's training had clearly included a masterclass on which parties to avoid. Obviously another secret code I hadn't cracked. How could I have been so pathetically excited? What had I seriously thought was going to happen? Gracious conversation with a glittering crowd, sharing a joke with Jay Jopling before being swept off to dinner at Lucien Freud's old table at the Wolseley?

That would never happen to me, because I was just a grunt, wasn't I? A jumped-up tea lady. I felt humiliated. Even the paps outside had gone on to better things. The ancient supermodel had vanished, too, presumably stowing the fat cheque for turning up under the chicken fillets in her bra, on her way to where the smart people were actually hanging out. God, I was pathetic. I thought I should punish myself by doing the walk home but I was too depressed. What was another twenty on a cab? At least I could tell Dave I'd been somewhere fancy; he liked that sort of thing. But was it always like this? Was

London a series of ever-tinier enclosures, like Russian dolls, so that when you thought you had got inside there was just another smooth painted casket, screwed down to keep you out? I was already clawing the stupid dress off me as I paid the driver. The delicate chain snapped and I was so furious I grabbed the split in the leg and tore the fucking thing in half, much to the surprise of an elderly couple who were passing, clutching programmes from the Albert Hall.

The flat was lying in wait for me, humming with white rage. After I'd scrambled through the hideous maze of cycles and pumps and helmets that permanently blocked the hallway, I saw a box on the kitchen table with a note to 'Judy' taped to it. The box contained a fat pink ceramic mug with bunny ears. The note said, 'Really sorry. I borrowed your cup and accidentally broke it. I got you this instead!' My roommate had drawn a smiley face, the silly cunt. I looked in the bin. There were the pieces of my cup and saucer, a perfect Villeroy 1929 glaze in absinthe green that I'd gone all the way to Camden Passage to agonise over for two weeks. It had only cost forty quid, but that was not the point. It was just not the point. I thought there might be some Superglue in the drawer of the horrible fake-Victorian buffet, but the handle stuck and I kicked the leg of the fucking thing so hard it just flew off, and the cabinet lurched to one side so that all the shitty china smashed, and then there were a regrettable few minutes which took quite a long time to clean up, after I'd calmed down.

7

I woke at five with my head fizzing. I lay naked on my bed, staring at the usual aching ceiling. I'd let the club addle my brain. The camaraderie with the girls and the easy money had put me off my game. I was going to do this right, and that meant getting to the bottom of the Stubbs acquisition. A bad party was nothing. I just had to focus.

I was at the office early, dying to see Dave, but Laura cornered me and made me spend an impatient morning going through minimum sale prices for Stanley Spencers in order to help some hedge funder fiddle his capital gains tax. CGT was about the only area in which the department was remotely business-like. I went down to the warehouse at lunch, but Dave was out. I called his mobile and offered to buy him a drink after work, then went across to N. Peal and bought a beautiful pale blue cashmere crew neck that cost almost as much as I had spunked in Harvey Nicks. Somehow spending more money made me feel better about the Tentis debacle. I planned to change for the club in the ladies at the London Library in St James's Square to give me time to meet Dave in the Bunch of Grapes on Duke Street. When he limped in – he was too proud to use a cane – I got him a pint of London Pride and a tonic water for myself.

'Thanks for the drink, Judith, but my missus will be wondering where I've got to.'

I explained that my notes on the picture seemed to have been lost, and that the Stubbs had been acquired not direct from the couple in Warminster but through a mystery buyer. It did sound a bit lame, but I was so sure there was something wrong. I couldn't have explained it to Dave, but after my total failure the previous evening it seemed even more important to prove that I was right about the Stubbs.

'I want to have a look at it, Dave. It's in, right? You've got a better eye than me. I don't believe this overpainting stuff.'

Dave lowered his voice.

'You don't really mean Rupert would be flogging a fake?'

'Of course I don't. I think he might have made a mistake and I don't want anyone to look bad, that's all. If helping them not look bad makes me look good, then that suits me fine. But it wouldn't be the first time someone made an attribution error, would it? You know that. Please? Ten minutes and you can tell me I'm an idiot and I'll never mention it again.'

'Judith, there's the experts for this. I'd need, I dunno, tools.'

'Dave. You care about the real thing, right? You think what we sell should be the real thing? Regimental honour and all that?'

'We should really get permission.'

'I work there, you work there. We have passes – I could just be looking at the "works", like bloody Laura is always saying.'

'Ten minutes?'

'Max. Come on.' I made my voice softer. 'We're mates, yes?'

'Oh, go on then.'

Most of the staff had left, so Dave took us in using his code for the back entrance. We had to use torches in the storage room, which was kept dim to protect the artworks. Dave went straight to the correct crate and lifted the picture out. I pointed out where I had remembered the Newmarket sign being placed, and where I thought the signature had been moved.

'Judith, I can't say. It really looks alright to me.'

'But there was a sign, just here. How new is that varnish?'

Our heads were close together as we peered at the canvas, both our fingertips hovering over the emptied space.

'If it was cleaned,' Dave said, engaged now, 'there might be a trace on the underpainting. We need to get it under the right light.'

'Well, can we move it?'

'Where did you say the signature was?'

'Yes, where was it?' Rupert. They say that fat people can often move with surprising stealth. I laughed stupidly.

'Rupert. Hi, sorry, we were just –'

'Please explain what you are doing. You are a junior, you have no permission to be here.' Actually it wasn't that big a deal. I'd popped down after hours many times. Usually because Rupert had asked me to. He turned to Dave, his voice softer.

'What are you two up to, eh? Isn't it time you were getting home, Dave?'

Dave looked mortified and mumbled a good evening. I hated the way he called Rupert 'sir'. Rupert stayed affable, politely undramatic until he limped off up the stairs, then considered me for a long moment. In the bluish light he looked like a strangely bloated El Greco. I knew he wasn't going to make a scene. Power is so much more effective when it's quiet.

'Judith, I've been meaning to speak to you for a while. I don't really think you fit in here, do you? I wanted to give you a chance, but I've had several complaints in the department about your attitude. Your comments at the Stubbs meeting were inappropriate and frankly impertinent.'

'I just thought – that is, I was trying – I wasn't sure –.' I was babbling like a guilty schoolgirl, furious with myself but unable to stop.

'I think it would be better if you get your things and leave now, don't you?' he added calmly.

'You're – firing me?'

'If you want to put it like that, yes. I am.'

I was bewildered. Instead of protesting, instead of defending myself, I just started to cry. Absurd. All the frustrated tears I had kept down chose that moment to bubble up like a geyser, reducing me despite myself to the role of pleading woman. Even as I felt those hot, furious tears massing in my eyes, I knew that Rupert was hiding something. Even that the stupid party invitation had been meant as a sop to keep me quiet. Yet this wasn't how it was meant to be, was it? I was trying to do the right thing, the good thing.

'Rupert, please. I wasn't doing anything wrong. If I could just explain?'

'I have no interest in your explanations.'

He ignored me as we made our way back to the department. I walked in front of him through the narrow corridors, feeling like a prisoner. He stood with his arms folded as I gathered the bits and pieces from my desk and scooped them into my briefcase. My dress and heels for the club were stuffed at the bottom. I couldn't bear to see them.

'Are you ready?'

I nodded dumbly.

'I need your pass, please. I don't think there's any need to ask Security to see you out.'

I handed it over, mute.

'Off you go then, Judith.'

I thought of Colonel Morris. I thought of the skivvying I had done for Rupert, fetching his suits from the tailor, picking up his laundered shirts, phone calls I had fielded when he'd skived off, pissed after lunch, extra hours I'd spent in the library and the archives, trying to prove that I was better, that I was smarter, that I could run faster, that I could take more and do better. I had been humble and diligent. I had never allowed it to show that I felt slighted and excluded. I had never let any of them – Laura, Oliver, Rupert – see that I even noticed the differences between us. My Oxbridge degree was a better degree than any of theirs. I had actually believed that with time and hard work I could make it, that I could get up there amongst them. I'd never pretended to myself that Rupert respected or valued me. But I had believed I had been useful, and that I was worth something. Pathetic.

'I suppose you'll be giving my job to Angelica?' I hated the way it sounded, whining, bitter.

'That's not your concern. Please leave now.'

I looked him in the face, knowing that my own was grubby with tears. I thought about how it would feel waking up in the flat and not getting up to go to Prince Street. The cool lobby, the reassuring grain of the banister under my hand. This had been my chance. I might not have got much beyond the gate, yet, but I was in, I was part of the world that I belonged to and every day I had thought I was climbing a little higher. I thought about how I would have to send out my CV and where that would get me. I had fucked it up. I had lost control, I had let myself want too much, been over eager, thoughtless, stupid, *stupid*. I had let myself stop being angry enough, had been tripping around like Pollyanna thinking that goodwill was everything and we could put the show on right here in the sodding barn. Rage had always been my friend, and I had neglected it. Rage had kept my back straight, rage had seen me through the fights and the slights. Rage had propelled me from my no-mark comprehensive to university; it had been my strength and my solace. For a moment I felt the white heat of it deep in my body and had a flash of Rupert's bloodied face sagging over his computer. Come, Rage beckoned, just for once. Come on. My tatty briefcase had brass hinges on the corners; I imagined swinging it at his temple, but I wouldn't need it. I could feel the ache in the sinew of my arms, in my teeth. I wanted to savage his throat like a dog. He watched me, and for a tiny second I saw a flicker of alarm in his eyes. That was all I needed.

'You know, Rupert,' I said, casually, 'you're a cunt. A fat-arsed, overprivileged, talentless, bent cunt.'

'Get out.'

I didn't know which of us I despised more.

To make up, I took Rage drinking. Good company, Rage, matching me glass for glass. By the time James arrived at the club I was halfway down a second bottle of Bolly with another client and this time I was swallowing. I didn't bother saying goodbye, just left the john looking surprised and plumped myself down next to James while Carlo did the business with the Cristal.

'I think I might drink some of this tonight, if you don't mind.'

'Rough day?'

I nodded. This wasn't going to be a happy drunk. I felt cold and cruel and reckless. I raised my bowl in a dry little toast. Sure, I found him obscene, but we were drinking in the last chance saloon, Rage and I.

'James. Let's cut to the chase. How much would you be willing to pay to fuck me?'

He looked bewildered, then rather disgusted.

'I don't need to pay for sex.'

'Why? Is it less important to you than money?'

'Lauren, what's the matter?'

If this had been a movie, it would have been a montage moment. A swirl of memories, plucky little Judith getting her degree, Judith plodding home late from work, sitting up over her catalogues, a tear sliding poignantly down Judith's cheek as Rupert fired her, the wide-eyed recognition that here she was in a sleazy basement believing that this filthy old punter was her only hope. *That* Judith would have got up and politely walked away into her fabulous future because she didn't need to compromise her integrity for anything. Yes, well. I was all over new fucking beginnings. This felt like my only hope. If this was what I was born to do, then I would do it properly. Me and Rage, we were going places.

I let the tears I had been suppressing for hours well prettily to the brims of my eyelids, that wet hyacinth effect, a little tremble and bite on the lower lip. I lifted up my face to him.

'James, I'm sorry. That was vulgar of me. It's just this place – I can't bear to think you would think I was – like that. I was testing you. You see, you're so wonderful, and I – I –'

Even his gargantuan ego might balk at the word love, so I had a little sob instead. Another one, Jesus. He gave me his handkerchief, which was large and white and smelled cleanly of Persil. I remembered my mum, on one of her good days, giving me a bath and wrapping me in a clean white towel that smelled just the same, and after that the sobs became real. So then we had a chat and I told him I was frightened, that I had lost my job (as a receptionist in a gallery) and when he proposed that I might like to get away for a weekend I pretended

I'd never been to the South of France, and wouldn't that be heaven, but we'd better take my friend too, to show I wasn't really that sort of girl. Or not entirely. I did a bit of whispering about how he might persuade me otherwise. In truth, it was the possibility of having to share a bed with him that made me want someone else along. Plus if he felt like a threesome it was better to come equipped. It wasn't hard to hint that the persuasion might involve, say, £3,000, just to help me along until I could find work. So when he left there was a thousand on the table, to cover two tickets to Nice, and I lurched over to Mercedes and told her we were going to the Riviera.

'Christ, Jude,' she said admiringly, 'what've you got up there? Crack?'

8

I'd used some of James's fifties to get together some gear for the trip. A tan braided leather weekend bag and matching tote from a little shop in Marylebone that could pass for Bottega Veneta, a black Eres tie-side bikini, Tom Ford sunglasses, a Vuitton Sprouse scarf in turquoise and beige. When we landed at Nice airport, I was pleased to see that the accessories meant I looked like many of the other women coming in for the weekend: super-groomed but not too effortful. Mercedes (we said we'd try to use club names so as not to slip up) was uncharacteristically restrained in simple jeans and a white shirt. James was waiting for us in the café next to the arrivals lounge. I took a deep breath as I saw the unselfconscious sprawl of his bulk, the patches of sweat on his pale pink shirt. Sure he was fat, but did he have to be such a slob? There was something conceited about it, as though his money meant he could afford to disregard the effect he had on other people – which of course it did. I took a deep breath. I had a sudden weird longing to be back in my horrible flat. I'd spent so many hours there, planning, dreaming, safe in the fantasy that the future was going to happen. But this was it. This was the future. Or at least, in the absence of a better plan, the next few months. I could do this, I told myself. More than ever now, I *had* to do this. It was just about control.

A young Moroccan-looking man in a dark jacket with 'Hôtel du Cap' on the breast loaded our bags into a long black car.

James heaved himself into the front and the car immediately sagged like an old bed on his side. I couldn't look at Mercedes.

'*S'il vous plaît, Mesdemoiselles.*'

I slipped through the door he held for me and sat back on ivory leather seats. The car was cool, the windows tinted, the engine had a low purring hum. This was what it felt like, then. James was fiddling with his phone so I didn't need to try to make conversation. When we arrived at the hotel, Mercedes squeezed my hand excitedly.

'It's gorgeous, James,' she breathed, giving me a nudge.

'Really lovely,' I added enthusiastically.

We waited discreetly in the black marble-tiled hallway while James checked in. One of the receptionists asked us for our passports, and I told her quickly in French, with a calm smile, that they had gone up with the bags and we could bring them down later. I didn't want James to have any chance of seeing our real names; it would spoil the mood.

'Your French is dead good!' said Mercedes, surprised.

I shrugged.

'We'd probably best not let James know that.'

We were shown to a suite on the second floor. Two bedrooms opened off a huge drawing room with white sofas and a vast arrangement of calla lilies. Double doors opened onto a balcony over a long lawn that dropped down to the famous pool I had seen in so many magazines. Beyond that, to the right in the direction of Cannes, a pod of giant boats swarmed the old port. Big seemed to be a theme.

Even amongst those giga-yachts, one in particular stood out, its vast hull rearing up like the Kraken. I had seen that in photographs, too. Mikhail Balensky, 'The Man from the Stan,' as the English papers called him, was an Uzbek industrialist whose career, according to even sober reports, read like something from a comic. Beginning in oil fields, he'd diversified into the arms trade but, finding that there weren't enough wars going on to make a decent profit, had decided to start a few. Fund some disaffected rebels in a small country of which we knew nothing, arm both sides, sit back and let them slug it out, then buy up whatever hard assets remained in the hands of the government he'd helped to install. Very efficient. That was two decades ago; nowadays Balensky appeared at galas with heads of state, popped up at the Met Ball or the Serpentine summer party, or was photographed sloshing out a couple of million at whatever repellent philanthropist's shindig represented the cause *du jour*. It's amazing what you learn by keeping up with *Hello!*

'Mademoiselle?'

The bellboy, discreetly distracting me from my Riviera reverie. I had a ten-euro note already folded in my hand. I gave him his tip and told him to put our bags in the bedroom to the left, and monsieur's to the right. Whatever James had in mind I had no intention of sharing a bed with him. In case he had anything to say I stepped onto the balcony with my back to him and looked determinedly at the view. I felt him come up behind me and his hand reached for mine.

'Happy, darling?'

Darling. Oh God.

'It's beautiful,' I said, with wondering hesitancy.

'And I bought you this,' he added, handing me a crumpled plain black plastic bag with what he obviously thought was a roguish grin. 'Something to slip into. Later.'

I wondered what horrors it contained, but I managed to give him a little tiptoe kiss on the clammy slab of his cheek. 'Thank you, darling. That's so thoughtful of you.'

'I thought we'd have lunch at the pool and then go to Cannes for a bit of shopping. Thought you girls might like that.'

'Super. I'll just get changed.'

Mercedes was whirling round the bathroom, examining the Bulgari toiletries.

'Oh my God, this bathroom is bigger than my whole flat!'

'Find the minibar,' I hissed. 'I need a fucking drink.'

James appeared for lunch at the Eden Roc, the hotel's cliff-side swimming pool, wearing a vast pair of garish Vilebrequin swimming trunks under a white hotel robe, which hung meekly on either side of his milky gut. From behind my sunglasses I saw two blonde children in the water, pointing and giggling until their nanny shushed them. We all ordered lobster salad and Perrier water. James speared whole pats of butter from their little bed of ice, cramming them onto rolls and into his mouth. A little party of crumbs descended the folds of his chin and lodged in the grey mat of hair on his chest. It was like watching an animated Lucien Freud, but that didn't make it easier to look at. While Mercedes picked at her salad and played with her phone (I thought I'd have to tell her to stop holding her knife like a pen) I prompted James to tell me again about his patently fictional days as a Riviera playboy, pretending to be fascinated by his exaggerated stories of dancing with Elizabeth Taylor at Jimmy'z and partying with Dionne Warwick at Golfe Juan. It wasn't that he was trying to convince me that he was quite the catch, I realised, it was that he actually believed he was.

We were driven over to the Croisette after lunch. On the beach below the Carlton hotel a group of women in burkas splashed wretchedly in the surf. The sky had dulled, it was incredibly humid and James was irritable, rudely insisting to the driver that he knew the best place to park then berating him in pidgin French when we had to drive three times round the block. I didn't think his patience would hold out for much of a trolley dash, so I suggested we stop outside Chanel and have the car wait. I walked into the boutique first and asked the saleswoman if she could possibly bring a chair while Mercedes and I looked at the bags. She looked faintly appalled at the suggestion she might do something so menial. But then she glimpsed James in the doorway.

'*Tout de suite, madame.*'

I knew what I wanted: the classic quilted shoulder bag in black with leather and gilt handles. Mercedes was dithering, looking through a rack of unseasonable tweed coats. They were beautiful; I would have loved to try one on, to feel the silk lining against my bare arms, the swing of the tiny gold chain stitched into the hem, but James clearly felt the role of sugar daddy was wearing a bit thin.

'Which bag do you want, Mercedes?'

'The big one.'

It seemed to take an age for the saleswoman to pack up the bags in their tissue paper and black cotton pochettes stamped with the Chanel C's, finally placing them in pleasingly stiff ribbon-tied carriers. I'd gathered by now that James's short temper sprang from the fact that he couldn't admit to himself that the fact that he was constantly exhausted and uncomfortable was not the world in general's problem but his, as he was too fucking fat to fit in it. Still, he gamely handed over his

Amex while Mercedes and I pretended to be interested in the scarves, discreetly keeping our eyes away from the cash till. Result. But when James declined my admittedly rather cruel suggestion that we take a stroll round the steep cobbled streets of the old town in favour of going back to the hotel for a 'siesta', I knew I was going to have to earn it.

When we got back to the suite I shoved Mercedes into our room.

'Why don't you have a nice relaxing shower, darling?' I trilled over my shoulder. At least I wouldn't have to get covered in that filthy sweat.

'I hate you,' I said as she collected her things to go back to the pool.

'Don't worry. He'll only want a bit of a cuddle. Anyway, look at these.'

She showed me a couple of pill jars in her overflowing make-up bag.

'What's that?'

'Nothing much. Xanax. A few Vallies.'

'Hand it over, then.'

'Not for you. For him.'

'I don't get it.'

'Duh. We'll slip him a Mickey Finn. I don't want to spend an evening with that fat bastard. We're in the South of France, Jude!'

'Lauren.'

'Alright. Listen,' she whispered, though I could hear the sound of the water from the other room. 'We'll go for dinner, then I'll grind up a few of these and you can slip them into his brandy.'

'He doesn't drink.'

'Fizzy water, then. Half an hour and he'll be knackered. We can go out on the town and in the morning he'll have had a lovely rest. He'll never know.'

'He's really fat, Mercedes. I'm not sure dead punters are a good look.'

'Don't be soft, they're not strong. I take them all the time. I'll get it ready in the loos by the pool now. Or will you be feeling like another session on the rubber mattress later?'

'Don't be a cow. This is a free ride for you.'

'I know. I'm just saying why shouldn't you have some fun? We'll go down to where all them big yachts are. Come on, it'll be a laugh.'

Maybe it was the insouciant air of the Riviera, but I was feeling a lot more cheerful. Sod it. Even if James found out, he could only get furious and pack us off home with a £2,000 handbag each, not bad going for a single day. Something else would turn up.

'Go on, then,' I said. 'But be careful. Look at the labels.'

'Best get your glad rags on then. Knickers off, ladies!'

When Mercedes skipped off, I examined James's little bag of tricks. It contained a pair of crotchless PVC panties, a fishnet camisole which laced like a corset, open at the nipples, and a pair of black hold-ups with PVC trim. Nasty stuff, the sort sold in touristy Soho sex shops. I hauled it all on, washed my cunt and rubbed a trickle of monoi oil over the stripe of my pubic hair and between my buttocks. Adding black stiletto sandals and mussing my hair, I looked at myself in the mirror with the opulent marble bathroom behind me. Well, if what he wanted was low-rent hooker . . . it could have been much worse, I supposed. If I squinted, I could almost pretend it was more *Cabaret* than streetwalker. 'Mama thinks I'm living in a convent, a secluded little convent, in the southern part of France,' I sang under my breath, trying out a slow, voracious smile. Good. Very good.

I sashayed across the drawing room and tapped on James's bedroom door.

'I'm ready, darling,' I purred.

'Come in.'

The room was empty. From the bathroom I heard the splatter of an explosive crap, followed by a ricochet of bubbling farts. I paused in the doorway. Oh God. A few moments later there was a flush and James emerged, along with a steamy waft of shit and Penhaligon's Extract of Limes.

'Bit of a runny tummy,' he said, in an accusing voice. Why couldn't he keep his foulness to himself? He was naked now, under the gaping robe. As he looked at me, a slow leer spread across his face, but he hesitated to approach me. He hasn't done this before, I realised. Feeling more confident, I took a step towards him. I closed my eyes and ran my fingertips along what passed for his jawline, down his throat, across the hillocks of his chest.

'So,' I murmured breathily, 'what do you want to do with me?'

Silence. I braced myself for a kiss, peeking under my eyelashes.

'James has been a naughty boy.' I opened my eyes. He was pouting, the fat on his face suddenly making him appear like an inflated toddler.

'James has been a naughty boy and he wants his mistress to punish him.'

I could have laughed for joy.

'Then lie down on the bed, *immediately*!'

I held my breath and ducked into the bathroom to detach the belt from the spare dressing gown. James was spread out on the bed, his weight challenging even the hyper-technical mattress. As I flipped his arms over his head and tied his wrists together I took a quick look down over the vast mottled belly. Would I actually have to lift up a skirt of flesh to get at his cock? Jesus. I didn't have much to improvise with, so I worked on my script as I slid the belt from the loops of his trousers where they hung over a chair. Holding the buckle, I looped it around three times and swallowed hard as I approached the bed. Three thousand pounds. A few months' grace. Admittedly I had never let anything as hideous as this near me, but I told myself all cats were grey in the dark.

'Turn over!'

He rolled onto his side, he couldn't have got any further without a hole cut in the bed. His arse looked like a pair of cheap battery chickens. I had to concentrate or I was going to either laugh or chuck. I stroked the makeshift flail along one puckered buttock.

'James deserves a good spanking. I saw him looking at those girls by the pool. I was very jealous. Naughty, naughty boy!' With each 'naughty' I gave him a tap, trying to measure how hard he wanted it.

'Yes, mistress, I've been a naughty boy.'

'And you deserve to be punished, don't you?'

'Yes.'

Harder this time.

'Yes, what?'

'Yes, mistress.'

Harder again, enough to raise a red stripe. He sighed. So did I.

I went on with that for a bit, but there was really no way of telling whether he was excited; his face was already scarlet from the sun at lunch. So I rolled him back over, unlaced the camisole to give him a peek at my tits and crawled around him until my face was above his crotch, with my bottom in the air so he could see my cunt through the split in the panties. His cock was tiny, a two-inch stub poking jauntily from a thatched cushion of flesh. I'd tucked a condom into the sole of my sandals, but there was no way I could see to get it on him, let alone him in me. Thank Christ, but I was going to have to get him off somehow.

'Do you deserve to come, you bad boy?'

'Yes, please, please!'

Crack.

'Please what?'

'Please mistress.'

'And what do you want?'

He screwed up his face again, lisping now, even more revolting.

'Jameth wanth hith pudding.'

I had done a lot of stuff sexually. Most of it I'd liked, and some I hadn't, but I'd forced myself, sometimes from curiosity and sometimes because I wanted to know what I could take. Girls and boys and threesomes and moresomes; sometimes I'd been scared and sometimes hurt, but it was the only real power I'd ever had and I wanted to test its limits. Each of those acts had been another veneer on the enamel of my strength; this was just one more. Nothing. I pushed my hair away and took it in my mouth and he came in about twenty seconds, a little mucus dribble that I knocked back like medicine. Kerching. In my own bathroom I yanked off the nasty lingerie and took a quick shower. I wondered briefly how I ought to feel. I didn't feel like anything except swimming laps, so that's what I went and did.

James insisted we went to a place called Tétou for dinner. He claimed it was the only place to eat bouillabaisse in the South of France.

'Ugh, fish soup,' muttered Mercedes. 'Don't have any of that garlic paste, we'll stink.'

As soon as the valet opened the door I trotted inside the restaurant, which didn't look like much more than a glass-walled beach hut, and had a quick look at the chairs. I wanted to keep James in the good temper he'd enjoyed since our little encounter.

'Monsieur will need a different chair,' I whispered quickly to a waiter in French. 'He's very – robust.'

The waiter gave me an odd look, but by the time James plodded in an armless chair had been found. Mercedes was excited. We'd both spent a long time dressing, she in one of her pour-on sub-Léger numbers, me in a very plain lemon silk shift, a childish, soft tunic cut that finished inches below my knickers, with six-inch Zanotti platforms in buff suede. I noticed the gratifying second of stillness among the customers around us as we sat down, though I doubted anyone thought that James was taking his nieces out to celebrate their graduation from finishing school. With a roguish grin, James suggested champagne, and a bottle of Krug appeared.

'Come on, James,' prompted Mercedes, 'Go mad! Have a sip.' James's jowls chortled to themselves as he held out his glass.

'Why not? Just this once.'

The bouillabaisse came in two servings, first the intense shellfish broth with croutons and rouille, then a white tureen of fish. The saffron sauce looked delicious, but Mercedes had a point about the garlic. It was quite a jolly dinner, really. I'd told Mercedes to put her bloody phone away, and she listened attentively to round three of James's anecdotes, laughing in all the right places and making unobtrusively sure, accomplished as she was, that his glass always contained a few fingers of fizz. When the plates were cleared and we were handed the dessert menu, James excused himself.

'Touch of the runs,' he confided.

I felt my own guts contract in horror. What was the *matter* with him? We both looked away as he lumbered off between the tables and asked loudly for *la toilette*.

'Quick,' said Mercedes. 'Move your serviette. I've got it here.' In her hand was a little homemade wrap, folded from a sheet of Hôtel du Cap writing paper. She tipped it into his glass like a Jacobean villain while I ordered *tarte tropézienne* for three.

James declined my offer of a romantic stroll on the beach, as I knew he would, and the waiting car took us back to the hotel. We could have a drink on the terrace, I suggested instead, to enjoy the wonderful view. It was a short drive, but James's head was lolling on his shoulder like an overblown cabbage after five minutes. He emitted loud, viscous snores. I caught the driver's eye in the mirror.

'Perhaps you'd like to wait while we help monsieur inside? Perhaps a little too much champagne –'

The banknote crunch of Hôtel du Cap gravel roused James. He pretended, of course, that he hadn't been sleeping, but added thickly that he might turn in. I followed him solicitously up to the suite and steeled myself for an affectionate goodnight kiss, but he was already shambling towards the bed. I heard him banging about for a few minutes, then the strip of light beneath the door vanished and there was silence. I counted slowly to sixty, twice, until the snores resumed.

Mercedes wanted to go to Jimmy'z, the famous nightclub on the port at Cannes, but it was too early, and besides I had an idea it would be lame. I asked the driver to take us somewhere '*décontracté*' and he swung the car right, towards Antibes, climbing away from the coast and into the hills for about a quarter of an hour, until we arrived at a low stone building done out Ibiza-style, all in white and silver, with a huge terrace and a gaggle of black-suited doormen. Two Ferraris were being parked as we pulled up.

'This looks alright, eh?' said Mercedes, and suddenly I started giggling. I'd never had anyone to do this with before and I felt giddy and even affectionate towards her. I told the driver he could go; we'd get the doormen to find us a taxi.

'Come on then, girl,' I said in a voice that hadn't been my own for a decade. 'We're going to have a right laugh.'

The bouncer gave us a quick once-over and unfastened the redundant velvet rope.

'*Bonsoir, mesdames.*'

We took a table on the terrace and ordered Kir Royal. There were a few groups of older Euro types, all open-collared white shirts and giant watches, one gaggle of etiolated Russian hookers and several younger couples. As I wondered if Balensky himself might make an appearance, two coupes of champagne appeared.

'With the compliments of the two gentlemen,' intoned the waiter solemnly.

I followed his gaze and saw two young Arab guys in absurd sunglasses nodding to us.

'We're sending them back,' I whispered to Mercedes. 'We're not prostitutes.'

'Speak for yourself, love.'

'Bitch.'

We drank three Kirs as the club filled up, then moved inside to the dance floor. I watched the men watching us. I think this is the moment I like best, the flirting, the choosing. Shall I have you, or you, or you? We did a bit of fairly half-hearted shimmying while we made our minds up.

'What about them?'

'Too old.'

'Or them?'

'Too fat. Too fucking fat.'

We collapsed shrieking. It seemed like the funniest thing in the world.

'Or them?'

'Promising.'

Mercedes was doing some frantic false eyelash signalling to a raised alcove, obviously the VIP section. Two men sat at a table with an ice bucket of vodka, both texting while a waiter unloaded a tray of sushi. They were young and presentable looking, though we were too far away for the watch and shoe check.

'Go on then.'

'I'll go and say hello.'

I clutched her back. 'You can't! I'll be ashamed!' This was how it was meant to feel, wasn't it, being a girl? 'We'll sit down and wait for them to come to us.'

'What if they don't? What if someone else gets in first?'

'They will. Watch.'

And then somehow, an hour later, we were in a Porsche cabriolet driving stupidly fast towards the old port at Antibes, with Dom Perignon drying on my yellow dress and Mercedes necking one of them madly in the back. Everyone was smoking and a little podgy guy whose name no one knew was doing coke from a Guerlain compact in the parcel shelf.

'I wanna go to Saint-Tropez,' yelled Mercedes, surfacing for a second.

'I wanna see the Picassos!' I yelled back.

Then we were veering crazily over the cobbles of the old town, nearly knocking over a weary paparazzo kneeling on the dock, the podgy guy had vanished and Mercedes was being carried down a gangplank, legs waving like a beetle.

'Take your shoes off!' I called after her.

'Friggin' 'ell, Lauren,' she screeched, 'get in here!'

The driver of the Porsche and the owner of the boat, which was as bright and new and shiny as his money, was called Steve, and if I was a Russian hooker he'd have smelled like Christmas. But I'd noticed that he hadn't touched the vodka or the coke, so nor had I, and while Mercedes made some low-rent porn noises with his friend offstage he made me a hot chocolate and we looked at his three Picassos, which were rather good, and he told me about his contemporary art collection, because of course he collected contemporary, then Mercedes and Thing reappeared and we all stripped off and got into Steve's hot tub on the deck of Steve's enormous boat and drank some more Dom and he tried to look as though this was happy. Maybe it was. Maybe being happy is, just for once, not being on the make.

We lurched into the Hôtel du Cap about three, carrying our shoes wincingly over the gravel and past the impassive night porter. Once we'd opened the door to the suite with painful care, it seemed necessary to crawl commando style to our bedroom, but Mercedes caught the table with her shoulder as she performed a teddy roll, bringing down the baroque vase of lilies with a crash that seemed loud enough to be heard in Saint-Tropez. We froze, but the only sound was our sudden harsh breathing. For a few seconds I felt as though I had swallowed a balloon, but James didn't stir behind his door. There wasn't even any sound of snoring. Which meant that by the time we were safely in our own bed we were helpless with giggles. I don't ever remember having fallen asleep laughing before.

A shaft of strong white sun cutting between the heavy drapes woke me about nine. I slipped out from beneath the sheet and looked into the sitting room. The lilies had magically been replaced and *The Times* was fanned out on the table, but there was no other sign of life. James must still be sleeping. I fumbled in my bag for a couple of Nurofen and hauled myself under the shower, letting the water stream through last night's make-up. There was just today to be got through – maybe I could persuade him to go to the Picasso museum in Antibes? He would enjoy feeling cultured. After last night I almost felt a bit sorry for him. Wrapped in a huge towel, I went to wake Mercedes.

'Come on, he's not up. We'll leave a note and get some breakfast in the garden.'

We slipped robes over our bikinis, and with sunglasses and crystal goblets of sweet fresh orange juice everything felt sort of fantastic. I thought it looked more considerate to order breakfast for three, but though we took our time with the exquisite warm croissants and tiny kilner jars of quince and fig preserve, James didn't appear. Looking at the other guests breakfasting, and the hotel gardeners in their red jackets raking the paths and practically polishing the grass, I almost forgot him, as though we were there in our own right. And that was fantastic too. Mercedes lowered her glasses, cringing a bit at the strong sun.

'D'you think he's OK?'

'Sure. Maybe he got breakfast upstairs.' Though we had left him a note, and he seemed the type to want the full value of my company at least.

'I'll just run up and check,' Mercedes offered.

When she came back she was carrying two of the hotel's monogrammed towels.

'I knocked on his door, but he didn't answer. Let's go swimming!'

9

It might sound funny, but I knew there was something wrong when James didn't appear for lunch. Mercedes had immediately fallen back asleep in the sun, the strings of her bikini top trailing untied across her back, and I had passed the time reading a biography of Chagall that I'd brought in case we had the chance to go up to Saint-Paul de Vence. At half past twelve, I started to worry, and though I tried for a few minutes more to concentrate on the book, I knew something was strange. What if he was ill? He had been going on about his gruesome diarrhoea. He might need a doctor. The last thing we needed was bother. I tied my robe and went back up across the lawn, too impatient when I got inside to wait for the lift. On the second floor I barrelled down the corridor, muttering '*Désolée*' at a maid who was bent over a vacuum cleaner. I went straight to James's room and as soon as I saw him, I knew.

I had never seen a dead body before. But there was a vacant immobility to the flesh, a strange hollowness to the features, which signalled a total absence of vitality. James didn't look as though he was sleeping. He just looked dead. His huge body in the white sheets was covered in a cotton nightshirt; with his rinded, thick-nailed feet sticking out he resembled a grotesque elderly *putto*. I knew, but still I went through some motions I had learned from films – I went and fetched a blusher compact from my make-up bag and cautiously held the unsnapped mirror over his face. Nothing. I couldn't bring myself to try to open his eyes, but I gingerly lifted the ham of his arm and tried to feel for a pulse.

'James?' I hissed urgently, trying to control a gulping scream. 'James!' Nothing.

I walked round the bed to pick up the phone and call reception, but I checked myself. I felt dizzy and like I wanted to vomit, but I couldn't lose control. He'd been drinking – he didn't usually drink, maybe he couldn't. I took a huge, shuddering breath. I saw it all, the swift, discreet staff, the ambulance, the police station. If they did an autopsy they would find whatever stupid cocktail of tranqs Mercedes had given him, and it would be manslaughter. I saw the newspapers, our names, my mother's face. The unimaginable impossibility of prison. I suddenly heard the sound of the vacuum getting closer. The maid was on her way to clean the room. I jogged to the main door, fumbled with the hangers of breakfast and safety cards, dropped them, scrabbled for the 'Do Not Disturb'. In a place like this, that would give us hours. I sat slowly on one of the white sofas. Breathe, Judith. Think.

I had never sent our passports to reception; I had just forgotten. I had scrawled LJ on the breakfast tab, just notional initials. We had called each other by our club names, worn sunglasses most of the time. The staff had seen us coming and going, but this was the South of France – they would simply assume we were whores, rented as a double act for a weekend. If we could get out, they had no way of tracing us beyond our descriptions, and this was a major hotel, with staff who were trained not to be too observant, I guessed. Fingerprints? I had no idea, really, how that worked, but I certainly had no criminal record and to my knowledge nor did Leanne. Didn't they have some bureau where they were held? Some mega-tech international DNA databank?

I couldn't think that. I'd often dipped into my roommates' medical textbooks but I wasn't sure if there were any visible signs of sudden cardiac arrest. He was obese, it was hot and he'd had sex – surely that would be the obvious conclusion? I thanked God for the fact that nice girls always swallow: there wouldn't be much evidence of me on the sheets. By the time anyone worked out there was more to it than that, we would be back in our lives. And if anyone came looking. . .

The night porter had seen us coming in last night. We could say we had come out for a laugh, that we couldn't really go through with it. Two silly girls taking an old man for a ride. We could say that James had been angry when we didn't want to follow up on the promised sex, told us we had to go home today and we'd gone out on the town without him. We didn't say goodbye because we thought he was sleeping, furious. Plausible. I took my mobile from the robe pocket and texted Leanne to get upstairs immediately. My thumb slipped greasily across the screen. He had a wife – Veronica. They would find her, through his passport, perhaps she would want to keep things quiet, to avoid scandal. Surely she would have been expecting a heart attack in the not too distant future anyway.

My phone buzzed. Leanne was at the door. I opened it and pulled her into the suite.

'Sit down. Don't say anything and for God's sake don't scream. He's dead. No joke, no mistake. Whatever you gave him, it was too much. He's in there.'

I had never seen anyone go white before – part of me was interested to see that the blood did indeed drain from her face, leaving it greenish under her tan. I went to the bathroom, fetched one of the fine linen towels hanging by the bidet to wrap round my hand and fetched her one of the mini bottles of cognac from the bar, no glass.

'Drink this.'

She swallowed obediently in one gulp, and began to sob, burying her face in the sleeves of the robe. I took the bottle and padded through to James's room. I didn't look at the thing on the bed, just set the empty down on the bedside cabinet. There was already alcohol in his system, so that couldn't hurt.

I tried to make my voice as gentle as I could.

'Leanne, this is bad. It's very bad. We can't tell anyone, do you understand? If we do, it's a crime, even though we didn't mean it. We would go to prison. Tell me you understand.'

She nodded. She looked incredibly young.

'I can handle this. Do you want me to handle this?'

She nodded again, grateful, desperate. I hardly believed it myself, but my instinct was all we had. I just needed to keep my actions as quick as my thoughts. Leanne started gasping, the hiccupping in her throat moving towards hysteria. I gripped her arms tightly.

'Look at me. Leanne, look at me! Stop that. Breathe. Come on, just take a deep breath. And another one, that's it, come on now. Better?'

She nodded again.

'OK. Now all you have to do is exactly what I tell you. They don't know who we are – it will be OK. Listen! It will be OK. Get dressed, something neat and smart. Put everything in your bag. Check the bathroom carefully, no make-up, bottles, anything.' I didn't think that really mattered but having something to concentrate on would keep her quiet. She shuffled into our bedroom like a hospital patient.

I went back to James. If I kept my eyes away, it was alright, but I had a queasy fear that one of those fat dead hands was suddenly going to reach out and grab me. Looking round the room, I saw his navy linen jacket hanging on a chair. Using the towel again, I reached inside and found his phone, which was switched off. All the better. There was a wallet with credit cards, driving licence, a few fifty-euro notes and a silver Tiffany money clip. Probably a gift from Veronica. I took out the cash. Most of it was in pink 500-euro notes, some yellow 200s. I counted it, disbelieving, and counted again. Then I remembered. This was the Eden Roc. The hotel was famous for only accepting cash – I remembered reading some vulgar restaurant reviewer boasting about it. God knows how much a suite here cost, but James had obviously withdrawn all the money ready for the bill, plus what he had promised to me. There was just over 10,000 euro. I took two of the fifties from the wallet, added 200 and placed them back in the money clip in the jacket. For a mad second I thought of removing his huge gold Rolex but that would be way too dumb. The rest of the money I rolled up tightly and stuffed in the pocket of my robe.

Leanne was sitting patiently on the bed in her jeans and a grey tee, staring at her feet in their platform wedges. I tossed her my beige canvas Alaïa jacket. It was a sacrifice, but I guessed I could get another one now.

'Put that on, and your glasses. I won't be long.' She tried, but she started shaking and couldn't get her arms into the tightly seamed sleeve.

'If you start having hysterics, I'm going to hit you. Stop it. Just be fucking grateful I had the sense not to call the police.'

I scrabbled my things into my weekend bag, including the trashy lingerie I'd worn just the day before. Heels, make-up, phone charger, books, hairbrush, laptop. Then I took out the Chanel bags from their carriers and stuffed our other bags inside, shoving the branded pouches back on top. This way we wouldn't look as though we were leaving, just sauntering off for a bit of Saturday shopping. I wondered what time check-out was. If it was noon tomorrow, or even eleven, we'd have lots of time with the Do Not Disturb up. I dashed back into the sitting room. The note I had written, a jaunty 'Gone for a swim! See you downstairs, darling x' was on the Eden Roc pad. I removed it, and the sheet underneath for good measure, in case the pen had left an imprint. I scrunched them up and shoved them in my pocket.

'Right, we're going. Have your phone out. When we get to the lobby, start texting, keep your head down. Don't hurry.'

The maid was still hovering in the passage. I thought I was going to throw up when she spoke to me.

'*Voulez-vous que je fasse la chambre, madame?*'

I managed a casual smile. She was not much older than me, but her face was sallow and pitted. I guess she didn't get to see much Riviera sun.

'*Pas pour l'instant, non merci.*'

We passed on, took the lift to the lobby and stepped onto the drive.

'*Vous avez besoin d'une voiture, mesdames?*'

It was the same bellboy I had tipped yesterday. Damn.

'*Non merci. Nous avons besoin de marcher!*' Pissed English slags walking off their hangover, I hoped he was thinking.

Then we were walking down the drive, Leanne's ankles lurching precariously on the slope. The hotel was a fair way out of Cannes, and for a while we walked along an empty road, banked on both sides with white walls and security gates. We passed several green plastic wheelie bins, so I lifted the heavy lid of one and pushed the torn-up scraps of paper inside. It was the hottest time of day and the cord handles of the carrier were digging weals in my fingers. I had a headache and I could feel a wet patch of sweat on my back. Leanne plodded silently beside me.

'It's fine, Leanne, it's going to be fine. Just keep going.'

Eventually, the road wound round to the seafront. Up to the left we could see the windows of the hotel emerging serenely from palm fronds like a showgirl's eyelashes. The bay was busy with jet skis and sailboats, further out the ferry to Sainte Marguerite island was crossing. We stopped at the first small bar, where I ordered two Oranginas and asked the waiter politely but not too correctly if he could possibly help us order a cab to Nice airport. He did a bit of French grumbling, but as I was paying for the drinks a white Mercedes pulled up.

Leanne stared dully out of the taxi window. I remembered her bawdy defiance back in the National Gallery and felt a little twinge of schadenfreude. Who needed good old Rashers now? Maybe it was something in the submissive way she inclined her head, but I suddenly remembered the Friday that the bailiffs came.

My mum wasn't a drunk. Mostly, she held down whatever job she had that month; mostly, she got up in the morning. Sometimes, though, it just got too much for her, and then she drank. Not joyously or recklessly, just a steady sip towards blissful oblivion. Which actually might have been a perfectly reasonable response to her life. I remembered I'd just got her to bed when the bell rang, tucked up under her pink chenille bedspread with a cup of tea and a plastic tub on the nightstand in case the room started to spin when she closed her eyes. I must have been about eleven.

'Who's that, Mum?'

She was a bit beyond speech, but she eventually got it out that it was the hire purchase on the telly. She'd not paid the bill for months; the company had obviously sold on the bad debt.

'Do you want me to take care of it, Mum? I'll take care of it.'

'Thanks, love,' was all she managed.

I opened the door, still in my school uniform. I tried saying there was no one home but me, so I couldn't let them in. They weren't bad blokes, for all the bouncer outfits. Just trying to make a living, same as all of us. They even said they were sorry, as they carried it out of the kitchen. We didn't use the front room; it was just another cold space that cost money. That left us with the fridge and the cooker and the table and the sofa. I thought fitted kitchens were posh, then – at least, we didn't have one. They came back for the fridge, though they took the food out first. They were even quite gentle, laying the bread and jam and vodka on the sofa. One of them had returned with a packet of frozen sweetcorn from the freezer compartment. I cannot say how lonely that room looked. The neighbours had come out to stare; it would be all round the estate tomorrow. I stared back, shivering in my polyester school shirt, trying to look proud. I was glad Mum was too out of it to see, she might have made a scene for them all to gas about. That would not happen again, I'd thought then. That was never, ever going to happen to me again.

But nor was this exactly the moment for nostalgia.

* * * * *

'Talk,' I said to Leanne. 'Tell me about last night.'

I managed to keep her going, laughing hilariously now and then, as though we were reliving our adventures. If the driver remembered us I wanted him to think that we were cheerful, normal. He didn't even bother pretending that he hadn't ripped us off when we got to the airport, so I acted a bit frosty, while paying him what he asked.

'Right,' I said, once we were in the cool of the check-in area. I shoved one of the rolled-up 500-euro notes into her hand. 'Take this, go to the BA counter and buy a one-way ticket to London. It's Saturday, they'll have space. When you get back, don't text or phone; I'll text you to let you know everything's OK. I won't be back at the club and if anyone asks just say you think I met someone and went off on a holiday. Ibiza. You think I'm in Ibiza. Do you get that?'

'Judy, I can't take it all in.'

'Don't try.' I gave her a hug, like two friends saying goodbye. 'You'll be fine.'

'But what about you?'

'Don't worry about me.' As if she would, anyway. Her greedy naked eyes were already scanning the departure desks, looking for BA. 'When you get home, act normal, totally normal. You'll forget this ever happened, OK?' Then I walked quickly away before she had time to say anything else.

I took another cab to the centre of Cannes, had him let me off at the port, then found a tourist placard and worked out the route to the station. The Chanel carrier snapped on the way, forcing me to hoist it like a recalcitrant toddler. There was a train to Ventimiglia in forty minutes. I thought crazily of border guards, of trying to find the British Consulate and throwing myself on the mercy of some nice young chap in the diplomatic corps, but I made myself remember James's body, still in that close shuttered room with its funereal scent of lilies. I had time. I bought a copy of *Gala*, a bottle of Evian and a packet of Marlboro Lights and sat with the magazine open on my lap, chain-smoking and hiding behind my sunglasses. I didn't have any plan, but I had 9,000 euro, and I was on my way to Italy.

10

Until the train crossed the border, I didn't allow myself to think. I took slow sips of water and tried to look interested in French reality-TV stars I couldn't recognise. Then I stared at the Chagall biography, reminding myself to turn a page now and then. Outside the window, what must once have been enchanting hill villages went by, muddled with motorway and newly built villas amongst huge low greenhouses. At Ventimiglia I changed for the Genoa train, and suddenly I was in Italy proper. The last time I'd been there was on that month-long study bursary to Rome after my undergraduate degree, and I remembered the feeling, the shift in the light, the enveloping chatter of the language. The carriage was now filled with young men with huge watches and huger sunglasses that would have looked really gay were it not for that ineffable Italian self-confidence, neatly groomed women with good leather shoes and too much gold jewellery, an American couple with backpacks and guidebooks and appalling sandals. At Genoa I changed again. I'd always wanted to go to Portofino, but apparently the train didn't go there, a station clerk told me in Italian, only to a place called Santa Margherita. Then there was a bus, or a taxi. No one had yet asked to see my passport, but I knew I'd have to show it if I wanted to get a hotel. I went over the trail in my head: Judith Rashleigh lands at Nice airport – we had not arrived with James – and a few days later she turns up in Portofino. What was there to connect her with a dead man who for all I knew was still waiting in the fragrant darkness of the

Eden Roc? Nothing, necessarily. I'd have to risk it, or else sleep on the beach.

Santa Margherita looked idyllic, the sort of place I could imagine Audrey Hepburn going on holiday. Tall old houses in yellow and ochre framed a double bay, cutting off at a headland with a marina where super yachts bobbed next to wooden fishing boats. The air smelled of gardenias and ozone; even the children scrambling about on the beach looked chic, in neat linen smocks and shorts, not a hideous sequined T-shirt in sight. By the time I had staggered down the grey slate steps from the station to the seafront, I'd really had it with the broken Chanel bag. Portofino could wait. I needed a shower and some fresh clothes. There were several hotels on the first curve of the bay, opposite the public beach and an enclosed private bathing area with red-and-white striped umbrellas and sun loungers arranged in precise Italian rows. I didn't think, just turned into the nearest and asked for a room. I spoke English, thinking that it would make me less conspicuous. When the woman at reception asked for my credit card, I said something quick and complex that I didn't expect her to catch, and cheerfully waved a couple of 200-euro notes. She let me pay in advance for two nights and asked for my passport. I had the same feeling I used to get at the cash point at the end of the month as she logged the details laboriously into a computer, and tried to keep a pleasant smile on my face. She reached for a phone. Christ, was she calling the *carabinieri*? Don't panic, don't panic. I could drop my bags and be out of there, the roll of notes safe in my pocket, in seconds. There was a taxi rank just outside, a single Audi idling as the driver smoked out of the window. I had to struggle to keep my breathing even, to resist the urge in my muscles to sprint for it.

It was housekeeping. She was calling housekeeping to check that the room was made up. She handed me an old-fashioned key with a heavy brass fob and wished me a pleasant stay. I gestured that I would take up my own bags. Once in the room I dumped my stuff on the bed, opened the window and ignored the 'No Smoking' sign. I was surprised to see that the sun was low behind the headland, making purple ribbons of the waves. I had been travelling all day. No, I was on the run. On the lam.

The pale pink curtains bellied in the sea breeze. I started, gasped aloud. A second in which the fabric formed two swollen arms, reaching for me. I froze, my heart banging so loudly I could hear it even over the regular beat of the surf outside. Then I giggled to myself. James might have looked like the bogeyman, but he was gone. I had 8,470 euro in cash, no job and a dead man behind me in another country. I thought briefly of texting Leanne, decided against it. I'd get a new phone tomorrow, transfer the numbers, drop the old one in the harbour. I dragged on my cigarette and waited for the fear to return. It didn't. I was in Italy in high summer and for the first time in my entire life, I was free. I didn't have to worry about money for quite a while. I considered a little celebration, but told myself to calm down. I couldn't wipe the stupid smirk off my face, though. For once, I didn't need to get laid to feel untouchable.

I showered and changed, took a walk along the port, drank a modest glass of white wine outside a bar, smoked and read my book and looked around me. I had forgotten the effect that Italy has on English people, the way everyone does seem to be so good-looking, the waiters so charming, the food so delicious. Life really does seem to be *bella*. After eating *trofie* with real, luminous-green pesto and slivers of potato and green beans I went back to the hotel. No messages on my phone. I stripped and inserted myself between starched pale pink sheets and slept perfectly.

Next morning I found my way to the main square, irregular around the white façade of a baroque church. A few stalls selling bunches of basil and bulbous tomatoes had been set up. Older women in nylon housecoats, clearly residents, were poking amongst them with string bags, while what were obviously summer people, discreetly wealthy, did some immaculate ciao-ing between two cafés. I collected *Nice Matin* and *La Repubblica* from the news kiosk; no point in bothering with day-old English papers. I ordered a *cappuccio* and a brioche *con marmellata* and looked through them carefully, scanning the columns at the side for any brief mention of the Eden Roc, or an English body. Nothing. The jam between the delicate layers of brioche was apricot, still warm, and the bartender had left a chocolate heart on the beige hood of my cappuccino: '*Per la bellissima signorina*'.

I spent the morning wandering slowly round Santa Margherita's many tiny boutiques. This was a destination for rich people, as the bemused faces of the cruise ship passengers chugged in for the day showed; it might look quaint and old-fashioned, but the prices were twenty-first-century Milan. Still, the day was so lovely it would have been an insult to the universe to economise just yet. I picked up a couple of bikinis, a wide-brimmed straw hat with a thick black silk band that made me smile to look at it, some neat caramel ballerinas from a cobbler who fetched my size out of a heap of boxes in his dark, leather-scented cubby hole of a shop, and splurged on an irresistibly charming Miu Miu sundress, orange flowers on a white background with a bandeau neck and a flared, Fifties-style skirt that made my waist tinier. Italian Judith, it seemed, was more demure than her English cousin. I didn't want to think too much about what I should do. After a night's sleep, the horror journey from France felt, itself, like a dream. I had had no thought beyond getting away, but now I needed a plan. But the town was so pretty, a pastel of jasmine and sunshine, sensible had rather lost its appeal.

Maybe Italy was sensible, though, for a time. I could spend a couple of weeks there, if I moved on somewhere cheaper, and still have enough to manage carefully for a couple of months when I got back. Some of poor old James's fifties were still racked up in my savings account. I hesitated for a while, then bought a pre-paid phonecard from a *tabaccheria* and left a voicemail for one of my flatmates. I hadn't bothered to tell them I was going anywhere, and didn't imagine for a moment that they'd care, but they might notice after a while. My rent was paid up quarterly, so there was nothing to worry about there. I said that I'd gone to visit some friends abroad and might stay on for a few weeks, remembered to add that I hoped the summer exams went well. In a back street away from the port, where the smart restaurants gave way to estate agents and electrical goods shops, I found a phone store and replaced my mobile. I got the wi-fi password from the hotel and used the new phone for a quick check of the English papers on the web. Still nothing. In the afternoon I went to the public beach, mostly full of teenagers who stared but didn't bother me. Then I showered the salt from my hair, fastened my new dress and applied a little make-up – mascara, gloss, a touch of blush. Pretty, not shouty.

I wanted to ask the cabbie if he was having a laugh when he told me it would be fifty euro for the five-kilometre drive to Portofino, but he looked bored and said, '*così*'. They had a monopoly, I supposed – the kind of people who could stay at the Splendido wouldn't be caught dead on a public bus. The road unspooled in a narrow gap between the sea and steep cliffs, so narrow that only one vehicle could pass at a time. We got stuck in the Ligurian rush hour, Porsche SUVs and BMWs driven by irritable-looking mammas in the ubiquitous giant glasses, the back seats full of sandy children and plump, mournful Filipinas. The driver swore and drummed his hands on the wheel, but I didn't mind. Through the window I could smell the fig trees that overhung the deep emerald water of little rocky bays, and through the trees I glimpsed ridiculously palatial nineteenth-century villas. I'd read up on Portofino: it pleased me to know that people who thought these things mattered said that the best Bellinis in the world were made here, not at Harry's Bar in Venice. Tragic really, my little grasps at status.

The square of the tiny fishing village had featured heavily in the celeb mags at the Gstaad Club, Beyoncé teetering down a gangplank, Leonardo DiCaprio scowling from under a baseball cap, but the pap shots hadn't given a sense of how small the place was. Just a single street leading down to a space not much bigger than a tennis court, albeit a tennis court surrounded with Dior and cashmere shops. I crossed to the café on the left side and ordered a Bellini from a silver-haired waiter straight from central casting. Of course that was a cliché, but then the whole of Portofino looked like a cliché, everyone's fantasy of the *bel paese*. He reappeared with a thick glass goblet filled with snowy pink peach slush, reverently opened a half-bottle of Veuve Clicquot and stirred the champagne carefully into the fruit. Little dishes of oily smoked ham, caperberries, crostini and thumbnail-sized hunks of Parmesan surrounded it. I sipped. It was delicious, the kind of drink you could swallow until you slid down the wall, but I made it last, watching the last tourist ferry pull away from the harbour in a flutter of Japanese camera phones. The sun was still strong, but gentle now, softening the sky behind the promontory to the west of the village, capped with its wedding-cake church. I licked salt and peach juice from my lips, a sensual Instagram. I knew I should feel sad about what had happened to James, but if only because it had so strangely given me this moment, I couldn't.

An elegant wooden boat was tying up at the dockside, one of the traditional Genovese fishing boats called *gozzi*, with smart navy cushions and a white sun-canopy. A group of people were scrambling out, about my age, calling their thanks to the driver, who was naked except for cut-off denims and a nautical cap, with improbable bright blond hair poking out underneath. I remembered that the Vikings had sailed along this coast long ago, and that blond, blue-eyed Italians were not uncommon here, or in Sicily. I was fascinated by the group, four men and two women. There was a relaxed possessiveness to the way they moved through this space, as though there was nothing special about being in Portofino, as though they were unaware that this was the locus of so many cramped commuter dreams. They sprawled at a table close to me and lit cigarettes, ordered drinks, began to make phone calls which, from what I could overhear, concerned whose house they were going to meet up in for dinner later, with other friends. I watched. The girls were not strictly beautiful, but they had that show-pony sheen that comes from generations of confident money, long legs and narrow ankles, glossy hair, perfect teeth, no make-up. One wore what was obviously her boyfriend's shirt over her bikini top, a monogram discreetly visible in the linen folds, the other was in an embroidered white tunic, with just a pair of green suede Manolo sandals, flat and rather scuffed, that I knew would have cost at least 500 euro. I was embarrassed that I noticed that, because, of course, a girl like her never would. The men were identikit, thick dark hair falling to their collars, broad-shouldered and slim as though they had never done anything but ski and swim and play tennis, which they probably hadn't. They were – effortless, I decided. Compared with Leanne and myself in our fussy Riviera finery they had an air of belonging which no amount of expensive shopping could ever produce. This is what properly rich people looked like, I thought, like they would never, ever have to try.

I spun my drink out, taking them in, until they wandered off. The girl in the shirt let herself into a building across the square, and a few minutes later appeared on a terrace above the Dior boutique, talking to a maid in a pale pink uniform. Maybe the dinner would be at her house, not that she'd have to shop for it, or cook it, or clear up afterwards. I didn't like these thoughts, they were bitter. I was too used to being on the outside, looking in. The bar was filling up now, a few overdressed American couples, perhaps guests at the Splendido on top of the hill who'd strolled down for an *aperitivo*. I thought about another drink, but the ticket in its tiny saucer already said forty euro. Perhaps I could walk back to Santa on the decked pedestrian path. I put two notes and a couple of coins on the table and got up to leave.

Three huge boats were docked at the right side of the harbour, absurd, like whales in a goldfish bowl. Two crew, in white knee-length shorts and polished leather belts, were letting down a gangplank on one of them, the hugest of the lot. The blunt lines of the hull and the sheen of the finish, like rubberised charcoal, gave it an almost military air, as though it might vanish beneath the waves to transport a James Bond villain to his undersea lair. It was ugly, but certainly impressive. After a minute, two pairs of chunky Nikes appeared, followed by Levi'd legs and garish Polo shirts with huge logos. Both their owners had their phones clamped to their ears, indifferent to their surroundings. I wondered if they even knew where they were. Then I looked again, and saw it was Steve. Steve whose boat I had been on at Antibes just two nights before.

And then something switched. The dreamy, soporific air about me was brusquely charged with an adrenalin kick so sharp I thought the whole piazza must feel it. The soft colours of the square flared into tropical life as I watched the two men approach. My brain fizzed awake, because I had seen, suddenly, what I could do. I took a deep breath and stood slowly. This was what rich people did, wasn't it? They bumped into one another all the time, in St Moritz, in Mégève, on Elba or Pantelleria. I had to act like one of them, airy, casual. I twitched my sunglasses into my bag. They were making for the green-awninged restaurant facing the dock. Puny, another famous place I had read about. I timed my walk so that I crossed them diagonally, letting my full skirt swing so that it almost brushed Steve's legs. He was still messaging. I turned, caught his eye.

'Steve!'

He looked up, and I saw him trying to place me. I stepped forward confidently and kissed him on both cheeks. 'Lauren. We hung out in Antibes!'

'Hey, yeah. Lauren? Hi, how are you?'

At least he did seem to genuinely recognise me. I said hi to Thing, Leanne's Jacuzzi paramour, who turned out to be called Tristan, which I wouldn't have had him down for.

We stood for an awkward minute. Social chit-chat obviously wasn't Steve's thing, but I could not let this go. Steve didn't know it yet, but he was about to play Sir Lancelot.

'Great night, wasn't it?'

'Yeah, great.'

Oh God, we could be here for decades.

'My friend, that is, she's more of an acquaintance really, went back to town. I've been staying with some friends – over there.' I waved my arm vaguely in the direction of the villa-speckled hills. 'But they've left already for Corsica. I'm going back myself tomorrow.'

'We've just got in. We're planning to take her along the coast – Sardinia,' proffered Steve.

I acted like he hadn't already told me that over hot chocolate.

'Plans for tonight?' I tried to look flirtatious but not too desperate, though in fact I'd have done them both sideways with the polished crew as cheerleaders if it got me on that boat. Boats jump borders in a way that corpses just don't.

'Just checking in with a few people. Why don't you have dinner with us?'

Don't rush him, Judith.

'Well, my stuff's over at Santa.'

'You can pick it up later.'

Result.

'Sure, thanks. I'd love to.'

So Steve ordered a magnum of 95 Dom, which might have impressed me in another life, and two older guys with mahogany cleavages and sullen Estonian mistresses appeared, and we ordered some baby octopus antipasti, which nobody touched but me, and then Steve ordered two bottles of lime-coloured Vermentino, and then a group of Milanese bankers who'd turned up from Forte dei Marmi appeared, and one of them took time out from fawning deferentially over Steve to whizz me back to Santa in his vintage Alfa to collect my bags, and then we had to go to a floating bar at Paraggi where the Estonians did a bit of listless pole dancing and everyone ordered sushi, which no one ate, then it was back to the boat for Cohibas and coke in the hot tub and Steve showing off his underwater stereo system which meant you could listen to Rihanna even while you were swimming in the upper deck pool, if that blew your hair back. I took every glass that was offered and didn't drink a drop – thanks, Olly – and stayed close to Steve when one of the old walruses reached a proprietorial hand out of the bubbles towards me, and, eventually, lay down meekly in Steve's huge bed quite ready to sing for my supper if required. But all he did was hold my hand and turn over quietly, and let me sleep in the soft unsteady cradle of the waves.

He was gone in the morning. I sat up, glad of my clear head, and pressed my face to the porthole. Sea and sky. Fuck. I'd done it. There was a tray on the bed, orange juice, a silver coffee pot, scrambled eggs and toast under a silver cover, fruit, yoghurt, croissants. A tiny crystal vase with a single white rose. Today's

FT, *Times*, *Daily Mail* – because everyone reads that. Presumably billionaires had a special press connection, no day-old news for them. I scanned them rapidly; nothing. My bags had been unpacked, my shoes lined up and neatly stuffed with tissue, my few dresses looking forlorn on padded charcoal-silk hangers, each with a striped linen bag of rose petals. I showered in the bathroom, where the double shower and personal sauna made the Eden Roc look a bit basic, knotted up my hair and added a plain grey tee to the briefest of the bikinis I had bought in Santa. In the stateroom, Steve was in shorts, bare chested, chugging coffee from a jumbo Starbucks mug, his eyes travelling over a bank of blinking screens. Currents of money. Through the glass doors to the deck I could see Tristan lifting dumbbells.

'Hey, babe.' Babe was good. I wasn't yet sure how to play this. I didn't want to be relegated to Estonian slut category, but then I obviously was the kind of girl who hopped a boat with a virtual stranger at a moment's notice. The kind of girl who checks into a hotel in Santa Margherita for two nights and then disappears, no passports, no tickets, no borders. I let my hands rest briefly on his shoulders, smelling his clean skin and cologne, planted a kiss on his slightly receding hairline.

'Hey, you.'

'We're putting in at Porto Venere tonight.'

'We' was also good. Very good.

'Lovely,' I answered casually, as though I always spent my summers popping from one exclusive Italian resort town to another. Inside, I was running a victory lap of the deck, punching the air. What's the appropriate selfie pose when you've just got away with manslaughter? But I'm a quick learner, a very quick learner, and I knew that the only way to pull this off was never for a moment to let it show that I didn't have a fucking clue what I was doing. So I went out to sunbathe, noticing all the same that he didn't give a glance to my tie-sided back view as it swung through the doors.

After lunch – grilled fish, *salsa verde* and fruit served from more old crystal and thick modern china, bright orange, stamped with the boat's name, *Mandarin* – Steve gave me an enthusiastic tour. I inspected the helipad, heard quite a lot about the Russian military-grade casing of the hull, the folding balconies on the sundeck, the sliding glass wall of the stateroom, the extending box release of the passerelle – whatever that was – revisited the Picassos. The crew glided around Steve like pilot fish to his shark, with a kind of trained telepathy that produced a steadying hand in a doorway or a frosted glass of Armani mineral water without a need ever being expressed aloud. Steve introduced his captain, Jan, a stern-looking Norwegian who smiled along professionally with Steve's awkward attempts at mateyness.

'Show her the lights, Jan!'

Jan's tanned forearm brushed mine as he leaned over to flick the switch. A second's flash of erotic Morse code, but that could wait. I peered dutifully over the prow. Despite the sunlight, the dark margin of the waterline was suddenly filled with a pink neon glow. Jan flicked a switch and the illuminations fireworked through orange, cobalt, purple, throbbing diamond white. At night the thing would have looked like a Las Vegas cathouse.

'Great, isn't it! I've just got them.'

There was something endearingly boyish about his enthusiasm, though Jan's opinion of the decorative scheme was visible from Genoa. We inspected the cabins, which apart from the room which I now seemed to be sharing with Steve were surprisingly poky. When we had finished, Steve showed me his new toy, a personal planetarium installed in the wheelhouse.

'It has lasers, so you can track the constellations against the real sky.' Even the stars, here, could be rearranged for pleasure.

'It's a shame I won't see it in action,' I said hesitantly. 'You'd probably better drop me off, tonight.'

'Do you have somewhere to be?'

I looked at him from under my lashes. 'Not specially.'

'Why don't you stay then? We can hang out.'

There was no flirtation in his eyes; I adjusted my own.

'Sure. I'd love that. Thanks. Is it cool to keep my stuff in your room, though?'

'No problem.'

So that was that.

PART TWO

INSIDE

11

I once read somewhere that people would worry much less about what others thought of them if they realised how seldom they did so. As a day turned into three, then a week, then two, I got by through simply offering no information. Steve was essentially incurious, uninterested in anything except his business and his possessions, though he had obviously travelled far enough from whatever geek cellar he had crawled out of to attain a semblance of social functionality. As far as I could surmise from Steve's minimal observations, Tristan was his sidekick, the rent-a-friend, nominally employed in one of Steve's funds, but basically there to deal with the crew, call ahead to the clubs, produce the coke and the almost-model girls, because this was fun, wasn't it? This was how you had fun, when you'd made enough money to make Abramovich feel shifty.

But sometimes, across a dance floor or a dinner table, when it was time for Steve to produce his nuclear Amex and suddenly everyone turned their eyes away, I'd see him move his head dumbly from side to side, bewildered as a dancing bear. Sexually, I couldn't work him out. The first night I had assumed he was just tired, but though he called me 'baby' or 'darling', he didn't even try to kiss me, except for brief pecks of greeting. I slept with him as though by default; we lay quietly side by side like brother and sister. He never tried anything and I wasn't stupid enough to initiate it, though I was careful to go to bed each night looking as though there was nothing I'd rather do. Of course, I wondered if he was gay, whether old Tris was more than a major-domo, but that didn't seem to be the case either; Tristan gaily indulged in all the girls who shoved themselves his way. After a while, I concluded that Steve was simply asexual, that the furthest his desire went was liking to have a pretty girl around, that he had worked out that picking up women was what he was supposed to do, like owning a huge boat and a plane and four houses and God knew how many cars: because he could. That was how you kept score, wasn't it? I realised that the mistake people make about people like Steve is to imagine that they're interested in money, when it's impossible to get that rich if money is what you care about. To play those kind of hedge fund odds, the real guys, the serious guys (and Steve was gleefully dismissive about his peers whose funds moved only five or six billion through the labyrinths of finance), require indifference to money. The only interest is the game. I understood that.

The longer I stayed on the boat, the further I was from that gelid body, that reproachful pallid face. I tried not to think too much about Leanne. Our brief moment of complicity belonged to another world now, yet in many ways, I could have been back at the Gstaad Club. Girls everywhere, ubiquitous on the drag down from Saint-Tropez to Sicily as rosé and bougainvillea. I've never met the girl who wasn't prepared to hawk it when there was a bona fide billionaire in the room, so I realised in a while that in a sense my presence protected Steve. I made sure to be vaguely possessive in company, mirroring Steve's 'babes' and draping a casual arm around his shoulders, which made me an object of irritation and fascination to the girls, but kept them off. Seated next to Steve at dinner, I would overhear them talking gaily like suburban housewives about the terrible cost of things, until sometimes I wondered why he didn't write them a cheque for a million quid just to buy a bit of quiet.

Tristan's assiduous messaging produced a facsimile of a social scene – hopping from tender to drinks to restaurant, then the inevitable club or sometimes a house party in the hills above a resort – though we never met anyone who resembled the *figli d'oro* I had spied in Portofino. The men were in funds or banks or property; once we drove up into the hills of the Tuscan Maremma to lunch at the house of an English TV pundit with a terrifying hair weave who'd been big in newspapers in the Nineties, and his crowd of incredibly pleased-with-themselves minor celebrities who spent the whole time trying to cap each other's jokes in a monsoon of name-dropping. Every guy, no matter how paunchy or bald or vilely cigar-breathed, had a girl. Wives were not what you took to the Riviera, and glittering conversation was not what was required of the girls. They never left their men's sides, sitting next to them, cutting up and forking in their food for them as though they were babies, not speaking unless spoken to, but laughing at everything their man said just in case it was funny, creating a force field around each couple that no other woman could penetrate. At the pundit's lunch the only exception was a successful television comedian, a big, ungainly woman who had won several prestigious awards, who began by dominating the talk, matching the men quip for quip, but gradually descended into a bewildered and furious silence as the rosé flowed and her colleagues stopped even pretending to listen to her. I pitied her, as the faces reddened and the noise round the table swelled and her erstwhile civilised, BBC-valued peers reverted to braying Neanderthals, pawing at their harem and,

I could see, taking a savage pleasure in besting her at a game she couldn't even enter.

Our job, the girls' job, was to wear delicate K-Jacques sandals around our pretty tanned ankles, to swish our pretty hair and sip delicately at our wine, to play with our pretty Rolexes around our slender tanned wrists. We were the prizes, the gold made delectable bronzed flesh, Galateas who unfroze at the touch of money. No wonder she was fuming. She had been stripped of her currency as swiftly as a Neapolitan pickpocket would have relieved her of her boring Mulberry handbag. I should have said something, done something to shut those smug cunts up, but I just smiled and let my hair swing over my collarbone and fed Steve tiny bites of iced coconut soufflé. Watch and learn, baby.

Wealth creeps under your epidermis like poison. It invades your posture, your gestures, the way you carry yourself. From the moment I stepped aboard the *Mandarin*, I don't think I opened a door. I certainly didn't carry a heavy bag, or lift a dirty plate. If the price is cosying up to some ancient boor who eyes you in the Jacuzzi like a rutting hippo, the pay-off is being surrounded by young, uniformed men with broad shoulders and clean nails who hold out your chair, fetch your napkin or your sunglasses, adjust the cushions on your sun lounger, pick up your dirty knickers and thank you for permitting them to do it. They don't look you in the eyes; you are not for them. They clear away the ashtrays and the smeared mirrors, discreetly replenish the aspirin by the bed and the Xanax and Viagra in the bathroom cabinet, repair the insults to your flesh in hundreds of subtle, complicitous ways so that you stalk amongst them immaculate as a goddess, and, in a while, between the brim of your Ray-Bans and the tip of your imperiously tilted chin, they disappear from your sight. But don't let the accoutrements distract you. If you don't get the ring on your finger sharpish, you're fucked. The real difference between the Riviera hotties and the crowd back at the Gstaad was that these girls had climbed to the next tier, which only made the precipice before them all the more appalling.

In Porto-Vecchio, we were joined by Hermann, a reedy, silent German colleague of Steve's, and his fiancée Carlotta, the diamond on her ring finger as spectacularly disproportionate as her tit job. Carlotta went in for the cooing princess routine when Hermann was present, playing with his earlobes and calling him 'baby' every five seconds. In private she took no prisoners.

'He's a fucking pig,' she confided casually as we lay topless on one of the huge orange sun mattresses on the upper deck.

'Who?'

'Hermann. Yeah, like I was in St Moritz last season and I was meant to be joining him in Verbier and he sent a car. A fucking car to pick me up.'

Her accent was vaguely European, but I couldn't place it. I wondered if she still could.

'Oh God, that's awful.'

'Yeah, I made my own bed in the chalet for like a week, and he can't even be bothered to send the fucking heli for me. You should only fly private, you know,' she added seriously. 'Like, don't let them take advantage.'

'Are you going to marry him?'

'Sure. We got engaged when I got pregnant last year, but he already has like six kids from previous, so he made me get rid of it.'

I touched the warm skin of her shoulder sympathetically.

'That's awful. I'm so sorry.'

She bit her overfilled lip theatrically. 'Thanks. But I got a flat on Eaton Place for hoovering it out, so it wasn't that bad.'

Once I'd started breathing again Carlotta was noodling on her phone.

'Did you hear about the Swedish girl at Nikki Beach?'

Of course I'd heard about the Swedish girl at Nikki Beach. Everyone from Antibes to Panarea that year had heard about the Swedish girl at Nikki Beach.

'She was in the pool for, like, a day' – five hours, two days, it varied – 'before anyone noticed she was dead.'

'Gross.'

'Yeah, gross. She was already, like' – Carlotta fished for the word – 'mouldering.'

Carlotta shared the vulnerability of the classless; I understood that. But I wasn't like her; I didn't want to snag a rich husband and spend the rest of my life as flotsam on the tide of Euromoney. Dressing the part was a different matter. Steve might not have been the cockrocking king of Mayfair, which suited me fine, but his few fixed ideas about women conveniently included their need to shop. The acquisition of clothes was apparently my sex's highest calling, and since I had the brains never to ask him for so much as an ice cream, I did rather well.

As we glided slowly south through the sparkling breezes, and July slipped into August, whenever we docked, Steve would ask me if I needed to pick up a few things, then solemnly hand me a boggling wad of notes. At first I was careful, keeping much of it back, so that I could at least offer to pay my share of drinks and dinner, but after a few days it didn't seem relevant. So I bought expensive things, things I would never be able to afford again, a lifetime's rainbow of cashmere, a hammered linen Vuitton raincoat, a perfect chestnut crocodile Prada tote. I'd catch a glimpse of myself in the boutique windows or the glassy smoothness of a harbour, tanned in my simple white shirt and cut-offs, hair tied up messily in a Dolce & Gabbana scarf, swinging my ribboned bags of loot, and wonder whether I ought to be surprised at my metamorphosis. But I wasn't, really. I looked in the water and there saw, finally, myself.

Philip Larkin once wrote wistfully of a world where beauty was accepted slang for yes. Fucking can be such a very uncomplicated pleasure, as ancient and elemental as the salt-earth taste of an olive, or a glass of cold water after a long, dusty walk. So why say no? Monogamy must be so much easier for the plain.

After a few weeks as Steve's pseudo-girlfriend, I was climbing the walls. If you're like me, the trick is to learn to spot the other ones who feel the same. When Jan had given his slightly contemptuous tour of the *Mandarin* that first day, I had made sure my attention remained on Steve, but there had been one other moment, a few days into the trip, when I had passed him on the deck and watched his eyes follow me precisely the way Steve's didn't.

I had to let it sit for a while. I wasn't dumb enough to fuck up my chances for the sake of a shag, but it was a wonder Tris hadn't noticed Jan's looks and given him his P45, he was so mercilessly appealing. Thick through the shoulders and tight through the waist, eyes blue and deep as a fjord, framed by thick grey lashes like a cartoon donkey. *Caveat emptor*: I wasn't complaining. So one afternoon, as we were gliding through the Maddalena archipelago, I asked Steve if he wanted to go for a picnic.

'We can take the tender, go snorkelling!' I enthused.

'Sorry, babe, I have stuff to do. Get Tris to take you.'

'Of course. I didn't mean to disturb you.'

I barged into Tristan's cabin without knocking. He was watching porn on his laptop in his underwear, pasty and hungover under his tan. I just glimpsed a POV of Jada Stevens lifting her famous spherical arse to the camera before he flipped the lid shut irritably.

'Steve says will you take me snorkelling?' I put just enough spoiled petulance into my voice to get on his nerves even more.

'Sorry, Lauren, I don't feel that good.' What he meant to say was 'fuck off'. It was a poignant little power negotiation.

'But I really want to go,' I pouted.

'Get one of the guys to take you in the tender.'

'Great idea! Thanks,' I chirped brightly. 'Hope you feel better.'

'Sure. See you later.'

I found Jan actually swabbing the deck. He was very Scandi like that, always joining in with the dirty work. Still, he looked glad of an excuse to put down his mop.

'Tris says will you take me snorkelling, please, Jan?'

He stood up slowly, all six foot heaven of him.

'Snorkelling?'

'Yes, please. He says to take the tender.'

'OK. The other guys can manage. I'll speak to them and get my stuff. Be ready in ten minutes?'

'Perfect. Thank you.'

* * * * *

The spray stung my face as we bounced away from the *Mandarin*, heading round the point of one of the tiny bare islets. Jan steered, I lay back on the cushions and let a hand trail in the frothing water. I was wearing denim cut-offs, a white Fernandez bikini top and a floppy straw hat, bound heavily round the brim with a retro Pucci silk shawl. Jan had swapped his crew kit for knackered khaki Bermudas and a faded navy linen shirt that matched his eyes. I'd fetched a bottle of Vermentino, a corkscrew and a heap of pulsing figs from the galley.

'Do you like sea urchin?' Jan called over the noise of the engine.

'I don't know.'

He slowed the boat to a putter and began to peer over the side. We glided over cups of white sand, the clarity of the water belying its depth, until we came to a clump of rocks, just protruding from the surface, iridescent with sea lichen in the wash of the waves, gleaming like petrol.

'Here will do.' I liked his voice, clipped, precise, the twist of the Norwegian accent. I liked that he spared his words.

'Open the anchor hatch.'

I crawled, rather ungainly, over the flat sunbathing bed and unsnapped the trap which concealed the anchor. Jan reversed the boat.

'Throw it when I say. Wait, wait, now.'

I watched the anchor plunge, playing out its chain, as Jan moved the boat away until it held taut.

'Good. Now you can try a sea urchin.'

He had a battered canvas backpack at his feet, from which he took a mask, a clasp knife and a steel mesh glove like a medieval gauntlet.

'Put your snorkel on. You can watch. Do you know the difference between the males and the females?'

Oddly, I didn't.

'You can only eat the females. They collect little shells, stones, to decorate themselves. They make themselves beautiful, like women.' He held my gaze for a second too long, then slipped off his shirt and dropped over the side.

I wriggled out of my shorts and joined him. For a moment, the water felt cold after the concentrated heat of the boat. I floated off, bobbing like a starfish, watching as Jan dived, pulling himself down with long strokes. He gripped the base of the rock and, using the knife in the gloved hand, worked away at something fat and black. Then he popped up, placed the thing on the gunnel, inhaled and dived again. I lifted my head to look. The sea urchin was a sinister underwater hedgehog, its spines twitching in the air. Jan retrieved two more, then we climbed out of the water by the short ladder beside the engine.

I opened the wine while Jan used the knife to scrape the spines from the shells overboard.

'I forgot glasses.'

'No problem.' He took the bottle and raised it to his mouth. I watched his throat move as he swallowed.

'Now, here.'

The cleaned shell was beautiful, hatched in delicate pink and green. Jan worked the knife into the underside, splitting it in two like a mango, showing dark orange flesh edged with black.

'It's loose. Take it with your fingers.'

'Show me.'

He scooped a piece and held it out to me. I opened my mouth and closed my eyes.

'Good?'

'Mmmm.'

It was strong, viscous, salty and almost gamey. I took a slug of wine and felt the minerals meld on my tongue. I lay back with the sun on my face and the slick of raw flesh on my lips.

'More.'

He fed me the rest, then I fed him. Then there was that delicious moment when his face was so close to mine that I could see the salt crystals gleaming on those ridiculous eyelashes. I was wet before he even kissed me. He didn't hurry, let his tongue find mine, twine, push, twine. Then he sat back, on the seat behind the tiller, and looked at me.

'Do you want to fuck, now?' he asked.

'Yes, I want to fuck now, Jan.'

So many twists had brought me to this particular moment. I knew that I might never get free, that James's arms might still twine about me, deadly as a siren's, and drag me to the depths. But for a few moments, I could be liberated, I could stop time.

I kept my eyes on his as I lay back again on the cushions. Holding his gaze, I unfastened my bikini top and dropped it next to me. He tilted his chin in a minute gesture of acquiescence. I undid the ribbon ties on either side of the bikini bottoms, lifted them off me and placed them with the top.

'Show me.'

Slowly, perfectly slowly, I let my thighs open. From where he sat, my cunt was on a level with his eyes. I dipped the middle finger of my right hand into my mouth, then trailed it down between my breasts, across my stomach and between my legs. When I held it towards his mouth it was slick with my juice. He rose to his feet, easy on the swaying boards of the boat.

He had a beautiful cock, thick around the base, the straining tip tight as watered silk.

'Turn over. I want to see your arse.'

I had a brief flash of Jada Stevens before I flipped over on all fours. He put a hand between my shoulder blades and pushed me down so that my spine curved back to meet him, and slid his fingers inside me.

'Move. I want to see your hips.'

I pushed against the hardness of his hand, swaying a slow figure eight. It felt so good I thought I might cum just from that. I turned and took the head in my mouth, slid it deep into my throat, let it rest there. It was thumping. I sucked him again and again, letting my nails play across his tight balls, then withdrew, looking up into his eyes, letting him look at the swollen tip against my lips.

'Fuck me. I want you to fuck me.'

He got on his knees behind me, buried his hand inside my cunt once more, spreading his fingers at the top.

'Move. Move your ass. That's right. Show me. That's how you get me hard. Move it like that.'

'Give me your cock now.'

I caught the tip between the lips of my pussy, manoeuvred the head into me, then paused, clenching my muscles.

'Be still,' I told him. I pulled myself forward a little, releasing him, then took the head back into me, corkscrewing, taking him deeper each time until I could feel his balls against the soaked lips of my cunt.

'Go faster now.'

He grabbed my hips, pulled me tight, gasping against him, started to work me.

'Fuck. This is perfect. Don't stop.'

'You like that. You like it hard?'

'Yeah. I like it hard. Just – don't – stop.'

The boat was rocking crazily; a wash of water splashed us both. I could feel my wet hair heavy down my back. He grabbed it, pulling my head back so that my back curved deeper and his cock hit the sweet spot and I was going to cum, begging him to go harder.

'Now, with me. Cum. I want you to flood me.'

He slapped my ass as he came, and that got me there, that and the short stabs of his fat cock as it pulsed three great gouts of cum up me. I screamed and ground my cunt against him, then we both fell forward, all his weight on my back, as the boat swayed slowly back to stillness. Then we ate the figs ravenously and drank some more wine, and he asked me if I wanted to go again, and I did, me on top this time, his hands gripping the muscles at the side of my waist, bringing me down on him over and over while I stroked my clit until I came and lay over him, his cock hammering up at me until he was ready, then he pushed me back, knelt between my lolling thighs and gave it to me across my mouth. I licked his cum from my lips. Salty, viscous, mineral. Then we slept a while under the sun, hand in hand, and then it was time to go back to the boat.

It had been a fantastic matinee, but we both knew, wordlessly, that there wasn't going to be an evening performance. I knew Jan wouldn't kiss and tell. We barely spoke for the rest of my time on the *Mandarin*, and that was just fine.

12

The summer migration across the Mediterranean moves to a rhythm as mysterious as a skein of geese in flight. A rumoured sighting of celebrity, a Kate or a Kanye, will have the unwieldy tubs of the wealthy suddenly nosing their way to a particular bar or beach, indistinguishable from its fellows: the owner will triple the prices on the chalkboard and for a few days or a week the customers will glow with the elusive fairy dust of imagined fame, the knowledge that this place, and this place only, is the right place to be. Then the rumour will skip once more across the waves, and the boats will tack clumsily off in another futile pursuit, leaving the locals to a hyenas' feast of scraps.

This year, it was Giacomo's near Gaeta, a baroque town on the coast south of Rome. In the nineteenth century, Pope Pius IX had promulgated the doctrine of the Immaculate Conception after meditating in the Golden Grotto of the Church of Santissima Annunziata there, and Tris announced our dinner reservation with similar awe. As we trailed up the uneven cobblestoned alleyway from the harbour to the restaurant, there was definitely a sense of mystery in the air. Before the night was out, someone was surely going to dance on a table. Giacomo's did have an enchanting view across the bay: a terrace was built out dramatically on a promontory above the town, above a cliff draped in creamy yellow jasmine, creating a flying carpet of scent.

After we had played with the tuna tartare and grilled sea bass with fennel (if I saw another sea bass soon, I'd have to stick a fork in my eye), Steve drew me aside to look out at the harbour and the massive fortress of the one-time kings of Aragon.

'Having fun?' he asked dutifully.

'Of course, darling. It's beautiful. You?'

'Sure,' he replied unconvincingly.

Steve may have been fundamentally uninterested in people, but I couldn't afford to be. I had to sweat what few assets I had, which meant being alert to the tiniest calibrations of this strange new world, to work out where I could find a foothold in its nexus. I scanned the view, looking for something to liven Steve up.

'That's Balensky's boat.'

I couldn't have done better if I'd announced that there was a run on the rouble.

'*He's* here?'

'Guess so. The boat anyway. I saw it back in Cannes.'

I'd never seen Steve look nervous, but he was suddenly shifty, fiddling aimlessly with the permanent pacifier of his phone.

'I want to meet him.'

'Why?'

'Not here. Later, when we get back to the boat.'

I was intrigued, something of a novelty in Steve's company, but I kept quiet until we were safely in his bedroom. As I stooped to unfasten my Lanvin wedges in just my knickers, I realised I'd stopped noticing or caring whether Steve looked at me or not. We could have been married. I slipped on an embroidered Antik Batik kurta and patted the bed next to me.

'So. What's this all about?'

'I need some information.'

'And you want me to get it?'

Of course he did, and of course it was majorly out of order. And then, with the same sudden rush of clarity I'd experienced back on the dock at Portofino, I saw that I had been adrift, just allowing the days to unroll. Maybe a shrink would have said it was delayed shock, but I preferred to see it as getting into character. Steve had never asked anything of me. But this could make him vulnerable, put him in my debt. This was a tipping point, a chance to change the game. So far, I'd been a passenger on this trip, but now I wondered if I could start to feel like a player.

'Steve, you're asking me to do something totally fucking illegal.'

'Tell me about it.'

I sat up from my nest of pillows. 'No, you tell me. I might need to tell it to the judge, after all. Why do you need this?'

Steve looked weary. 'It's just . . . he's here, in Italy. I wanted to check up on something, something I'd heard, that's all.'

'What?'

'I'll tell you when I know.'

'Well,' I said carefully. 'For a start he needs to know you're here, too. Put it on Twitter if you have to.'

'But I don't do Twitter.'

'Fine. Get Tris to call his PA then.'

'But what should he say?'

Oh God. I reached for my phone and googled Balensky. 'He collects art,' I said as I held out the screen to Steve. 'Just like you,' I added encouragingly. 'Get Tris to say you want to pick his brains, that'll flatter him.'

'Brilliant.'

No shit, Sherlock. I took a deep breath, and suggested a few refinements to Steve's plan. To leverage the trade between us, I was going to need knowledge, not to mention a decoy. Steve seemed pretty impressed with my solution.

It was a simple ruse, but it worked as I had hoped. The following afternoon, Steve joined me in the plunge pool.

'Have you got an evening dress, Lauren – you know, something long?' I'd been on the boat a month, and an evening gown was about the only thing I hadn't yet bought.

'Not with me, no. Why, darling?'

'We're invited to a dinner.' As ever, Steve had half an eye on Bloomberg on the flat screen installed just above the water line. 'Black tie,' he added, morosely.

'Where?'

'On Balensky's boat.' He raised what he obviously thought was a dashing eyebrow.

Result.

'We're meeting him tomorrow, near Ponza.'

'Sounds grand.'

Above us on the sundeck, I could sense Carlotta pricking up her ears, or maybe her tits. Her nipples probably had built-in oligarch radar. I flipped over and swam a couple of side strokes to bring me next to him.

'I could pick something up.'

'Yeah, you need something smart. Get Tris to sort it.'

Carlotta's face popped over the rail. 'I hate you,' she mouthed sulkily, condemned to a romantic supper for two with her beloved.

'Get over it, Cinderella,' I called. 'It's your lucky day. We're going shopping.'

* * * * *

Like all the charming fishing villages we'd passed on our way down the coast, the port at Ponza, the tiny strip of an island where the Romans go to play, no longer took the fishing part that literally. Most of the ramshackle ochre and yellow houses tumbling down to the sea contained million-euro *pieds à terre*, though a few still displayed washing at the windows and old ladies gazing placidly from their doorways. Maybe they were actresses sponsored by the government to give the place some colour. And even the sleepiest village square would contain a boutique or two where the women of the floating tribe of Eurowealth could pop in to make an offering. I pulled Carlotta into the nearest shop, which featured a window display of thousand-euro La Perla bikinis.

'You need a dress. You're going to be Steve's girlfriend tonight.'

'You mean, like, a threesome?' I didn't have the impression that this was a particularly novel request.

It was a struggle not to roll my eyes. 'Duh. No. Just for this party. You don't have to do anything except look devoted. Now, how about this?'

'What about Hermann? He won't like it.'

'Tris'll square it. He'll have a fine time, don't worry.'

Carlotta picked out a full-length white Marc Jacobs shift with the tiniest of spaghetti straps that made her breasts look more improbably gravity-defying than ever. With her hair down and simple jewellery she would look like a Fellini goddess. I chose a vintage-style long-sleeved lurex dress in gold, much more covered up at the front, but scooped out and draped down to the coccyx behind. We found nude python Giambattista Valli sandals for us both – I assumed that a black-tie evening would dispense with the no-shoe nonsense – and two Fendi python clutches, emerald and silver for Carlotta, pink and gold for me. Carlotta watched appraisingly as I peeled off just over 7,000 euro in 500-euro notes.

'He really likes you, Steve.'

'Maybe.'

'Still, whatever. You want to get good stuff you can keep.'

Before we went back to the Mandarin we stopped at the café and snarfed down two *pizzettes* and a *gelato affogato*, swimming in Baileys and espresso. Carlotta speculatively pinched a fold of skin above her elbow.

'I'm always starving. Hermann hates me to eat, but two prawns and a piece of watermelon is not lunch, you know? When I'm old, I'm going to get like totally fucking fat.'

As we boarded the tender that evening. Carlotta was really getting into character, holding Steve's arm and playing with his collar. He actually looked quite handsome in a dinner jacket, though at the last minute he'd defiantly left off the tie. I hissed at Carlotta to take off her engagement ring and she whipped it into the Fendi. She'd happily have chucked it into the sea, I thought, if there was a chance of her method acting becoming reality. Hermann had been diplomatically removed by Tristan for a scuba excursion, a night dive to some famously inaccessible caverns, from which Carlotta reluctantly had to be excluded as she didn't have her PADI scuba certificate. Maybe I'd better see about doing that.

'So did you hear about that father and son last year in the caves at Capri? They got, like, stuck, and the father had to decide whether to save himself and leave the son or die with him, so like –'

'Jesus, Carlotta,' I said, 'It's like being on holiday with Edgar Allen Poe.'

She looked blank.

'Nothing. You look gorgeous. We'll have a great time.'

The trip in the Riva took a while, as Balensky's boat was moored further out, in deeper water. Five decks loomed up at us; it seemed the size of a shopping mall, so huge that we drove inside it into an inner dock and were shown into a copper-lined lift to whizz us up to the deck. I'd had many moments since being on the *Mandarin* when I wanted to freeze-frame my surroundings, to look at myself and remember incredulously how it felt to be hauling my briefcase along the Piccadilly line. This was one of those moments.

The biggest of the decks was decorated with garlands of pink orchids, twined around the rails and the staircases. Globes of heavily sherbet-scented pink roses formed an aisle along which waiters stood with magnums of pink Krug. Carlotta and I refused grilled tartines with caviar of truffle and tomato confit and tiny dishes of pink lobster bolognaise. Balensky was waiting at the top of the aisle, in a midnight blue silk jacket with padded shoulders that was working overtime to disguise the fact that he was practically a dwarf. His sallow skin hung in wattles from his Botoxed forehead, which sported a few strands of carefully woven in, weirdly henna-coloured hair. Maybe this was the one thing money couldn't buy, I thought. No matter how much wedge you threw at it, a restored scalp still looked like a nuclear disaster. I thought Balensky must be in his eighties, but his face was timelessly malicious. He supposedly had a wife and children stashed away somewhere, although braver Web gossips also claimed that he gave boys-only parties at his restored Roman villa outside Tangier. Balensky shook Steve's hand with a politician's enthusiastic pump, then bowed over Carlotta's wrist as Steve introduced her. I hovered behind, the spare friend, but made sure I turned my hip so he could glimpse my naked back as he greeted me.

'Thank you for coming. Lovely to see you.'

'Thank you for inviting me. What wonderful flowers.'

His eyes were already elsewhere. I stepped back to allow the next guests to be received. Behind Balensky, in the shadows of the stairwell, were two huge men, standard-issue American football physiques, with ill-fitting black suits (why are billionaires so stingy when it comes to their bodyguards' suits – surely a proper tailor could accommodate the concealed guns?), folded arms and earpieces. At the sight of them, I felt a delicious icy caress of adrenalin sink into me like the first sip of a perfect martini.

I moved backwards into the group, pretending to wave at someone I knew, until I was out of their range, then I discreetly asked one of the waiters for the ladies' room. He escorted me slowly down a flight of stairs and along a corridor decorated with a replica of the Villefranche Cocteau mural of St Peter and the fishes and opened a door to a bathroom. I shut myself inside and waited to hear the sound of his footsteps retreat. They didn't. Rats. I counted to sixty, flushed and ran the tap, then allowed him to accompany me back to the party, counting the number of doors we passed on the way.

It had been pretty easy to obtain the layout of Balensky's boat. An email from Steve's office to the yacht-builder suggesting he was looking to upgrade and asking for a 'similar' plan to Balensky's had produced a virtual blueprint from the slavering designers in a couple of hours. Since Balensky's was obviously a unique custom build, we could be sure the layout would be fairly accurate. The stateroom was the third door after the guest bathroom on the right, the first corridor as you came down the stairs.

Back on deck, Carlotta was curled under Steve's shoulder as he spoke to a heavy-set man with diamond studs in his starched shirt front, trailing a disdainful teenage blonde from his fingertips like an ornamental poodle. I managed to get a conversation going with one of the other girls, a South African swimwear model we'd met at Marina di Massa, the usual exchange of where we were going next and what parties we'd been to. I liked her earrings, she admired my shoes.

Bikini Babe and I soldiered on until we were ushered up to the next deck for dinner. It wasn't that large a party; despite decorations worthy of the debutante ball at the Crillon we were only about twenty at table, and Balensky directed the seating himself, placing me three seats to his right with Steve and Carlotta opposite. I had diamond studs to my left, and next to him, in the seat of honour beside the host, was an Italian actress/model in a sequined gown slashed to her navel, whose face I recognised from the pages of *Gente*. She had a lingerie range and had once dated George Clooney. I assumed she was being paid to attend as she and Balensky ignored one another completely.

To my right was another girlfriend, and what conversation there was began in fits and starts between the men, as we were served with poached oysters stuffed with caviar, lacquered quail stuffed with foie gras and *vitello tonnato* with truffle cream. Pink pansies and shavings of gold leaf adorned every plate. Long silences endured while the waiters ponderously changed the dishes, interspersed with staccato bursts of talk from the men in response to a remark from Balensky. At least we had chairs to sit on, not like the poor French aristocrats at Versailles, forbidden to sit in the presence of the king. Pudding was a rose petal parfait in a violent cerise nitroglycerined gelee, sculpted into such a perfectly realistic flower that we might have been eating the arrangements. Perhaps we were. I was grateful that little was expected of me on the dazzling repartee front; the quiet scrape of my spoon on the plate was measuring out the moments before I would have to strike. I was savouring what I was about to do far more than the parfait.

As the waiters went round with coffee and pyramids of pink Ladurée *macarons* and the men began to light their cigars, I excused myself to go to the loo, carrying my heels as soon as I reached the staircase and tying a knot in the skirt of my gown so I could move more freely.

As I descended, my eyes were casting urgently for the bodyguards, whom I had left standing behind Balensky's chair. They hadn't followed me. I paused to listen, rising on my toes a few times like a high jumper preparing a run-up, lengthening out into a run, low, wolflike, down the next flight and along the corridor. Vision twitching neatly along the doors, one, two, three, I streamed towards the stateroom like a missile, loving the focused suppleness of my limbs, the predatory high. Heart drumming, I paused again at the correct door. Behind me, the corridor was still empty. I pushed gently at the doorhandle, and I was in.

The cabin was lined in white carpeting, with piles of white fox stoles on the bed. Certainly the old chap would need them; it was freezing in there. With the air conditioning turned up to maximum the place felt like a luxury morgue. One door at the side of the bed led to the bathroom, another to a dressing room, a row of tiny Rumpelstiltskin shoes neatly lined up, carefully moulded wedges slipped in the soles for extra lift. At the back of the dressing area was the second door I'd seen on the plans. Either an office or a private dungeon. Again, I pushed the handle gently, half expecting an ice pick to shoot out from the spy hole. A small study, just a plain built-in desk and a bank of screens like Steve's on the *Mandarin*. The Nokia burner was ready, though my hands were sweating so much despite the cold I thought I might drop it. I moved the mouse and the screens came to life.

Football. Bloody football. Steve was not going to be impressed. I photographed the screens anyway, then took a few shots of the bits and pieces lying on the desk – a pile of receipts, a cigar case half-covering a few scribbled notes, a copy of the *Spectator* with the page folded back at the wine column. Should I try the desk drawers? They could be alarmed, and Balensky probably had a personal tiger shark in a tank somewhere for nosy guests. Something crunched under my bare foot, a piece of A4 paper from a cheap jotting pad. Quickly I rolled it up and hooked it into the elastic of my Fifi Chachnil panties. As I was trying to haul my long dress into place, I heard a voice, a man's voice, speaking Russian. Fuck. What was I doing? Hadn't I learned anything from playing spies with the Stubbs?

A crazy squad of images tumbled across my mind, old footage of Balensky posing with a gold-plated machine gun, his malevolent leer as he accepted a charity award, humped roadside corpses in wars I'd half read about. Balensky wasn't a comic-book joke, he was real. This was real. It would take a minute for his guys to snap my neck and dump me over the side, and if a fraction of the rumours I'd seen about their boss were true, they'd had the practice. Didn't pissed holiday girls drown all the time? I froze, trying to hold my breath, but I was shaking, shuddering as though I'd been punched in the stomach. I hugged my arms around my body and squeezed my eyes shut for a moment, trying to force out the fear.

Think. There was nowhere to hide except the cubby hole beneath the desk. I looked frantically round for a security camera. The carpeting in the bedroom muffled any footsteps, but I heard the bathroom door open. Fuck fuck fuck. Better the wardrobe than the study. I chanced it, racing across into the dressing cubicle while the bodyguards peered down the plughole. They were going to be in here any second. I yanked down the knickers and shoved them in my bag, fumbling to get the paper into my half-empty fag packet.

When the first guard opened the dressing-room door, he found me naked except for the Valli sandals. 'Darling!' I gasped, rushing into the black expanse of his chest. 'I thought you were never – oh! Oh my God! I'm so sorry.'

We looked at one another for a long moment. I forced myself to meet his gaze. If he was amused, I lived. If he wasn't, I was more than prepared to beg. He said something and the second man joined him, both of them doing a combined bored-slash-deathly menace expression.

'What are you doing in Mr Balensky's bedroom?'

'Waiting for Mr Balensky,' I answered, as haughtily as I could, which wasn't easy in six-inch stilettos and nothing else.

'He tell you to come?'

'Not exactly. I – um – I wanted to give him a surprise.'

The second man translated for the first. They both laughed. I breathed for the first time in what felt like hours.

'Please, miss. Is not allow to be in Mr Balensky's bedroom.'

Thank God, they were being polite. I'd assumed this kind of thing must happen all the time.

'You have phone?'

I opened my Fendi bag and handed over my iPhone, all innocent.

'Of course.'

Another exchange in Russian, then the second guard spoke again.

'I check phone. You are staying here with him. Phone is OK, we are not saying anything to Mr Balensky. OK, miss? You open phone now.'

I tapped in my code and he closed the door. It was rather cramped in the dressing room, but we didn't need much space for what was expected of me.

When I'd wiped my mouth on one of Balensky's starched Turnbull & Asser cuffs I put my dress back on and we sat side by side on the bed. After a few minutes of listening to the air conditioner he managed, 'You like party?'

'Yes, thank you. Very nice party.'

Number two reappeared and threw my phone and bag at me. Another line in Russian, containing 'shylukha'-sounds like 'slut', means 'whore'.

'Phone is OK.'

'Good. OK!' Why were we talking like we were in *The Sopranos*?

'You go back to party now. Naughty girl!' He wagged his finger at me.

Two minutes later I was back on the upper deck, hair smoothed, heart quiet. I asked a waiter for a Brandy Alexander to take the taste away. I took it to the rail and watched the waves for a moment. There's a lot to be said for being bullied as a child. After all, as every misery memoir triumphantly confirms, you're only being picked on because you're special. You become isolated, but also adamantine. I had learned a particular set to my spine, a disregard for the whispered taunts, even a kind of pleasure in them, because I told myself that it made me different, and then I'd just carried on believing it. Perhaps a therapist would have confessed it out of me, but I'd never had either the money or the interest, because that knowledge of pain became, in time, a source of defiance, a source – though I was embarrassed to even think the word – of strength. I could take things that others couldn't, and that meant I could do them, too. I had done this, and the relief was glorious.

Anyway it could have been worse. The goon could have wanted a fuck. And even if his cock was as tiny as I imagined his boss's was, it might have been a bit cosy, what with the second mobile already jammed up there.

13

Like emotion, humour wasn't Steve's thing, but even he saw the funny side. I couldn't tell him, of course, until Carlotta, rock reluctantly back in place, had been reunited with Hermann, then we curled up in Steve's bed and laughed until I thought I might pee.

'Let it be noted for the record,' I gasped, 'that I cannot be accused of not taking one for the team.'

'Did you wash it?'

'Eeeew. Of course!' I chucked it over. 'You so owe me.'

'You're good, you know. Thinking of the two phones. He didn't notice a thing.'

'If they'd found that phone I can't think what Balensky would have done, to all of us. They don't mess about, those people.'

'Believe me, I'm grateful.' He wasn't, he was just impatient.

I went to take a shower while Steve hooked up the phone. When I came back he had a screen up, the picture of the notes I'd seen under the cigar case, spinning it, zooming in and out.

'Anything?'

'Nope.' He sounded irritated, which worried me.

'I got everything, I'm sure I did. All that was up on his computer was Premier League summer transfers.'

'There's nothing.'

'You weren't the one risking a broken neck from Lenny back there.'

'Who?'

'Doesn't matter.'

'Whatever, Lauren. Fuck.' He reached for his phone. 'I need to make some calls now.'

There was a hardness to his tone I had not heard before; in fact I had never seen Steve so expressive. Those abstract trails of money may have represented a game, but it was one he was fearsomely committed to winning.

'Wait, there was something else, a bit of paper. I'll get it.'

I dumped the contents of the tiny Fendi bag on the duvet. Fags, lighter, lip gloss, comb, mints, one pair black silk chiffon knickers and the crumpled sheet of paper I had hastily stuffed in the cigarette packet.

'This. Here.'

Steve scanned it slowly, and as he did the tension was ironed out of his face.

'Lauren, you are a fucking genius. Where did you get this?'

'It was on the floor by the desk. I didn't think he'd miss it – the maid could have picked it up easily. What is it?'

Of course, I'd already read it. A name, a date two days from now and a question mark, scribbled in Biro.

'Rivoli. Hotel group. He's bidding for it. I really do need to make some calls now. Thanks, doll.' Steve wandered out, yelling for Tris.

All that cloak-and-dagger nonsense for a bit of insider share dealing. If I hadn't read up on the penalties for that kind of thing, I wouldn't have been able to see what Steve was so excited about. But if he wasn't going to prison, he stood to make some serious money, and whilst I supposed I could ask him for a cut, there was something else that he could do for me now. And it was useful to know that even the financial masters of the universe were so unsophisticated when it came to dirty little secrets.

* * * * *

Something else I discovered while the *Mandarin* was off Ponza was James's obituary notice. It was in *The Times* online, no photograph, presumably out of respect for the family, but it mentioned James's wife, Veronica. Rhodes, like Cecil. I'd never registered his surname. JR, like me. I could have read that as a sign. It mentioned various charities he had contributed to, the bank he worked for, the fact that he'd once played for Harrow at Lord's which I couldn't really picture, that he left one daughter, Flora, that a memorial service was to be held in a month. He was sixty-three, not a bad innings, considering. The piece only mentioned that he'd died of a heart attack whilst travelling on business, but it still made me antsy. I locked myself in the bathroom and took out the seamed Loro Piana carrier where I kept my personal stuff. My money was crammed into a paper sandwich bag. There was still about 8,000 euro of James's cash left, plus what I'd creamed off from my shopping trips, a good few thousand. I'd made a few withdrawals from my own English account, small sums, just to keep up the idea that I was on holiday, but it wasn't as though I could stay on the boat forever. Steve was obviously getting a bit over the whole idea of leisure pursuits, dying to get back to moving some serious money. I could keep the bank off my back for a few months, until I had some work, but the cash wouldn't stretch much further, not in London. I also had to consider that it might not be so easy to find a job in the art world, given that I'd called one of London's major experts a 'bent cunt'.

The immediate issue was where to put the money. I didn't want to deposit that amount of cash in my English account; it felt dubious. Of course I could just hold onto it, but that didn't feel right either. Maybe it was stupid, but I wanted that money to mean something. I'd always thought that people who believed in horoscopes should be denied the vote, but equally, when the universe tries to tell you something it's dumb not to listen. And I couldn't quite bear the thought of going back to the flat, to textbooks and toast crumbs and tights drying over the shower rail.

Trailing back to London with a stash of pocket money that would dribble away in rent and bills felt too much like defeat. It was one step closer to Sky on the box and the pub on Friday night, to the slow ooze of sugar bloat and the wind at the bus stop on College Road, to pebbledash and Tesco and the vomit in the doorway of the Social, to the bottles stashed in the microwave and the unanswered doorbell, to the smell of cold fat and Rothmans and lurid curry that was my own little bouquet of despair. All the things I knew it was indecent to despise, because they were just the fabric of most people's lives, yet my contempt for which kept me flinty clean inside.

I needed to think, so I wandered up to the deck. We were anchored a few miles along the coast from the main port; the only other craft in sight was a fabulous Thirties teak racing yacht, whose owners probably referred to the likes of the *Mandarin*, disparagingly, as 'Tupperware'. It was very quiet, just the lulling creak of the hull in the waves and the thrum of crickets from the low hills backing up from the shore. Carlotta was taking a siesta with Hermann, being disgusted; Steve was hunched over his screens as usual, intent as an alchemist. The water was peacock-coloured, gold and turquoise and green, so clear that I could see shoals of tiny silver fish fanning below the surface. I pulled off my Heidi Klein caftan, then my white Eres bikini and hopped over the bow rail, the afternoon heat throbbing on my bare skin. It suddenly looked a long way down. It would have been easy to jump, let myself fall into that delicious blue, but even though there was no one watching, I couldn't let myself be sloppy. Arms stretched until my sternum opened, flex the calves, abs held tight, tuck in the head, a perfect swallow dive, opening my eyes after the report of my body in the water to feel the salt streaming across my eyeballs, crystals at my fingertips as I arched to the surface. I pushed my hair back and trod water. The sea cradled my body and a dazzle of tiny salt crystals blurred my vision into a smooth panorama of blue and gold and white. Above me the *Mandarin* cut a neat geometric shadow over the soft waves, a reassuring island of money. This was where I belonged, I thought. I just had to work out a way to stay here.

That night, we trooped to Billionaire. Never mind that the Chinese had bought it, we were going to paaaarty like Briatore. As we walked to a VIP table, I could feel the girls watching us, in their hooker shoes and spaghetti straps, pretending to dance. When did nightclubs start to look like strip clubs? They were on the banquettes, on the tables, practically swinging from the chandeliers. There was enough booty-shaking going on to cause an earthquake. Carlotta scowled as a rogue buttock nearly knocked Hermann's Oliver Peoples off. Steve was bored, fiddling on his BlackBerry, not even looking up when the waiter brought the champagne. Tris looked nervy; any minute now it would be back to school. He touched Steve's shoulder, indicated two gorgeous black girls with impossibly tiny waists and arses just beneath their shoulder blades who were writhing nearby. Steve shook his head irritably. It was impossible to talk over the music, so I leaned forward and bawled in Steve's ear, 'Darling, I'm really sorry, but I've got the worst headache. Will you take me back?'

Steve didn't do gent stuff, but it was clear to me that he had no interest in staying, so when he got up I caught a look of gratitude from Tris. He took my hand and held it in his own smooth, dry palm all the way to the car, and I couldn't help a little flip of triumph as I carried off my prey.

I made him a Tanqueray and tonic, carefully wiping a lemon slice around the rim of the glass, and carried it through to where he was idly flicking through the news channels on the vast plasma screen.

'How's your head?'

'Fine, really. It was just too much, that place.'

'Yeah, I know what you mean.'

We looked at CNN for a bit. There was no way to open this conversation subtly, but then subtlety wasn't his thing.

'Steve?'

'What?'

'I've been thinking. You've been so amazing to me, the trip, the shopping, everything. I want to thank you.' I really meant it, too.

He looked suddenly nervous. I put a hand on his shoulder.

'Not like that. I think – we're friends, aren't we? Kind of?'

'Sure.'

'So I had this idea –'

I'd learned enough from the endless capital gains racket back in London to be able to talk a good game. I wanted to open my own gallery, I explained, dealing privately. I had some money saved, but it was cash, awkward. Could Steve help me to get started? If I made a profit, I could buy for him; we'd talked enough about his collection for him to believe I shared what he thought was his taste, I had a good eye, and I knew how to make it convenient for him, tax-wise. If there's one thing that really gets rich people razzled it's the prospect of saving entirely negligible amounts of tax.

'Where do you want to put it?'

I hesitated. 'Well, it's chump change, really. About ten grand. I thought – maybe Geneva?'

Ten grand happened to be the minimum deposit required at a small and not particularly successful private bank called Osprey. I'd checked it out on my laptop at a café in the port.

'I have an apartment in Geneva.'

'Nice. Shall we go?'

'OK.'

'Just like that, OK?'

'Sure. I'll get Tris to see to it in the morning. I'm getting fucked off with all this, anyway.'

I straddled his lap and nuzzled his face. 'Steve, I love you. It's going to be great, I promise!'

He held my shoulders at arm's length and looked into my eyes.

'Sure you do, Lauren.'

Of course, he had heard it all before. He would never know for sure if any woman ever meant those words. I held his gaze. There might have been a little moment when we both felt human.

'Ooops, sorry, you two!'

Carlotta.

'No worries.' I sensed Steve wasn't sorry for her to misunderstand. I left him watching the second half of *The Matrix* and went to have a good bitch about the quality of the sluts at Billionaire.

* * * * *

Flying business class from Sardinia to Switzerland was the first time I'd ever turned left on a plane. It was practically the first time I'd been on a plane – my European travels had mostly been conducted by train. Steve was going on to the States while Tris took the boat back up the coast to Genoa. If he was annoyed with me for cutting short his free cruise he had the sense not to show it; besides, he'd have a few days of pretending the *Mandarin* was his. I left a handwritten thank-you note and 300 euro for the crew, crammed all my swag into bags and said goodbye to Carlotta and Hermann, who made polite noises about seeing me at their wedding. I'd asked for my return ticket to be to Rome; it seemed a shame not to see it again when I had the chance.

We didn't talk much on the flight. Conversation was an effort for Steve if he wasn't discussing things he owned; I assumed that was why he kept buying them. I appreciated the space and the leather seats and the extra-voltage smiles of the Alitalia hostesses with their gleaming chignons. Steve didn't, but then his own plane was picking him up the next day. If it was anything like his flat, I couldn't envy him. All I could think of when we got to the apartment was that God never resists a chance to show His contempt for money. Now I knew where Ian Schrager went to die.

'Got this place last year. Used to have a house on the lake, but I thought an apartment was more me. Alberto Pinto did it.'

I wondered if there had been much marble left in Carrara by the time Alberto had finished. I wandered about a bit, looking, admiring. Everything that wasn't black or white or golden marble was lacquered shagreen: the bathroom looked like Oscar Wilde's cigarette case.

'It's very impressive,' I said, managing to look serious while wondering why new money always has such appalling taste. Perhaps it's just a matter of time – this century's gruesome opulence is the next's priceless baroque.

'Most of the art is in the study,' said Steve, pressing a button which opened a dividing door disguised as a mother-of-pearl screen. The room was larger than the whole of my old flat in London, with one entirely glass wall looking over the rather lugubrious sights of Geneva. You could tell it was the study because of the books, at least three of them, retro French novels from the Sixties laid out on a nineteenth-century washstand, the only pretty thing in the place. How much had Alberto charged for one of his assistants to break the spines? Emin, Hirst, check, check, a huge Pollock, check, Schnabel, check. Entirely predictable.

'What do you think of this?'

A concrete cast of a gravestone, like a Bronze Age *stela*, engraved with a thug-necked young man in a flashy suit, Rolex prominently displayed, an Uzi dangling from his right hand as casually as a young man about town might have held a riding crop in an earlier century.

'It's clever. The definition of a swagger portrait. Whose?'

'It's real, a real tombstone. The guy's family sold it to the artist. Leni Kravchenko?'

Not that clever then, just sad and sneering and cheap.

'You have some nice things. This,' I indicated the boy gangster's memorial, 'this is the kind of stuff I can see you getting into. I'm thinking Eastern Bloc, maybe China. Not *so* certain as an investment, but more interesting for that. Witty, ambitious.' Just like you, Steve.

His eyes were already wandering towards the screens in the sitting room. So much for Art, gotta get to work.

'Sure, that would be great, when you get your thing going,' he answered vaguely.

I said that I was sure he had a lot to do, and why didn't I come back for him after lunch? I'd love to see the city. He was already sinking gratefully into his desk chair, tapping open the veins of the world's money, but he didn't forget to release a lump of it for me from the silver clip in his back pocket. So I tripped prettily off and found a taxi to take me on a tour where I could ask a few questions, followed by a little light shopping and a *croque monsieur* in a café overlooking the lake, surrounded by muffled Middle Eastern women and their beer-bellied offspring and men on their phones, tapping, tapping, in the green shadow of the sublime Alps.

I reflected that I didn't really know all that much about contemporary art, but I didn't see that being a reason to hold me back. Firstly because there wasn't much to know and secondly because no one buying it knows anything, either. The expertise is in spying out the trends, working out what will be hot when your client comes to sell. The idea of a patron buying for aesthetic reasons went out with the Grand Tour, and I'd been unbelievably lucky so far in convincing Steve that I knew how to buy, though his tastes weren't exactly a hard sell. After all my serious work for Rupert in my three years at the House, it seemed a bit cheap, but I'd got over worse things. Like, my entire life so far. And, maybe, if I could do it, if I could really do it, then I'd have a crack at being someone, being the person I'd always known I was meant to be.

Back at the flat I changed into one of my new purchases, a beige Stella McCartney shirt dress with an Hermès foulard, a pattern of pink and orange clocks. I'd bought a plain leather tan clutch to hold the cash; I didn't want to be rootling it out of a paper bag. Steve was in his usual jeans, Polo and Nikes. He held my hand in the cab to the bank, although the other was busy spidering away on his BlackBerry.

I'd once been sent to Hoare's, up on Fleet Street, to cash a cheque for Rupert, and I suppose I had expected something like that – imposing pillars, old oil paintings, white-gloved doormen. But Osprey looked like any other office, not a grand hotel. Just a lobby and a lift and a discreet plaque by the bell, a sofa and a water cooler and an ancient fax machine. Steve explained briefly in his surprisingly good French that he needed to open a personal account for a new employee. As soon as he gave his name, I could see the manager drooling. We were shown to an even smaller room, just a cubicle with a table and three chairs hastily squashed in, I flashed my passport and they brought the paperwork.

'Just sign here, Mademoiselle Rashleigh, and here, and here.' I pushed over the tan clutch and the manager took it with a pained smile, as though I'd handed him a dirty nappy. Actual cash was obviously not the thing to display in Geneva, though dodgy money was what the place was built on. He pressed a button under the table and a slim girl in a black trouser suit appeared to take it away, using her hand as though it was silver tongs. I saw her looking at Steve and allowed my hand to rest for a moment on his wrist. A few minutes passed, during which the manager ventured a remark about how I liked Geneva, then the girl came back with the now flaccid purse and a passbook with my name miraculously printed on the front.

'And where would mademoiselle like the correspondence to be sent?'

Fuck. I hadn't thought of that. I could hardly have Swiss bank statements turning up on the Koreans' breakfast table.

'I'm, um, looking for premises at the moment,' I managed lamely.

'Of course, mademoiselle. But you will be passing through Geneva?' He was helping me, with his eye on Steve's potential.

'Yes, naturally. Art Basel and, um, so on.'

'So we have an arrangement here at Osprey. A numbered box, a key for yourself, only. Just for correspondence, you understand. Our clients find it helpful while they are . . . travelling.'

I liked that. 'Travelling', like Holly Golightly.

'That would be very suitable, thank you.'

'Just one more form then, mademoiselle.' Black suit reappeared, I signed. Steve had barely registered anything; he was still tapping.

I got to turn left again on the flight to Rome early that evening. I declined a glass of champagne with the weary air of the seasoned business-class traveller, which obviously I really enjoyed. My goodbye to Steve had been awkward, though I doubted he had felt it. Even though he didn't know quite what he had done for me, he had been extraordinarily kind, and had it been any other man I would at least have given him an assiduous farewell going-over on Alberto's carefully selected Pratesi sheets, but I had the sense not to suggest it. Still, saying 'thank you' didn't seem enough, and there was nothing else I could give him, at least nothing I could explain and expect him to understand. To know that someone sees you is a gift, even love, of a kind, but if there was a part of Steve that remembered what it felt like to be a fearful geek, it had long ago been veneered beyond recognition. To tell him that I saw what he wasn't and liked him anyway would merely have puzzled him, momentarily. So I settled for a hug and a promise, which he took as lightly as all the hugs and promises I imagine he encountered these days, and left him to the dancing enchantments of the markets.

I spent a while fantasising about what I could do with the money, but that didn't last long; 10K wasn't much more than dinner for six at Billionaire. On my hoarded fund of Steve-euros I could have a couple of nice days in Rome, see some pictures, eat some good food. When I got back to London I could wire a couple of hundred quid to my mother, stay in the flat until I could find some work in a contemporary gallery, carefully buy a few pieces on the side and then see. Maybe in a while I could afford a little studio of my own, once I'd paid off the bank loan. Small beginnings, maybe, but a clean start. I wouldn't be desperate, and somehow that gave me the courage to face down the prospect of Rupert blacklisting me. It would be OK. Actually, it was going to be a lot bigger than OK.

As we waited on the tarmac to pull up to the gate at Fiumicino, every Italian on the plane pulled out their phone. I did the same and texted Dave. I hadn't dared to contact him before, in case there had been any fuss over James, but this felt like the right time.

'Hi, it's Judith. Back in town in a couple of days. Can I take you for a drink? So sorry about that awful scene, hope all OK. Jx'.

He pinged back. 'I lost my job because of you. Think about that. D.'

Suddenly I was back in the Gstaad Club, poring over some boyfriend's cramped textual inarticulacy. What did one kiss mean, two? I knew what no kiss meant. Fury. Why would Rupert have fired Dave? He had been acting on my instructions; it was hardly a sacking offence. I pressed 'Call sender' immediately.

'Judith. What do you want?' I could hear a TV in the background, but it didn't disguise the weary tone of disgust in his voice.

'Dave, I'm so sorry, I had no idea. I'll call Rupert, explain it was all my fault – I'd never, ever have asked you if I thought your job was at risk. I knew how much it meant to you. Rupert had no right to sack you,' I finished weakly.

'He did though.'

'I'm so sorry.'

'Don't bother. We'll be fine.' I remembered Dave's wife and felt even worse, if that was possible.

'Dave, I'll make it up to you. I will, I promise. Can't your friend Mike help you? Maybe I –'

'Leave it, Judith. Just get on with your life.'

He hung up. I felt sick, sicker than I'd felt when I'd found James's corpse. I knew how much the porters earned and I guessed Dave's army pension would be predictably pathetic. I covered my face with my hands. I'd done this to him with my stupid conceited meddling. I'd give him half the money, as soon as I got back to town. But then I thought of the bank and the rent and the way I'd felt in the water in Sardinia, of the sour milk of James's cum in my mouth and what I'd just pulled off in Geneva and I knew that I couldn't. I just couldn't.

PART THREE

OUTSIDE

14

The second time was much less of an accident. I had thought of a room at the Hassler, overlooking the Spanish Steps, for my last hurrah, but unsurprisingly, and despite my attempt to bribe the concierge with a 100-euro note and a winning smile, all their rooms with a view were taken. There didn't seem any point in spending the money to look at a Roman wall, but as the receptionist was checking the register, I saw a name I recognised: Cameron Fitzpatrick. I'd last glimpsed him chatting to Rupert at the gruesome Tentis party. Fitzpatrick was a dealer I had sometimes contacted for the department; he had a poky, old-fashioned gallery in one of the forgotten eighteenth-century closes up by the old Adelphi buildings in London. His generally raffish air and the slight blush of the whisky in his cheeks made him appear as though only his blarney charm stood between him and the bailiffs, but the manner belied him – he had a good eye for quirky second-rank pieces; thinking on it I recalled a newspaper piece last year about an impressive price for a self-portrait by Oscar Wilde's mother. The clock behind the reception desk read 12.05 p.m., just about time for an *aperitivo*. Maybe it would be worth hanging around to see if I could bump into him? I was keen to know if the Rupert debacle had caused any rumours, not that I had been remotely important enough at the House for that to be likely, but, still, he was a potential contact now it looked like I might actually be in business. Perhaps he'd even have a job going. I asked the receptionist to let me know if Signor Fitzpatrick came in and took myself off to the terrace at the back of the hotel for a glass of prosecco and a spot of people-watching. Half an hour later it didn't seem as though he was going to appear, and I was walking back to the front door when I heard my name.

'Judith Rashleigh?' The accent was a soothing bath of Irish bonhomie. Cameron was a big, shambling man with a thick head of coffee-coloured hair, attractive for a straight guy who worked in the art world.

'Cameron – what a nice surprise!' I didn't think I needed to mention that I'd been lurking about hoping to see him.

I stepped up to him and offered my cheek for the now-obligatory metropolitan kiss and we bobbed awkwardly at one another the way Londoners still do.

'I'm just checking in. Are you staying here?'

'Sadly not. But Rome in August? It must be business. How's the gallery?'

We chatted for a few moments while he went through the business of handing over his passport and credit card. It was an appointment with a client that brought him to Rome. I got in quickly with the information that I had left British Pictures – I didn't imagine Rupert and co thought enough of me to bother saying anything unpleasant, but it was better not to seem to be hiding anything.

'You staying here?'

'No. With some friends, actually. The de Grecis.'

I said it as if he ought to know them. There had been a Francesco de Greci at my college; we'd screwed once. His family had a street named after them in Florence.

'Lovely.' He seemed taken in. I made as if to leave. 'I was just collecting something. So . . . it was nice to see you.'

I hovered, knowing he would ask me to lunch, and when he did I pretended surprise and looked at my watch and said that would be lovely. While he went up to his room I quickly loaded my bags into a cab and paid the driver to take them to a small hotel I remembered in Trastevere. The de Grecis, I decided, had a charming old villa up beyond the Borghese.

'Do you know Rome well?' He still wore his navy suit, though the collar and tie had been replaced with a crumpled white linen shirt. There was a swag of paunch at his waist, but he was a good-looking man, if one liked things on that scale.

'Hardly at all.' Always better to play the novice.

So we talked of other places we knew in Italy as he led me down through the gazing crowds. After the thick gold blanket of dusty heat that lay across the open spaces, the tight, dim streets felt vicious and secretive. We came out in a small piazza whose dinginess suggested the restaurant would be good. The groups of men eating under the awning spoke with Roman accents, a few beleaguered politicians' lawyers, I imagined, imprisoned here while the rest of their city's inhabitants were spread over the beaches of the peninsula. A solitary tourist in a baseball cap and sweat-ringed shirt read a French guidebook. I let Cameron order, saying nothing but an appreciative *grazie*. I wanted to charm him, to make him feel good. He drank a negroni *sbagliato*, we had razor clams and a delicate fresh pasta with rabbit and candied orange peel. After the first bottle of Ligurian Vermentino he asked for another, though I was still finishing my first glass, topped up with water. He was a good man for talking to women, I had to give him that, full of easy compliments and gossip and taking the trouble to ask for your opinion and look like he was paying attention to it. When I judged he was sufficiently confidential, I asked him who his mysterious client was.

'Well,' he said, leaning forward conspiratorially, 'would you believe I've a Stubbs to be selling?'

'A Stubbs?'

I practically choked on my makeshift spritzer. Why was Stubbs doing this to me? I'd always rooted for him, the northern boy pushed aside by the London snobs. Was he my personal chimera, a kind of horse-headed albatross?

Then Cameron pulled a folded catalogue from the breast pocket of his jacket and the razor clams nearly reappeared for an encore. I didn't need to look at it to recognise it, just the way I didn't need to look at it to guess immediately what Rupert had been up to, and why he'd fired poor Dave and me for snooping. The only thing that surprised me was how extraordinarily thick I'd been, swotting along, playing the ideal employee, when anyone with real experience would have twigged straight away that Rupert had been working a scam.

Cameron hadn't bothered asking exactly when I had left British Pictures and I hadn't bothered telling him, so I could exclaim as though I was seeing the Stubbs for the first time. I scanned the pages, making appreciative noises, noting that Rupert had at least bothered to add my research on the Ursford and Sweet sale to the provenance. Cameron had had it on a tip, he said, wasn't quite sure until it had been cleaned up and then offered it for auction, until he'd thought better of it and found himself a private buyer. I could hardly believe my own dimness. They were in it together – presumably that was what they had been whispering about at the Tentis party. They had put up the money to buy the picture from the Tigers together, listing it at British Pictures to gloss over any doubts about authenticity, then they would have withdrawn it from the auction and sold it on beyond the eyes of anyone who could say otherwise.

I had been right. It was not a Stubbs and Rupert had never believed it to be so. He would have called Mr and Mrs Tiger to ruefully confirm that their 'Stubbs' was merely a 'school of', an imitation by a minor artist of the period. Hence the cross-purpose awkwardness of our conversation on the phone. Then Cameron, pretending to be acting independently, would have purchased it. Once it was legally in Cameron's possession, the painting would have been 'cleaned' by a man in from Florence or Amsterdam in an industrial workshop in the East End, and, lo and behold, it turns out to be genuine after all. The hoo-ha of the projected sale rendered the provenance impeccable via the stamp of the world's greatest house; it would all make the buyer feel they were getting a bargain. The two of them had never intended for the painting to reach a public sale. That explained the low reserve – if a seller withdraws a piece too close to the auction, they are required to guarantee the reserve fee as a fine to the house. The 800K was a manageable amount for Cameron to produce, assuming he and Rupert were expecting a much higher price from their buyer. What had they paid the Tigers? Mrs T had sounded pretty pleased when I had called her. Say 200K, which meant that with the reserve fine a million all told. Serious money, then, which made me wonder how much they were coming in for from the eventual buyer.

It was brilliant, and perfectly legal, if the picture was real. Mr and Mrs Tiger might have seen their picture offered as a Stubbs and made a noise, but then it was withdrawn before the sale, false alarm. Any enquiries and Rupert could say that they had bought it and thought they'd got lucky, then reverted to the original valuation on investigation. Probably blame the 'intern'. And even if it wasn't genuine, and I was convinced of that, the client could sit it in a vault for a year and then offer it to some even more naive buyer, new money from China or the Gulf somewhere, with the back-up of the catalogue I held in my hand, and take the profit.

If there's anything that being a woman has taught me, it's when in doubt, play dumb.

'That's wonderful, Cameron,' I breathed. 'Go on, how much?'

'Judith!'

'Go on. I can keep a secret. Who would I be telling?'

He held up five fingers with a gleeful grin. Five million. Still low. Stubbs could easily fetch ten. The 1765 canvas 'Gimcrack on Newmarket Heath' had made over twenty from Piers Davies in New York a couple of years ago. But five would be cash, effectively. High enough to be genuine, low enough to make the client feel they'd been brilliant. Clever.

And then, just for a moment, I felt outside time. I saw myself again, ten years ago, my first time in the Uffizi, standing in front of Artemisia's *Judith Slaying Holofernes*. It's a standard subject, the Jewish heroine murdering the enemy general, but Artemisia makes it raw, almost unpainterly. When you look at the delicately enamelled sword at Holofernes' neck, you see that it's not laid there ceremonially, suggestively, but caught in the flesh at an inelegant angle, quite the wrong angle for a graceful composition. This is from the hand of a woman who had sliced off the head of fowls in the kitchen, wrung rabbits' necks for the pot. Judith is butchering him properly, grimly sawing through the sinew, her muscular arms tense with effort. There's something domestic about it; the plainness of the sheet, the ungainly spurt of the blood, a curious sense of quietness. This is women's work, Artemisia is saying, impassive. This is what we do. I saw my wrists resting lightly on the edge of the table next to my espresso cup with its twist of lemon as though from far away, yet in the sudden amber stillness of that moment I felt surprised that the jump of my pulse wasn't rattling the china. I had made her so many promises, that girl in the museum. I owed her. So I knew then that I was going to steal that painting.

'I don't suppose you might be good enough to let me see it? I'd so love to.'

'Sure. Why not right now?'

I demurred. My friends were waiting for me. But perhaps this evening – for a drink? And then dinner and a whole lot more, I implied, if his etchings were up to scratch. I looked into those smiling Irish eyes and reminded myself that they had lost me and Dave our jobs. I'd been right; Rupert *was* bent and so was Fitzpatrick.

I told Cameron that I had to run, but I waited while he keyed my number into his snazzy thumbprint-recognition phone, bent to kiss him goodbye, letting my mouth hover just a moment too long at the very corner of his own, so that my hair fell across his face in a dappled curtain of Roman shadow.

I was already working it out as I strolled away. I could do this. I could really do this. But I had to be calm now, to think of the next thing and nothing else. I had to be sure of the connection between Cameron and Rupert. Cameron had said he had had the painting on a 'tip', but that didn't necessarily prove it had come from Rupert. I had to confirm the mystery buyer whose name Mrs Tiger hadn't been able to recall. I found a cab back to my bland modern hotel on the other side of the

Tiber and after finding my room asked for the business centre. While I waited for the slow Italian dial-up to connect, I made a shopping list on the back of a napkin. I Googled Cameron first, then a couple of previous pieces he'd sold, then the Stubbs picture, the Goodwood fake. If I was going for a job interview it was only reasonable I'd do a bit of research. The sale of the Goodwood picture was indeed no longer due to proceed. I looked at my watch; it was just after four Italian time, so there was a good chance Frankie would be in the department. I still had her mobile number.

She answered and we exchanged a few rather awkward remarks about our summers before I asked her.

'Listen, I need a favour. The Stubbs – the one that was withdrawn. Can you find me the name of the seller? The one who bought it from the original owners?'

'I don't know, Judith. I mean, the way you left like that. Rupert said –'

'I don't want to embarrass you, Frankie. I understand. I can get it for myself if it feels difficult.'

A pause on the line.

'OK, then,' she answered hesitantly. I could hear rummaging and then she read out from what was obviously the catalogue.

'It just says "Property of a Gentleman".'

'No, I know that. You'll have to go to accounts – they'll have it because they'll have issued a scrip for the reserve and then the withdrawal fee. It won't take a minute.'

'I really shouldn't do this, Judith.'

I felt a horrible stab of guilt. I'd already lost Dave his job. But I knew I could make it right. Consequences can be a form of cowardice. I'd been a coward when Rupert confronted me, but after all that had happened I knew I just wasn't like that anymore. While Frankie hesitated, I considered the trajectory that had brought me here. All I needed was a few more breaks and I'd be ready to unfurl my new iridescent wings in the sun. Poetic, really.

'I know, but I'd really, really appreciate it.' I tried to make my voice both embarrassed and pleading.

'I would help, but really – I don't want to do anything wrong.'

Good old Frankie. She wasn't bent. But then, she could afford not to be.

'There's a chance of a job and I need to look good. You know Frankie . . . I'm really short.'

Mentioning actual poverty to someone like Frankie had the same effect as the word 'period' on the games teacher at school. I heard her making up her mind.

'Alright then. I'll try. I'll text it to you. But you mustn't ever, ever tell.'

'Honour bright.'

I had a good look at a map of Rome and bought an open train ticket to Como from the Trenitalia site. Just rehearsals. I might not do anything at all. My phone pinged.

'Cameron Fitzpatrick x.'

'Thanks a million!! xxxx' I pinged back. Or maybe five.

15

Later, I had a lot of time to think about when I'd made the decision. Had it been swelling inside me all along, waiting, like a tumour? Was it the moment when Rupert packed me off like a servant without a reference, or the drained resignation in Dave's voice? Was it when I agreed to work at the Gstaad Club or to Leanne's stupid plan to have ourselves a night out, or when I closed the door on James's body and took the Ventimiglia train? If I was being romantic, I could argue to myself that the decision was made for me long ago, by Artemisia, another young woman who understood hate, who had left her no-mark husband and come to these very streets to paint a living for her family. But none of that would be true. It happened when I went upstairs to my room and quietly changed my teetering cork-heeled wedges for flat sandals. My hands shook as I fastened each buckle. I stood up slowly and set off straight away for the Corso Italia.

In Zara I found a plain linen dress, a short A-line, with deep pockets. Close up, it was easy to see it was poorly made, but it was simple enough that with good accessories it looked expensive. I took two, one in black and one in navy. In a sports store I bought a pair of shorts, two sizes too big, and a pair of chunky white trainers. I added an 'I Heart Rome' T-shirt from a tourist booth on a nearby corner. I paid visits to two more tacky souvenir shops, then at the bottom of the Via Veneto I found a lightweight Kenzo raincoat in a bright fuchsia-and-white print. It looked quite striking. In a smart *tabaccaio*, the kind that sold silver photo frames and humidors, I bought a heavy cigar cutter and one of the fat leather pocket tubes that the guys back on the boat had used to transport their Cohibas. I also picked up a black nylon backpack, loose enough to slip my own leather tote inside, and called at a *farmacia* for a pack of maxi-sized sanitary towels and some wet wipes. By the time I had finished, it was after six. I felt a moment of regret for the Pinturicchios at the Vatican. I wouldn't get to see them now, but I wanted to take the time to bathe and blow-dry my hair for my date with Cameron.

I rejoined him at the Hassler around eight. He was waiting for me in the lobby and suggested a drink, but I said I'd love one later. On the way to the third floor in the lift I dropped a few unsubtle hints about how eager I was to work for a private gallerist when I returned to London. The de Grecis, conveniently, were dining with relatives that evening. As soon as we entered his room I slowly slipped off the new Kenzo coat and dropped it over the back of the chair. I could feel his eyes moving slowly up my legs, and I let him feel me feeling it and flashed him a smile under lowered eyes. The room felt too intimate, as hotel rooms always do. Behind elaborate triple curtains the window was open onto a scruffy ventilation shaft. A small wheeled suitcase lay unzipped on the luggage stand and a pile of papers and keys occupied a corner of the desk. On the bed lay a cheap black plastic case, the kind art students use, but when Cameron bent to unfasten it I saw that it was expertly padded and lined. Reverently, he lifted out the picture in a plain metal frame.

'You didn't crate it?'

'Too much fuss – Italian bureaucracy.' So no one knew he had brought it in, except Rupert and the client.

There it was, the Duke and Duchess at their eternal picnic, the trio of horses thundering over the gallops. It looked gaudier in the bluish twilight of Rome – perhaps the Chinese appreciated a nice shiny varnish. He stood behind my shoulder as he looked, but he was no Colonel Morris. He would wait for his pudding.

'So,' I said, 'I'm very impressed by the business part. Now, d'you fancy yourself as Marcello Mastroianni?'

'La Dolce Vita at your command, signorina.'

I told him I'd found the restaurant in my guidebook, though it was one I had known when I'd been studying in the city. It was very old-fashioned, off the Piazza Cavour opposite Sant'Angelo, on the *piano nobile*, with a covered loggia where one could eat outside. By the time we had finished the stuffed courgette flowers and the grilled fish Cameron was ordering a third bottle. I might have been chewing straw, it was so difficult to force anything past the bolus of tension in my throat. Cameron was not an easy man to read – sure, he'd give you the stars from the Oirish sky to pin on your jacket if you asked him, but beneath the charm I was seeking what it was that he longed for, the little switch that, if I pressed it just right, would deliver him to me. It's there in all men, and the trick is simply finding it and then, if you care to, making yourself into whatever it is they can't quite admit to themselves that they want you to be. As the falling light turned the remains of the wine in the bottle from dull jade to viridian, Cameron took my hand across the table. I turned my wrist and he brought it to his lips.

'It's strange, Judith. I have this feeling that we're alike, you and I.'

'How so?'

'We're . . . loners. We stand outside things.'

Oh please, I thought, not the childhood. What half-buried pain makes us both so special? Ugh. Sharing was not on tonight's agenda. I retrieved my hand and traced the knuckle pensively along my jawbone.

'Cameron. We are alike, you and I.' I paused for one breath. 'I think you should fuck me.'

'I'll get the bill.'

As soon as we were outside the restaurant he pressed me against the wall and kissed me, winding his tongue around mine. It felt good to be enveloped like that, wrapped up against the breadth of his chest. I could hear his blood, pumping strong against my ear. I grabbed his hand and stooped to release the ankle straps on my sandals, tugged at him so that for a few minutes he was running with a barefoot girl through the August streets of Rome. We crossed the bridge at the Castello and picked our way down one of the stairs, kissing again at the bottom, and then walked hand in hand along the quay. One bridge, two. The Tiber is not like the Seine, polished up and gleaming for the tourists. Weeds swayed between the cobbles and piles of refuse were heaped on the banks. Under the second bridge we passed a huddle of winos and I felt Cameron stiffen and straighten his shoulders, but they barely glanced at us.

'I'm cold.'

'Have my jacket, darlin'.'

He draped it round my shoulders and I laughed and began to run again, the warm stone smooth beneath my feet. He lumbered to keep up with me. I wanted him breathless. Under the third bridge I pulled him round towards me, shimmying the jacket off my shoulders, and kissed him urgently, running both hands up his thighs to where his cock was already bulging.

'I want you, God, I want you, now,' I murmured. 'I want you to fuck me right now.'

His back was to the water. I dropped to my knees and took his belt between my teeth. I began to unfasten it, easing it through the buckle and catching the hook with my tongue, flipping it back. It's a cheap trick, but not difficult and it has the virtue of arresting the attention. His hands were already in my hair.

'Oh Judith, Jesus.'

I chivvied the head of his cock free from his shorts with quick laps and took it in my mouth. I almost wanted to giggle at the sudden flash of myself singing in the Eden Roc bathroom, of James's bulk spread-eagled expectantly on the bed. 'Well, Judith,' a snide little voice whispered, 'here we are again.' Push it down, focus. I closed my eyes. Only the next thing, nothing beyond that.

Cameron didn't say anything when I opened the flick knife from my pocket and drove it into the hollow in the flesh of his ankle, just above the Achilles tendon. He gasped and toppled sideways like a dropped marionette. I had to follow his trousers down from their open fly to wrench it out. He screamed. The knife had been in my right pocket; I took a sanitary towel from my left, rolled up with the sticky strip torn off and worked it between his teeth, pushing it against his tongue, holding my palm flat against his mouth to stop the gag reflex. There's a trick to that too, when you're blowing a guy. You have to open your throat slowly, retract your tonsils. Cameron was a quick learner.

The concentration of nerves in the Achilles means that a wound there will temporarily shut the body down. Cameron wouldn't be able to react for a few precious seconds. I got to my feet and moved my handbag and discarded shoes neatly out of the way. He was hunched up, sucking in great rasps of air against the pain; there was nothing for him beyond that. Straddling him, I took a handful of his thick hair and twisted his head, turning his face roughly away from me into his shoulder. As I felt for his ear, his eyes flared open. I realised he still thought I was trying to help him.

I guessed those eyes would have been frantic and bulging, but I didn't look too hard. I pushed the knife straight in just beneath the ear lobe, all the way to the handle. It didn't quite go in like a watermelon, more the toughness of a pumpkin. I thought of the rabbit we had eaten at lunch. Still no noise, but a second later I saw the dark patch against the glow of his linen shirt and felt a warm wetness across my thigh. His big body was bucking and jerking, then his left arm swung up and caught me a crack across the jaw. The blow sang in my windpipe, driving me back, wrenching for breath. It had been a long time since anyone had hit me like that. Would it bruise? I had no time to worry about that yet; I had to do it now. Hideously lithe, he twisted and hauled himself towards me, head sagging, those powerful hands scrabbling at my legs, reaching for me. I was still dizzy from the punch. I tried to move back, further into the shadow of the bridge, but I was too slow, and the whole of his weight against my knees brought me down again. Cameron was clawing up towards my face. I tried to kick him off but he was too heavy, creeping up my body inch by inch, a rich bubbling surging from his throat. The hands reached my neck and he began to squeeze. I had forgotten how strong men really are. I clawed at the grip, but it was hopeless, I began to gag for air, I couldn't move my lower body; I was pinned beneath him, trying to twist him off, but he was heavy, so heavy, and there were strange dancing lights in front of my eyes now as his grip tightened, tightened. And then unclenched. He was still. I resisted the impulse to shove him off me, gulped for air, three, four times, until I was breathing again. He lay slumped across me, his arms trailing like dead branches over my breasts. I inhaled again, clenched my muscles tight, then released, twisting my hips to shift his weight, rolling on all fours as he fell to the side.

It was not the most dignified position. I looked up, quickly ran my eyes along either side of the quay. If there was anyone coming I would have to pretend we were making love, but the riverbank was empty. I eased myself from him, my dress rucking up and the cobbles rough against the bare skin of my stomach, until I was stretched out, as far away as I could get, only my fingers on the knife connecting us along my arm, like some horribly inverted umbilical cord. Then I pulled. I didn't look at the result. I turned away and took the backpack from my tote bag, steadily removing the things I would need and counting Mississippis under my breath. He would need a few minutes. I folded myself up and buried my face in my knees, pixelated with stray gravel. The wheeze of breath from his nostrils became shallower and more rapid. Hypovolemia. If I touched him now he would be getting colder.

I had read something once about soldiers in the First World War who went over the top, then lay down in no man's land and promptly fell fast asleep. All the warmth in my body had concentrated into my chest, the push of my own breath against my skin lulled me. It wasn't until I heard the sound of a motor that I came back to myself, shuddering. Shit, shit shit. The white of his shirt . . . I raced through the contingencies. We had been attacked, I had pulled out the knife . . . I rocked back and forth, practising for being traumatised, but when I peeped through my fingers I saw a small boat with a fat prow, tacking upriver like an ungainly shark, a stooped figure in the stern. A fisherman. There were still eels in the Tiber. Only when he had passed and the water was a smooth sheet again did I notice that the panting had stopped.

Now the thumb. He had used his left hand to access his phone. I pressed his open palm onto the stones and splayed the fingers, put the knife to his digit and my knee on top of that, pushed. Once I'd made a deep incision the cigar cutter took care of the bone. I threw the cutter over my shoulder and heard it splash as I slid the thumb into the cigar case. I had been afraid of how difficult it was going to be to get him into the river, and that was before I learned how much that bulk really weighed. I had to put my bare feet in the puddle around him to get hold of his shoulders, but adrenalin gave me strength and I got his torso over the quay in one heave. His left arm jerked again, a zombie's twitching grab. He arched back, as supple as a gymnast, and the back of his head cracked against the stone of the embankment. That couldn't hurt. I put my knee on his chest to ease the stuffing from his mouth, then shoved against his thigh to work the body round until it rolled into the water. One of his loafers came off as I shoved him over the bank. I picked it up and felt the snaffle. Gucci. Sharp. I chucked it after him.

In the silence after the splash, I heard a high-pitched squeak and caught a flash of black fuzz in my peripheral vision. I gave a shrill gasp and stumbled, almost pitching myself into the water after Cameron. A rat, just a rat. But I was gasping and my hands were shaking. I half expected a figure to step out of the shadows, so strongly did I feel I was being watched. Just a rat. Probably attracted by the scent of fresh blood, which was a disgusting thought.

Forcing my breath to come steadily through my teeth I stripped, did a quick clean-up with several wet wipes and a half-bottle of Evian from my bag. I stuffed the wipes through the neck of the bottle and buried it in the weeds in the urine-drenched midden at the back of the bridge. The flimsy navy dress I had been wearing was wadded in another huge sanitary pad and tied up in a sheer plastic bag for later disposal. No dustbin man would be keen on opening that. I removed the black dress from my bag and knotted it around my waist to add bulk, then pulled on the ugly shorts and T-shirt. It seemed to take an age to get the shirt over my head. Hair knotted up, shoes in my handbag and then into the nylon backpack along with the cigar tube and his phone. I went through the pockets of the jacket before it went into the water, putting the room key inside my bra. No passport or wallet would slow down the identification. The darkness was frustrating, but I was grateful for it – no folksy streetlamps to encourage strolling lovers. I waited for the arc lights over the Castello to turn, then watched the glint of the knife as I slowly ran my tongue against each flat of the blade, sucking the ferrous juice between my teeth. Superstitious, but I felt I was licking away my reflection. Then I threw it, watching it curve and fall to a tiny, oily splash.

When the Borgias wanted to make a point, their assassins would bundle their targets, throats slit, into sacks and loose them into the Tiber, where they would drift down to the Castello. Sometimes special reed screens were set to ensure that the bodies would be found. How quickly did the river tide flow? I thought I would have at least an hour, perhaps until morning if I was lucky, before someone noticed him. Earphones in, phone clipped to my collar, I pounded back along the bank, AC/DC shaking me all night long

I was back at the Hassler in fifteen minutes, having taken the Spanish Steps at a run. By the time I panted into the lobby, I could almost believe that I was what I appeared, a tourist running the *gelato* off those American thighs. I bopped my way to the lift, and no one looked at me. The room had been turned down, curtains drawn and air conditioning humming, chocolate on the pillow, cotton mats spread on either side of the bed. Once inside I splashed water on my face, taking a quick look to see that Cameron's blow to the jaw hadn't left a mark. I changed back into the black dress and heels and pulled on the bright coat which was still waiting for me on the chair. If anyone had seen me coming up, they would see an entirely different woman coming down. I quickly checked the folder on the bed in case a maid might have touched it, but the picture was still there.

Now the phone. I grabbed a bathtowel and spread it on the carpet, unscrewed the cigar tube. The thumb fell out, white and grey where it wasn't bloodied, like an obese maggot. I slid my finger across the screen, held the thumb to the keypad. The display shuddered, and a message popped up: 'Try Again'. Fuck. What if it was heat sensitive as well? I ran the hot water and rinsed the thumb, tried again. It opened. The thumb rolled across my lap – oh God. I placed it carefully on a corner of the towel. I wanted to read Cameron's mail and messages, but there was no time. I flicked quickly through the apps until I found the calendar. I hoped Cameron might have noted the meeting with his client there, but there was nothing except the details of his flight back to London from Fiumicino the day after tomorrow. OK. I knew that the meeting must be set for the next day then. What else? Passbook. I needed the codes for wherever he was planning to put the money. British Airways, Heathrow Express, Boots, all banal stuff. HSBC looked promising but the account was in Cameron's name and, besides, it needed a password and security code. Would he seriously have been planning to stick five million there? Think, Judith, think. The thumb regarded me perkily. Wouldn't Cameron have had a back-up? Rome was notorious for pickpockets and the phone was almost new. Why keep anything sensitive on it?

As I stood, my knee ruched the towel and the thumb rolled again.

'You can fuck off,' I told it. But then I looked. The mangled stub of the joint was pointing towards the luggage. Maybe there was another passbook in there, a paper one? I had to have those codes, all this *effort* would be pointless without them. I ran my hands through a couple of folded shirts, socks, underwear, a paperback. I flicked through that; perhaps he had hidden a note to himself on the pages. Nothing, though it occurred to me that one feels less guilty about murdering a man who reads Jeffrey Archer for pleasure. There had to be something written down. I couldn't think about what it would mean if I was wrong. There would be a passbook, there had to be. I checked the pocket and the inside flap for any scraps of paper, then thought of the shaving bag I had seen in the bathroom.

Sure enough, there was a small red Moleskine notebook in the pocket of the toilet bag. The bathtowel had only a small smear of blood, his blood, so I left it on the side of the sink and squirted a bit of shaving foam on the rim for good measure. The thumb I wadded in toilet paper and flushed down the lavatory. I folded the backpack and stuffed my gear into my handbag, picked up the portfolio and after a quick look up and down the corridor I put the 'Do Not Disturb' sign on the door, a little tribute to old James.

I've always believed that hiding things in plain sight is a good maxim. I took the lift back down, hoping my face wasn't too flushed from the run, crossed the lobby back to the reception desk and asked if Mr Fitzpatrick had left any message for me. No, signora. Could they please call his room? No reply, signora. I thanked the concierge and walked slowly out of the back entrance. I pulled off the coat in a doorway and rolled it tightly into my bag. I walked calmly to the Piazza Navona, disposing of the bloodied dress in one dustbin, the cigar tube in another, kneeling to adjust my ankle strap and losing the passport down a drain grating. I took the cash and credit cards from the wallet, added the notes to my own and deposited the cards in another bin. There were a couple of photos and what looked like a folded letter, dirt in the creases from refolding; I made sure not to look at those. Presumably Holofernes in Artemisia's painting had had a family, too. The wallet and the phone could go into the river on my way back to my hotel. I chose the café nearest to the Bernini fountain and ordered a cognac and a *caffè shakerato, amaro*. Then I opened the notebook. I turned the leaves with slow deliberation. Shopping list, reminder to buy a card, the name of a restaurant with a question mark next to it oh come on, come on. On the last written page, I found them. A name and an address, 11 a.m. next to it, underlined. And on the facing page, the numbers. Joy. I drank the iced coffee and sipped the cognac while I smoked three cigarettes, watching the tourists throwing coins and taking pictures. The brandy felt warm as it oozed into me. I touched my hand to my cheek and found the skin of my face was cold, despite the warmth of the evening. I made sure to leave a large tip and exchange a polite goodbye with the waiter, hoping that he would remember me if anyone ever asked, then walked back across the river.

In my room I undressed, placed my clothes neatly in a pile and flipped up the loo seat, and then I vomited until all I could cough up was strings of bile. I took a long shower, as hot as I could stand, wrapped myself in a towel and sat cross-legged on the bed to study the notebook. I called up the account on my laptop, entering the numbers carefully. They had been quite clever, my little duo of art crooks. The account was in the Cook Islands, obviously recently opened as it held $10,000, the international minimum, just as mine in Switzerland did. There was the IBAN, the SWIFT code, the beneficiary name. Not so clever that one, 'Goodwood Holdings Inc.', whilst the password, 'Horse1905', was just moronic. I shut it down. I guessed that Rupert would have access to the account, too, imagined him waiting tensely tomorrow for the numbers to roll through. Tomorrow. The appointment. The name of the person Cameron was meeting was Moncada. Maybe Fitzpatrick had had a date with a snazzy Roman hairdresser, but somehow, I didn't think so.

My blood was sputtering with weariness; I couldn't bear to look at the clock. Still, it wouldn't be the first time I had pulled an all-nighter. I made myself some disgusting instant coffee with the miniature hotel kettle and took a health break at the window, then turned back to the laptop. The name Moncada drew a complete blank. I tried art galleries, smaller dealers, sale reports, guests at art-world parties, curators, journalists – nothing. Then I tried the Roman address, looking first for any art-related businesses nearby, then Google-Earthing images of what appeared to be a fairly grotty suburban neighbourhood. Why would Cameron have been doing a hugely lucrative trade in such a place? Either Moncada was a reclusive private collector or he was dodgy, and I had my money on dodgy.

I checked the index of *Money Laundering Through Art: A Criminal Justice Perspective* on Google Books. I'd looked at it for my Master's, but the name Moncada was absent. I tried a few random search terms, and 'art fraud Italy' soon got me to the word I had expected. The Mafia had their beaks in the art world, but that didn't mean much – the Mafia remained as much a fact of life in Italy as half-naked hostesses on TV gameshows. One of the things I love about Italians is that they take culture so seriously. One wouldn't have thought that art could be too important to the mob, in between corrupting the government and covering the south with tarmac, but the gangs were real professionals. One group had successfully substituted fake Renaissance canvases for twenty real works in one of the smaller Vatican museums here in Rome, and had sold the real pictures underground in order to fund arms-buying for a territory war in Calabria. It had been decades before the fakes were revealed and some of the canvases recovered. More recently, arrests had been made in a money-laundering case involving fake Ancient Greek artifacts supposedly excavated from a tiny islet off the Sicilian coast, Penisola Magnisi, famous for its wildflowers, and for being the site where the nymph Calypso holds Odysseus an erotic prisoner for seven years in Homer's *Odyssey*. Those involved in the scam were clearly less than enchanted by their treatment they received from the Roman police force, and responded by blowing up several of them as they enjoyed a cappuccino break at a beach-front café. If Cameron's man was connected with this sort of thing, it was rather discouraging. Gaudy straplines kept popping up, detailing the fates of those who crossed the gangsters. Concrete and explosives featured prominently, which would have been funny if it wasn't true. It was the kind of stuff that Dave would have enjoyed.

My research and my vision were starting to spin in circles, so I gave up. If this Moncada character was the type to carry thumbscrews in his briefcase, maybe the less I knew about it the better. Dawn was glowing beneath the acrylic hotel blind, but even after a busy day, it's vital to consider your skin, so I drank both the bottles of mineral water in the minibar and flopped on the bed for a couple of blessed hours' unconsciousness.

16

Next morning I was in the lobby of the Hassler at 9.30. I took a seat in the lounge, ordered a *cappuccio* and looked at *La Repubblica*. Nothing in the early edition. After ten minutes or so I pretended to make a call, waited another ten and did the same. I ordered a glass of water. I went back to the desk and repeated last night's performance. No, Signor Fitzpatrick had not left a message, no he was not in his room. I waited a bit longer, looking agitated now, playing with my hair and smoothing my sober tan linen skirt over my knees. Finally, after forty minutes, I asked if I could leave a message. On a sheet of hotel writing paper I wrote, 'Dear Cameron, I waited for you this morning as we agreed, but I'm sure you were busy. Perhaps you'll be in touch when you're back in London? I hope you enjoy the rest of your stay in Rome. Many thanks for dinner. Yours, JR'. The letters could have been that, or they could have been GP or SH. Another bit of stalling.

At eleven I stepped off a tram near the address I had found in the notebook. It was a little way out, a scruffy residential area of eight-storey apartment blocks perched on islands of yellow grass and dog shit. I found the shop easily enough from my map, between a pizzeria and a cobbler's. It was a framer's, with a couple of big gilt mounts in the window and a section of modern photographs, mostly Chinese brides in hired white nylon and faux-baroque borders. A tracksuited Chinese woman watched a small television behind the counter. Behind her was a door to what must be the workshop; I could smell resin and glue.

'*Buongiorno, signora. Ho un appuntamento con il Signor Moncada. C'è?*'

'*Di fronte.*'

She turned back to her programme. Politics, probably, from the shouting. Across the street I could see a small bar with aluminium tables under a green striped awning. Only one was occupied, by a man in a pale grey suit with collar-length silvering hair. I could see the glint of his Rolex as he picked up his espresso cup.

'*Grazie.*'

There was sweat prickling under my arms and between my shoulders; my grip on the portfolio was so tight it hurt. I didn't have to do this, I thought. I could just get a tram, then a train, then another, and be back in London tonight. All my planning had been focused on this moment only. I had refused the enormity of what I had done. I had ten metres to offer myself a reason to stay, and I couldn't find one, except that I thought this was possible. I'd proved to myself that I could do it, so now I felt compelled to see it through.

'Signor Moncada?'

'*Si?*' He was wearing Bulgari sunglasses and a beautifully knotted pale blue silk tie. Why can't all men carry off clothes the way Italians can? I handed him one of the cards I had removed from Cameron's jacket and my passport.

'*Sono l'assistente del Signor Fitzpatrick.*'

He shifted into English.

'The assistant? Where is he, Signor Fitzpatrick?'

I looked embarrassed.

'I couldn't find him this morning. He sent me a text last night.' I showed him my phone. Before I'd flushed the thumb, I had sent it to myself at 11.30 last night. I'd slightly misspelled instructions to keep the appointment without him, for an authentic drunk-text look. No one else was ever going to read it – the phone, minus the SIM card, was becoming archaeology in the Tiber sludge. I shrugged apologetically.

'I have the picture, of course. And everything else which is necessary.'

'I need to see it.'

'I imagined you would have planned somewhere to do so, Signor Moncada.'

He indicated the frame shop and set down some coins for his coffee. We walked past the Chinese lady without acknowledgement, into the workshop. The ceiling was low; it must have been a modern front built onto a much older building. Moncada had to incline his neck, and I could scent that faint watery smell of cool ancient stone in shadow. The workbench was empty, as if in anticipation. I opened the folder, gently lifted out the Duke and Duchess, placed the catalogue and the provenances next to it and stepped back. He took his time, to show me he knew what he was doing.

'I need to speak to Signor Fitzpatrick.'

'Please call him.'

He stepped outside to make the call and I waited with my eyes closed, all my weight in my fingertips on the glass-topped bench.

'I can't reach him.'

'I'm sorry. But if you are satisfied, I have his authority to go ahead.'

Another call, another wait with the inside of my eyelids for company.

'*Va bene*. I'll take it now.'

'Of course. But I'm not to hand it over until you make the transfer, Signor Moncada. I know Mr Fitzpatrick wouldn't like it.' I didn't add, because Mr Fitzpatrick knows you are a crook and you know he knows it. Or knew, anyway.

'How?'

I straightened my shoulders and switched back to Italian.

'You have a laptop? Good. Then we find somewhere with wi-fi, you make the transfer, I watch it come in, I leave the picture with you. Very clear, no?' Before he had a chance to reply I ducked my head into the shop and asked the woman if the restaurant nearby had broadband.

So we went to the pizzeria and ordered two Diet Cokes and two margheritas and logged on. I wrote the codes from the notebook on a napkin and pushed it towards Moncada to copy for the transfer. I felt as though an elastic band was squeezing round my heart. I opened Cameron's account again on my own laptop. The little beachball appeared on the screen, and as it whirled I poured Coke from the can to stop my hand from shaking. The site loaded. I entered the passcode. Nothing had changed since last night. Now I could watch the money arrive. Moncada typed slowly at his own machine, his hands hovering before he punched the keys. That made me feel young, which was a nice change.

'*Ecco fatto*.'

We both sat there in silence, as I watched my screen.

There it was – 6.4 million euro.

'I need to try Signor Fitzpatrick. Would you mind?'

'*Certo, signorina. Prego.*'

His courtesy encouraged me. Had I been a man, he might have questioned the beneficiary, asked for some proof that I hadn't already done what in fact I was just about to do. Luckily Italian men don't have a high opinion of the young female mind. Or men in general, come to that.

Outside, he lit a cigarette. I hooked my phone under my ear, paused, then pretended to leave a message, my hands still working on the laptop keys. Open the account Steve had set up for me, hold it at the bottom of the screen, select the transfer option from the Goodwood account. Send. I called up my own numbered account. SWIFT, IBAN, password. Happy days at Osprey. It was in. I left the folder on the table, next to the untouched microwave pizza. It was truly tragic, what was happening to Italian food.

'I got his voicemail. I left a message and of course Signor Fitzpatrick will call you. I'm very sorry he couldn't be here, Signor Moncada, but I hope you and your client will be satisfied. It's a very lovely picture.'

I took a taxi back to my hotel and made a point of asking if there had been any messages from a Signor Fitzpatrick. As I checked out, I gave the clerk my number and asked her to be so kind as to pass it on if the signor called. I was going on a trip, I said chattily, up to the Lakes. Just enough details for her to remember. There was a place near the Campo di Fiori that made white Roman pizza, the real thing, spiked with rosemary. I thought I'd have one of those before collecting my things and catching the Como train. I'd never seen the lake. I could sunbathe, I thought, and take a ferry trip to Bellagio, while I waited for the police.

17

It couldn't be an accident that the baroque had been invented in Italy. There was just too much beauty here, too many perfect views, too many delicately melded colours in too much startling Mediterranean light. The abundance was excessive, almost embarrassing. After the train had left the disquietingly elegant cavern of the Stazione Centrale in Milan and crawled through the bleak high-rise suburbs, their streets holiday-vacant, it began to pass through a series of tunnels in the first reaches of the Alps, emerging to brief flashes of green slopes and blue stretches of water, vivid and dazzling as a suddenly opened jewel box. And in the way that the rhythm of train tracks will always catch one's mood, the carriages crooned to me, 'You are rich, you are rich, you are rich.'

All the same, when I reached Como, I checked into the most modest *pensione* I could find, a place so old-fashioned I was astonished it was still open, green lino on the floors and a communal bathroom shared with various hearty Dutch and Germans who went off cycling or hiking each morning, with rolls furtively assembled from the meagre breakfast buffet tucked into their lycra onesies. I sorted through my clothes, putting the expensive items aside, and bought a cheap checked plastic holdall from the supermarket to store them in, concealing it under a bile-coloured blanket at the bottom of the rickety wardrobe.

The first evening, I took a seat in a snack bar, ordering a Coke which I didn't drink and a mineral water which I did. In a square-ruled school exercise book, I made a list of names.

Cameron. Dealt with. He obviously wasn't going to be talking to anyone ever again.

But how soon would news of the killing make the press? That led me to Rupert. He would have been frantically trying to contact Cameron, panicking that the deal had gone wrong.

It gave me a certain pleasure to imagine one day on the sodding Scotch grouse moor ruined. I had to assume that Rupert had access to the Cook Island account, that he would see that the money had come and gone, and, moreover, where it had gone. When he heard of Cameron's death, as he unquestionably would, he would have to think that Cameron had got involved in something too dodgy, offended someone, taken a risk. Rupert could hardly go to the police to try and get the 'Stubbs' back. And if the papers threw up my name? It was perfectly reasonable that Judith Rashleigh could have been in Rome, perfectly reasonable that she could have been angling after a job from Cameron. Rupert knew that Dave and I had been snooping round the Stubbs, but even if he credited me with the intelligence to have worked it out, and Cameron with the stupidity of having told me, the picture was gone. He was powerless. Mostly.

Which left two names: Leanne and Moncada. Leanne wasn't the type to pay much attention to newspapers, but she wasn't entirely stupid. If my name was published, she would be able to associate me with two dead men. Yet I knew her well enough to recognise that her only interest in life was Leanne, so why would she get involved when there was nothing for her to gain but trouble?

So, Moncada. He didn't strike me as the type to have a very friendly relationship with the police. There was no law against being a private dealer, but he was too well dressed to be clean, even for an Italian. I hadn't ripped him off; his clients would be satisfied and pay up. My performance as Cameron's assistant had been convincing enough to get Moncada to hand over the money; indeed it must have seemed in his eyes that I had acted correctly, given that I was ignorant that my boss was a gore-sodden lump in the Tiber at the time we made our deal. If anything, would *he* be afraid of nice little Judith going to the police? For a few seconds I felt incredibly cold. Would he come after me? Would he remember my name from my passport? I'd had to flash it, to make it convincing. If Moncada was in any way connected with organised crime, as I somehow felt he must be, he would have no trouble finding me while I was in Italy. Perhaps right now he was slipping through those same rock tunnels like a vicious rat, homing in on the rank scent of my fear. My heart was banging and my hands began to shake. Stop it, stop it, breathe. Moncada knew that he personally had nothing to do with Cameron's death. Nor could he suspect that I did. He had paid Cameron, he'd thought, not me. But what was the worst-case scenario? Moncada discovers unsuspected qualities of civic-mindedness and goes to the police. There was no evidence to charge me with, only circumstance. For fuck's sake, I sounded to myself like one of those morons who think they understand the law from watching *CSI*. Think. At present, Judith Rashleigh is a skint ex-art dealer who has been unfortunately connected with a horrible incident – two, if they pulled my flight records and somehow connected me back to James. There were records of cash withdrawals from her UK savings account, which proved how she had funded her modest travels before returning to London to look for work.

The only flaw, then, was the possible connection between Rupert, Cameron and Moncada. If Rupert succeeded in reaching Moncada, he would discover that we had met and that I had handed over the picture, at which point he could dob me in. An anonymous phone call to the Italian police . . . The only evidence would be if the authorities could subpoena my bank accounts. To put me on trial for murder, Rupert would have to ruin himself, and it wouldn't get his money back. My brain was writhing, a twitching began in the base of my right wrist. I could hardly hold the pen. How long did I have?

In through the nose, out through the mouth. Calm. I couldn't control all the possibilities, but nor could Rupert. He would hang fire until he knew about the killing, at least. So, I had to move the money from Switzerland, just there, reassuringly close on the other side of the mountain. Then I could go anywhere, be anyone. All I had to do was wait for the police and give them my story. I crumpled up the paper I had scribbled on and walked over to the shore of the lake, dipped it into the water in a clenched fist until it drifted away in lumps of sodden pulp. It was the waiting, I realised, that was going to be the hardest.

There was something close to the almost unbearable quality of desire to those next three days. The white noise of the beloved's absence which hums and whispers constantly in the ear, in the veins. I waited like a woman in love, like a hidden mistress who will only be delivered from the languorous torment of lack by her lover's tread in the passage of a cheap hotel. Each morning I ran, pushing myself up the vertiginous hiking tracks until my thighs shook and my calves burned. I ordered lunch and dinner, but could barely eat. I smoked until I retched water and lit cigarettes through the metallic taint of my own guts. I bought a bottle of cheap brandy and some over-the-counter sleeping pills and tried to knock myself out every night, but woke before the light with a thin wire of pain in my skull, watching my own heart beat under the frail, dawn-blue sheet. I felt the skin hollow out under my cheekbones; the plane of my hip became hard against my palm. I tried to read, on benches overlooking the postcard views, hunched on my windowsill, stretched out on the little shingle beach, but all I could really do was stare into space and endlessly, endlessly check my phone. I played games, like a crush-struck teenager. If the man in the blue baseball cap buys a chocolate *gelato* they'll call me, if the ferry horn sounds twice they'll call me. Each time my phone buzzed I grabbed at it like water in the desert, my fingers stumbling over the keypad, but apart from a single message from Steve – 'Hey you' – there was nothing except advertisements from Telecom Italia. I didn't buy a newspaper; I didn't trust myself to react authentically otherwise, though I knew that was probably stupid. I had wanted before – I had wanted, and I had coveted – but perhaps I had never yearned in my life as I did for Inspector da Silva's voice when it poured like medicine into my ear, after those days which dripped by as slowly as amber oozing through a pine.

He spoke English hesitantly.

'May I speak with Judith Rashleigh?'

'Speaking. This is Judith Rashleigh.'

'Signora, my name is da Silva, Romero da Silva.'

Inexplicably I found myself wanting to laugh. It had begun.

'Signora, I am member of the Italian police force. I am working with the *carabinieri*, in Rome.'

I had practised this.

'What's the matter? Has something happened? My family? Please, tell me!'

I didn't have to act breathless because I was practically fainting.

'No, signora, no. But I have some distressing news. Your colleague has been murdered.'

I waited a strangled breath before answering.

'I don't understand.'

'Your colleague, Mr Cameron Feetzpatrick.'

I took a deep breath. 'My God.'

'*Si, signora*.'

They would be waiting for my reaction, I'd considered, maybe even taping this call. Mustn't overdo it. I let him – them? – hear me breathe again before I spoke.

'I saw him in Rome. I don't understand.'

'Yes, signora, you left your number at the hotel.'

'But what happened? I –'

'I am sorry to give you this shocking news, signora. Tell me, are you still in Italy?'

'Yes, in Italy, yes, I'm in Como.'

'Then, if you will permit, I have some questions for you. This is possible?'

'Yes, of course, of course. I should come to Rome? What happened?'

'That will not be necessary, signora. If you would give me the details of your address –'

'Should I call the consulate? His family, I don't know, have they been –'

'The procedure is taken care of, signora. We will only take a little of your time. Again, please accept my sincere condolences.'

They arrived five hours later. They had called ahead; I was waiting in the cramped lobby of the *pensione*, scrubbed face, the black dress I had bought in Rome belted with a leather thong. I had crazy ideas about DNA, maybe there would be splashes of blood from the thumb on it – if I wore the evidence they could hardly drag it off me. The woman at reception looked up curiously from her blaring game show when she saw the *Guardia di Finanza* car with its Roman plates. I could feel her stare as I stepped out into the heat of the late summer evening towards them. I thought da Silva would be the older of the two, but in fact he was about thirty, with a stocky, gym-worked body and short dark hair. Clean nails, wedding band. Not bad, actually. The colleague, Mosoni, looked about fifty, saggy, with hunched shoulders. Both men wore ordinary clothes, smartly pressed jeans and sports polos. I couldn't work out if this was good or bad – would they have come in uniform if they were going to arrest me? I held out my hand to each of them, then waited.

'We may speak somewhere, signora?'

I answered in Italian and they broke out in smiles, obviously relieved not to have to struggle on in English. I suggested we talk in my room; it was more private and it would show that I had nothing to hide. The reception woman looked as though she was going to ask a question as the three of us made for the staircase, but I didn't look at her or answer her tentative

'Signora?' as I led them up to the second floor. I took the only chair and gestured to them to sit down on the sagging three-quarter bed, making an apology with my face. I smoothed the skirt of my dress over my knees and asked, calmly, how I could help them. Da Silva spoke first.

'Well, signora, as I explained, your colleague –'

'I think I should tell you that Mr Fitzpatrick was not my colleague. I used to work at British Pictures' – I noted their recognition of the name of the House – 'so I knew him a little, professionally. I bumped into him in Rome and we talked about the possibility of my working for him, at his gallery in London. I hoped he would call me, but obviously . . .' I trailed off. I was trying to look shocked, but tears would have been too much.

'Signora, I must ask you, did you have a relationship with Signor Fitzpatrick?'

'I understand. No, I did not. As I said, I don't really know him very well at all.' I hoped they would notice the deliberate slip in the tense, but they might have put that down to a mistake in my Italian.

They took me through my presence in Italy, my meeting with Cameron at the Hassler. I said that we had lunched and dined together, then that Cameron had left, saying he had an appointment and that I was to meet him in the hotel lobby the next morning. I had waited about an hour, I said, then left a note. I was planning to continue my holiday, as they could see. I confessed, looking modestly under my lashes, that thinking about it, perhaps Cameron hadn't wanted to offer me a job, that he'd just been wanting a bit of company while he waited for his client in Rome. I said that I had gone to Rome alone, planning to study some museums. I gave them the name of the hotel I had stayed at. I guessed my insistence on receiving a message from Cameron had given them my name and number, as I had intended. If I hadn't been so terrified, if the effort of controlling my slamming heart hadn't been so intense, I might have felt rather proud.

'His client?' Da Silva went back to the point.

'Yes, he said he was in Rome to meet a client. He seemed quite excited about that. He didn't tell me anything more, though.'

'Is that usual?'

'Yes. Art dealers are always discreet.' Trying to sound professional.

'Did Signor Fitzpatrick seem disturbed in any way? *Agitato*?'

'No, I wouldn't say so.'

'Do you know who Signor Fitzpatrick was meeting? Was it the client?'

'I don't know. I couldn't say.'

'Could it have been a woman?'

The woman in the Hassler in the garish Kenzo coat, which was safely stowed in a rubbish bag in a dustbin in the austerely splendid Fascist architecture of Milan station.

'I really don't know.'

'A member of staff at the Hassler said there was a woman asking for Signor Fitzpatrick the night he was killed.'

Were they about to produce a blurred CCTV photo of me at the desk? Was this the moment they would catch me in the lie and get the cuffs out? I had a sudden wildly inappropriate memory of Helene and Stanley, back in Chester Square. Mosoni was watching me intently. No quarter, Judith.

'No, it wasn't me. We had said goodbye at the restaurant. I'm afraid I can't remember the name of it. It had a balcony . . .

I went to Piazza Navona, had a coffee, I think. Do I need an alibi?' I half laughed, then looked ashamed, my attempt at a joke in bad taste.

Da Silva cut in. 'Did Signor Fitzpatrick say anything about a woman?'

'No, nothing.'

Mosoni added, 'No, signora. No alibi. But you are planning to stay in Italy? We may need to contact you again.'

'Just a few more days. I was planning to keep travelling. Of course, I will help in any way I can. Poor Cameron. I still can't really take it in.'

'Of course, it is a terrible shock,' responded da Silva gravely.

'Yes, a terrible shock.'

We were all silent for a few moments, being terribly shocked. Then both men rose and we said the usual things. I opened the door and heard them go down the stairs, heard them politely say goodbye to the goggling receptionist. I stood a few steps away from the window, listening for the police car's engine. As it swung away I remained perfectly, perfectly still. Could they have planted a spy camera in my bedroom? Mosoni, while da Silva had me distracted? Wasn't that illegal? I couldn't look for anything, because then it would spy on me looking and that would show I was suspicious. Christ. They hadn't asked about the knife, at least. I sat down gingerly in the chair again, smoked a cigarette, got up, began to pack my things. There was still a decent amount of Steve's money rolled up in my washbag. I would stay in Italy at most a couple of days, then take a train to Geneva. Cash for everything, until I could find what I needed there.

I leaned against the window and let my hand stray between my legs. It felt good, seeing what I could take. Better than good. I could feel the lips of my pussy swell against the tight cloth of my panties. I had endured, and I had got away. Well, almost. In the meantime, I thought I'd find a nicer hotel and do what I'd been dying to do for weeks. Get laid.

18

I'm not interested in being pursued. I'm not interested in flirting, or going on dates, or being lied at, which is all that eventually amounts to. I like choosing. That's why I like going to parties, because all that boring business is already out of the way. Everyone knows why they're there; no one is looking for another soul to gaze into their eyes and reflect their own. Flying solo, out in the world, is more complicated. Once I'd discounted the married fathers – not that they wouldn't, but the work, the bother, the inconvenience – and the local teenagers – unlikely to be talented – I was pretty much left with the staff of the considerably nicer hotel I'd checked into in Bellagio. And not that one is proud about fucking the help – fond recollections of Jan – but they were a depressing bunch. I was antsy after my meeting with the police; I needed to smooth out the tension.

Matteo seemed perfect. I let him pick me up in a scruffy bar on the shore of the lake, a place I'd picked for the line of motorbikes racked up outside, though I'd noticed that the bikers who toured through Como usually had a conveniently pint-sized girlfriend perched between the topcases. Matteo was alone; when we got talking he explained that he was from Milan, staying out at his grandmother's house. He had just finished university, which in Italy made him a few years older than me. His face wasn't much, but he was tall, and the shoulders under his washed-out black T-shirt were broad and tight. He bought me a glass of nasty prosecco, then I bought myself another one and offered him a beer. I hopped on the back of his Vespa and we puttered off to Granny's (Nonna, I'd confirmed, was away at the seaside). I called myself Lauren again, gave the same story of a tour of Italy between jobs. For a moment, as the Vespa chugged up the steep road away from the little town, with the lake below us pink in the sunset, I rested my face against his jacket, letting my hands gently grip his hipbones, and felt a little lonely. This was how it was going to be, I thought. If I went through with this I'd never be able to be myself again. Still, we'd never been that close.

The thought of an old-lady cottage had been a bit lowering, but Matteo's house was rather nice – Seventies in that way that Italian architecture can be without being disgusting, with lots of white wall and dark wood, and a huge terrace with a spectacular view of the water. It was growing cool, so Matteo lent me a cashmere sweater to throw over my jeans and we sat with a bottle of strange fizzy red wine watching the fairy lights of the last ferry receding towards Como. He lit a joint, which I pretended to take a toke on, and told me that although he had studied architecture he was thinking of writing a novel. Then he asked if I'd like to hear him play the guitar, and I could see where that might end, so I murmured, 'Maybe later' and put my tongue in his mouth. He seemed surprised, but keeping in mind that Italians think all English women are slags, he soon got the idea. I allowed the kiss to deepen, twisting myself over his lap so he could feel my breasts against him, working my tongue deeper into the sweet taste of grass in his mouth until I felt him hardening under his jeans.

'Let's go to your room.'

I saw the painting as Matteo led the way upstairs, and only then did I understand what I had done in Rome. I hate it when the world does that cheap leitmotif thing. A reproduction in oils of Turner's *Campo Vaccino*, the last painting he had made of the city. Some people see regret in the picture, the soft vagrancies of the light across the Forum, the great man's dancing farewell. A tourist memento, the kind of thing you'd see slung against a fence on the banks of the Tiber river. Where I had been, not so long before.

Matteo paused to push me against the wall in another kiss, more urgently now. I shimmied out of my boots and jeans, bunching my knickers in my hand, and lay back while he removed his sweater and T-shirt, then I pulled him down and flipped him onto his back, running my tongue over the clean young lines of his chest, rubbing the flat of my tongue against his nipples. Just the smell of a man after so long was getting me wet – I pushed my face into his armpit and sucked the musk of his sweat like a hummingbird seeking nectar. I traced the narrow line of hair over his flat belly with my tongue, paused at the first button of his Levis, opened his fly to take him in my mouth. His cock was a bit morose – long, yet too narrow, with a displeasingly childish amount of foreskin, but achingly hard. From the tenor of his breathing I guess this didn't happen all that often on a quiet night in Como, and I wanted him to fuck me before he came.

'Have you got a condom?'

He got up and switched on a light in the bathroom, his thin buttocks vulnerably exposed as he crossed from the bed. I stroked the lips of my cunt, opening myself, rubbing a little of my own juice on my mouth. I was so wound up I thought I could come like that; it seemed to take him forever to get the damn thing on and position his hipbones between my spread thighs. I guided him in and let his head fall in the hollow of my collarbone, squeezing him tightly to slow him down.

'*Aspetta*. Wait. Take your time.' He moved more slowly, pushing deep, a good regular rhythm. I manoeuvred my right hand between us to reach my clit.

'Harder. *Vai*. Harder.'

And then, for a second as he came into me, that first, exquisite moment of opening, of taking, I got distracted. His breath in my ear was a vespertilian caress, a demon's love poem. It was dark in the bedroom and my gaze searched out a few objects on the bureau next to the bed – a paperback, an ashtray, a touching silver sports cup. You could grab it, I thought, you could grab it and crack it against the back of his head. The blood would flow down around his ear, drip onto your face. He wouldn't know what had hit him. He would collapse softly on your breast like a puppet, twitching out his life through his cock, a hanged corpse. I closed my eyes. I was starting to cum, but behind my eyelids there was a film playing, a pair of pleading eyes, the brass corner of a briefcase, a crimson swaddle of sanitary towels, a bloated, greyed face. I feared that I was fucking another dead man, and I found I liked those thoughts. I was panting deep in my throat, almost grunting, I could hear Matteo's gasps rising to meet mine, and then for a few perfect seconds I was lost until there we were, lying like real lovers, panting on the shipwrecked shore. I couldn't speak; I couldn't look at him. We were silent for a while and then he nuzzled me, kissing my shoulder, my hair.

There's a device called anamorphic perspective. An object is painted on a slant, so that its true identity is only revealed when you view the picture from exactly the right point. The most famous example, perhaps, is Holbein's *The Ambassadors*, where a white smear in the foreground of the portrait becomes a human skull. There's a worn patch on the floor of the National Gallery, to the right of the picture, where you have to be to see the conceit. But I think that all great painters create a form of anamorphism. You have to stand in the correct place, and suddenly it's as though you have fallen into the picture. Briefly, you exist in two states, inside and outside, a quantum trick. Neither state can exist in isolation from the other. So there I was in Rome, in Matteo's bed, doubled.

'*Ciao, cara. Ciao bellissima.*'

'*Ciao*,' I whispered, against his throat.

I tried to put some warmth into my voice, stroked a hand idly through his hair. It wasn't Matteo's fault, he was sweet enough. He fetched a glass of water but I shook my head, snuggling into the duvet and pretending to doze off. I was still wearing his sweater; it made me feel more naked as he spooned his body around my bare thighs. I waited until his breathing softened and then my eyes flicked open like a horror film vampire. I counted down slowly from a thousand in Italian, then in French, then in English, gently lifted the arm holding me and slowly, slowly, wriggled out of the bed. I left the sweater, grabbed my jeans and boots. I'd been planning to hold my knickers against his face when he came, letting him inhale me as he let go in my cunt, but I'd been too busy thinking about how sexy it would be to murder him to recall that little trick. I went half-naked down the staircase with my heels on the edge of the tread and pulled on the rest of my clothes in the hall, beneath the hazy glow of the Turner. I could see the lights of Bellagio below and started down at a jog. My room key was behind the desk at the hotel. Matteo hadn't asked where I was staying. Even if he wanted to find me, I'd be gone by the time he woke up. This wasn't how it was going to be, I told myself, this is how it is, now. I had been overwrought, it was just my brain playing games, a technicolour dreamshow of stress. Nothing more, nothing to worry over. There was no moon, it wasn't late and I knew I wouldn't sleep. I would pack my things, pay the bill, ask for a cab at 5 a.m. to drive me round the lake to the station. I needed to be stronger than ever now; just a few more days, that was all. Matteo had been a mistake, I thought, irritated. What was I, a fucking junkie? There would be time enough for that, so much time. Just the next thing then, and the next and the next, until I had finished in Geneva.

19

In about 1612, in Rome, Artemisia Gentileschi made a small drawing of Danae, the princess of Argos, to whom Zeus made love in a shower of golden rain. It was a startling choice for a female apprentice who was heavily chaperoned whenever she left her father's house. Artemisia's *Danae* wouldn't be much of a beauty by contemporary standards, her flesh too pale, her belly too pouting. Even reclining, audaciously displaying her nudity, there is a touch of doubling to her thrown-back chin. I loved the picture because, unlike most examples of the subject – a popular choice for seventeenth-century soft porn – it is witty. Danae's eyes are closed in ecstasy, but not quite. Beneath the languor of their lids she is appraising, glancing slyly at the number of gold nuggets tumbling on her compliant flesh. Her right hand entwined with marmalade-gold hair rests on her substantial thigh, but the muscles of her forearm are clenched, her fist is tight as she clutches a handful of loot. Danae is making a fool of the god who believes he has bedazzled her; she is laughing beneath those knowingly lowered lashes at the viewer, at the man who cloaks his own need to gaze at her nakedness in the respectability of a classical subject. This is what we are, Danae is saying; even when we play the nymph you have to fill our cunts with gold. But it is not cruel, the teenage painter's laughter. She is sharing her giggles, inviting us to see what erotic cripples we are. If Danae had a cartoon bubble spilling from the peachy purse of her mouth it would be saying, 'OK, then, big boy. How much?'

It was a good thing to think of, that picture, as I sat in the lobby bar of the Hotel des Bergues in Geneva. Unlike other European cities, it hadn't become a necropolis in August. Inside, the air conditioning might be purring discreetly, but out there under the sullen Swiss sky, the city still throbbed with the hidden gleam of money. I remembered reading the memoirs of a famous call girl, who said that if you want to find the hooker in a smart hotel, look for the woman in the conservative suit. I remembered my poor little flop of tweed, a lifetime ago at the Ritz with Leanne. Obviously, I thought wryly, destiny had just been biding her time. This new number was courtesy of Steve, an investment made from the prefall collections on my last visit: Valentino in the lightest navy wool, softly yet rigorously cut, plain high Jimmy Choo sandals in black. Hair up, no jewellery, mani-pedi in pearly beige. I looked so like a banker I had to be a whore.

I ordered a glass of Chenin blanc and scanned the room. A couple of Arab guys at the next table, giving me the glad eye, an ancient exiled-dictator type with an implausible blonde, a group of German women with laptops scowling at her, two youngish men in jeans and IWC watches drinking vodka tonics. No good. Hedgies wear jeans. I needed someone dressed like me; I needed a banker. So I took myself and my copy of the *Economist* to Quirinale for dinner and ordered fresh foie gras for the hell of it, and scanned an article on North Korea while I waited for the music in the adjoining bar to start up, the aggressive house that Eurotrash need to know they're having a good time. I ordered a *mousse au chocolat* with jasmine syrup for the hell of that, then slid over to the bar and abandoned the pretence of reading. The place was filling up. Two women in black suits occupied the next stools, standard blonde and brunette combo, though by the look of the brunette's over-large hands and the slightly taut set to her jawline I thought whoever *she* ended up with might be getting a surprise extra. Within minutes they had annexed a couple of suits, and were soon halfway down a bottle of champagne, laughing and tossing their highlights and generally acting like they were absolutely thrilled to be in precisely that stuffy bar with its lame DJ and lamer floating candles in ice troughs, with precisely those fascinatingly witty men, while their luckier colleagues were doing bad Russian coke on the Riviera. I gave it ten minutes and then I asked the doorman to get me a cab to the Leopard Lounge.

There, I ordered bourbon. No one was bothering to pretend that this was anything other than a meat market. A gaggle of D-list teenage models, lingerie catalogue level, with a gay fixer in white Dolce jeans and a couple of ageing-player types whose hair looked like it had crawled off the seating of their doubtless slightly crappy boat. More blondes with varying degrees of tit job, more four-inch starched collars, more Rolexes, more lasered teeth and undead eyes. The two hedgies I'd seen at the Bergues getting loud and brawly on vodka, a girl in leather-look skinnies on either arm. Girls everywhere, Grazia'd up and ready to do anything. Girls alight with the hope that tonight might be the chance, the springboard, the moment that would make the dawn horrors and the bad blowjobs worthwhile. Girls like me, once.

Geneva is a small town, full of young single men with money, and two and a half per cent of its population is engaged in the sex trade. I wasn't overly concerned with competition, but by eleven thirty I was beginning to feel a bit desperate. I couldn't risk another bourbon. The list I had made back in Como was spinning like a juke box behind my eyes: Rupert, Cameron, Leanne, Moncada. How long did I have? If I couldn't swing this I'd have to get what I could from the bank and make a run for it. How much cash could I legally get away with carrying? It could only be a couple of days, and at this rate I'd be lucky to get any money out of Osprey and myself out of Europe before one of da Silva's colleagues came looking for me.

And then, because sometimes, just sometimes, if you close your eyes and wish really hard, life can be just like a movie, he walked in. Fiftyish, greying, not too handsome but sheeny with money, wedding band, Savile Row, Bulgari cufflinks (excellent – not aristocratic and a bit insecure), shoes and watch *impeccable.* Especially the shoes. If there was one thing I wanted never to see again if this little European tour came off it was another fucking tasselled loafer. He was alone, which meant things had gone badly and he was having a drink, or that things had gone well and he was having a drink. Either way, he was having it with me.

20

It wasn't until we were back in my hotel room and I'd poured him the drink and not asked for the money up front, that it began to dawn on Jean-Christophe that I wasn't a hooker. And even after he'd spent fifteen minutes with his face in my cunt, and about three banging me from behind with suitably orchestral encouragement, and I'd fluttered and shivered a bit in his surprisingly hairy arms, he still couldn't quite believe it.

'So, I wasn't exactly expecting that.' He spoke French.

'Is this the part where I tell you I'm not usually this forward, it's just that I really couldn't help myself?' I wriggled free and got up from the bed naked to fetch a glass of water, ensuring he could get his first proper look.

'Well, I do really like you,' I went on, 'but I'm a grown-up and games bore me.'

'I see.'

'But I'm not the clingy type. You can stay if you want.' I got back into bed and arranged the duvet around myself. 'Or not.'

He slid his arms back around me from behind, holding my breasts and biting the nape of my neck. This might not have to be such a chore.

'I have to be at the office in the morning.'

'What's your collar size?'

'Why?'

'I'll call the concierge and see about a clean shirt. He'll like a challenge.'

* * * * *

Jean-Christophe did stay, that night and the next. Then he asked me if I would join him in Courchevel for the weekend. The season was on my side, I thought. Not only were the wives safely tucked away *en vacances* (I wondered whether Madame Jean-Christophe was amusing herself with the tennis coach at Cap d'Antibes or assiduously starving in Biarritz?), but also, for all my many gifts, I didn't actually know how to ski, which could have proved awkward for Lauren the nice English art dealer to explain had it been winter. Lauren was the kind of girl to be childishly delighted, but not excessively impressed, when Jean-Christophe's Jaguar turned into the General Aviation sector at Geneva airport. Obviously I'd never flown private before, but now I could see Carlotta's point. Twenty minutes in the Sikorsky helicopter, exclaiming over the sublime views of the Alps gleaming below us, and we were touching down in 1850. The kind of thing that could corrupt a person for life, really.

We were to stay in a chalet borrowed from Jean-Christophe's old schoolfriend. His own place was in Verbier; I imagined that this was a longstanding arrangement which suited the pair of them. I had a poke around while he finished off his Friday-evening calls to the office. It wasn't one of the gazillion-euro glass-walled palaces that the Russians were constructing on what in winter were the pistes, more a solid family home, three bedrooms, everything in wood, decorated in a mixture of shabby Alpine chic with a few mediocre but pretty pieces of Oriental art. The beds were made up with colourful striped Basque linens. The only glamorous touch was a cedar hot tub built out on a wooden deck, with views right down the valley. There were tatty paperbacks and family photos, the friend with his highlighted wife and his three wholesome blond children on the slopes or what looked like tropical beaches. The daughter looked about ten years younger than me. I wondered what her life was like, about her boarding school and her clothes and her holidays, about what it would be like to grow up that secure, that safe. No doubt she probably spent her days smoking fags and bitching to her friends on Facebook about how crap her existence was.

Jean-Christophe apologised that he couldn't take me to La Mangeoire, the restaurant which turned into Courchevel's most expensive night club at ten thirty, but I assured him prettily that I'd much rather do something simple. We changed into jeans and cashmere sweaters and walked hand in hand through the town, stopping at a small bistro where the owner obviously recognised Monsieur. Jean-Christophe asked politely if I thought *raclette* was too heavy, and I answered politely that it was just cold enough, up here, to make it a delight. So we carved oozing cheese from what looked like a medieval torture instrument onto thin shards of cured ham and venison and drank a bottle of Burgundy. I quite liked Jean-Christophe, though obviously not as passionately as I pretended to. Unlike James, he had nice manners, and an easy store of chat which mostly revolved around travel. He didn't ask many questions, but I made a point of telling him briefly that I had plans to start my own gallery. Towards the end of the bottle he reached for my hand across the table and kissed it.

'*Mais, que tu es belle.*'

I wanted to giggle. In another life this might have been all that I dreamed of. Distinguished older man, exclusive location. Jesus. As it was, I was counting the minutes until I could get him safely settled in the hot tub. So we strolled back, and I did a bit of exclaiming at the beauty of the stars, which really were extraordinary, touchably luminescent, and I ran ahead of him indoors to fetch a bottle of champagne and two glasses and fiddle with the buttons, so that when he came out onto the terrace I was already naked under the deliciously steaming water with my hair trailing sleek along my back. Jean-Christophe joined me, lit a cigar and let his head fall back and we were silent for a few minutes, sipping and staring at the night. His fingers swam towards me, reaching idly for my nipple, but I sat up a little straighter.

'Darling, I want to ask you something.'

Immediately, he was tense. If this was the hard sell he would be ready, and no doubt perfectly courteous, but furiously disappointed, perhaps even a little sad. I could let him stew a moment.

'You see, there's something I need help with.'

'*Oui*.'

His tone was flat and discouraging. What was it going to be, I could see him wondering suspiciously – the intractable landlord, the exorbitant college fee? The sick mother? Surely not the sick mother?

'I would pay, of course. A fee. Maybe a hundred thousand euro?'

'*You* would pay?'

'Well, of course. You see, I was thinking . . . remember I told you at dinner about the gallery?'

'Yes.'

'I was in Geneva because I have an investor. He's a serious buyer and he's prepared to back me. I was seeing to the practicalities. The funds are with Osprey at present.'

He was interested now, beginning to think like a money man, not a john.

'Osprey? Yes, I know someone there.'

'But I want to move them. My client is very . . . exacting. He wants to gather an important collection and I'm very conscious that he's taking a chance on me. But he also needs to be very discreet – you understand? He doesn't necessarily want the world to know what he's buying. And I don't think Switzerland is as quiet as it could be. Not after all that UBS stuff last year.'

'*Alors?*'

'So I want to move it. I want to move the money. But I need to do it quickly, because I think my client has a fairly short attention span and if I'm not picking up pieces for him soon he might lose patience. Shanghai Contemporary starts in early September and I need to be ready. And there's some artists showing at Art Basel Hong Kong in the spring – I just can't afford bureaucracy. So I thought you could help me,' I finished simply, looking him as clearly in the eye as the tea lights and the swirling steam would allow.

'What did you have in mind?'

'Jean-Christophe, I don't know you very well. But I feel I can trust you. It's a fair amount of money – about six million euro. I want you to move it to a corporate account in Panama for me, as quickly as you can. I want to arrange to draw funds and my own salary as a corporate employee from the account. I will pay you a hundred thousand euro, wherever you want the money sent. Nothing more.'

'Six million?'

'A cheap Rothko. Not that much, really.'

'You are quite a surprising young woman.'

'Yes,' I answered, before I slid under the water. 'Quite surprising.' I was glad I'd got my life-saving certificate. It was true, what the instructor had said: those skills always do come in handy.

So I had a rather strenuous weekend and Jean-Christophe had a very relaxing one, then we took the heli back to Geneva on the Monday morning and a taxi straight to the Osprey building. I told Jean-Christophe I didn't want to go in, but he said I had to accompany him or they wouldn't agree to close the account. But it seemed that the benediction of Steve's billions still hovered over me like a fairy godmother. The contact was if anything more sycophantic and obliging than the manager had been. I handed over the codes and decided in the end to leave the original 10K where it was – you never knew. I planned to send Steve something in about that price range as soon as I was settled and then we'd be quits. If Jean-Christophe's connection at Osprey was surprised, he didn't show it, but then that's the point of Switzerland. If you have the money, you can hide anything there. So when we walked out Jean-Christophe was 100K richer and I was the proud and solitary employee of Gentileschi Ltd, registered with Klein Fenyves, Panama, on a salary of a hundred thousand euro a year with discretionary release options for purchases, funds to be released into the account of my choice. All taxable, all open, all safe, all in my own name. No more connections to the Moncada transfer or to that meagre account in the Cook Islands. It was too early for a celebratory drink, so we shook hands awkwardly on the steps of the bank and I made a few noises about getting in touch next time I was in town, though we both knew I wouldn't. His driver brought the car round and he disappeared, though I was sort of touched that he bothered to look back out of the window until they turned the corner before reaching for his phone. I wondered if he felt he'd been played for a mug and decided he probably did, though not many mugs are that well paid, in every sense.

I walked back to the Bergues through a surly drizzle. I seemed to have acquired a surprising amount of stuff, looking at the mismatched pile in the luggage room. I could treat myself to a better set now. Matching luggage, dead posh. Somehow that didn't lift my heart quite the way I thought it would. Wearily, I went to the lounge and ordered a coffee, logged on to the *Corriere della Sera* site. There it was: 'Brutal killing of British businessman'. I forced myself to read it through slowly, three times. No mention of my name. Just 'Police have interviewed a colleague of the victim, who confirmed he was meeting an unknown client.' If it was out in Italy today it would definitely be in the English press tomorrow, especially as August was the slow season. But I was clear, wasn't I? Rupert would have been frantic, seeing the money had gone to the Swiss account, but now it had simply vanished. Osprey wouldn't hand out the details of where it had been sent, no matter what strings that fat fuck pulled. I had worked out a story now. Even if he knew I had met Moncada, even if he found me, I could say I had guessed the Stubbs stunt and talked Cameron into letting me in on it for ten grand. The kind of pathetic amount of money someone like Judith Rashleigh would be in need of. And then he didn't show, and I went alone and saw that the money was transferred to where Cameron had directed me, and that's all I knew. Rupert could blame Moncada, he could blame Cameron, he could blame whoever he liked, but they had nothing on me. And why had I kept quiet about Rupert's involvement to the Italian police? Residual loyalty, playing the game, not letting the school down. Again, the kind of doglike fidelity to their values which I had once thought might impress them.

I closed my eyes. How long had it been since I could breathe properly? I should be moving, gathering that bloody luggage, taking a cab to the station, doing the next thing, and the next. But I didn't. I just sat there, watching the rain.

PART FOUR

OUTSIDE

21

The Stubbs came up at auction that winter. Ten million pounds through a Beijing dealer bidding for a private client. Five million profit to Moncada's invisible seller and the whole dairy department of Fortnum's on Rupert's face. Mr and Mrs Tiger obviously didn't read the trades, or if they did they were happy to keep their mouths shut. I did try and follow it, just to discover if there was anyone I'd need to avoid, but it vanished from sight. Stashed in a safe somewhere with a few Nazi Chagalls, maybe, ready to emerge in a few decades.

Here are some things that happen when you have murdered someone. You jump at the sound of the radio. You never walk into an empty room. The white noise of your knowledge will never silence, and sometimes there are monsters in your dreams. Yet with the disappearance of the Stubbs, the last link with my own life had gently snapped. Until Rome, I saw that I had been reacting, harried by circumstance; I had believed I had a plan, but it hadn't really consisted of much except getting the hell out of Dodge, howsoever I could. I wasn't like that anymore. The incident with Cameron had been regrettable, certainly, and da Silva was something of a fly in the La Prairie face cream, but as time passed, I found that I barely gave either of them a moment's thought. A hundred suspicions don't make a proof, after all. I had a new life now.

By the time the picture was sold, I had everything arranged. When I left Switzerland, I had no real doubt as to where I would go. Since I didn't believe that *Sex and the City* was a documentary, I'd never seen much point to New York, and, besides, America meant paperwork and hassles with green cards. I'd considered the South American classic, Buenos Aires, but my Spanish was schoolgirl; Asia just seemed too distant. I don't see my mother much, but somehow I still didn't like the thought of being so far away. I'd posted a card before I left Como, saying I was going travelling for a while. It made me a bit sad that she probably didn't expect much more. Since I was legitimate, Europe made much more sense, and there was only one city I wanted to live in – Paris. I'd had my gap year there, though it didn't much resemble the gap years I heard about at college. Endless shitty jobs to make the rent on a horrible studio outside the *Périphérique*, studying French grammar weakly after a 2 a.m. shift, Sunday trips to the Louvre when I'd rather have been sleeping. Poor little me. But the city had got under my skin in a way that nowhere else ever had, and as soon as I could please myself, for the first time in my life, that's where I went.

While I organised everything, I spent a week or so at the Holiday Inn on the Boulevard Haussmann, in the part of the city I liked least. Those wide streets that always seem dusty, dull with office buildings and windblown, disappointed tourists. I opened two bank accounts, personal and business, and applied for a *carte de séjour* – the long-term residency permit – all correct. I didn't need a map of the city to know where I did want to live. Over the river in the fifth, above the Pantheon, in the streets running down to the Luxembourg. I used to go there, after those dutiful gallery trawls, to watch the rich men playing tennis in Marie de Medici's garden, or sit by the fountain where Sartre and de Beauvoir first met. I had loved the quarter then, and it still danced with spells for me, spun on the familiar scents of roast chestnuts and plane trees. The flat I found was in an eighteenth-century building on the Rue de l'Abbé de l'Epée, off the Rue Saint-Jacques, second floor, overlooking a paved courtyard with a proper concierge, squat and waddling in a pussy-bow blouse and leisure slacks, a stiff bright yellow perm and a martyred air. I think I chose it for the concierge, really, but the flat had golden parquet floors, the old kind, laid criss-cross like the famous Caillebotte painting, a huge bathroom, white walls and painted roof beams above the bed, crudely done rinceaux in crimson and turquoise. Rilke had lived on that street, I saw in my guidebook.

The first thing I bought was a hideous Ule Andresson from Paradise Galleries in New York, a dull green canvas with a faecal smear in one corner. I had it shipped to Steve's office on Guernsey, and sent a text with a smiley face that said 'Thanks for getting me started.' I'd been following the results of my little research trip on Balensky's boat in the *FT*: Steve had done well from it. He'd hidden the trade in the classic manner, building up his fund's interest in general hospitality along with the Rivoli group, then watching his shares catapult when the Man from the Stan acquired it. Neat, and entirely illegal. But Steve didn't return my message; he was gone, to New York or Dubai or Sydney, and I was surprised to find I minded, a bit. I wanted to send some money to Dave, my only non-Asperger's male friend, but I couldn't work out a way of doing it that wouldn't seem conspicuous. Also he was pissed at me.

I couldn't let that sit any longer. I texted him apprehensively, asking how he was doing. He pinged back the word 'Bonhams', with an exclamation mark and a smiley face. No x, but what a relief. Bonham's wasn't quite up there with the Big Two, but it was a decent house and Dave was working again.

When I replied, asking discreetly if there was any way I could help him out, he returned the words 'Mercenary fees only. X'. He'd used to joke that he would have ended up fighting as private security in somewhere like Somalia, as had many of his former army pals, that it was only his missing leg that had spared him. I was delighted, but not entirely surprised that he had forgiven me. Dave was smart enough to recognise that grudges are not an efficient use of one's time

So then, I went shopping. First to Hôtel Drouot for an eighteenth-century writing desk, a real *bonheur du jour* with a hidden compartment in the back and a chased strawberry leather lining, then to La Maison du Kilim in Le Marais for a square Anatolian rug in bronze and emerald and turquoise, to Artemide for lamps and Thonet for a sofa, to the *marché aux puces* for a nineteenth-century rosewood *credenza* and an art deco dining table. Gentileschi forked out for a Lucio Fontana, a cool half-million, but I could afford it. I would sell, in time, and my home would be my gallery. I found a 'school of Orazio Gentileschi', *Susanna and the Elders*, nothing very special, apprentice work, but it pleased me, the tense silent space between the limbs of the terrified young girl, the evil mass of the two filthy old men whispering over her shoulder. I hung it on my white wall, alongside the Fontana and a Cocteau sketch of a Negroid profile with a fish for the eye. I even insured them.

I thought I would just keep my head down for a year, practise living as I had always dreamed I should. And then, if it seemed safe, I could start to buy seriously. True, London and Paris were very close, but pretty girls with rich indulgent boyfriends play at being gallerists all the time. That would be my story if it got back to the House that Judith Rashleigh was in business. And I did mean to be in business. I intended to gather a few less expensive pieces to show with the Fontana, to visit the European art fairs to build up contacts, then start to deal. I knew how it was done, and if I could hold back on spending the money like a navvy, in time I could start to think about renting a real gallery space, to travel, to find artists of my own. But I needed to wait, give myself time to learn, to become as sure as I ever could be that the old men would stay safely enframed on the wall.

I wasn't remotely bored. For a start, I never stopped loving my flat. Sometimes I'd spend a creepy little ten minutes just . . . *stroking* it, running my palms over the contours of the wood, tracing the line of the sunlight through my crisp linen blinds along the battlements of the kilim. I loved how it smelled, of beeswax and Trudon candles and tobacco. I loved opening a bottle of wine and pouring it into one of the heavy jade-coloured art nouveau glasses I'd found on a junk stall near the flower market. I loved the heavy clunk of the closed door and the silence inside. Sometimes it made me so happy I'd pirouette naked along the wide hallway from the bathroom to the bedroom. Not that I entertained there. For that, there was what Parisians call *la nuit*.

Real Paris is a small town, neat in its protective belt of *autoroute*. The suburbs, crammed with weary *fonctionnaires* and disaffected, violent Arab boys, don't count. Like any city, it has its tribes, but they are tidily arranged like matryoshka dolls, one inside the other, with what the mags call '*les happy few*' at the centre, but I wasn't interested in fashion parties or the rich kids of Paris *ouest*, I was looking for something more particular. I ignored the neat ads in the back of the *Pariscope*, too. I'd tried them a couple of times on my gap year, the cellar bars thinly populated with middle-aged masturbators and tourists out for a thrill. I wasn't opposed in principle to fucking ugly people, I'm democratic like that, but I could afford to raise my standards now. So I went to the obvious places first, Le Baron and La Maison Blanche, even poor old Queen on the Champs and le Cab in the Place du Palais Royal, went diligently and often until the bouncers said '*Salut, chérie*' and undid the ropes as soon as they saw me. I sat and chatted and drank, and bought coke to give away and hundred-euro bottles of bad vodka to share with lesbian DJs and Italian playboys, concentrating on the women, always the women, until the inbox on my new phone was full of inane texts and kisses and somebody else might have thought she'd acquired some friends.

I met Yvette at a private party at Castel, full of skinny boys in velvet jackets and models with ostentatiously bare faces. She was wearing a white Stetson, dancing on a banquette, because if you're crazeee you can't dance on the floor, swigging from a bottle of Jack Daniel's, contemptuously twirling a lasso over a crowd of drooling Eurotwinks, platinum dreads bobbing to Daft Punk. I liked her style, the way I always like people who are their own invention. I offered her a line and by 4 a.m., the white time, we were best friends. She introduced me to that night's crowd: Stéphane, a dealer who looked like a philosophy student; a pair of six-foot Midwestern runway models who sure as hell weren't in Kansas anymore; and a random Vicomte in Harley leathers who claimed to be a film producer. Everyone was shiny, everyone was pretty.

Even later, Yvette took me on to an 'after' in a penthouse in the seventh, trompe l'oeil corrugated copper walls and blackout blinds pulled against the dawn, a huddle of bodies crowded round a table covered with art books, jaws working, noses running, chasing their high off a Marc Quinn retrospective, the joyless air dense with nicotine and bullshit. A girl reared to her feet and began a impressionistic striptease, clutching vaguely at an imaginary pole, tugging at a ruined scrap of peach-coloured Chloé chiffon. A few hands, equally lackadaisical, fastened themselves over her flat breasts, tweaking the tan nipples like knobs on an old-school stereo.

'I'm leaving,' I hissed to Yvette.

'What's the matter, baby? Not your scene?'

'I like that' – I jerked my head to where the lost girl was jabbing her dry mouth at the crotch of the nearest guy, helpless as a baby vampire – 'but not like this. You see?'

Yvette nodded knowingly.

'Sure, baby. No amateurs, right?'

'No amateurs, got it.'

'Call me tomorrow, I'll take you somewhere better.'

Somewhere better was an evening hosted by Julien, who I got to know later at his club, La Lumière. I met Yvette in the bar at the Lutetia. She was sober, if a little twitchy. The dreads, it turned out, were clip-ons, her own hair was a severe white-blond crop, dramatic against her perse skin and this season's orange Lanvin shift, which she had accessorised with python Louboutins. No jewellery. I looked closer.

'Nice dress.'

'Mango. Don't tell.'

'I won't. You OK?'

'I will be in a minute. Want one of these? Just a little beta-blocker. Slows you down, takes the edge off.'

'Sure.' I mouthed the little tan pill into my *kir framboise*.

I asked about her day, in a desultory way. She was a stylist, she said. I told her I worked with pictures. We were neither of us really interested, now the coke had worn off, but it felt important to go through the motions.

'So where are we heading?'

'I told you about Julien? He has a club in the centre, but he also organises parties – something a bit more special.'

'Sounds perfect.'

At ten, we took a cab up to Montmartre. I could see her watching the meter. 'My friend, Julien,' she whispered anxiously, 'his nights aren't that cheap, you know.'

'No worries. I'm inviting you.' Her face relaxed visibly. Ligger.

Julien greeted us at the street door of a sombre nineteenth-century townhouse. A slight man who compensated for his lack of looks with a slim-cut Italian suit and mirror-polished Aubercy wing tips, too dapper to be anything but sleazy. Yvette introduced us, and I reached into my bag, but he waved us casually through to the courtyard, 'Later, darling, later.' Inside, coloured glass lanterns and discreet electric heaters made the air feel cosy despite the April chill. My heels snagged; I looked down and saw that I was walking over a Persian rug. Heavy mahogany chaises-longues and armchairs, brass plant stands and ormolu side tables had been dragged in to make an outdoor drawing room. A stolid-looking young woman in a long black dress played a harp. It looked like the setting for a bourgeois Victorian novel, were it not for the fact that the waitresses handing round trays of iced Sauternes and oozing morsels of foie gras were naked except for black button boots, long black satin gloves and straw boaters with thick black grosgrain ribbon bands. Maybe thirty people were smoking and chatting in the warm glow of elaborate Fortuny lanterns, the women in simple, elegant cocktail dresses, the men in dark suits.

'Wow,' I said to Yvette, and I meant it. She smiled, a genuine smile.

'You like?'

'A lot. Thanks for bringing me.'

'So . . . in a while we'll have dinner, and then –'

'And then.' I smiled back.

Yvette greeted a few people she knew and introduced me. The women used the formal '*vous*'; the men stooped punctiliously to kiss our hands. None of the anxious status confrontations of Balensky's boat here – if Yvette's 'career' was not quite what she pretended, and I suspected it wasn't, it didn't matter. Beauty was enough, and were it not for shadows, there would be no beauty. We might have been at an old-fashioned society wedding, juggling canapés and small talk, were it not for the confident, measured glances passing between the guests, the humming radar of sex. One of the waitresses beat a small dinner gong and we trooped obediently indoors, through an anteroom to a staircase. Julien bobbed up again: 'Ladies upstairs, please, gentlemen to the right, just here. *Voilà, comme ça*. Dinner is served in fifteen minutes.' I followed Yvette's heels upwards, to a large room with dressing tables and bright lights, presided over by another woman in black, compact and serious, her mouth full of pins. 'She's a hand at Chanel,' whispered Yvette – *les mains*, the artisans who hand-stitch the beading and feathers for the couture. Around us, the women were undressing, folding their clothes to reveal expensive lingerie in coffee lace or fuchsia silk, slipping on heavy, delicately embroidered kimonos. The air was thick with our mingled perfumes. As each woman fastened her robe, the little 'hand' bustled up with a basket. The women looked elongated and alien, towering over her squat shoulders in their high shoes, like creatures of a different species, which I suppose was how we were meant to feel. With considerable muttering and comparing, the woman pinned a favour on a kimono, fastened a flower into a chignon or on a choker, wound a jewelled and plumed chain around a wrist. After looking at me for a long time, she rootled in the basket and brought out an exquisite white silk gardenia, so perfect that I wanted to smell it.

'Bend down.'

I inclined my head and felt her fingers unpinning and refastening my simple up-do.

'Nothing fussy for you, mademoiselle. *Très simple*. Yes, like that.'

She stepped back, speculatively inserted another pin, withdrew it.

'Very good.'

As she moved on I sat at one of the dressing tables. My hair was twisted up, with the flower held in the cornet. I had been given a dark bronze kimono with white and cobalt embroidery, the silk stitching picking up the pale gleam of the petals. The table looked like a counter at Sephora, every kind of cream and cosmetic. I took a cotton pad and swiped off my make-up, which looked too modern for this setting, replacing it with just a dark red stain on my lips. My reflection looked strange, as though I had been redrawn by Ingres, and looking about, I could see that the other women were altered, too. Yvette wore a scarlet gown, with wide sleeves to the elbows, both her arms bound by a filigree of gold chains interwoven with leather and peacock feathers, like a hawk's jesses. The little woman clapped her hands, though the room was curiously silent, concentrated, none of the giggling or exclaiming that usually feature when women are dressing together.

'*Allez, mesdames*.' Her voice was as matter-of-fact as if we were a troop of schoolgirls being herded worthily around a museum.

Heavy hems and vicious heels swooped and clacked over the parquet. We crossed the hallway to a set of double doors, the low hum within indicating that the men were already inside. The room was lit with candles, small tables positioned between sofas and low dining chairs. The waiting men were dressed in thick black satin pyjamas with frogged jackets, the sheen in the weft of the fabric offsetting their starched shirts. An occasional heavy cufflink or slim watch flashed gold in the candlelight, an embroidered monogram rippled beneath a flamboyant silk handkerchief. It would have felt silly, theatrical, had the details not been so perfect, but I felt hypnotised, my pulse slow and deep. Yvette was being led away by a man with a peacock feather pinned in his cuff – I looked up and saw another man approaching me, a gardenia like my own in his lapel.

'So it works like that?'

'While we eat, yes. Afterwards you can choose. *Bonsoir*.'

'*Bonsoir*.'

He was tall and slim, though his body was younger than his face, rather hard and lined, with greying hair swept back over a high forehead and large, slightly hooded eyes, like a Byzantine saint. He led me to a sofa, waited while I sat and handed me a plain crystal glass of white wine, clean and flinty. The formality was arch, but I liked the choreography. Julien clearly appreciated the pleasure of anticipation. The mostly nude waitresses reappeared with small plates of tiny lobster pastries, then slices of duck breast in a honey and ginger paste, tuiles of raspberries and strawberries. Gestures at food, nothing to sate us.

'Red fruit makes a woman's cunt taste so beautiful,' my dinner companion remarked.

'I know.'

There was some quiet conversation, but mostly people watched and drank, their eyes moving from one another to the swift movements of the waitresses, who had dancers' bodies, I saw, slim but strongly muscled, their calves full over their tight boots. Moonlighting from the *corps de ballet*? I saw Yvette dimly across the room, being fed almond-stuffed figs with a sharp-tined silver fork, her body laid out like a serpent's, one dark thigh a hint between the red silk. Solemnly, the waitresses circled the room with candle snuffers, dimming the lights in a cloud of beeswax, and as they did so I felt the man's hand on my thigh, circling and stroking, entirely unhurried, and an answering tautness between my legs. The girls set out shallow lacquered trays containing condoms, small crystal bottles of monoi oil, lube decanted into bonbon dishes. Some of the couples were kissing, happy with their matched partners, others rose politely and crossed the room to find the prey they had selected earlier. Yvette's robe was fully open, her man's head dipped to her cunt. I caught her eye, and she smiled, luxuriously, before letting her head fall back among the cushions with the ecstatic motion of a junkie nodding out.

Saint's hands had reached my cunt. He stopped, unfastened my kimono and traced his fingers over my breast, twisting the nipple gently. I thought of that poor girl last night, coked out and whimpering in the penthouse.

'Do you like this?'

'Yes. I like it.'

I did. I liked the slip of his hands over my body, easy as water. I liked his mouth as he began to flick his tongue from my collarbone, over my stomach, to the lips of my cunt, changing the shimmering tap to firm strokes, wet, penetrating. I opened my legs a little.

'Deeper.'

He moved so that he was kneeling on the floor, one hand still caressing me, his eyes level with the gaping lips of my cunt. He worked one finger inside me, two, then three, opening me fully, his tongue never leaving my clit. I closed my eyes, but it was no good, I wanted more.

'Do you have a friend?'

'Certainly. Come with me.'

We stood, he took my hand and looked around. The room was all bodies now, twisting and melding, sighs of pleasure and requests for more muffled by skin. He nodded to a man being straddled by a vanilla-fleshed brunette; he lifted her off and her mouth sought that of the woman next to her, a blonde, their hair mingling as they kissed, hands groping for another man who slipped off his jacket as he sank down between them.

Even in the low, flattering light, Saint's friend was worn-looking, youngish but pale, his shirt with its initials straining a little over the beginnings of a paunchy belly.

'Mademoiselle needs some assistance.'

If I hadn't been so hot, I would have laughed then. When were they going to stop with the faux fin de siècle manners?

He reached for my other hand, and I walked carefully to keep my heels from skewering the skirt of my kimono as they led me through to a small, dim boudoir, entirely filled with a low divan, lit only with a stemmed candelabra. An incense burner released a dense scent of cinnamon and musk, leather straps hung from the ceiling like the tendrils of vines. I reached for one, gripping it between both palms, feeling the length of my legs, my breasts taut and erect against the cool silk, knowing I was lovely, knowing I was powerful. I nodded to Saint and he got into position behind me, fumbling a moment with the condom, then he was in me, good, firm and very confident, hands flat on my buttocks, thrusting hard.

'Do you like that?'

I nodded to Saint, reached for my clit, closed my eyes and lost myself in him pounding me. The second man's hands were stroking my back, the insides of my thighs. I tightened the muscles of my cunt, flattening my thumb against my clit, dark red and black waves at the centre of me, deeper, harder. I came, ramming my hips down on his cock, and felt the swell of his own orgasm before they changed places.

'You want to fuck some more?'

'Sure.'

'What's your name?'

'I don't have one.'

'I want to fuck your arse. May I?'

Saint was lying back, on one elbow. He handed up a little porcelain dish of lube and propped himself up, watching avidly.

'Go ahead.'

I took a deep breath and bit my lip, readying myself for the first quick shot of pain. He was a beauty, obviously proud of his unexpected treasure, and he eased himself in skilfully, not pulling back until he was fully inside, his fingers working deep in my pussy until they rested against the wall of flesh that separated them from his cock. I moaned a little, pushed myself back and started grinding him, answering the pressure. I felt glutted, crammed. I wanted him to get me off before he came. I loved this. I love being mined by a hard cock; I like it better without a condom in the arse, the balm of the sperm after that first hot wrench of opening. He slapped me, hard across the buttocks with the flat of his hand.

'Again.' I felt the blood rushing in, the exquisite heightening in my nerves.

He knew what I wanted, did it again, putting his back into it this time, so that I tottered and spun on my strap.

'Like that?'

'Yes. Yes, that's what I –'

The cuff came from nowhere, a boxer's jab across the jaw. I felt my eyelids judder.

'And that?'

'Thank you.'

'Spread wider, good girl, like that.'

My hair was tumbling down; he looped it into a knot around his fist, pulling my head back, giving it a tug as he slammed into me, so that I felt his cock was going all the way into my throat. He was fantastic. I worked two fingers inside myself, feeling that swollen head through the fine wall of flesh. He slammed me until I came, once, twice, three times. I was sweating, sagging like a broken marionette on the leather. He pushed me forward and hooked the straps under my arms, harnessing me, fucking me the whole time. He lifted my thighs around that thick waist, one arm tight against my ribs, so that I was suspended against him, the angle taking him even further into me. I couldn't keep my fingers off my clit; I had stopped counting now. I was gasping, growling in my throat, wanting him to come, to flood me, but then I felt his hands releasing my wrists from the straps, lowering me, spread-eagled, to the divan, where Saint was waiting on his back, ready again. He pulled out. I was soaked, so wet that the first push took Saint into me with a speed and depth that made me grunt, then I sat back and found the sweet spot, riding him with my face bowed beneath the curtain of my hair, his friend's voice murmuring rhythmically in my ear yes, like that, like that, darling, take that cock, take it in you, until I came, as I felt him jerk and give inside me and I rolled off him, slick with sweat beneath my robe. The friend reached across us for a glass, filled his mouth with wine, pulled me to him so I could suck it from his lips, its coolness spreading through my lungs. I took three cigarettes from a case which had appeared on a side table and lit us one each. The friend took my hand, turning it until my wrist was exposed to his kiss, then wandered off to the drawing room. I rested against Saint's chest while we smoked, his hand playing gently on my neck. I felt glorious, molten gold inside. He took the stubs and leaned forward to tamp them out, releasing me. I gave him a soft kiss on the side of his mouth, scenting the fresh tobacco, restored my hair, pinned back the fallen flower.

'*Ça a été?*'

I leaned back down, put my mouth by his ear. 'Thanks. You were fucking great. But I'm busy now.'

'Go ahead, darling. Have fun.'

So I did. Until I felt – what was the right word? Slaked. When Yvette and I wandered out hand in hand onto the pavement several hours later and a thousand euro poorer, I felt a rush of soft affection for her, gratitude for her having given me so exactly what I needed. Julien's card was in my bag, along with the crushed silk flower.

'We can go down to the boulevard, look for a cab.'

'I think I'll take the Métro. It's still running.'

We were sober and oddly polite, as though what each of us had seen the other do had occurred in a dream, far from us. I wanted to do something for her.

'I'll lend you the fare. Sorry I haven't got anything smaller. You can bring me the change another time.' I shoved a crumpled 500-euro note at her hand. The bells of Sacré-Cœur chimed three. We were passing a boulangerie that was spilling out yellow light and the thick sweet scent of butter and flour as the ovens were started.

'Take your shoes off.'

'What?'

I took a quick peek round the door, grabbed a few hot *pains au chocolat* and threw them into my bag, pastry flaking everywhere. 'Breakfast. Run.'

We scuttled down towards Rochechouart barefoot, carried by the steepness until we couldn't stop, Yvette started laughing and so did I, our dresses flapping round our knees, until the running and the laughing were the same, and somewhere above us a man's voice shouted what was going on, which made us laugh and run harder, until we clutched each other to a stop at the edge of the road, gasping and rubbing our eyes. The gutter was swirling with purpled water; we sat on the kerbstone with our aching feet in the blissful dirty stream and stuffed scorching handfuls of dough and chocolate into our mouths, spluttering and swallowing, sucking the butter from our hands.

22

It was some months later that I first noticed him, at the café on the corner of the Place du Panthéon. From the moment I set eyes on him, I sensed something odd. There was no reason for it; he was just another customer in another pleasant Parisian spot. Over the sticky city summer, I'd made a routine of starting my day there, after my laps of the Luxembourg and a shower; it was a short walk from Rue de l'Abbé de l'Epée, with a fantastic view up to the severe monument on the right and down to the gardens on the left. It was always full of university students, huddled in a fug of Marlboro Lights in the enclosed smoking terrace, not hipster types but bourgeois bohemians from the sixth and seventh *arrondissements*, their wealth subtly visible in their complexions, the turn of their collars, the girls with shiny hair tucked into vintage Hermès scarves. I never failed to take pleasure in how perfectly I fitted in, though equally I never spoke to them. A couple of times one of the guys would nod to me, and I exchanged '*Saluts*' with some of the girls, even, but that was all. I couldn't have those sort of friends, even if I wanted them.

When you're no one from nowhere it's best to know your limits. Rich kids can play at bohemia, but wealth has long tendrils – it twines into a safety net which can also be a trap for the unprepared. Rich kids have families and backgrounds and connections, they ask questions, because their world functions on being able to place people. I couldn't expose myself to that. Still, I ordered my *grand crème* and an *orange pressé*, and after a while the waiter brought them without asking, with that familiar Parisian efficiency which made me feel again, pleasingly, that I belonged. I usually brought a couple of auction catalogues with me, as well as the *Pariscope* to catch up on shows and private views and *Le Monde* for conversation. In case I ever needed conversation. Of course, every day I did a scan of the press online for safety.

He didn't stick out immediately amongst the early crowd; I think it could have been several days before I became aware of his presence. But again, when I did, my body registered a tension that I realised had been there for some time. Not a polished lawyer or banker, but one of those awkwardly dressed French businessmen whose jackets are always too boxy, ties too bright for a nation with such a reputation for chic. A civil servant or middle manager of some sort. His blue shirt had a monogram over an unhealthy swag of stomach that looked recently acquired, the fat of an active man who is too busy or unloved to care anymore, but the shirts themselves were cheap, button-cuffed, the initials an affectation stitched on at a dry cleaner's, probably. I began to watch him. No wedding ring, bad shoes, usually a copy of *Le Figaro*. He ordered double espresso which came with a glass of water he never drank. He looked as though his breath would be dry and stale. How long did it take before I realised that he was watching me?

At first, I simply assumed that he fancied me. I didn't acknowledge it with my eyes or a polite nod – he was hardly my type. Then I thought he might have a little crush – he was there whenever I arrived and remained at his table until I had smoked my luxurious after-breakfast cigarette, gathered my things and placed six euro fifty in the saucer. I began to look over my shoulder as I made for the door and turned right up to the square. His eyes were always on me, hovering on the horizon of his folded paper. So then I got scared. I took a snap of him with my phone while pretending to make a call and studied it. I was still telling myself it was just a precaution. Nothing. Completely bland face, no one I recognised. Just a middle-aged sentimental nutter with a secret passion for a girl with swingy hair and good taste in newspapers.

I knew he was following me when I went out to the Arab convenience store on my street corner for cigarettes one evening and saw him at the bus stop down towards the boulevard, still reading his bloody paper. I tried to tell myself it was a coincidence – this was Paris, after all, a city of neighbourhoods where one did recognise people from one's own *quartier*. He could perfectly well live round here, in a twenty-three square-metre studio with a huge flat-screen and the photos of the children of his divorce on an Ikea bookshelf. But I knew. In that tiny, plenteous moment of recognition, the monsters swarmed, chuckling and gibbering, tweaking at my chilled flesh with severed thumbs. He saw me, and in the line of his vision I watched the walls I had so carefully constructed around my life suddenly disintegrate, their solidity spun intangible as air.

I felt savage, hunted. I had a crazy urge to rush down the pavement and push him into the traffic. Of course I didn't. I went into the shop and lingered, buying a few things I didn't need, cleaning liquids, gum, a packet of string dishcloths, took my time finding the change, exchanging the time of day pleasantly with the leather-jacketed son of the couple who kept the store. As I looked down the street when I left, a bus was pulling away from the stop, but he was still there. He could be meeting someone, waiting? No. He was only waiting for me. I tried to keep my breathing smooth, but I couldn't help looking round as I punched in the door code. I called '*Bonsoir*' to the concierge, although I'd only just done so on the way out, letting him know another human was there, in case he was lurking behind me, in the twilight. I let myself into the flat, dropped the thin plastic bag and leaned against the wall. I didn't turn on the light. Whoever he was, did it matter? I could call a cab to the airport right now.

Every day, after I'd scanned the international news on my laptop, I checked the bag, a plain leather holdall I'd bought from a Tunisian street vendor. Five thousand euro cash, the same in American dollars, carefully changed in small amounts in the tourist den of the Latin Quarter, wadded in towelling sports socks. A few changes of clothes, toiletries, a couple of paperbacks, a steel Rolex still in its box and some gaudy gold earrings in case I wound up somewhere money didn't work, photocopies of my documents and the papers for the paintings. Not a professional's scarpering kit, but I thought it would do.

Yet I had a sick feeling that wherever I took a plane, I would turn round as the seatbelt signs went off and see him, watching me. Stop. This was insane, stupid. If he was following me it was because he wanted something. Always, desire and lack. Find the space between, Judith. I took out my phone and scrolled back to his photo, scrolling through my memory at the same time, my excellent recall of faces. Still nothing. I poured myself a whopping cognac, got a cigarette started. My phone blinked dumbly up at me, maddening. Who are you going to call, when you're alone in the night? No one, that's who.

The sound of the street bell was so loud its wire could have been connected direct to my tendons. I stubbed out the fag, set the glass carefully on the floor and crawled to my window. One of the things I loved about the flat was the recessed window seats in the thick eighteenth-century walls; now I angled myself over the cushion, squinting down into the courtyard, trying to see without showing a silhouette. The bell rang again. I had time to count to ten before I sensed, rather than heard, the low electric pulse of the buzzer in the lodge. The door clicked, swung heavily back. He was in. I saw his shape in the entry of the lodge, outlined in the rays of the concierge's TV. Impossible to know what he was saying. Then I saw the concierge heave herself with maximum Gallic disgruntlement from her comfortable chair, pass through the lodge door and cross the courtyard to the staircase. I held my breath. She trod heavily up the stairs; I could hear her muttering to herself in Portuguese. She buzzed my door. I held myself as tight as a cat before it pounces. One more buzz, then her weight in her sloppy Dr Scholls receding, a creak on the banister, and she reappeared, returning to where he waited. I saw her flip her hand contemptuously, shake her head. He stepped back into the courtyard, careful, I noticed, to stand directly beneath the security light so that his face would be invisible. But I could feel him looking. He called '*Merci, madame*' to the concierge, pressed the illuminated release button next to the street door in its plastic envelope, and then he was gone.

It took me a while to stand up straight. I felt like an old woman. I closed the bathroom door before turning on the light and took a long shower, as hot as I could stand, mechanically going through the motions of soap, body scrub, cleansing oil, facewash, exfoliator, shampoo, conditioner. I shaved my legs and underarms, applied a moisturising mask, spent a few minutes rubbing in body cream, monoi where it mattered, deodorant, scent. I made up my face – primer, foundation, concealer, bronzer, blush, eyebrow gel, eyeliner, mascara, flipped my head upside down and blew out my hair. None of that stopped my hands shaking, but it calmed me enough to think. I chose a short trapeze-line grey dress from APC, black hold-up stockings, added ankle boots, a scarf, diamond studs, my Vuitton raincoat. I called Taxis Bleus and drank a glass of water while they put me on hold, ordered a cab from my building, locked the door, lost my keys in my bag, went back to check the lock.

The concierge was still glued to a Brazilian *telenovela*. A woman with improbably sculpted breasts and buttocks stuffed into a laughable business suit was screeching in Portuguese at a guilty-looking man with a moustache. Every time she yelled, you could see the set tremble.

'Excuse me, madame? I'm very sorry to disturb you, but has there been a message for me?'

There had been a caller, a man, didn't give his name, what were those mobile phones for, the concierge would like to know, disturbing people at night, no, no message, but he had asked for me by name, Mademoiselle Rashleigh, not that the concierge had anything better to do than go trailing up and down stairs of an evening, no certainly no message, didn't say if he would call back and if he does could he buzz mademoiselle directly please, it's like that, isn't it, people have no manners. And on and on, until I had apologised and agreed with her enough times that she was mollified and we had agreed that people were dreadfully inconsiderate, especially with regard to the concierge's gammy hip, until the taxi tooted impatiently in the street and I departed in a hustle of '*vous*' and sympathy.

* * * * *

It was still early, just after midnight, when I got to the Rue Thérèse. I had visited the club alone several times since the party at the townhouse, and I liked the way it worked. Julien's door policy was democratic, if mercurial, balancing the two powers which mattered in the night world – money and beauty. The prettier you were, the less you paid, though the discreet bill handed over as the clients left was still fairly eye-watering. Expense bought secrecy: La Lumière was known to be frequented by some surprisingly respectable figures, though despite, or perhaps because of, its notoriety there were never any journos lurking outside the plain black door. Inside was a different matter. As I wandered down to the bar and ordered a terrible cognac (the cognac in these places is always terrible), I noticed that the banquettes had been recovered in zebra skin, and wondered, as I always did, which came first, the decor or the instinct. Are Europeans hardwired to associate animal skin and red paint and black leather with sex, or is it just habit? Though one could hardly imagine a *partouze* club decked out in tasteful neutrals.

There was no sign of Julien in the bar, so I slid off the stool and crossed the dance floor to the darkroom. Several groups were already gathered on the divans. A slim brunette was engaged in a complex daisy chain with three guys, one in her mouth, one behind, one underneath, the steady pant of her pleasure sighing and dipping between the glossy walls. The murmurs and gasps were decorous, though, unostentatious; the clientele here went in for action rather than performance. A young, very young man looked up at me expectantly, coffee-coloured hair falling across the tight line of his jaw. South American, maybe? I wouldn't have minded, but I didn't have the time tonight. Reluctantly, I shook my head and walked along the corridor past the individual changing cubicles, their short black-lacquered doors concealing shower, mirror and thoughtful Acqua di Parma toiletries. I found Julien back in the bar. He nodded in recognition as I approached him.

'I'm not staying downstairs,' I explained. 'Do you have a moment? I should like to speak to you.'

Julien looked baffled and slightly offended. This was not form. But I noticed he didn't look surprised, either. I followed him back up to the small, velvet-curtained lobby. I leaned forward over the counter, letting him see the 500-euro notes bunched in my black-gloved hand.

'I'm sorry to bother you' – this was obviously a big night for apologies – 'but I need to know: has someone been here looking for me? A man? It's quite important.'

Julien took his time, relishing my attention.

'Yes, Mademoiselle Lauren. A man did come looking for you. He had a photograph.'

'A photo?'

'Yes, mademoiselle and another young lady.'

'What did she look like – the other one?'

'I couldn't say, mademoiselle.'

I handed over a smacker.

'Perhaps she had unusual hair. Red hair?'

Leanne. Fuck. It had to be Leanne.

'And the man? Did you tell him you knew me?'

Julien's eye was on the second note. I closed my fingers slightly.

'Naturally, mademoiselle, I told him I had never seen you before in my life.'

'Did he say anything else? Anything?'

'No. Nothing. He was very correct.'

I released the money, which he pocketed whilst holding my gaze.

'Would you like to leave a number? I can let you know if he calls again.'

I wondered who Julien thought he was kidding. I wondered how much the guy had given him. There was a faint noise of music from the basement, the sound of a woman's heels crossing the floor. Down there, it was so easy to let people see who you really were, that's what made it so curiously gentle. We both knew that, Julien and I. He traded on the differences between those two worlds. I couldn't hold his cupidity against him.

'No, no thanks. Maybe I'll see you some time.'

'Always a pleasure, mademoiselle.'

I walked slowly down towards the river, crossed through the Louvre to the *quais*. Always so preposterously beautiful, Paris. I hadn't eaten, but I wasn't hungry. I called Yvette, who didn't answer, because no one actually answers their phone anymore, but she returned the call in a few minutes.

'Hey, *chérie*.'

We hadn't spoken for ages, not since the party at the townhouse, but everyone's a darling in the world of *la nuit*. There was music and loud conversation in the background. She would be outside in some smoking area, crowded under the fairy lights next to the thrumming heater.

'I need a favour. Can you text me Stéphane's number, please?'

'Stéphane? Are you having a party?'

'Yes. Something like that. A private one.'

'Sure thing. Have fun. Call me, *chérie*!'

I waited until the text came through, then sent a message of my own.

'I'm a friend of Yvette. I need a little favour. Please can you call me on this number? Thanks.'

I couldn't face the flat yet, so I turned left and made for Le Fumoir. It took Stéphane about an hour to reply, by which time I'd drunk three Grasshoppers and was feeling more equal to the world.

'You're Yvette's friend?'

'Yes.' I doubted he'd remember me from the club way back, but better to be someone else, keep more distance. 'I'm Carlotta. Thanks for getting back to me.'

'So, you need something?'

'Yes. For a friend. But not the usual. Something . . . brown?' My French wasn't quite up to this; I felt comic.

He hesitated.

'I see. Well, I could get you that. But not tonight.'

'Tomorrow evening is fine.'

We agreed that he'd meet 'Carlotta's friend' at eight in the café at the Panthéon. I wasn't troubled that my *Figaro*-reading pal would be there. He would have packed up his stuff and taken the first Eurostar back to London, eager to report to whoever had employed him. He'd had a clear sighting, he had confirmed my name and address. With that photo he'd had of me and Leanne it had to be London. Someone in London was trying to find me. I was regretting the Grasshoppers now. I needed a clear head.

I forced myself awake at six, jittery and underslept. My running gear was next to the bed, no excuses. It had begun to rain as I was getting home, but now the late autumn sun was daffodil gold in the sky and the city looked scrubbed, lucent. I felt better by the second lap of the Luxembourg, ran a few sprints, sit-ups in the damp grass, stretches. I jogged slowly back to the Rue de l'Abbé de l'Epée, running over my day's programme. Up to the tenth, where the shops specialise in African ladies' hair, over to Belleville to a pharmacy, a pit stop at a café for some research, my local Nicolas for a bottle, a doctor's appointment to make. That would take up most of my time. I'd give myself an hour to bathe and change ready to meet Stéphane.

The drugs trade had moved on since I'd last bought gear in Toxteth. Stéphane was white for a start. I'd positioned myself outside despite the heavy damp that followed a perfect autumn day, promising rain, but when he pulled up on his natty vintage Lambretta I didn't clock him immediately amongst the *intello* crowd. Skinny and earnest-looking, with a bad-good Eighties haircut and heavy, black-framed glasses, he was doing his best not to look like a pusher. I saw him slowly scanning the crowd under the awning and stood up a little so the hair would catch the light. It was a bit awful, the wig, but I'd done my best with it, screwing it into a messy chignon to make it look more natural, wrapping my big Sprouse scarf tight around my neck so it covered the nape. I was casually dressed but deliberately over made-up, and we spoke in English. I wondered how convincing my old voice was after so long, but I guessed Stéphane wouldn't have too precise a take on it. He sat down and waited until his espresso order was taken, then set a Camel Lights pack on the table, next to my Marlboro Gold. He smiled encouragingly – did he actually think I looked nice?

'So, you know Yvette?' he asked. I relaxed, no worries that he recognised me.

'A bit. Carlotta is my friend.'

We sat for a few moments in silence.

'Well, have fun. D'you want my number?'

'Sure.'

I put it into my phone. 'I'm not here for long, but you never know.'

'So, bye-bye, then.'

'Bye.'

He kicked the scooter over while he checked his phone, no doubt for the next drop-off. He probably had an app, I thought. I waited until he was gone, then made my way through to the loo and unpinned the hair. It looked spooky, voodooish, stuffed in my bag, but if there was a chance of seeing Leanne on my way home I couldn't risk it.

If you'd asked me how I knew Leanne was going to appear, I couldn't have said. Somehow, I just knew it was the obvious thing to happen. If da Silva had been going to arrest me, he would just have arrested me, not given me time to disappear. Assuming my new chum had a London connection, and given Julien's mention of the hair, London meant Leanne. She didn't turn up until after ten, by which time I'd begun to doubt myself. I began to feel sick; maybe my casual assurance about da Silva had been wrong. I'd showered and put on white pyjamas, men's, from Charvet. The concierge had already been primed with a bunch of nasty cellophaned chrysanthemums, to assuage the inconvenience of showing any late-night guests up to my flat. I'd lit candles, poured a meditative glass of red, Mozart's 21st piano concerto on the stereo, the latest Philippe Claudel novel open on the arm of the sofa. A lovely quiet night in, I was having. Buzz, click, buzz. Voices, Scholl schlump, click, schlump, click of heels on the flagstones, '*Allez-vous par là*,' click click click on the stairs, buzz.

'Oh my God! Leanne! What a surprise! Come in, come in. It's been what, more than a year! Ages!You look great! Come in.'

Actually, I was glad to note that she didn't look that great. She was thin, but her face was pale and puffy, a crop of spots on her jawline heavily rubbed out with chalky concealer. The hair was still wildly red, but the gold-weave highlights were gone, dulling her skin further. She carried the Chanel bag we'd got in Cannes, but it was battered now, her tan coat was chain store and her boots were worn out at their pointed toes.

'Look at this, eh? Fab.'

'It's only rented.'

I followed her eyes around the room. She wouldn't know that the plain black sofa was Thonet, or that the Cocteau drawing was real, if she'd even heard of Cocteau, but as I echoed her gaze, I saw with pleasure that my flat sang with taste, and the money to supply it.

'Still, you seem like you're doing really well.'

I lowered my eyes. 'You remember that guy with the boat. Steve? Well, we've been seeing each other ever since, on and off. He helps me out. And I have a new job, a proper dealer's job. It's . . . OK.'

She reached up and pulled me into a Prada Candy-scented hug.

'Good for you, Jude. Good for you.' She actually sounded like she meant it.

'Let's have a drink. I'd have got Roederer if I'd known you were coming,' I smiled. I waved my own full glass and fetched her one from the cupboard. She took a long swallow and rooted in her bag for cigarettes. I joined her on the sofa and we lit up.

'And how are you? Still at the club?'

'Yeah. I'm a bit over it now, though.' Her voice was flatter, more Estuary London; somehow it made her seem older, the sparkiness gone.

'When did you get here? How come you're in Paris?'

'A guy at the club. Asked me for a weekend, you know.'

I answered brightly. 'Cool! Did you stay anywhere nice?'

'Yeah, dead nice. The something de la Reine? In that square?' Perfect; she thought I was buying it. 'So, um, then I heard you were here and I thought I'd look you up.'

'You heard I was here. Right.'

I let the silence sit until she looked at me appealingly, floundering.

'It's great to see you,' she muttered. 'We had a laugh, right? In Cannes?'

'Yes. It was a laugh.'

The 21st is a bit obvious for serious tastes, but there's something in the tension of it, the hovering space between the notes, that makes me ache. I crossed the parquet in my bare feet, unplugged my phone from where it was charging, let her see me turn it off. Wordlessly, she retrieved hers and did the same. I held out my hand and she let me take it, as though hypnotised. I placed them side by side on the table. I sat down on the other end of the sofa, sipped my wine, tucked my legs underneath me, leaned forward.

'Leanne. Please tell me why you're here. It's obviously not a coincidence. How did you even know I was in Paris, let alone where I live? Are you in trouble? Can I help?'

I could see her working out how much to tell me, setting it against what she thought I knew. Which was nothing much, right now.

'Leanne. What's up? I can't help you if you won't tell me.'

I didn't ask anything else. We sat there on the sofa like a therapist and a patient, until the music came to its poised, protracted end.

'There was a bloke came asking at the club. He had a photo. It was on a security pass from that place you used to work.'

I made my voice a little harder. 'And what did you tell him?'

'Nothing, I swear. I was bricking it. Olly recognised you, said you didn't look like a Judith. But all I said was that you'd left. Nothing, I swear.'

'Why do you need to swear? What's the problem?'

'I didn't know. I thought it was about, well . . . you know . . . James. So I kept schtum. But there was this other girl, she'd been in the club a couple of weeks, started after you left. Ashley. Blonde, very tall? She told him she knew you.'

Ashley. The hooker from the party in Chester Square. *Quelle* sodding *horrible surprise*. I looked at Leanne, who was on her second glass, chain-smoking. I felt sorry, then. I believed her; she had kept quiet. And I'd been grassed up by a fucking Svetlana whom I'd last seen with her gob full of a stranger's prick.

'What happened then?'

'They went off and talked. He left. I tried to find out what they'd been talking about, but she was a snotty bitch. Russian. She left, anyway, a few nights later. Sacked. Got caught with a client.'

'That figures. So, the guy, what's his name?'

'Cleret. Renaud Cleret. He's French.'

If Ashley had been a shock, that hit me like a rabbit punch in the solar plexus. I laughed, madly.

'What's funny?'

'Nothing, nothing Leanne. Sorry. It's just, just such a French name, you know. Renaud Cleret. Like a bad film. Whatever.'

And then she told me the rest. That she'd panicked, been convinced that the story about James was out. She said she'd tried to text me, but of course I'd changed my number. So she'd gone to British Pictures, braved the receptionists until they let her in to see Rupert.

'Your old boss? The one you used to do the impressions of? They were dead good, when I really met him.'

And Rupert had told her that he believed I was mixed up in a faking scam, that they needed to find me, partly in case I was playing on the reputation of the House, partly out of concern. How touching. He'd hinted darkly that these things could get very nasty, that I probably didn't know I was playing with fire. So they'd hired Cleret, he explained, to find me. And now here was Leanne, my old friend. Would she try to talk to me? Cleret would let her know where I was; she just had to drop by. They'd pay the fare to Paris, and a bit extra on top. He emphasised that it was urgent, that he was concerned for my welfare. Really, Leanne would be doing a favour to her friend.

'How much on top? Go on, it's OK.'

Two thousand pounds. Thirty pieces of silver, I said, but she just looked blank.

'I didn't believe them, anyway. I made out like I did, I made out like I was as stupid as they thought I was. The Cleret guy gave me your address last night, said I was to come at once.'

'Where is he now?'

'London. He's French but he lives in London.'

'And so you came.'

'Yeah.'

I took another swig of wine, poured her some more. She sat up a bit straighter, her confidence renewed by her confession, cunning little eyes glittering at me.

'So, now I've told you, what have you got to tell me?'

'What do you mean?'

'I mean, I'm not soft. That Rupert said you were mixed up in something. He said a guy had been killed in Rome, that was why he was so worried.'

'What guy?'

'Cameron Fitzpatrick, he said. I looked in the papers, online. A bloke was murdered. Cameron Fitzpatrick, in Rome. Not too long after you'd left the South of France. He was an art dealer, like you, Jude. And this Cleret bloke, he said you had been in Rome. You were there. When it happened.'

Fuck. Fuck. How could Cleret have known that? Wait, breathe. My name would have been in da Silva's report, even though the newspaper had been discreet. It was public knowledge, and supposedly this Cleret was some kind of detective. Concentrate on what's in front of you, for now.

Leanne might have been ignorant, but she wasn't thick. As far as cash potential went, she was a rat on an open wound. I was genuinely impressed she'd managed to put so many pieces together, but seriously – what did she expect? That I would confess all and allow her to blackmail me?

'So what? I was there. I had to speak to the Italian police. It was awful. I'd hoped he might give me a job. I mean, it was awful for him, poor man. I imagine Rupert knew I was there too, even if he didn't tell you that. Maybe that's where he got his suspicions from, but so what? He could have got in touch, just asked me. None of this stupid cat and mouse business. What's your point?'

'Why is Rupert so keen to talk to you? Why was he so pleased to see me?'

'How the fuck would I know? Maybe he fancied a cheap screw.'

That hit her like a slap, but she let it go.

'I didn't come here to argue, Jude. You're into something, right? That's why those blokes want me to talk to you. To find out. But what do we owe those posh cunts? We did it in Cannes, didn't we? We did it together? So I thought maybe I could help you. Two's better than one, right?'

'What was it that we did? That we did together? I don't know what you're talking about.'

'Come on Jude –'

I tried not to let the contempt show in my face, mostly succeeded. I managed a wry, cards-on-the-table smile.

'Come off it, Leanne. You're not here for Rupert, or because you want to get one over on him, either. How much do you need? To keep quiet about James, to go back to Rupert and tell him you couldn't find me, because that's what you think I'm scared of, isn't it? How much?'

I never got to find out how much the poor dumb bitch wanted because the half-dozen benzodiazepine I'd mixed into a rather nice bottle of Madiran had kicked in and Leanne's head had fallen back against the cushion, her half-empty glass tipping from her limp hand and spilling over her lap. Sedatives and slimming pills: French doctors are so obliging. That's why French women don't get fat. Lucky I'd got the sofa in black.

If only French cabbies were as compliant as their medics. It took forever to slap Leanne into a semblance of consciousness and get some water down her. It took an age to half-walk, half-carry her down the stairs and along to the boulevard, an eternity for a cab to draw up, and then he wouldn't take us because she obviously looked pissed and he was afraid she'd chuck on his nice synthetic seats. I hoped she didn't throw up; I couldn't have that. I was murmuring encouragingly, don't worry, no problem, just a bit too much wine, you'll be fine. I got her into the second cab, where she immediately passed out again, solid against my shoulder. It wasn't far across the river to the Place des Vosges. I had time to hunt for her room card in her bag and pass a twenty over to the driver and we were there. Hauling her through reception was even worse, with her weight and both our bags over my spare shoulder, not to mention the large umbrella I'd unfolded to protect her from the showers, but with my left arm gripping her around her back I managed to stagger to the lift. If anyone raised an eyebrow I'd just say apologetically that she was English, but there was a party of Japanese tourists arriving and the receptionist and porter were busy. Her room was on the third floor; I had to put the brolly down to fiddle with the key card, and Leanne slumped almost to the floor, her legs splaying in a puppet's plié.

I got her coat off and propped her on the bed with a couple of pillows behind her, half-sitting. I locked the door and put out the good old 'Do Not Disturb', turned the TV on, flicked through until I got MTV, not too loud. As I turned back to the bed she moaned and her eyelids flickered, startling me, but she slipped back under in seconds. I pulled on antiseptic plastic gloves and took the works I'd picked up in Belleville from my bag, along with a black sequined elastic belt from H&M. Then the pack of Camels I'd taken in the café, where I'd also lifted a teaspoon. I hoped to God Stéphane hadn't gypped me – there hadn't been time to have a little chase of the gear, even if I'd felt like passing a couple of hours monged out, but Yvette used him; he was bound to be reliable. I'd seen it done, most recently by Lawrence in bloody Chester Square. I took off Leanne's boots, fetched an Evian and a miniature of Johnnie Walker from the minibar and tipped a bit of the whisky down her throat. Most of it dribbled down her cheek, but that wouldn't matter.

I really, really don't like needles. Rihanna was singing about diamonds in the sky. I had my Cartier lighter and a cotton pad. The gear was the colour of strong tea. Holding the belt taut between my teeth, I fixed her up in the crook of her left elbow, half of what I'd bought from Stéphane, more than enough. She twitched a bit as I hit the vein, but I was pressing down on her shoulder and I was strong. A couple of minutes, I'd read, until the body forgets to breathe. One of the nicer ways to go.

It was the second time I had watched a person die. I could have run a little montage in my head – Leanne with her original chestnut hair at school, pleated navy skirt hiked up to her thighs, Leanne twirling her cocktail at the Ritz, Leanne and I dancing in a club on the Riviera. All swirly and happy and poignant. If I'd been that kind of person. Or I could have thought about the sound a thirteen-year-old girl's head makes when it hits the red brick of the sports hall, and a slim figure with carefully tonged hair who stood there and did nothing. But I wasn't that kind of person, either. So I waited until Leanne's body forgot, then I waited a little longer, and while I waited I opened Leanne's phone. I remembered her birthday; I'm good like that. She was twenty-seven, like me. I called Stéphane from her phone and hung up before he answered. I copied a French mobile number from her phone to mine, then I wriggled gently off the bed, letting her fall onto her side, and went meticulously through her things with the gloves on; the wheelie bag on the luggage stand, the cosmetics in the bathroom. There was a collection of business cards in the pocket of her Chanel bag, hopefuls from the Gstaad Club presumably. Rupert's card was amongst them. I didn't see much point in taking that. Her wallet contained a few hundred euro and an open-return train ticket. I pocketed that, her passport, her bank card, everything with her name, as well as her hairbrush and a stray lipstick, the kind of things that might fall out if the bag's owner was jacked up and careless. I was guessing the Cleret guy would have checked in, as he was shouting the room, and walked her in later. One look at her and the front desk would have known better than to ask questions: this was Paris after all, and the Pavillon is a stylish hotel. No photos, no book or magazine on the night table, the rumpled clothes low-end and obvious. A non-person, really. I didn't know where she lived, or what had become of her parents, she was nothing to me. Rihanna was singing her umbrella song. I picked up mine and left. Just like you imagine, it does get easier. Perhaps I didn't need to kill her. But then, I hadn't killed her because I needed to. That was the third time, and it wasn't an accident at all.

23

Two weeks. That time in Como had just flown by, in comparison. Two weeks of pacing and smoking and conjecturing, playing it out, over and over again. When, finally, I saw Cleret loitering at the end of my street one evening, it was all I could do not to rush through the traffic and kiss him.

Still, the Rules say that one must never be too eager to greet a gentleman caller. I went home and forced myself to pay attention to two long articles in the *Art Newspaper*. Some time later I looked at my watch, a slim pink gold Vacheron Aronde 1954: 9.45 p.m. I brushed out my hair and changed my sweater for a ruffled Isabel Marant blouse, swapped my boots for neat Saint Laurent heels, gorgeous claret patent, but not too high. Time to go out to play. I swung down to the boulevard and crossed next to the bus stop, passing close enough to him that he could smell my scent (Gantier's Tubéreuse, good and strong). I walked on to the corner, aware that my tight grey jeans and heels were snagging a few stares, and turned left down the Rue Vaugirard, cut down to the taxi rank on the Place Saint-Sulpice. There was a bar I was fond of on the Rue Mazarine, done out like Julien's orgy to look like a bourgeois drawing room, quiet in the week. They made good cocktails, but tonight I ordered straight bourbon, drank it slowly, looking out into the street over the artful net curtains. It took him twenty minutes to find a position in a doorway opposite. We were just metres apart as I exited the bar and turned left again, heading down to the river. No footsteps behind me;

the soles of those shoes, thick and brown like supermarket pastry, must be made of rubber. Not bad, stranger.

This was sort of fun. I came out on the *quai* and waited at the crossing in a crowd of tourists on a romantic late walking tour. I walked over to Cité, round Notre Dame and over to the Ile Saint-Louis. Quite the stroll for him, work off some of those spare kilos. It was an unusually warm night for November and the cafés at the head of the island were crowded, the queue for ice cream at Berthillon snaking along their terraces. I felt electric, vividly alive, aroused, the muscles in my thighs and arse alert to his seeking gaze. I took the Rue Saint-Louis en l'Ile, crossed once more at Pont Marie to the Right Bank. It was 11.15 p.m. There was the usual bunch of tramps carousing under the bridge. I could smell their filth under cheap spirits, my senses as vivid as an animal's. I perched on the thick balustrade, lit a cigarette, waited some more. He couldn't be that far behind. I felt almost sorry if he'd lost me that easily. Then, there he was, coming towards me, his face shadowed under the ornate streetlamp. I'd have bet he looked irritable. I had the number ready, the one I had taken from Leanne's phone. I pressed 'Call'. He paused to take it, his head moving as he scanned the bridge for me.

'*Allô?*'

'Monsieur Cleret, it's Judith Rashleigh. It's been a while.'

'*Alors, bonsoir, mademoiselle.*'

'I'm at the end of the bridge,' I said, and hung up.

I hopped down, walked a little further to the front of the cab rank that served the Hôtel de Ville, waited again. I could sense him quicken his pace as I opened the door and asked the driver if he was free – he couldn't risk losing me to the

Parisian traffic, perhaps, or he hadn't the funds for another taxi. I stepped back, holding the door open as he approached.

'I thought you might like a drink.'

He didn't speak, just slid along beside me on the broad seat of the Mercedes. I leaned forward and asked the driver to take us to the Ritz.

'Rue Cambon? I have a feeling for the Hemingway.'

He had been silent all along the Rue de Rivoli; now he turned to face me. He looked weary, but faintly amused.

'As you like.'

We waited while the bartender fussed impeccably, setting water glasses with floating cucumber and redcurrants on frilled coasters, producing a rose martini for me and a gin and tonic for him. As he reached forward to taste his drink his shabby jacket fell open over the slight swell of his belly, the absurd monogram. I felt a swift, alien spasm of desire.

'So. Shall we begin?'

'Where?'

'Well, since you've already fucked me, perhaps we can dispense with polite conversation.'

He raised an eyebrow, rather well.

'The monogram. On your shirt? The party at the townhouse in Montmartre. I believe you know Julien? At least you went to his club to check up on me, La Lumière on the Rue Thérèse?'

He inclined his head, faintly gallant. 'Indeed.'

For a moment, neither of us spoke. I'd worked it out a few weeks ago. We'd met at the club, that night we both behaved so naughtily in the darkroom. What I couldn't work out was the sting. Until I knew exactly what he wanted, I couldn't play this. But then, we knew one another already, he and I. That dim incense-scented room, the burn of the leather on my palms, his teeth in my neck . . .

I shook myself back into the present, took a long swallow of my drink. God, I wanted a cigarette; I wanted to be able to exhale a slow plume of smoke in his eyes. 'You remember?'

'How could I forget?'

There was something absurdly unreal about this Bogart-and-Bacall routine we seemed to be pulling. Stick to the point, Judith. So what if he's already banged you months ago in some lousy swingers' club? I sat up straighter, tried for a hard, flat tone.

'You were following me, then? Because you are now, obviously.'

'No, not then. Not exactly. But it seemed a – pleasing coincidence.'

'I want to know why.'

'I should have thought that was obvious.'

'Cheap shot. Why are you following me?'

'Because you killed Cameron Fitzpatrick.'

Now I really wanted a fucking fag.

'That's absurd.'

He sat back a little, drank some water and remarked conversationally, 'I know that you killed Cameron Fitzpatrick because I saw you do it.'

For a few seconds, I truly thought I might faint. I stared at the cocktail stick spearing the pale pink rose balanced on the edge of my glass. I wished I could faint. My instinct had been right, that sudden frisson of fear, the sense that I was being watched there, back under the bridge. A rat, sure enough. A rat who scented blood.

'I have no idea what you're talking about. Please tell me, now, why you are following me.'

He reached forward and gently touched the back of my hand.

'Don't worry. Finish your drink. I haven't got a squad of cops outside. Then maybe we can go somewhere more private.'

'I don't have to listen to a word you say. You have no right –'

'No, you don't. No, I don't. But I think you will. Now finish your drink.'

I let him pay the bill and walk me through the long corridors, glowing pink like the inside of a shell, past the naff glass cases of jewellery and scarves, past the disdainful porters, to the Place Vendôme. I followed him mutely round the square, across to the arcades of Rue Castiglione, right to Concorde. It was chilly now, and my low heels were beginning to rub after so much walking. I was glad when he sat down on a bench at the locked entrance to the Tuileries.

'Take this.' He handed me his jacket; I was shivering. I let him arrange it around my shoulders, a waft of sweat breezing from the synthetic lining, my eyes fixed on the lights of a bus crawling up the Champs. I tried to light a cigarette, put the filter in my mouth. Smooth.

'So, Mademoiselle No-Name, you can call me Renaud. I'll call you Judith, unless you prefer Lauren?'

'It's my middle name, Lauren. My mother was a fan of Lauren Bacall. Cool, no?'

'OK, Judith then. Now, I'm going to talk and you're going to listen.' He took my lighter from my shaking hand and lit my fag. 'OK?'

'You speak excellent English.'

'Thank you. Now I'm going to show you a picture. That's him, right, Cameron?'

I had to squint in the traffic glow from the crossroads. He held my lighter to the screen. It was. Caught on Renaud's phone, coming down the Spanish Steps, his face dipped away from the Roman sun. I had managed not to think of his face for so long.

'You know it's him.'

'Yes, but what you don't know is that his name wasn't Cameron Fitzpatrick. It was Tommaso Bianchetti.'

All that Oirish charm.

'He was pretty good, then,' was all I said.

'Yes, he was. Very good. Irish mother, maid in a Roman hotel. Anyway, this is what I need to explain to you. Bianchetti washed money for . . . associates in Italy. He'd been doing it for years.'

'The Mafia?'

Renaud gave me a pitying look. ''Ndrangheta, Camorra . . . Only amateurs say Mafia.'

My feeling about Moncada had been right then, too. 'Excuse me.' Weirdly, I was starting to feel better.

'Your old colleague, Rupert, he didn't call Fitzpatrick. Fitzpatrick called Rupert. Nice little scheme, one he's pulled hundreds of times. Real stuff mostly, not bothered with the effort of fakes. But times were getting a little tough in Italy, and the mark-up on a fake piece was so much better. Rinse the picture and the money. That's how I got involved.'

'I thought you were working for him. For Rupert.'

'I wonder who could have told you that? We'll leave that for a minute, shall we? I was hired by an extremely angry American. Banker, Goldman Sachs. Found out that the Rothko he'd been showing off at his pad in the Hamptons was a fake. Wanted his money back. Which led me to Alonso Moncada.'

'Moncada deals fakes then?'

'Sometimes yes, sometimes no.'

'Why you?'

'What did you think I was, some old-school shamus? I chase money, for people who want to get it back quietly.'

I couldn't help glancing at his terrible shirt, the awful shoes. 'You don't look like someone who chases money.'

'Yes. And you do.'

I took that one on the chin.

'Bianchetti was one of several guys who worked for Moncada. Moncada acquires the piece for cash, provided from a small Roman bank controlled by . . . associates. Covered as a business loan. They shift it to a private client for a profit, the client can keep it as an asset or auction it legitimately. Moncada provided the funds, Bianchetti the provenance. Everyone makes money. Very neat.'

'So?'

'So I went to the gallery where my man picked up his Rothko, talked them into giving me the name of the previous owner and persuaded him – no, actually, it was a *her*, nice woman, three children – to give me Moncada. She had no idea she'd been duped either. It took a long while to track him down, and in the meantime I began to pick up Bianchetti's name, under the Fitzpatrick alias. I went to London to trace him – Bianchetti, that is – followed him to Rome, and then you pulled your little stunt – don't interrupt – and I followed you to Moncada. It was the first time I'd been able to set eyes on him. Obviously I was quite intrigued by you, too. But I didn't know what it was you'd made off with, however you did it.'

'I didn't –'

'Shut up.' He scrolled through a file on his phone, showed me another picture, myself and Moncada, apparently enjoying a pizza. I was surprised by how calm I looked in the photo.

'So then, finally, the Stubbs comes up last winter, and it has Fitzpatrick – now tragically deceased – amongst the provenances. So then I knew what you had sold to Moncada.'

'But Rupert?'

'Well, by then I was considerably more than intrigued by you. So I had a look at the police report, found your name. I guessed you'd have something to do with art. I knew you were English. So I started at the top. Two calls.'

Only two auction houses in London worth bothering about . . .

'The nice girls on reception hadn't heard of you, so I spoke to the heads of department, in turn. And came up with your old employer.'

'Go on.'

'So, I went along for a little talk.' He gave a half-smile. I hadn't noticed that I had started shaking again, but he had. He pulled the jacket more tightly around me, solicitous.

'It gave Rupert a bit of a shock when I mentioned Fitzpatrick. I told him that I had seen his department's name alongside Fitzpatrick's with the provenance of the picture. And then I asked about you. When he heard you'd been in Italy he practically exploded. He was very eager to employ me, on the side, *comme on dit*, to find you. So he showed me your picture. I needed to check you were the same girl I'd seen, naturally. And there you were. The beautiful girl from Rome. You do have an unforgettable face.'

'Thanks. How romantic. And the townhouse? What were you doing at Julien's?'

'Blind luck. A lot of people know Julien, a lot of powerful people. I like to check up on him while I'm here, and one must amuse oneself now and again, no? We are in Paris, after all, *chérie*. I'd been trying to find you in London, nothing. Your mother didn't know anymore.'

'My mother?'

'Not hard to find. Social services.'

I swallowed in shock. 'Was she . . . was she OK?'

'You mean was she drunk? No. Just fine. I didn't say anything to worry her. But then I drew a blank. You see, your flatmates just said you'd sent a cheque for the rent, gone abroad. Soo and Pai. Nice quiet girls, the medical students. They suggested that you enjoyed going to parties. Not their sort of thing. Very much mine though. I was over here – just catching up with some friends for the weekend – and there you were again.'

'As you said, what a coincidence.'

'You perhaps need to be a bit more discreet. In your . . . amusements.'

'What about Leanne?'

'Ah. Leanne. Well, your face is very memorable, as I said. I'd seen your photo in London, seen someone who looked very much like you in Paris, but the lighting at Julien's parties is always so . . . considerate.'

He switched to French.

'*Encore*, I needed to be certain that it was the same girl. Julien didn't have a name for you, except Lauren, but he gave me the details of several professional girls who share your – er – proclivities. Girls with international reputations, to use the old-fashioned phrase. Again, it took me a while, I had to track down each of the girls individually and eventually one recognised you. I found your friend Ashley at your other former place of employment.'

'The Gstaad Club.'

'*Précisément.* And then Rupert seems to have found your friend Leanne about the same time, in the very same place. It suited him to use her – he didn't want your connection with British Pictures coming up any more than it had to. I came here with Leanne. She gave me a photo from the club to show Julien, to check. It was hardly a betrayal – we were both looking for you. She just didn't know the reason.'

I didn't dare to say another word. Fucking moronic selfies: the two of us snapped on her phone on a quiet night, gurning for the camera.

'You don't need to worry about them, Judith. Forget about Rupert. He's got too much to lose; he made a dumb call on something that was bigger than he knew. Leanne was just some junkie semi-hooker, right?'

'Was?'

'Judith, please. It wasn't very polite of you to leave a dead body in a hotel room I was paying for. Nice touch, though, leaving the dealer's number. The police were pretty happy to have him.'

'The police? I thought you said –'

'I said I wasn't a cop. That doesn't mean I don't have friends at the *préfecture*. I need them, in my line. How do you think I got your address?'

'I thought you followed me.'

'Form. Crossing the t's, that's all. Isn't that what you say?' He looked pleased with the idiom. 'They had plenty of questions for your Stéphane. I told my friend that Leanne was just some girl I'd picked up, didn't know her, didn't know she was using. They'll find her through the consulate eventually, ship her back. Don't sweat.' Another English phrase. I could hear his accent come through.

'Anyway, Rupert. I think he just wanted to keep an eye on you, make sure you weren't talking. You might even find a few doors open to you now, if you wanted to go back to London.'

I shook my head numbly. All that time. Over and over, I had thought myself so clever, and Cleret had only been waiting for me to stumble into his sights. I forced myself to speak.

'What do you want?'

'I want Moncada. I want my client's money and I want my fee. That's all.'

'You know who he is, where he is. Why not just find him?'

'I want him here, in Paris. He's too dangerous in Rome.'

'So what can I do?'

'Sell him a painting, of course.'

'And then?'

'You deliver Moncada, you're in the clear. We can even split the profit on your deal with him.'

I thought about that for a while.

'But if I do, then won't Moncada and his "associates" come after me? They won't want to pay up for the Rothko, the one that belonged to your banker. And you say he's dangerous.'

I hated the way I was feeling: childish, desperate, out of control.

'Who would you rather have looking for you – them or the police? Anyway, I can arrange the details for you. I know a guy in Amsterdam, he's good with passports. You'll have to disappear for a while, leave Paris. But I don't think you have a lot of choice, do you?'

I thought about *that* for a while. I could protest, deny what I hadn't even admitted; I could run. As I said, I don't like games, unless they're ones I can win. He didn't seem to care about Cameron or Leanne, at least not if I did what he wanted.

'So you want Moncada here? That's all? And I walk?'

'I need to find a way of speaking to him in private. They're wary, these people. You're getting the hang of this, Judith.'

He whisked the jacket off my shoulders as he stood. He looked different to me now, contained, powerful even.

'We'll go to your place.'

'My place?'

'Do you think I'm going to let you out of my sight? I can even run round the Luxembourg if I have to. As long as it takes.'

Renaud had his things in a tourist hotel in the Latin Quarter. We tried to flag down a couple of cabs as we walked, but in true Parisian form none of them wanted to earn any money. My feet felt like bleeding stumps by the time we arrived in the kebab-stinking alleyway. He made me go up the four flights of dingily carpeted stairs with him while he collected his bags. I looked out of the window at a picturesque fire escape and a shamble of satellite dishes as he rummaged in the tiny bathroom.

'The rooftops of Paris,' I said, for something to say. He ignored me, but as my shoulders began to heave I felt his hand on my back. I turned and pressed my face to that damned shirt front, and he patted at me with that clumsy necessary tenderness that men show to weeping women. I cried for a long time, cried properly with my throat full of tears and snot, until I heard a strange noise. It seemed to come from outside, a keening, a baby maybe, or mating cats. Then I realised it was me, howling. I cried out all the tears I hadn't allowed to fall since that day in London when Rupert had sent me to see Colonel Morris, and I was curious, even as I sobbed and gasped and writhed, at the alien sensation which had, finally, allowed me to let go. It was relief. Just for once, at last, someone else was in charge. For a few moments I even thought that it could end there, like that, with me molten and grateful in his arms, and occasionally, later, I would wish that it had. But, of course, it didn't.

24

I had hardly ever woken up with a man. Few heads had ever lain beneath my faithless arm till morning. At 5 a.m., opening my eyes in my flat, I experienced a moment of bewildered panic about the hump under the duvet next to me. Steve? Jean-Christophe? Jan? Not Matteo. Renaud. I could smell last night's drinks seeping from my skin, but for once I didn't haul myself straight out of bed, I turned on my back and lay there, listening to his thick breathing. I was sore and sticky and there was a tinny pain below my right ear where he'd slapped me as we fucked. Because of course we'd fucked. Not before he'd relieved me of my passport and credit cards to make sure I really wasn't going anywhere, but then against the closed door, tripping over his bags, me wriggling awkwardly out of my tight jeans, him on his knees, his face drenched from my already sodden and gaping cunt, his hand inside me, then on the floor, his teeth buried in the hollow of my throat. Then somehow we'd crawled to the bed, both of us naked now, and he'd smeared that beautiful cock and my exposed arse with some of my priceless body oil and battered into me, one hand gripping tight on my neck, the other stroking my clit in rhythm with his cock until my mouth found the soft hollow of his palm and I tasted the iron of his blood while he split and salved me. Nice, although the sheets were going to be a write-off.

He turned on his side, his belly shifting against my hip. Odd, given my preference for handsome men, but there was something about the heft of it, its unexpected firmness, that

I found erotic. Me and fat men. I lay on my back and listened. Where was Rage? Where was that little voice, teasing me, telling me to do it, do it now? Nothing. It was – peaceful. My eyes slid sideways and met his, creased with sleep and smiles.

'Open your legs.'

His breath was sour in my ear, but somehow I didn't mind that, either.

'I'm a mess.'

'Open. Good. Wider.'

I stretched my thighs until I felt the tendons strain. He opened me, manoeuvred himself heavily on top, his face on my shoulder, guided himself slowly inside. My cunt gave a wet slurp, greedy, but he didn't rush, just worked the length of his cock deeper, a centimetre at a time. His finger stabbed sharply into my arse. I gasped, but felt my muscles relaxing, already familiar. I was glued to his body by his weight, a leaf preserved in blotting paper, the muscles of my limbs twitching in fluttering arpeggios. I worked my hand between us, squeezed the head of his cock where it entered me, my clit and the lips of my cunt swollen against my palm, their heat spreading in waves, penetrating my guts.

'Harder.'

'No.'

'Please?'

'No.'

He raised his head as I caught him with my muscles, stalling.

'Relax, I'm going to make you come.'

Prettier in French. *Je vais te faire jouir*.

'Lick my face.'

I let my tongue loll softly from my mouth, licked his jaw, his cheeks, wetting him with my saliva.

'Yes, like that. Like that, my bitch.'

I was so wet, I could feel my own juice streaming over my aching thighs. It began, like a ripple of wind across water, my body stroked by a shimmering wave, swirling around the red need between my legs. I was nothing; I was only flesh where it was touched by his cock. My eyelids juddered shut, open, shut, I could see his own orgasm begin to shake his pale torso, his hand wrapped in a tight skein of my hair. He growled, deep from his lungs, threw his body back, the veins in his arms pulsing blue neon, and I let myself fall deeper, deeper into my own ecstasy, drowning in the gouts of his sperm.

He collapsed on top of me, shuddering, panting. I held him for a moment, feeling the sweat cooling under the hair on his back.

'Why are you laughing?'

I let my head bounce on the pillows. 'Because – because . . . like, wow!'

'Wow? Like?'

'OK. You're an exceptionally talented man. Surprisingly so.'

'Slut. What time is it? Fuck, that's indecent.'

'I wake up early.' But he was gathering himself to sleep again. It was a clever test. Without saying a word, he was giving me a chance to get away, but where was I going to run to? He would find me, and we both knew it. If I skipped out now, he could simply turn me in. So I hopped up, showered him off me, pulled on jeans and a sweater, grabbed my purse and ran down the stairs into rain-washed Paris. The boulangerie up the street was just opening. I bought *croissants au beurre* and a pot of salted-caramel jam, milk, orange juice. The concierge was grumbling into life in the lodge; she looked up as I smiled good morning. I made coffee, balanced spoons and knives on plates, then carried it through and curled up on the bed, watching him. There was something so soothing in the rise and fall of his chest that I must have slept again, too; at least when we woke the sun was in the courtyard and the coffee was cold.

That was the last time we were separated for three weeks. Renaud meant it when he said he wasn't going to let me out of his sight – he even made me leave my phone behind when I was in the bathroom, and took it with him when he used it. He put the flat keys under his pillow every night, though they often got dislodged. Sometimes I'd tuck them back before he woke so he wouldn't feel bad. I thought of asking him why he didn't trust me, but that was obviously a stupid question. The first few mornings, I had work to do. After he'd staggered round the Luxo with me, in an ancient Nike T-shirt and my largest pair of track pants, he'd read the papers while I checked lots and prices online. I considered Urs Fischer and Alan Gussow, but Renaud thought I ought to go for something more blue chip. I couldn't afford Bacon, but Twombly and Calder had pieces within the range of a million which Renaud specified. Finally I found a Gerhard Richter – more of a Richterette really, a small 1988 canvas in crimson and charcoal – in the autumn contemporary show at what I'd used to call the other place. Aside from my Fontana, it would be Gentileschi's first major acquisition. But I hesitated. Maybe Moncada would be more likely to go for something strictly classic.

I explained to Renaud that I wanted some advice, told him about Dave and his passion for the eighteenth century. 'Can I get him to send me some catalogues over? Recent sales?'

'Why?'

'Because I want to know how things are moving. In theory, I'm going to make a profit on this.'

'*We're* going to make a profit. Half and half.'

'Of course. Well, I just want to check, before I bid on the Richter.'

He tossed me my phone. 'Go ahead.'

'Frankie, it's Judith.'

'Judith! Oh my God, hi, how are you?'

'I'm great, thanks. You?'

'Oh Judith, it's so strange that you called today. I've just got engaged!'

'That's wonderful! I'm thrilled for you, Frankie, congratulations. Who's the lucky chap?'

'He's called Henry. He's in the Guards. We're going to live in Kenya. Army wife, can you believe it?'

'Is he heaven?'

'Well, Mummy's delighted.'

I could see Renaud looking at me quizzically. Time to stop with the Jane Austen stuff.

'Frankie, remember ages ago I asked you a favour?'

'Oh my God, I know. Wasn't it awful about Cameron Fitzpatrick? It was in all the papers.'

'Yes, I know, awful. And after you'd been so kind, too, helping me to try for a job with him. God, I didn't mean it like that –'

'That's OK, I know.'

'Listen, Frankie, I wondered if I could trouble you for something else?'

'OK.'

'You remember Dave, Dave who used to work in the warehouse?'

'Yes, he left yonks ago.'

'Do you still have an address for him on file?'

'I could find it.'

'Frankie, could you text it to me, please? I'm sorry to bother you again, I really don't want you to get into trouble, but –'

'No probs. Anyway, I don't care, I'm off to Africa.' She lowered her voice. 'They're all wankers here anyway.'

Wankers. Go Frankie.

I spent a bit of time on the computer while I waited for Frankie's text, ordering two copies of a book from Amazon I thought Dave would like. One for him, one for me. They turned up next day; thank goodness for Prime. Then Renaud walked me down to the bank and handed me my card. I mistyped my code on purpose.

'The catalogues will cost a couple of hundred, but the machine's bust. Will I just pop in?'

He waited outside, smoking, while I went in to the counter where I wrote myself a cheque for 10,000 euro. I used my *carte de séjour* for ID. They were a bit sniffy about handing it over, but I pointed out that it was my money, and I took it in 500-euro notes, most of which I stuffed in my bra Then we walked over to Rue de Sèvres, as I explained to Renaud I wanted to send a birthday present to my old colleague's wife. Not unreasonable. I wasn't sure what kind of scent Dave's wife would like, so I settled for Chanel No. 5, a gift box from Le Bon Marché with perfume, body lotion and soap. I popped to the store's powder room and lurked in a cubicle while I retrieved the cash and put it underneath the plastic mouldings for the bottles. I added a hastily scribbled note with my Paris address along with some page references for the books. At the bottom, I wrote 'Mercenary fee pending'. Renaud accompanied me to the post office, where I put the gift in a jiffy bag and had the package expressed to London. It turned out Dave lived up in Finsbury. I had to pray that he would understand.

In the evenings, we ate dinner together, another first. Sometimes we'd walk up to the Rue Mouffetard, Renaud solemnly carrying a straw basket, and buy ingredients to cook. It turned out Renaud could do fantastic risotto. I bought him a set of Japanese ceramic knives so he could prepare melting *osso buco*. He'd pour me a glass of wine while we chopped in our pyjamas and afterwards we'd finish the bottle and listen to music. Sometimes we went out, to the smaller, less obvious places we both preferred. I found I liked having company; maybe he liked it too. He told me a little about his work, about the calls he made to New York and LA while I read through the afternoons. It was apparently less dramatic than it seemed, chasing money. Mostly a waiting game. Testify. Often, though, we just chatted about articles we'd read in the papers – I was trying to wean him off *Le Figaro* – or about the latest sex scandals amongst French politicians now that the country's media was finally getting up to kiss 'n' tell sleb speed. A couple of times we went to the cinema, and he held my hand in the dark. One evening, though, he asked if I'd like to go to La Lumière. I thought about that.

'Or Regrattier if you don't fancy seeing Julien?'

'You know your stuff.'

'But of course, Mademoiselle No-Name.'

I smiled and let my hair fall across my cheekbone, twisted my wine glass.

'Do you know, I don't think I do? I'm . . . fine. Fine as we are.'

'We?'

I backtracked. 'For the present. Until you've talked to Moncada.'

Renaud reached over and gently pushed the fallen hair behind my ear. 'That's OK, Judith. I might like "we".'

Another time, while we were slurping Vietnamese in a tiny café in Belleville, he asked me about Rome. I didn't need to ask what he was referring to.

'I thought you said you saw.'

'I saw enough. I saw you go under the bridge. I saw you come out in your jogging gear. The rest I got from the police report. Inspector da Silva.'

'Renaud, you total cunt.'

He mimed a huge shrug. 'Saaarry.'

'But you speak Italian?'

'*Certo*. Well, a bit.'

I sucked a forkful of grilled pork noodles, considering.

'Why didn't you tell them – the police?'

'You were my way to get to Moncada. Besides, I explained, I'm not a cop. And I was – interested. Interested in you, in how it would come out.'

I wanted to tell him everything. I wanted to tell him about James, Leanne, all of it. I wanted to tell him about Dave, that I'd done it because Dave had lost his job, but that wouldn't have been true, and somehow that mattered. I wanted to tell him about being on the outside, about feeling trapped, because no matter how brilliant or beautiful you were, there was no place in the world for someone like me. But that wasn't true, either.

'It wasn't the money,' I said. 'The money was a by-product.'

'Revenge?' he smiled.

'Nah, way too simple. Not revenge. Not interesting.'

'Interesting. I think, that is, I –'. He broke off. Was he trying to trick me, by offering a confession of his own? Unlikely he'd try anything so obvious. It was his turn to take a contemplative slurp.

'So what, then?' he asked again.

Because I could, I suppose. Because I needed to see if I could. Why does there have to be a logic? It's like sex, people always wanting reasons, to know how you bloody well *feel*.

'Can I tell you some other time?'

'Sure. Any time.'

Dave came through with the catalogues, a glossy brick that must have cost a fortune to post. He'd sweetly included a cigar box containing three Wispa bars, remembering that I was always a sucker for hydrogenated vegetable fat. I felt all warm and glowy when I opened it up. In the end, though, thinking of Steve, I told Renaud I'd decided to go for the Richter: contemporary was more of a cert with new money. I had half a mind to go over to London for the sale, take old Frankie out for a celebratory drink, even, and Rupert could go screw himself, but Renaud thought it would be unwise to use my own passport.

'You'll have a new one, soon. I'm arranging it. When I've seen Moncada.'

I bought a copy of *Condé Nast Traveller* and thought about my future. Montenegro looked promising. Or Norway. Cold – suitable for murderers.

'Why can't I just stay here?'

'Don't be dumb, Judith.'

'What about my bank accounts?'

'Gentileschi will just have to take on a new employee.'

I settled on a phone bid, using the company name. We went to the FNAC to buy some headphones and Renaud set up my computer back at the flat so he could listen in. If I got the picture, it could be shipped in a couple of weeks. To compensate for missing the auction in person, I dressed for the occasion. My Chanel two-piece, black, with an artful leather camellia on the hip pocket, stockings, classic Pigalle 120s in patent leather, hair severely pinned up, red lipstick which didn't really suit me. I put crotchless Seventies-style Bensimon panties underneath. I felt a bit of an idiot, all that to sit at my own dining table, but it was worth it for the look Renaud gave me when I strolled out of the bathroom.

I'd applied online to bid, in Gentileschi's name, and received a number, 38, for the telephone auction. We'd bought a chuck-away pay-as-you-go phone for the sale, the bank details were what would matter if I got the Richter. At eleven o'clock the House called to say the sale had begun. I had a pad and a pen in front of me, I didn't know what for, just to make it seem businesslike. I'd been allowed to watch a good few sales at the House, enjoying the showmanship of the experts and the senior auctioneer, the vice-chairman of the House, and I tried to imagine the blond wood room, the tense stillness of the bidders. At 11.42 the cell rang again; the Richter was up. Renaud hunched forward over the computer, his hair a parrot's quiff under the headphones. I wondered which of the snotty girls I'd seen in the passage way of the other place was managing the Gentileschi bid I had a childish urge to shout down the line that it was me, Judith Rashleigh, but of course I didn't. I even put a little Fransh accent into my voice.

The starting price was 400K. The Richter quickly raised four point five, five, five five, then six. I stayed in. The bids continued rising in increments of fifty.

'I have 750,000 against you, number 38. Will you bid?'

Renaud gave me a sharp nod. 'Eight hundred.' He took my hand.

'Very good.'

I couldn't help it, I was excited.

'Number 38? I have 850,000 pounds. Will you bid?'

'Nine hundred.'

Renaud was sweating, his shirt sticking to his back, his palm slippery in mine, carried along by the tension. I sat straighter, poised and cool in my perfect suit. Down the line I could faintly hear the auctioneer's voice asking for any further bids. Pause.

'We have 950,000 against you, madam. Will you bid?'

Fuck it. 'A million. A million pounds.' We were into the straight now, the jockeys bobbing like monkeys, brandishing their whips for the last furlong. I was rushed.

'I'm going to come,' I mouthed at Renaud.

I knew she would be nodding to the podium, raising one finger.

'One million and fifty thousand pounds, number 38. Will you bid?'

'One point one.'

Renaud was scowling, making a cut sign at his neck. I ignored him; I was crazed.

'Very good.'

The handler was holding out her phone, so I could hear 'Ladies and gentleman, I have one point one million pounds.

Going once –' I squeezed my eyes shut, held my breath, my fingers shaking around the handset.

'Congratulations, madam.'

I pressed the little red button, carefully, let my head fall back and unpinned my hair.

'We've got it.'

'Good girl.'

I lit a cigarette and practically sucked it down in one. Then I went and sat on his knee and rested my brow against his.

'I can't believe I just did that. I can't believe it,' I whispered.

'Why not?' I liked that about Renaud, that unlike every other man I'd ever met he was genuinely interested when I said that I felt something.

'I just bought a million-pound picture. Me. It seems impossible, crazy.'

'Yet you've done much more difficult things.'

The high dissipated as suddenly as it had risen. I stalked a few irritable paces about the room. 'Do you have to keep going on about that? Can't you just leave it alone? I'm doing what you want, aren't I?'

He came towards me and crouched down by my feet, the absurd headphones still ruffling his hair as he pulled me close.

'I didn't mean that. You forget, I know a lot about you. I've seen where you grew up, I've seen what you must have had to do to get out. I suppose what I'm saying is that I admire you, Judith.'

'Really? You admire me?'

'I said it, don't make me flatter you. Now, I think we should go and celebrate your first major acquisition. What's your very favourite thing to eat in Paris?'

'Lobster salad at Laurent.'

'Then I'll get changed. I'll even wear decent clothes. I've got a tie, can you believe it? And mademoiselle shall have her lobster.'

But I'd already slipped off my skirt. The lips of my cunt were fat with desire, pulsing through the slit in the black mesh panties. I perched up on the table and opened my legs.

'Or we could dine at home?'

He pushed a finger inside me, so abruptly that I gasped, withdrew it slowly, a gossamer strand of cum stretching between us, brought it to his mouth.

'We could dine at home.'

25

I'd debated about having the Richter shipped to my own address, and eventually decided in favour. Gentileschi was registered, my money was clean, and what I did with my own property after I received it was nobody's business. It was a standard sale; there was no reason for Rupert to look up the buyer of a picture he hadn't even sold. It would appear in the trades, in the account of the sale, but there was no reason to connect my company to me personally, even if the name Gentileschi did tweak a memory. Besides, Rupert had other things to worry about, as he was down a cool half-million since his game with Cameron hadn't paid off. Renaud agreed. Once the paperwork arrived, expressed from London after the sale, I was ready to contact Moncada. Another throwaway phone, a list of numbers from Renaud's notebook.

'How do you know these will work for Moncada?'

'One of them will. I told you, I have good contacts.'

'Yeah yeah. You and your famous contacts. But he won't call me back on this thing. We'll have to find a payphone.'

'Good girl.'

'I found you can learn most things on the job, if you concentrate.'

We took the Métro over to the eighteenth arrondissement, found a call shack on the Rue de la Goutte d'Or where immigrants could buy cards to speak to their families among piles of plantain and limes and stacks of cheap African headcloths. Renaud bought a card and waited in line for the phone while I started on the list. The first two numbers were dead, the third was answered and hung up, the fourth responded '*Pronto*' but hung up again as soon as I spoke. I tried two more. Useless.

'What can we do if he doesn't respond? Is this all you've got?'

Renaud had reached the last place in the queue. A lady with a complicated fan of melon-printed cotton on her head swung her enormous arse at him as though she was brushing off a tick, then went back to shouting in impenetrable Creole patois. The shop smelled of acrid sweat and treacle, a game show blared above the counter, half-watched by the five or six people waiting behind Renaud for the phone.

'This could take forever. And even if we get him, this phone will be occupied till Christmas.'

'Just keep trying.'

This was pathetic. Did he actually want to get it done? I called over and over again until the mobile's credit was exhausted. We went out for a coffee and a dry-mouthed cigarette, bought another phone, started again. More coffee, more cigarettes; my head ached with exhaust fumes and nicotine. I called until I didn't need to look at the paper anymore.

'Renaud, this is useless.'

In his horrible jacket and shoes he fitted right in on the Goutte d'Or. We must have looked ridiculous, a pair of small-time hustlers from a film student's patternbook. By five o'clock, we'd been there for three hours, Renaud had given up his place in the queue so many times that even the game-show-watching cashier had started to peer at us.

'I want to go home. I want a shower.'

For the first time since he had stepped into my cab at the Hôtel de Ville, Renaud looked ruffled, uncontrolled.

'Wait here. I'll make a call.'

'Sure,' I said wearily. I tried to watch his lips through a window display of Hello Kitty phone cases as he placed the call but he squared his back to me in the street.

'Try these.'

Two more numbers. The first one was dead. The second one rang, and rang.

'*Pronto*.' A woman's voice.

'I need to speak to Signor Moncada. Judith Rashleigh. I worked for Cameron Fitzpatrick.'

Dialling tone. I took a few breaths, called back. 'Please give Signor Moncada this number. I'll be waiting.' I gave Renaud a quick nod. 'Maybe now.'

Renaud stepped forward, removed the handset from an etiolated Somali man in a nylon robe and hung it up.

'What the fuck?'

Renaud was opening his jacket, pulling a badge from the pocket.

'Police.'

For a second, it was as though all the oxygen had been vacuumed from the room. Then the whole crowd scrambled for the door, knocking over an open sack of rice and a box of fake Ray-Bans. The cashier stood up, two huge fists bunched with rings on the counter.

'Listen, monsieur, you can't just come in here –'

'You. Sit down and shut up. Better still, get in the back and stuff your fat face with fried chicken until I say so, or I'll ask for your fucking papers too, OK? And then I'll send you back to whatever fucking hole you come from faster than you can say "racial discrimination", you fat fuck. If your smashed mouth still works well enough to speak. Clear?'

We were left alone. The rice crunched under Renaud's feet as he flipped the sign on the door to 'Closed'.

'There was no need to speak to him like that. And what's with the badge?' I muttered in English.

'Spare me. This is important. And the badge –'.

'Yeah, I know. Your famous friend at the *préfecture*.'

'Just wait by the phone.'

Renaud lit a fag.

'It's forbidden to smoke in here!' the cashier called defiantly from behind the plastic shower curtain that served as a divider.

'Want one?' he asked me, ignoring him.

'No, thanks. Stop behaving like a dickhead, why don't you? You're acting like you are a fucking cop.'

'Sorry. I'm just nervous. There's a lot of money in this for me. I'll apologise to him, I really will.'

'Whatever. Could you just sit down or something? Read a magazine, let me concentrate.'

Renaud made a half-hearted attempt to scoop the rice into the sack, set the sunglasses to rights and took the cashier's chair behind the counter, turning off the TV. We waited in silence for twenty minutes or so, until I was already planning where I'd hang the Richter, when it rang.

'Signor Moncada? Judith Rashleigh.'

'*Vi sento.*'

He wasn't giving me anything more. I launched into my little speech in Italian – God knows I'd had time to rehearse it. I mentioned that I had something I thought he might like to buy, gave details of the sale so he could check it, suggested we meet in Paris if he thought it would be suitable. The real thing. No mention of money, no mention of Fitzpatrick.

'Give me your number. I'll call you back.'

It took another hour before he returned the call. We didn't really have to hang around in the shop anymore, but by that time I'd sent Renaud out to McDonalds, and he and the cashier had set aside their differences and were chatting like pals, sluicing down mega Diet Cokes and watching a football match. The little phone buzzed in my hand. So tense with sweat that I almost dropped it, I waved the cashier frantically back behind the curtain, cupping my hand behind my ear to signal to Renaud that he could listen in.

'No need. My Italian's not that good,' he whispered in English.

'Have you a price for me, Signorina Rashleigh?'

'As you will have seen, I acquired the piece for one point one sterling. That's approximately one point five euro. The price I require is one point eight euro.'

If he bought that, my half share of the 300K euro difference would amount to about 100K sterling. A fair price for the piece.

Silence on the line.

'My estimate is that the piece will be worth over two million euro in six months, more in a year.'

I wondered how much Moncada really knew about the legitimate art market. If he was knowledgeable, he would know that this was a genuinely good deal, based on the way Richter held value and the general, steadily climbing prices for post-war art.

'Very good.'

I was rather impressed with him.

'As before, then?'

'As before.'

I ran through my suggestion as to how we should meet, but he didn't speak again. When I'd finished I let the silence hang for a breath, then said goodbye, using the polite, formal *lei*. I remembered my fear of Moncada, back in Como, but it seemed irrational now. Moncada would soon be Renaud's problem. I'd be up on the money for the Richter, if it worked, and, besides, at the meeting Renaud would be there to protect me. Or if his affection wasn't equal to that, he would certainly want to protect his fee for getting the Rothko back.

All I had to do was wait for the picture to arrive from London, hand it over, do the business with the bank codes and it would be finished. Renaud would disappear and I'd be free. I wasn't about to let myself get sentimental about the thought of him being gone, but there was a part of me, perhaps, that hoped the delivery wouldn't be too quick. There was nothing wrong in wanting just a few more days.

As it was, I found myself quite busy while we waited for the Richter to arrive, dismantling my life in Paris like a film running backwards. I found a specialist art moving company to take my paintings and the antiques; they would be held in temperature-controlled storage in Gentileschi's name in a depository just outside Brussels. Reluctantly, I gave notice on my flat and called a second set of movers who would come to pick up the rest of my stuff when I was ready and transport it to a rented warehouse space near the Porte de Vincennes. When the guy turned up with the packing cases and bubble wrap, the concierge asked where I was going. I felt that I'd rather sunk in her estimation since taking up living in sin with such a scruffy character as Renaud, who definitely lowered the *bon chic bon genre* tone of the building, but she couldn't bear not to be up on the gossip. I told her I was going to Japan for my work. It sounded as good a place as any.

'And monsieur?'

I shrugged. 'You know. Men.'

'You'll miss Paris, mademoiselle?'

'Yes, I'll miss it very much.'

Perhaps because she asked that, I persuaded Renaud to become a tourist for a few days. Like anyone who lives in a city, I'd never seen it through a stranger's eyes. So we went up the Eiffel Tower and out to Père Lachaise to push our way through the crowds of emo-ghosts at Jim Morrison's grave, to the Conciergerie to see Marie Antoinette's cell, to the Chagall murals at the Opéra Garnier, to a Vivaldi concert at the Sainte-Chapelle. We went to the Louvre to say *au revoir* to La Gioconda and walked in the gardens at the Musé Rodin. When I'd been a student I'd sneered patronisingly at the Japanese tourists who saw nothing of the art works beyond the perimeters of their Nikons; now they held up iPads to film the city's treasures, so all they saw with their own eyes was the blank grey of an Apple tablet. Shuffling zombies don't deserve to see beautiful things. We bought disgusting kebabs at Saint-Michel, smearing them down our throats as we sat on the fountain, mugged for pictures in the Métro photo booth. We even took a *bateau mouche*, eating a surprisingly nice dinner of onion soup and tournedos Rossini as we chugged beneath the illuminated bridges while a slim Algerian girl in a sequined red cocktail frock crooned Edith Piaf. Renaud held my hand and nuzzled my neck and though I could see we must appear as odd a couple as any of the horrors I had seen during my stay on the *Mandarin*, I didn't mind. I did ask him about the affected monogram which still adhered stubbornly to all his limp shirts.

'I do them myself, actually. I'm very good at sewing.'

'How so? Did you do time, on the mailbags?'

'Funny. My dad was – is – a tailor. He's still working, even though he's in his eighties.'

'Where?'

'Where what?'

'Where did you grow up?'

We were eating a *plateau de fruits de mer* at the Bar à Huîtres on the Rue de Rennes. Renaud fanned at the dry ice billowing from the plate and swallowed a green-tinged Oleron with shallot vinegar before he answered.

'Tiny little town, you wouldn't have heard of it. What we call a hole in the arse of nowhere. *La France profonde*.'

I peeled a langoustine. 'So how did you come to do what you do? It's not the kind of job you can exactly train for. And you know piss about pictures, anyway.'

'I don't just do pictures. I told you – I find money that has gone missing. Corporate stuff, mostly, managers who've had their hands in the till. I studied business at university, spent a couple of years at an accountancy firm in London.'

'Ugh.'

'Exactly. I suppose I fell into this because I wanted to be something else. Like you, Judith.'

'What makes you think we're so alike?' I said it teasingly, fishing for a compliment, I suppose, but he reached through the oyster graveyard and took my hand.

'Judith. What makes you do it?'

'Do what?'

'The sex stuff. Julien's place, the clubs. That.'

I swallowed my last mouthful of zinc and sea mist and stood up. 'Get the bill and I'll tell you.'

I didn't speak as we walked along the boulevard and when we came to the Rue de Sèvres I found a bench, lit a cigarette, took his hand.

'You've seen my mother? I mean, you could see what she's like?'

'Yes.'

'So, well, usual stuff. I was dumped at my grandmother's half the time. Drink, men in and out. "Uncles" for a week or a month. Apparently it's classic, these types. They shack up with the mother, weak, vulnerable, needy, so they can go after the daughter. The kind of thing you see in the papers all the time.'

'Or like Nabokov?'

'Nothing so stylish. So there was one, he seemed pretty decent at first, he had a job, truck driver, treated my mum OK. But then he started to wait for me after school, offer me a lift home in his big exciting lorry. It was better than the bus, I was always getting beaten up on the bus, and he'd have sweets. Pear drops – you know, boiled sweets. I still can't face them. And then, well, he'd suggest we took a little drive. We had these blue school uniforms, short pleated skirt, tie and navy gym knickers underneath. He'd ask me to undo my pigtails and push up my skirt. I thought that if I didn't do what he said he'd leave my mum, and she would blame me, and she'd start on the drink again. So I let him.'

'God. I'm so, so sorry. You poor thing.'

I buried my face in his chest, and after a moment my shoulders started to tremble. He stroked my hair, dropped a kiss on the edge of my brow.

'So what happened?'

My face was muffled in the cheap cloth of his jacket. There was something reassuring, now, about the smell of its gathered sweat.

'I couldn't stand it anymore. So I took a kitchen knife, one morning, and I-I –'

I collapsed against him, out of control. I couldn't stifle it any longer. It took him a good couple of minutes to realise I was laughing.

'Judith!'

'Oh, for fuck's sake, Renaud, were you going for it? His filthy work-callused hands on my dainty pre-pubescent thighs? Oh God.'

I wiped the tears from my face and looked at him squarely.

'Look, my mum is a drunk and I like fucking, OK? I like fucking. End of. Now take me home to bed.'

He tried to smile, but he couldn't quite manage it. But when we got back to the flat, and I put on my white cotton knickers and we played a game, he liked that. He liked that a whole lot. Later, he worked a finger up my arse and held it to his nose.

'You smell of oysters. Try?'

I breathed the scent on his hand and it was true.

'I didn't know that happened.'

For real, I didn't. I licked his finger to taste the clean scent of the sea, inside myself.

26

And then it was Richter day. Renaud was withdrawn and tetchy, mooching round the flat, fiddling aimlessly. He was making me anxious, so I suggested a walk. We trailed around the smart shops in St Germain. I said that he would be able to afford some decent gear soon, but he didn't smile.

When I asked him what was the matter, he said that he was just nervous about the meeting.

'You're not the one who's going to be sleeping with the fishes,' I pointed out.

'Judith, shut up. You don't know what you're talking about.'

'What do you mean? I'm doing what you want, aren't I? You're the one who says there's no risk. For you, at least.'

'You always have to think you know everything. That you can get by just by knowing stuff, like they taught at your snobby university.'

'Sorry,' I answered humbly. I might have added that it takes something more than intelligence to act intelligently, but there wasn't the time for a philosophical discussion. His face softened, he put an arm round my shoulder.

'Nothing's going to happen to you,' he reassured me. I could have pointed out that we wouldn't have got this far if consequences had been an issue for me, but it didn't seem like the time to mention that, either. I sensed that trying to calm me down was making him feel better, so I asked if Moncada really wouldn't care about Cameron's fate.

'Look. Cosa Nostra distributes information on a need-to-know basis. It's safer if an operative carries out orders by communicating only with those directly above or below him in the chain of command.'

'So Moncada will just get on with the job?'

'Exactly. And his job is to acquire pictures with dirty money and sell them on so that money is clean.'

'I guess death is just an occupational hazard?'

He kissed me softly on the mouth. 'Yes, you might say that, *chérie*.'

I had arranged to see Moncada outside the Flore at seven. I got there a little early in case I had to wait for one of the always-crowded tables outside. I was astonished, looking back, at how incredibly naive – amateur, in Renaud's words – I had been when I had gone to him with the Stubbs. For all the suspicions aroused by my research in the hotel in Rome, I'd still been possessed of the confidence of ignorance. Now I knew for sure what Moncada was, I knew that he would be watching me, alert to the potential of a trap. Before, it hadn't occurred to me to fear him; now, despite the calmness I had affected to Renaud, I was terrified. I told myself that business was business, that even if Moncada knew I had been involved in Cameron's erasure, my product was still good. But if he thought I was dicking him about? Severed limbs and stabbing was for the boys; they probably had something especially Byzantine for women.

I had dressed casually: flats, a black sweater, a Chloé pea coat, jeans, a silk scarf, a new Miu Miu tote bag containing my computer, my freshly printed Gentileschi business cards and the paperwork for the Richter. I set my phone on the table where he would be able to see that I wasn't touching it, ordered a Kir Royal and flicked through a copy of *Elle*. Moncada was late. I couldn't stop glancing at my watch as I tried to concentrate on yet another piece advising me on how to shift those last stubborn five kilos. The only time I'd ever wanted to lose weight, I'd simply stopped eating for a week. That seemed to work fine. Seven thirty. Where was he? Why didn't *Elle* have an article on why women spend half their lives waiting for men? Even with the heaters, I was getting cold. I was lighting yet another cigarette when I saw him crossing St Germain in front of Brasserie Lipp. I only recognised him by the huge sunglasses, absurd for evening. He pulled out the chair opposite me, set down a black leather briefcase and leaned forward, brushing awkwardly at my cheek, close enough for me to smell his Vetiver cologne.

'*Buona sera*.'

'*Buona sera*.'

The waiter appeared. I ordered another Kir and Moncada accepted a gin and tonic. I talked doggedly about the weather until the glasses were set down. Sometimes it's an advantage to be English.

'So, you have it?'

I looked down at the creamy quilted leather of my bag. 'Not here, obviously. At my hotel, very close by. Everything as we discussed?'

'*Certo*.'

He left a few notes on the waiter's saucer and we set off for the Place de l'Odéon. Renaud had booked a room, cash in advance, in a pretty pink hotel on the square, the doorway surrounded by fairy lights. It looked enchanting in the dusk. I'd somehow forgotten it was nearly Christmas. The lift was uncomfortably small, and it didn't help that much of it was occupied by the unacknowledged bulk of Cameron Fitzpatrick's ghost. Moncada clearly wasn't a chatty sort, but I felt obliged to keep up a flow of remarks, bright exclamations about the architecture show at Trocadéro and the refurbishment of the Palais de Tokyo.

'Here we are!' I chirped when we arrived at the fourth floor. Moncada let me pass through the door first, but immediately ducked behind me to look in the bathroom, then another glance both ways along the narrow hallway before he was satisfied. I had the Richter laid out on the bed, in the same style of cheap art-student case Cameron had used for the Stubbs. I placed the paperwork next to it and took a seat in the room's only chair, a white Eames-y number.

'Would you like a drink? Some water?'

'*No, grazie.*'

He worked his way methodically through the certification before turning his attention to the picture, making a show of studying the provenances thoroughly. I wondered if he liked Richter, if anyone did, really.

'All in order?'

'Yes. You seem to be a good businesswoman, signorina.'

'As are you, Signor Moncada. I see that the Stubbs fetched an impressive price in Beijing.'

'The Stubbs, yes. So unfortunate, what happened to your poor colleague.'

'Dreadful. A dreadful shock.'

For a moment I was reminded of the scene in my hotel room at the lake, with da Silva. I mustn't overdo the concern.

'Still, perhaps we might do business again?'

'*Si. Vediamo.*'

While he collected the papers and re-zipped the case I reached into my bag and while I took out my laptop and set it up on the desk I pressed send on the text I had prepared.

'So.' I handed over a plain sheet of paper with the passcodes written in biro. 'As we agreed, one point eight euro?'

'As we agreed.'

We went through the same routine we had followed in the nasty pizzeria, except this time I didn't have to make the switch. Quite the little businesswoman, I had become. My phone rang, right on time.

'I'm sorry, I have to take this. I'll just step outside –'

I didn't even see his arm move before it clamped on my wrist. He shook his head. I nodded, fluttered my fingers acquiescently.

'*Allô*?' I hoped he couldn't detect the tremor in my voice.

'Leave now.'

Moncada was still holding my arm. I took a step backwards; we might have been jiving.

'Yes, of course. Could I call you back? In a couple of minutes?' I hung up.

'Sorry.' He relaxed his grip, but held my eyes a few seconds longer.

'*Niente*.'

He turned back to the bed to gather the picture, and in the few seconds his back was turned, Renaud was in the room, shoving me roughly to one side, his hands arcing over Moncada's bent head with the flourish of a magician dashing off his cloak. Moncada was the taller man but Renaud brought his knee up between his legs and Moncada dropped forward, his right hand scrabbling under his jacket while his left pulled at his neck. I didn't understand what I was seeing until Moncada twisted, throwing his weight against Renaud. As they gyrated clumsily, I noticed something I'd half-registered when we were in bed, but never thought about. Renaud might have been flabby, but he was incredibly strong. Abstractedly, I observed the thick muscle across his suddenly powerful shoulders bulking out under the loose jacket, a sense of the definition of the triceps beneath, as he strained to hold Moncada in front of him. The room was full of both men's stertorous breathing, but far above it I heard an ambulance siren, a dreamy counterpoint, as I glimpsed the white cord around Moncada's throat, some sort of short metal vice which Renaud was twisting beneath his ear, Renaud's face purpling so that for a moment I thought it was Moncada who was hurting him and nearly threw myself at them, but then, looking up, saw Moncada slowly folding against Renaud's knees. Renaud's elbows raised in a Cossack dance. Moncada's eyeballs reddened, his gaping lips swelled and then, as I understood, time began again, and I watched until it was over. The third time I'd watched someone die.

For a while, the only sound in the room was Renaud's panting. I couldn't speak. He bent over, clutching his knees like a sprinter after a race, exhaled slowly a couple of times. Then he knelt over the body and began to go through his pockets, removing a Vuitton wallet, a passport. I gasped when I saw the gun holstered at Moncada's waist.

'Put the things in your handbag. Quickly, all of it. Take the computer, too. Take the picture. Do it.'

I obeyed mutely. Stuffed the laptop and the papers into my bag, zipped the flat carrying-case. Renaud was stuffing the thing back into his pocket. When I found my voice it came out high-pitched like a wind-up doll.

'Renaud!' I coughed, breathed, hissed. 'Renaud. This is crazy. I don't understand.'

'The police will be here in ten minutes. Do as I say, I'll explain later.'

'But, fingerprints?' There was the beginning of an hysterical scream in my question.

'I told you, it's taken care of. Move!'

My bag was overflowing; I couldn't fasten it. I took off my scarf and did my best to hide the contents.

'Take the picture. Go. Take a cab to the flat, I'll be there soon. Go.'

'He-he had a briefcase.' I pointed. My body was a stream; I couldn't seem to find any purchase on the floor.

'Take that too. Now. Get. The. Fuck. Out.'

27

Waiting again. The sofa and my *escritoire* were wrapped in plastic sheeting, so I sat on the floor amongst the packing cases, my back to the wall. I drew my knees under my chin and closed my eyes. Some bit of my brain was reflecting that watching a murder was oddly more shocking than committing it. I didn't even feel like smoking. Again, the buzz of the street door, again the weight of his tread on the stairs. I lifted my head wearily; my eyes felt as though they should be black, desolate as a shark's. It was only when Renaud turned on the light that I realised I had been sitting in the dark. He looked jaunty, though perhaps that's normal for someone who's just strangled a notorious Mafioso.

'This had better be good.'

He came and sat beside me, put an arm around me. I didn't shake him off – I can't bear those female theatrics.

'I'm sorry, Judith. It was the only way. It was him or me.'

'But your client. How are you supposed to get the money for his wretched Rothko now?'

'Moncada knew who I was. He was looking for me. He was prepared to kill; you saw the gun.'

'But he had no idea you were in Paris.'

'Exactly. As I said, it was a matter of time. Which of us found the other first. You don't need to worry about the police. I have my friend at the *préfecture*, remember?'

I didn't smile.

'I tipped him off,' he continued. 'They know what Moncada was into, they'll see he was armed and they'll clear it up. You did them a favour, think of it that way.'

'And your client?'

'I'll be in touch with Moncada's associates. They'll see this as the warning it is. I'll get my money.'

'Hurray for you.'

'Don't be like that. Look.'

He took a folded brown envelope from inside his jacket and passed it to me. I had it in my hand before I remembered it would have been sitting next to the garotte. There was the photo from the Métro at Saint-Michel in a spanking new passport, a driving licence, even a *carte de séjour*.

'Leanne? That's low, Renaud.'

'A twenty-seven-year-old Englishwoman, recently deceased? It seemed too good to pass up. Anyway, it'll remind you to keep your nose clean.'

'How did you do it?'

'The *préfecture* contacted your consulate. A poor young lady who had been attacked and robbed, recovering now in hospital. Her parents anxious to take her home. You skip through as her. It's clean.'

'Pretty impressive contact you've got there. The *gendarmes* seem remarkably accommodating.'

'It's a quid pro quo.'

I gave him a long look.

'Don't feel bad.'

'I do feel fucking bad. Do I look like a Leanne to you?'

We sat there for a while, both our heads resting against the wall. After a while I asked him, 'So the Rothko, what was it anyway? I mean, which picture?'

'Dunno. I mean, they're all the same, aren't they? Big, reddish, squares, I think.'

If there's anything I've learned, it's that talking yourself into low expectations never works. You tell yourself to expect nothing, but when you get it, you still feel a tiny bit of irrational disappointment. I'd wanted to give him one more chance. I really had. He could have told me the truth and given me a head start, at least. I let my cheek fall against his shoulder.

'So,' I said. 'Job done.'

'*Oui*. I brought something. In the bag by the door.' I hauled it towards me.

'Cristal. My favourite. I'll open it.' In unison, our four eyes swivelled to my own bag on the floor, lying next to Moncada's briefcase and a million-pound painting. In it his things, the gun.

'No, I'll open it,' Renaud said quickly.

He caught my eye and we laughed, a real laugh, complicit.

'How about I hold the bottle and you get the glasses? They're in one of those boxes.'

I stood up so he could see me. 'Look. No sudden moves.'

A tiny, anamorphic moment. Slanted another way, we were doubled for a second, he and I, and I saw how things could have been. I went over to the window. God, I was going to miss this flat, I was going to miss the night sky over Paris.

'Can't find them.'

'Maybe in the other one? You'll have to peel the tape off.'

Still holding the bottle aloft in my right hand, I flicked the catch on the hidden drawer at the back of my writing desk. The silencer was already fitted to the barrel of the Glock 26.

'Here they are.'

Renaud stood with a coupe in either hand. He just had time to look surprised before I pulled the trigger.

According to *Women Serial Killers of America*, the 26 is the ideal lady's gun. In the same way that crimes in the movies can only be solved by a detective on suspension, the silencer is much misrepresented. The only one that really works is the Ruger Mark II, but it's over a foot long and weighs a kilo, not exactly handbag-friendly. And then there's the trade-off. The quieter the shot the less powerful the round that can be used, the less powerful the round the shorter distance the bullet travels and the less damage it causes. The Glock is half the weight of the Ruger, and apparently a sexy little number, if you like that sort of thing. It's amazing what you can fit into a hollowed-out catalogue if you try hard enough. A supersonic bullet has a loud crack that no silencer will do much about; a subsonic, on the other hand, is quiet but the shot has to be to the head, otherwise there's no guarantee the target will go down. Dave's army contacts had kindly provided me with six subsonic bullets in a Wispa wrapper, and since the nearest I'd ever got to a gun outside Southport funfair was hauling Rupert's Berettas to his Range Rover on a Friday afternoon, Dave had also enclosed a postcard of Boucher's *Madame de Pompadour* with '5 metres' written on the back. Luckily my drawing room wasn't particularly large.

I wove through the packing cases and put two more bullets in Renaud's head point blank, just to be sure. The silencer made a pretty loud whooshing suck, but even with the windows closed all I could hear outside was the concierge's blessed, eternal *telenovela*. And in cities, at least in good neighbourhoods, people don't hear shots. Or rather, they hear them, and think 'That's funny. Sounded like a gun', and go back to watching *Britain's Got Talent*. I opened the Cristal and took a spluttering swig out of the neck of the bottle. It was a bit warm. I put it in the fridge, which was splattered with Renaud's brains, like an angry Pollock.

There was a knock at the door.

'*Mademoiselle? Tout se passe bien*?'

Fuck. The downstairs neighbour. Fucking Left Bank intellectuals, why couldn't they be watching telly? He was a lawyer, I'd seen from the mailbox, older guy, maybe widowed. We'd exchanged greetings in the courtyard. I retrieved the bottle, took it with me towards the door, opened it a crack and inserted myself onto the landing.

'Just a minute.'

'*Bonsoir, mademoiselle.* Is everything alright? I heard a noise –'

I waved the bottle gaily. 'Just a little celebration. I'm moving out, you see.'

He wore glasses and a green cashmere cardigan over a workshirt and tie. In his left hand was a napkin. Quite the gent, using a napkin even when dining alone.

'I'm sorry if we disturbed you.' I had my hand behind my back, clutching the door handle to keep it from swinging wide. 'Would you care to join us?'

'Thank you, but I was in the middle of dinner. If you're sure that everything's fine?'

'Quite fine. I do apologise.'

Part of me felt like asking him in, just for the hell of it. Well, it felt sexy.

'*Alors, bonsoir, mademoiselle.*'

'*Bonsoir, monsieur.*'

Renaud might have looked at me reproachfully as I propped myself against the door and sucked down a gasper, but he didn't have a face left. I dropped the fag end into the fizz, then I found the packing case labelled 'Cuisine' and searched for the Japanese cleaver and a small toolkit I'd bought in the Arab convenience store. I took the plastic sheeting off the sofa, spread it on the floor and rolled the body onto it, removing the phone and wallet from the pocket of the ghastly jacket. Before I pulled on my gloves I gave a bit of thought to a musical accompaniment. Mozart again, the *Requiem* this time. Cheap shot, but then he'd been prepared to land me with 'Leanne' for the foreseeable. I dimmed the lights and found a candle under the sink for atmosphere. Then I set to work.

After her revolutionary *Judith Slaying Holofernes*, Artemisia Gentileschi left Rome for Florence, where she painted a more conventional version of the subject. *Giuditta con la sua ancella – Judith with her Maid* – hangs in the Pitti Palace. Initially, there's nothing violent about it. It's a picture of two women tidying up. The maid is in the foreground, her back to the viewer, her yellow dress protected by an apron, her hair twisted in a practical rag. Her mistress is in profile behind the maid's extended left arm, looking behind her to see if they are being followed, hoping they can get the job done in time. Her hair is carefully arranged, her dark, velvet-like dress richly brocaded. Over her shoulder she carries a sword; beneath its hilt the eye is drawn to the basket crooked in the maid's arm. Which contains Holofernes' head, bundled in muslin like a Christmas pudding. The women are poised in a moment of deadly tension, but the picture sings their silence. They are anxious but unhurried, pausing deliberately to see if they are being pursued before getting down to what they have to do. There is weight in the painting, the drag of the heavy sword hilt on Judith's shoulder, the solidity of the severed head in the basket supported on the maid's hip. This, for them, is the next thing.

Using the plastic sheeting for leverage, I dragged the body over the parquet to the bathroom. My shoulders and the muscles of my abdomen strained and I had to pause several times, but I got it in there. I'd always liked the luxury of a walk-in shower. I stripped to my knickers, bundled my jeans and sweater into the tub, then went back and filled the kitchen sink. I gave the whole place a good squirt of Monsieur Propre and started to swab it down, wringing the cloth until it turned from crimson to pinkish grey, running more and more hot water. The waste trap filled with viscous lumps. I gathered a wincing handful and flushed them down the lavatory. When the drawing room was clean I swilled water and bleach along the floor to the bathroom, everything immaculate for the next tenant.

I expected to cringe at the first cut but it turned out that I'd seen worse when I worked at the Chinese takeaway. With the shower running, the eight pints of blood contained in the human body streamed tidily enough down the drain in a few minutes. The neck gave a froglike belch as I hit the carotid artery, but there were no spouts of gore, just puddles and ooze and a surprisingly clean layer of whitish fat, like a ham sandwich. I left the head under the water while I dragged in the extra packing case I'd ordered. I cut off the blood-soaked clothes with another of the Japanese knives and chucked them into the bath. I unrolled a towel and shoved the body onto it, then spent some time drying it off with my hairdryer. I didn't want the box to leak. Two rubbish bags, top and tail, then a padded holder from the dry cleaner's, special jumbo size. The kind used to preserve wedding dresses. I padded back to the front door and collected Moncada's wallet and briefcase, laid them on the bottom of the packing case and rolled the body in sideways, braced myself against the sink with my hands under the lip of the case and hauled it upright. I turned Mozart up loud while I hammered down the lid. Finally I gaffer-taped all the seams several times, and attached some of the helpful stickers the moving company had given me – 'Heavy', 'This way up'. Renaud was ready to go to Vincennes. What was left of him, anyway.

First, I wrapped the head in clingfilm, then popped it in a Casino supermarket bag, tied the handles together, then put that into a snap-close Decathlon sports carrier, along with Moncada's gun and the manky Nikes Renaud had used to plod after me round the Luxembourg. I gave it an exploratory kick – no tell-tale drippage. I cleaned my way around the flat once more, using a toothbrush dipped in bleach for the inside of the taps and the bathplug, bundling the plastic sheeting together with our clothes and stuffing all that in another bag, backtracking to the shower to sluice myself down. Then I sat wetly on the floor and lit a fag. In front of me was a black bin liner of bloodied rubbish, the leather getaway holdall, the sports carrier and the black case containing the Richter. I could put the clothes and tools down the incinerator chute behind the concierge's broom cupboard off the courtyard. I packed the bag containing the head like a grisly picnic into the straw basket Renaud and I used to take to the market. I took track pants, sports bra, trainers and a sweatshirt from the holdall, shoved on a cashmere beanie and trotted out into the night. I made it to the river in under ten minutes, pretty good, tracing the same route as the one when I'd played cat and mouse with Renaud.

Like most portentous moments in life, our goodbye descended into bathos. I had given some thought to our final farewell, the Pont Neuf, the lovers' bridge to Ile de la Cité, but even at this hour there were couples entwined in the bays, watching the lumen-drenched currents of the Seine. I took the stone staircase down to the scraggy garden at the tip of the island, freezing as two patrolling *gendarmes* paused at the foot to allow me past. They said '*Bonsoir*' politely, but I could feel them watching me as I walked over to the statue of Henri IV, the basket cradled under my arm. I didn't dare risk a splash, so after a while I passed them again and crossed over to the *quai*, keeping my eye out for sleeping tramps. I sat with my feet dangling towards the icy water and lowered the bag by the handles until it was submerged, the current tugging at my fingers. Gently, I let it go.

When I was finished, finally, it was dawn. I thought that was the time I'd remember Paris best, in the end, the littoral moments between night and day when the city shifts on its axis, between the stripped-retina shame of the party's end and the clean-aproned bustle of the morning. The white time, the negative space, the gap between desire and lack. Renaud had always slept through the dawn, with a tiny bit of help, of course. All those cosy suppers, none lacking my special secret ingredient. Nothing heavy, just something to take the edge off, just to make sure he was out for the hour or so after we'd made love when I could retrieve the spare laptop I kept hidden behind the bookshelf and go hunting.

Exceeding the mark can sometimes be just as much a mistake as missing it. I'd been fooled, I admit, by Cameron Fitzpatrick's knack with the blarney, but one word had shown me that Renaud was not what he said. *Certo*. Of course. The roll of the 'r' too precise, the tiny lifted inflection at the end of the word. The real thing. That and the *osso buco*.

Plus, the casual drop of da Silva's name. The car in which da Silva had arrived last summer in Como to begin his investigation was a *Guardia di Finanza* vehicle. The Italian police force is split into many divisions, and, oddly, Mafia investigations are not dealt with by the *carabinieri*, the sexy poster boys in their tight uniforms who set the gap-year girls' hearts a-flutter, but by the more prosaically titled Financial Guards. I had guessed Moncada was Mafia in Rome, known it when I saw the car.

Da Silva. Facebook friends never *had* been my style, but they were certainly Signora da Silva's. Franci, short for Francesca, couldn't seem to throw a pot of spaghetti on the stove without uploading the latest detail of her thrilling life. With over 800 friends, I figured one more random acquaintance wouldn't make a difference to Franci, and a random snap culled from a local paper, with a suitable name amalgamated from the Roman phone directory, made me a new friend. I eagerly posted a picture of my new sofa, and a cute little Kinder hippopotamus with coconut frosting – 'Naughty!' – and then sat back to scroll through the details of Franci's existence in a Roman suburb. Christmas, Easter, a Prada purse her husband had given her for her birthday, a family holiday in Sardinia, a new dishwasher. Franci was certainly living the dream. The da Silvas had two children, Giulia, four, and baby

Giovanni, who must have been photographed more than the Beckham brats. And there, in the corner of a shot, next to the proud mamma trying to disguise her baby weight in an unfortunate red suit with a peplum, and *Papà*, neat and fit in suit and tie, was a familiar soft swell of paunch, and on the paunch, when I'd magnified it and spun it, and looked again and again, a monogram. R.C. Renato, Ronaldo? It didn't matter. A simple online search found a Chiotasso, *Sarto*, listed in the business section of the Italian phone book in the same suburb where Franci da Silva filmed the ongoing documentary of her life. *Sarto* – tailor. He'd told me that his father was a tailor, still carrying on the business in that doughty Italian way, and the initials fit. So they'd grown up together, Renaud and da Silva, stayed true to the old neighbourhood. They were friends, not professional acquaintances. A real pair of wiseguys.

I took the final gift Dave had sent me from the holdall and laid it on the floor. The latest *catalogue raisonné* of Rothko, produced for the Tate Modern exhibit in 2009. It had taken a lot of emails to New York gallerists from Gentileschi, who were looking out for a Rothko for a private client, but I'd been able to trace the sales of nearly all the pictures that had passed through private hands in the last three years and none matched Renaud's details. He had been too confident, naming the bank, Goldman Sachs.

Still, that wasn't enough to confirm it. That Renaud had lied about who he was didn't necessarily make him a cop. Yet the ease with which he'd taken care of Leanne, the sirens appearing in the wake of Moncada's death? I don't think he fully understood the power of Google. In a programme for the proceedings of a conference entitled 'Cultural Methods of Money

Laundering' at the University of Reggio Calabria, I found a scheduled talk by one Ispettore Chiotasso, R. on the use of artworks as 'capital covers' for illegal funds. He and da Silva were colleagues, after all. Renaud had spoken at the conference at 3 p.m. I could imagine him, shirt damp under the arms, in some dusty southern classroom, the delegates nodding after a heavy lunch. So he did chase money, after a fashion. It was only when I read the abstract of the talk that I'd had an inkling of what Renaud might have planned for Moncada. He wanted revenge.

In the early Nineties, a magistrate named Borsellino was murdered in Sicily by the Mafia. It was an easy name to remember, because it happened to be the same as my favourite Milanese hat-maker. The killing shocked Italy, and in its aftermath, police squads were drafted into Sicily from different regions of the country in an attempt to break the pattern of collusion between official forces and the Mafia. The Direzione Investigativa Antimafia was made up of combined teams from across Italy, amongst them several divisions of Financial Guards from Rome, including one Chiotasso, R. The Sicilian case twenty years later, where the police investigating the fake Greek artifacts got a lot more than froth with their coffee, had involved Renaud's colleagues. The culprits were never arrested, but they were believed to have been connected with the established international art scene.

Renaud must have known that Moncada was involved in the bombing that killed Renaud's fellow police officers. Sure, he and da Silva *were* investigating Mafia art fraud, but, as I had learned from my research, Mafia cases could drag on for decades, a few gains here, a few losses there. Cracking the money laundering ring hadn't been Renaud's real motive. Revenge, and a warning to Moncada's employers in the true Sicilian style. That's why I hadn't stiffed him sooner; I liked him enough to want him to have his moment of triumph. His story had been pretty damn good, all told. And I had to admit, I'd been amused by the game.

There were many things I could never know. Had da Silva's apparent belief in my innocence back in Como been an act, too? Either way, Renaud had obviously convinced him at some point not to haul me in, because it suited the long game with Moncada. They'd assumed they'd have me in the end. I was the bait for a little old-school justice.

How much da Silva knew of the way Renaud worked the sting wasn't my business, and I guessed since he was a family man, he didn't want to know more than he had to. It might have upset Franci. Nor did he look like the sort of guy who would cheerfully fuck his suspects. Renaud was the maverick cop, working the case on his own terms, regretfully bringing the *femme fatale* to justice. The awful clothes had been a nice touch, though. Quite a sacrifice, I guessed, for an Italian. So, Renaud planned to deliver his warning to Moncada's associates, da Silva would plausibly smooth over the killing as an officer's self-defence and I'd be stopped at the airport with a murdered girl's passport.

I thought about sleeping, but I didn't want to miss the post office opening, so I went out for a walk, circling the perimeter of the Luxembourg to keep warm until seven, when I found a *café-tabac* that was open and bought myself a *noisette* and an elderly postcard of a Parisian panorama. I borrowed a pen from the waiter, his day's scowl already in place, and wrote out the address of my white knight in Finsbury, then added:

D,

This is not a gift. You owe me £1. I'm sure Rupert will handle the sale with pleasure.

J xxx

Capital gains, after all. The money I'd pocketed from Moncada was unofficial: by selling the Richter to Dave for a quid, I'd got my original investment back, plus the profit, and let myself in for 28p in tax. At least I'd learned something in the department.

After that, it was eight, and the Richter and I were the first in line at *la poste*.

28

I gave the concierge a garish potted carnation and a Rykiel print scarf I'd never much liked. The sleepless night and the endless cigarettes had left me with a tinny ache in my ears and a twitch in my hands, but behind my eyes my mind was as shiny as the bathroom in the flat. The purple shadow of my eye sockets was also useful when I handed her a neat cardboard carton containing Renaud's few clothes (minus the plastic wallet in which he'd taped up my passport and credit cards) and asked, as a great favour, if she could look after it in the lodge in case monsieur ever came back for his things. Feckless lovers doing a moonlight flit were standard fare in the *telenovele*, and despite her voluble commiserations I managed to imply that it was just too painful to talk about. I reminded her that the movers would be arriving later that day and explained that a friend was giving me a lift to the airport, thanked her in between agreeing that No Man Was To Be Trusted and lugged the holdall to the end of the street, waiting at the bus stop where I had once watched Renaud waiting for me. The bus was crowded with passengers on their way to work, I had to stand clutching the rail with my bag wedged between my knees as we swayed across the city. How long since I had been on a bus? How long until the mysterious friend at the *préfecture* realised that 'Leanne' wasn't turning up at the airport? I had a day or two, I reckoned, before they came to question the concierge. At least she'd enjoy that. I'd miss my things, but I could always buy more. It was time for a new look, anyway.

By the time the bus had waddled through the commuter traffic to the depot behind Sacré-Cœur I was the only occupant. I trailed behind a tourist coach staggering up to the church, then flopped down on the steps amongst the early-morning backpackers. Someone was playing the bongos and I could already smell weed. I rooted in the holdall and pulled out Renaud's wallet. Empty, as I thought, except for a couple of notes, the 'fake' police badge he'd used on the Goutte d'Or and a postal slip, a receipt for a special delivery to be collected from Amsterdam. It had been a convincing touch, the fake passport. And the Amsterdam address would be useful, as I'd be needing another new one imminently. Next was Renaud's crappy old-school Nokia, the same model as the one I'd used on Balensky's boat. I assumed he must have had something more up to date somewhere, but he hadn't been taking any chance on having it near me. Bless. I didn't expect to find much, that would have been too neat, and the log lists and inbox were wiped clean, except for an offer from France Telecom that morning. The only call registered was the one he'd made to me while I was in the hotel room with Moncada.

What I did find was photos, beginning with the sequence he'd shown me from Rome, then from the period when he was spying me out in Paris, buying the newspaper, smoking a cigarette in the Panthéon café, running in the park. And then shots I'd never seen him taking, me sleeping, a close up of my hair on the pillow, me sprawled naked on the wreck of my bed looking like a pornographic Hogarth. Eeeew. But then, the heel of my shoe as he followed me upstairs, me stooping to spit as I brushed my teeth, a half-angle, caught through the bedroom door of me fiddling with a shopping bag. Hundreds of them. I looked for a long time, and the more I looked, the less voyeuristic and controlling they seemed. There was something softly intimate about the pictures, even a tenderness in the way he had recorded so many glancing moments of my life.

'Excuse. You take photo, please?'

A Spanish couple, hefty and acne-pocked, brandishing a phone. Another effing phone. I smiled, and snapped as they posed with their arms round one another with the marble façade behind them. Happy times.

I looked around for a dustbin, preparing to chuck Renaud's Nokia, but it buzzed in my hands. It began with 06, a French mobile number. The text read merely 'No sign yet'. How thoughtful of them to remind me. The one thing which had been nagging at me was that when Renaud vanished, da Silva would blame me, not Moncada's crew. And now, Renaud was still alive, texting away from Montmartre, where the two of us had first met. So, take a punt, Judith. I texted back, 'En route. Does the name Gentileschi mean anything to you?' I had to know if Renaud had told them where I kept my money. The dustbin stank of the vomit of putrid fast food. A vendor came up and offered me a tray of plastic friendship bracelets.

Another buzz. '*Bien. Non.*'

So he hadn't told them, which meant they wouldn't be applying for a warrant for the depository in Vincennes, which meant that if his head was ever fished out of the Seine it would be attributed to old-fashioned *omerta*. I wasn't dumb enough to think that this phone contained the only evidence of my meeting with Fitzpatrick and my tie with Renaud. Da Silva would surely have the shots by now, and there was the small matter of the dead junkie, but Gentileschi could be hiring again tomorrow. Definitely time for a new look.

I tapped back. '*Merci. A plus*.' Until later. Still, I somehow didn't want to relieve myself of the phone. I'd never had a love letter before.

I spent the afternoon wandering the west of the city. I could have gone to a museum to pass the time, but there were no pictures I wanted to look at. I trudged to the Parc Monceau and despite the cold managed to sleep an hour or so with my head on the holdall, waking to the offended glance of a chic young mother whose toddler was fiddling with my shoelaces. She probably thought I was a street drunk or a runaway, not the sort of thing one would wish to find in this most elegant and lifeless of Parisian gardens. I bought a coffee and a glass of water to wake myself up and looked at the papers to pass the time, more from habit than anxiety. It seemed remarkable, how many people one could kill without making the news.

At about seven that evening, I texted Yvette. 'Are you at home? I need to come over.' We'd been messaging from time to time. I'd explained my disappearance from the scene during the weeks with Renaud by saying I'd hooked up with a fantastic new guy. When she replied I waited at a cab rank, thinking about how city life was turning back to a time when everyone lived in lodgings and conducted their existence in public spaces. I'd known Yvette nearly a year and it had never occurred to me to learn where she lived. It turned out to be the fifteenth, one of the rare ugly modern buildings that disfigure the façades of Paris like bad dental work. She took a while to buzz me in, as though she'd thought better of it, but in the end I heard her '*Allô*' over the intercom and hauled myself up five flights of concrete stairs.

It was obvious Yvette had just got up. Her hair looked like an old Brillo sponge, her skin patchy without foundation, arms and legs liverish where they showed under the skimpy crumpled sweatshirt she'd dragged on over her knickers. I thought she must make up her limbs too. The small studio was close and stuffy, a cheap patchouli incense stick failing to disguise a heavy fug of scent, smoke and garbage. Yvette's clothes were heaped everywhere, toppling pyramids of leather and lace that half-obscured the futon mattress which was her only furniture. She looked defiant, as I would if I'd had to show off a home so squalid.

'So. This is me. Do you want some tea?'

'Thanks, that would be lovely.'

She had an electric ring, a kettle and a microwave in a cupboard. While she took out two cups and two peppermint tisane bags I asked for the bathroom. 'There.'

Another cupboard, a tiny shower, loo and basin, smeared with grime, toothpaste coagulated on the tap. The towel on the floor stank of mildew, but I ran the water hot and rubbed myself down, brushed my teeth, quickly moisturised and made up my face. The Glock peered snubly from the jumble in the holdall. I'd thought of just killing Yvette to take her identity card, but I'd never get away with the skin colour.

'So,' I said brightly, emerging. 'Feel like going out? My treat.'

'Sure,' she said, suspiciously. 'It's early, though.'

'We can have a drink, and then I thought Julien's place?'

'OK.'

We drank our tea and I spooned in a couple of mouthfuls of Nutella from the friendless jar in Yvette's tiny fridge. While Yvette began the long process of assembling herself for the night I lay on the futon and flicked through the TV news. Now she was focused, there was something concentrated, even balletic about her movements, a professional appraisal of her back view in a vintage emerald shantung sheath, the grimaces that accompany eyeliner and mascara, securing the ankle strap of a perilous Tribute sandal. When she was done it was impossible to believe, looking at her, that she might have crawled off this dungheap of a flat. My own toilette took two minutes, a simple Alexander Wang black jersey minidress and plain black pumps, no fuss.

'Shall we get some coke?'

'I'm good now, maybe later. You ready?' She nodded, fiddling with her phone, sensing that something was off, but the thought of a free night on the razzle was too much for her.

'You can leave that here. I mean, you can stay if you like.'

'Nah, I might need my stuff.'

'Meeting your new bloke?'

'Maybe later.'

I hoiked the holdall unsteadily onto my shoulder, thrown off by my heels.

'Let's go, then.'

Freed from her squat of a home, Yvette was more herself, telling me about a massive night someone was organising in a warehouse by Saint-Martin, an art and fashion happening that was bound to get a lot of attention. Yvette was 'styling' it, though as far as I could see from the swag in the flat, her styling career began and ended with half-inching whatever samples the press offices were mug enough to let her call in. It was still only nine, so we had an aperitif at a neighbourhood place before making for the Rue Thérèse. Apart from the Nutella, I couldn't remember the last time I'd eaten, so I grabbed a handful of urine-soaked peanuts from the bar. I couldn't have my hands shaking.

We got to Julien's about ten, just as the door was opening. I'd hoped to put Julien off from asking any questions by going in with Yvette, but it was the bartender on reception. He waved us through and we made our way down into the deserted club. He dashed after us to fix us up with a cognac.

'This is lame,' Yvette said pointlessly, kicking her leg against her stool.

'It'll warm up. Look.'

Two guys were coming in, tall, fair, gym-toned.

'Check out the Hitler youth.'

They came straight over and offered us a drink. The music was switched on and after half an hour of chat the room started to fill up. Yvette was getting a little drunk on the cognac, left for the cubicles and returned in a black lace thong and bodice, oozing herself round her Aryan, who didn't need any more invitation to drag her to the darkroom.

'Are you coming?'

'In a while.'

They skipped off, while I watched the girls intently. There weren't too many of them, and I needed someone with roughly my hair colour at least. The last Amsterdam train from the Gare du Nord left at twelve minutes past midnight, but it was 11.20 when they walked in. A youngish woman with a much older man, he clutching her hand possessively, she more composed, experienced. She brushed his lips lightly and headed for the cubicles while he approached the bar. In a few minutes she was back, in a pink high-cut lace leotard, her nipples squashed and dark against the fabric. Perfect. I nodded to my blond, who was already checking out the bon bons, slid off my own stool and went the way she had come, still clutching the bulging holdall. Only one of the changing booths was closed. I had no idea how to pick a lock; I just crawled under the slatted door and made straight for the bag, a soft black Prada clutch. I tipped it out, riffled through the usual detritus for the wallet, scattered a few credit cards and receipts until I had the ID in my hand. It was hard to see in the dim light, but Marie-Hélène Baudry was my lucky doppelganger for the night. She was married, and somehow I doubted it was to her old chap. Naughty girl. I considered leaving her Leanne's passport, but it had my picture on it, so I reassembled the wallet, scooped the junk back into the clutch and slipped the ID into the pocket of the holdall. It was 11.32. Tight, but possible.

I took a quick peek into the darkroom before I left. Yvette was under her blond boy, heels spiking at his back. She'd be stuffed for the bill, but then she'd never even offered to pay back that 500 – not that I'd have taken it, but, still, good manners. I was in the lobby at 11.35, the curtain ajar, my hand on the door, when Julien swam up out of the shadows.

'Mademoiselle Lauren?'

'I'm sorry, Julien, I've really got to leave.'

He reached around and gently closed the door. 'Not just yet. I need to speak to you.'

'OK, OK. But quickly.'

'*Bien sûr, mademoiselle.*'

He stopped under the reception counter and showed me into the back office. No pretence of louche luxury here, just a desk with a computer, a cheap office chair, a spike of receipts in the glare of a striplight. I put the holdall on the desk.

'Mademoiselle Lauren, I've had another visit. The police this time. Asking questions. Again.'

'When?'

'Today, yesterday. I can't quite remember.'

I really didn't have time for this elegant cat and mouse shit.

'How much do you want?'

He eyed the bag. 'Are you planning a trip?'

'None of your business. Just tell me how much.'

'Five thousand.'

'For what? What do you think I've been doing?'

'Why don't you tell me?'

'I don't have that much on me.'

'Then whatever you do have. And you're not welcome here anymore.'

I'd like to say I hadn't meant to do it. That I was reaching into the bag for the cash and the gun just sort of jumped into my hand, your honour. The thing was, I really didn't have the time. I could have given him a line, that it really wasn't his lucky day, that he shouldn't have made me angry, because he wouldn't like me when I was angry, but this wasn't the moment for style, either. I leaned over the desk, shot him twice in the chest, tugged off my shoes and hit the Rue Thérèse running.

I'd been having drinks with Renaud once at the bar of the Crillon when a couple had a row at the next tiny marble table. They were young, even younger than me, he unshaven and scruffy enough to be a famous actor, she properly beautiful in an Uma Thurman-before-Botox-happened way, ash-blonde hair drawn severely off a Picasso-planed face. Her coat was exquisite cream cashmere, a little heavy for the weather. She had ordered two martinis; he arrived late with a shabby bunch of corner-shop flowers. They spoke quietly for a while, then as the drinks went down she started to cry, prettily, Swarovski tears dripping from alarmingly turquoise eyes. Then she stood, and the way she did it let me know she was aware that she had the eyes of every man in the room. She gathered the soft collar to her long throat and leaned forward.

'I'm sorry, I just can't do it anymore. I've had enough.'

Then she picked up the sagging blooms and cracked him across the face with the bouquet before dropping it to the floor and stalking towards the lobby. He rose slowly, plucked a single carnation petal from his jaw and stared round, the picture of wounded bewilderment. As one, the waiters lined up like a cheerleading squad with cries of encouragement, 'She went that way! Go on, monsieur, that way!' and he ran after her. We spotted them later, over the river, kissing and giggling on the *quai*. Her coat was open and under it she wore a cheap denim skirt and a man's pyjama top. It was a beautiful way of cadging a drink. Maybe they were film students, or actors. The point being that the citizens of Paris are brand-aware – they know that theirs is a city which is supposed to love a lovers' quarrel, so barefoot girls with desperate faces running through midnight streets rarely attract attention. As I ran, I thought of another girl, running barefoot through evening streets, but even that summer's evening seemed so innocent now. It's 1.6 miles from the Rue Thérèse to the Gare du Nord, and I made it in sixteen minutes, not bad going with a heavy bag.

I slipped panting through the usual gaggle of drunks and gypsies at the station entrance and bought a single to Amsterdam from the ticket machine. Of course, it wouldn't take the fifty-euro note, but I couldn't use a card. I smoothed the banknote against my thigh, an eye on the clock. Not a train ticket, not now. I couldn't get done on that. Like Al Capone with the taxes. There was a strange bubbling noise; it took a moment to realise that it was me, giggling crazily. Twice, three times, the machine spat the note rudely back. I stood, breathed, twitched the corners hospital-neat, fed it in again. For twenty seconds I might have believed in God. *Aller simple, 1 adulte.* Thank you, Jesus. I even had time to punch the ticket in the machine at the end of the platform before my filthy soles clambered after the holdall into the train.

EPILOGUE

INSIDE

It was the first big night of the Biennale, nearly a year since I'd left Paris. The sky above San Giorgio Maggiore was an improbable pink and blue; everyone said that it looked like a Tiepolo ceiling, as everyone always does in Venice. A supple line of Rivas bobbed by the island's jetty, waiting to ferry a squawking gaggle of dealers and art-whores across the lagoon. Up towards Zattere, I could see the *Mandarin* tucked between two brushed-carbon leviathans. Their bulks squatted over the white Massari church, a surrealist installation in themselves. Steve would have to get a bigger boat if he wanted to keep up. I was to dine with him later. I wouldn't let him take me to Harry's; we'd have drinks on the perfect floating terrace at the Gritti, then La Madonna in San Polo for sea urchin risotto whether he liked it or not. I had three Quinn casts in mind for the garden of his new London house, magnified renderings of embryonic babies, curled in granite like mysterious sea creatures. Actually rather pretty, for once. But first there was the Johnson Chang party at the Bauer, for the Hong Kong gallerists, and I thought I'd have time to look in at the Prada Foundation too, before I met up with Steve. I held out my hand for the water taxi driver to grip and stepped neatly down into the boat, followed by a posse of stylists and photographers who were covering the shows for *Vanity Fair*. I made vague conversation with Mario Testino's buyer on the short crossing, but really I just wanted to take great heady gulps of the view.

The Chang party was strictly invite-only; I had my exquisite scroll of antique Chinese parchment in my floppy Saint Laurent clutch. A couple of paps and tourists were hanging around to gawp. I skirted them and walked up to the greeter. As she checked me off on the clipboard I looked beyond her to the long, bronze marble lobby of the hotel, opening onto the delicate Byzantine stonework of the terrace. Ranks of waiters with trays of the inevitable Bellinis stood between incongruous lumps of Shanghai street art.

'Are you going in?'

'Lorenzo! *Ciao, bello.* I wondered where I'd find you.'

Lorenzo represented the Other Place in Milan. He was Venetian, with the tawny hair and pale eyes of the lagoons. One of his great-grandmothers had famously given Byron the clap, or so he'd told me while I was fucking him in Kiev.

'You know Rupert, of course?'

Rupert. Rounder and redder than ever, the perennial Englishman abroad in a crumpled linen suit and a jaunty Lock Panama. I looked him straight in the face.

'No,' he said, 'I don't believe we've met.'

'Elisabeth Teerlinc.' Lorenzo had already been whirled inside. We stood at the centre of a sudden caesura in the crowd.

He offered his hand, sweaty naturally. I scanned his eyes, searching for some flicker of recognition, but there was nothing. How could there be? This woman in her cobalt suede Celine shift, her impeccable pumps, existed in another dimension from Judith Rashleigh. One should never notice the servants. I hadn't even bothered to change my hair in the end.

My hand was still in his. I let it rest there.

'And you're with?'

'I have my own gallery. Gentileschi. I have a space in Dorsoduro.'

'Ah. Gentileschi. Of course.'

I extracted my hand and fished in my purse for a card.

'You should come to our opening tomorrow. I'm showing a group of Balkan artists. Quite amusing.'

'I'd love to.' He was leering at me. Rupert. Like he had a hope.

'Are you coming in – Lorenzo's waiting?'

His skin flushed a deeper red under the claret tan.

'No, er, NFI actually.'

No fucking invite. Oh Rupert.

'That's a pity.'

'Too many bodies.'

'Yes. Quite the crush. Well, see you tomorrow, Rupert.'

I offered him my cheek, and then turned my back as the greeter lifted the velvet rope. I felt his eyes on me as I walked tall through the bodies and out into the Venice twilight. The lapis lazuli water shone at my feet. I took a glass and stood alone at the parapet, and looked at the waves, and they lifted my heart.

TO BE CONTINUED